Dear John

Thank you
continued a
Best wishes
Rufus (Ken.).

GW01458191

Golden Eagles

RUFUS STONE

Printed and bound in England by www.printondemand-worldwide.com

FastPrint Publishing

http://www.fast-print.net/bookshop

GOLDEN EAGLES
Copyright © Rufus Stone 2016

A catalogue record for this book is available from the British Library

ISBN 978-178456-378-3

First published 2016 by
FASTPRINT PUBLISHING
Peterborough, England.

To my wife Diana, the busy artist D. Lynch,
for her continuous support and encouragement
even with my constant amendments.

Suggested by actual events and carefully researched this series of stories ranges throughout Britain and, including the governor and admiral, many of the characters actually lived and worked as described at this time.

These books are the result of the author's lifelong interest in Roman Britain.

A glossary of places and other information is contained in the appendices at the rear of the book.

Titles in the Pax Romana Series

GOLDEN EAGLES

Chapter I

"Following our success in capturing the bullion wagon – and what a sweet taste that left – we are indebted to our new friend, Firmus, for news of another."

Mercurialis was in high spirits as he glanced from one to the other of his fellow conspirators, both of whom had apparently been reduced to silence by thoughts of so much treasure falling into their hands for a second time. Then he added, "We shall avail ourselves of it just as soon as he returns from Isca Silurum."

"I like the idea of all that gold – even the silver and copper coin for that matter," commented Flavius Silus finally, his thin features not unlike those of the group's leader, with the exception of Mercurialis' jug-ears which he often smiled at inwardly. He was smiling now only to let it fade as he continued, "What I don't like is this continued absence from us on so-called official business – about which we know virtually nothing!"

Publius Lucius nodded his agreement saying, "It's a dilemma I wrestle with as well. Silus speaks little but says much which, as we all know, is why he led us originally. This observation is in the same vein. I think you should make your own views clear," he observed, turning to Mercurialis and shrugging his shoulders as if to ask whether this was a satisfactory situation.

Justinian Mercurialis shrugged in reply, as he regarded the still solidly-built ex-soldier who had first spoken, before looking away to Lucius who had pursued the issue.

"We understand your impatience as our senator-in-waiting, as it were, but you surely must realise how important it is to move carefully. With care this further treasury shipment will bring the day closer that we become the governing body.

Our friend is delayed at Isca, but if he is unable to return shortly then we shall proceed without him."

"How?"

"Why?"

Frowning at having simultaneous questions Mercurialis fiddled with the creases of the toga fold he carried over his left arm, before replying, "If you doubt my judgement in this then I suggest you form your own insurgent group so that you can be responsible for your own decisions!"

Neither spoke but Lucius waved a hand as Silus simply shook his head.

"Then shall I take that as the *status quo*?"

Silus and Lucius nodded briefly, both disgruntled at having been routed so easily.

"Then as I was about to say," the tall, angular Mercurialis went on, his jaw muscles taut, "our young officer has verified that the additional wagon guards allocated after our first sortie have now been stood down in the light of no further attacks.

We shall wait further, giving them a false sense of security. However, we'll use that time in observation to confirm what we know and learn what we don't.

My own view is that we should expand our area of activity in order to take as many of these mobile treasure houses as are available to us. Those we cannot take will still tie down troops as escorts. It 'll cause massive disruption, out of all proportion to what is lost."

"Once the wind blows it cannot be returned from whence it came," Silus remarked quietly.

Lucius stared at Silus while Mercurialis said equally quietly, "We take your point but it's surely too late for cautionary philosophy. Our journey along this road started with the first wagon.

Firmus has given us the basic data and intends to fill it out sometime soon. After that we'll make such arrangements as will save the treasury clerks having to distribute the cargo.

As we've already discussed in times past, any irregularity in being paid will unsettle the legions themselves – let alone the auxiliary troops based on the Walls.

We shall buy the cooperation of the dissident Northern and Caledonian tribes and presumably the Silures from Cambria. The Cymru are not as settled as our masters would wish – obviously why the Second Augusta is still based in Isca Silurum."

"You haven't mentioned land. To my mind that is the most important acquisition. Land equals power." Lucius' furrowed brow matched the questioning in his voice.

Any reply was interrupted by the door to the private chambers opening. Quintus stood in the doorway as though waiting to be invited in.

Mercurialis stood and held out an arm in his direction. "Quintus! Good – we were finishing here. Let me thank you again for allowing us to meet privately in your home. We welcome you to the group now that our pre-meeting is over, just in time to talk about Haruld-The-One-Eyed."

"Yes – a good idea. He's still to fulfil the contact he took out with my late uncle, when *he* led the group."

As Quintus took his place Mercurialis said, "So I understand. We must certainly ensure he fulfils it, but getting rid of that damned Tribune, Albinus Felix, is paramount. With him gone our idiot of a governor will be emasculated – at least for a time."

"I would rather have him castrated permanently, " retorted Quintus. "Him and his bastard admiral are continually jeopardising our smuggling arrangements. My family has no wish to pay duty on our imports – the goods are only on the water for about thirty miles. We wouldn't ship them at all if we could float the wagons!"

The other three laughed, as much at his youthful enthusiasm as at the biting humour.

"I would gladly provide a blunt knife for the deed, as and when," Lucius commented, thinking of the yet more wasted time before they could usurp the governorship and set up a Britannic senate in isolation, on which he would serve in a major capacity.

"When we rouse the Caledonians the navy will need to support the New Wall of Antoninus Pius. Maybe then you'll slip across the narrow water undetected. One-eye's ships could also come into their own – although they're no match for Roman biremes and triremes," Silus observed pragmatically, his old-soldierly mind thinking laterally.

"Where is this Norseman? Back in Thule."

"I believe him on his way to Hibernia at this time of year – or he'll need to winter in the north," explained Mercurialis, "and he'd be no use to us there!"

★ ★ ★

Julia sat in the small, enclosed garden of the repaired villa in Waerham eating an apple, as she idly contemplated the scorched area marking the house wall opposite her. She had spend most of her life in the house and still felt violated by the attempt to burn it down, with her and her one-time paid companion, Dorcas, inside it.

Captured, both had been stripped and confined to one room by their attackers and she would be forever indebted to their disabled ex-soldier steward who had hidden himself, before killing the guard and rescuing them. Their lives might still have been forfeit had the local tribal chieftain, Stolus, not heard of the attack and brought his warriors to aid the small town's policing force.

Then she smiled broadly at the story of how Rex, her Canaan dog, had played his part my savaging the guard's ankle to help the steward. As though he was reading her thoughts she felt his tail thumping against the underside of the wooden bench, his favourite place in the garden. Yes, she told herself yet again, it had been a good day when Clemens had bought him for her before their marriage.

Suddenly a cramp-like pain took her lower abdomen and she leaned forward to ease it, but it passed almost as soon as it came. She smiled nervously at the thought of soon being a mother, until another cramping caught her and she decided to go inside to lie down.

As she made to get up so a flow of water wetted her expanded drawers before puddling the ground between her feet, making her gasp in anticipation as she realised her time had come.

Rex stuck his nose out from under the seat and looked up at her. Taking the cue Julia said hoarsely to him, "Go and fetch the master. Now, quickly." She watched him race into the house and disappear, barking urgently.

It seemed no time at all to her before Clemens was running out to help at the head of a number of servants, with Rex beside them wagging his tail happily.

"Are you all right, my love? Rex appeared quite agitated!"

"It's my time – it's arrived! I need the midwife to attend very soon" replied Julia, as the servants stood back in a group, uncertain but ready to assist as required.

They were all fond of their young mistress, some having known her all her life. Not to be outdone Rex put his head on her lap, wrinkling his nose at the unfamiliar scents.

Later, alone in her confinement room with Clemens, Julia turned her face to look straight into his eyes. He looked concernedly back at her and took a perspiring hand in his.

Calmly she said "I have no worries, my love, so you must try not to worry for me. I am only yet another wife presenting her husband with a child."

Pausing, as a pain came and went, she carried on, "But I just want to remind you of what we have spoken of before, in case a problem does arise."

Clemens squeezed her hand and bent forward to kiss her damp forehead. "I have already asked the spirits of this house to bless you, my dearest girl. I shall do so again, soon."

"I know you would have, Clemens – I know your feelings for me are those I have for you. But we must always be prepared for the unexpected."

"That's what your father has always said."

"He's right, my darling. Things can always go wrong. You know that well enough – all you soldiers do."

"I hope that midwife will be here soon," he responded, trying to change the subject.

"She will be. Your messenger was away like a flash of lightning." Julia gently patted his arm with her other hand as she attempted to reassure him.

She wished Livia was on hand but clearly her stepmother's place was with her father. In any case, Julia thought, no one had been anticipating this situation just yet. First babies were often overdue, she had been told.

"I just wanted you to remember that if anything did happen you should look for me in the garden. I shall be amongst the reflections dancing on the leaves and in the evening shadows playing on the walls."

Holding her hand tightly a worried Clemens told her he understood what she was saying and that she should look for him there too, if he was unable to return one day. "We often think so much alike, you and I. Look for me in the breeze that moves the leaves and my hand will brush your face to let you know I am there"

As their lips met each breathed the words "I love you, so much."

The curtain over the doorway was brushed aside at that moment and a strong, no-nonsense woman bustled in, followed by her eldest daughter and the perplexed steward, Comazon Valerius, who had not known whether to hold them back or rush them in, never having been a father himself.

"All you men shoo," the midwife ordered and forcibly waved them out as her trainee pulled the handily placed birthing chair into the middle of the room.

As Julia jumped at another contraction the two women gently pulled off her clothing and explained again how they would deliver her from the seated position.

"Child, go and fetch warm water – get a servant to bring it quickly. The cloths we need are here in the basket I brought, as usual. You must always check these things before you come out. Now go – quickly." The midwife turned back to Julia and asked casually, "This is your first? Of course it is, I can see it in your face – and you've no old stretch marks."

Cleaned up Julia was helped into the low-backed chair and, while her daughter put her arms around Julia's chest from behind, the woman began feeling around the extended abdomen, sometimes leaving her hand in a particular place as she felt or sensed movement.

★ ★ ★

It was sometime later that a bewildered Clemens was guided down a series of passageways from the far side of the villa and into the delivery room, where a newborn baby lay on a towel in the middle of the floor, its tiny hands and feet opening and closing.

Not having been able to hear the first cries of birth he had not known what to expect but, at once realising his legal position, he immediately stooped to scoop up the unwashed little body into his arms to signify his acceptance of the child, so that it would now be cared for by his family and household, before handing it to the midwife to be cleaned and passed to Julia.

"I'm so glad I gave you a son, Clemens, to carry on your family name," whispered a weary Julia from where she now lay propped up in bed.

Clemens gently kissed the clammy face and smiled happily. "You will be almost as much loved by my father as you are by me. Every grandfather wants a grandson first. Now you must have a daughter for yourself!"

The midwife ushered him out, clucking that there was plenty of time for that sort of talk but, more importantly, his good lady wife needed rest.

Ecstatic that he had a son and that Julia was safely delivered he almost floated back down the labyrinth, his slippered feet making no sound on the tessellated floors as he wondered what his absent father-in-law, Felix, would think about it – and what about names? Would he insist on any, as was his right, the three of them had never discussed it at any length. Why ever not? How strange, he thought. Of course, he consoled himself, there were still the usual eight or nine days before a naming ceremony. Still, what of any disagreement, since the birth had to be registered within thirty days to be legal. He resolved to deal with it immediately.

★ ★ ★

The commercial vessel was eventually drawn up to the Waerham quay by its tug and tied up. As soon as it was secure the gangplank clattered own and Felix almost bounded down it to greet his son-in-law.

They grasped each other in bear hugs and both had moist eyes, though neither would have admitted it. Only then realising what he had done, or not done, Felix turned back and was only just in time to help Livia step down onto the quay.

She moved towards Clemens to forestall any embarrassment on his part, which allowed them to hug briefly whilst she whispered, "It's difficult to say, simply, just how pleased we are – and even more pleased that Julia and your babe are both well."

"I have a *raeda* over there," the young man said pointing briefly in its general direction. "The four wheels will give you back your land legs on our way home. You know, Julia is so excited at the prospect of showing you your grandson it was all I could do to stop her bringing him down to meet you!"

"It's just as well," responded Felix through a smile, "it'll give you time to read a dashed note from the Governor."

"How is he, by the way," Clemens enquired, as they were assisted into the carriage by the driver.

As it jerked away, its wheels grinding on the quay's flagstones, Felix took Livia's hand in his and said, "Urbicus is basically fine but of late he's been looking ahead to the end of his Governorship. Not only his future, actually, but he's also disappointed that he won't be here to see in the celebrations for the nine-hundredth year since Rome's founding. Do you know, he even went to the trouble to calculate what the celebration date will be in that newfangled calendar, as he calls it, that's catching on in some places. One-four-eight AD, I think it was."

They each held on as the carriage quickly turned out of the little town's west gate and onto the dusty road that led to the house, rocking violently as the fixed rear wheels tried to follow the pivoting front axle.

Livia squeezed Felix' hand and remarked "Urbicus says it won't catch on but it's best to be prepared for it when he either goes home, or takes his nominated seat in the senate – just in case!"

Clemens had told the carriage crew to hurry and barely had time to comment that Urbicus' tenure would hardly be up sooner than in two or three years' time, when the running cursor guided the mules into the villa's yard and the driver pulled back on the reins.

"I'll let Julia read the Governor's note first," Clemens explained as he stepped down in their wake, "She did all the hard work, after all."

★ ★ ★

Later that evening, with the ladies fussing over the baby as it was put to bed by the wet nurse, Felix and his son-in-law made their way slowly down to the river that fringed the lower gardens, sometimes picking a way round storm-fallen trees that still had to be removed by the estate foreman's men. Both noted without remark that the old and blackened lightning tree still stood, cleft as it was. It was the storm damage, followed by the attempted sacking of the villa, that had set the train of thought in motion which had prompted Felix to suggest a wine-fuelled walk in the threatening dusk.

Sipping from his goblet and looking at his senior officer over it, Clemens finally asked, "If you go, when will it be?"

Startled by the accuracy of the question Felix fought to keep his face expressionless but realised the instant reaction would have been noted and he stopped trying.

"I've obviously trained you too well! Have you been picking up signs for long – and interpreting them to form an opinion?"

"For a while," he replied, "although you hold your counsel well, as always. Really it's what you haven't said, coupled with your abstraction, that triggered my thoughts in that direction.

You were as impressed with your grandson as anyone could be – but it never seemed to me that naming him crossed your mind. If it didn't, then whatever overrode it had to be important – at least on the spur. So what was it? Livia pregnant – no. That would have been obvious in her manner and Julia would have picked up on it anyway. Your role – no. That would have been official: you would have told me. Illness was a possibility – but you seem fit. What was left was another of life's burdens – removal."

Felix sighed heavily, "To be so obvious – I hate the idea of that. Do you think anyone else picked up on it?"

"No," Clemens said definitely. "The others were too busy purring over the new arrival. Now that you've reminded me – do you have any names on your mind?"

Frowning, Felix said he did not. Then he brightened and said, "Of course – my prerogative! But still no! As far as I'm concerned you did the deed, you take the responsibility! That said, my father's benefactor was mine, too, so if you put Augustus in the series both he and I would be grateful. It's up to you, beyond that."

Almost laughing Clemens took another sip. "I couldn't have wished a more prestigious name! It will be in there – and thank you!"

Now laughing himself, Felix stepped towards his son-in-law and they grasped forearms to cement the bond.

"What of your father's name?"

"It was his given name too, before mine. He'll understand."

"Augustus," they said together and broke away to salute one another with a draught of wine.

"It does well" Clemens repeated "Julia will love it!"

"Good," responded Felix saluting him again with his goblet, "but we must talk of my thoughts!"

Clemens returned the salute, then said seriously, "We must - indeed we must. I can only assume the girls don't know."

"Livia has the gist, but I'm not sure she realises I mean soon. Of course she's astute and may have picked up on things in the general way women have. Quite disconcerting, really. Still, there are questions and answers to follow in abundance."

"So. What do you want to tell me?"

"To tell it all, really. You are my daughter's husband and my grandson's father – how much closer can we be? I wish you had been my son. I'm proud of you and your record."

Felix paused but Clemens said nothing. The moment was too important.

"It's my belief, as I shall say at the next Triumvirate – only you know of that – the stakes are being raised. The possibility of a usurper as governor is increasing considerably. Alongside that I believe even more strongly that my own life is a target. The issues of that you will understand only too well. Those alongside me will be targets, too.

On the cautionary side, you will probably already be one, as my deputy. Take every precaution - and have men with you - as well as guards you can trust around the villa."

Taking a deep breath before he continued he went on, "As a target I involve you all. If I go – and I must – then the problem comes with me. By definition, any attacks on you then means you are a target anyway – and can take appropriate action.

We must halve the remaining century and put all the companions together. That will help cohesion. I doubt we could wholly trust replacements, even it they were available. The Walls need the recruits more than we do, regrettable as it is."

"I wish I could disagree with you – but I fear you're right. Still, we've about a half-century and the men are men I would always want at my back; or even half of them!"

"My own thoughts," agreed Felix. Then he added seriously, "Now, as I said, any problems should follow me if they're mine – as I think they will be. I'm being shadowed either because of our work or a vendetta from my past, whichever. Your problems on that front will probably be solved, or at least halved, on my move. What do you say?"

Clemens shifted uneasily and stared out over the narrow but deep and winding river noticing, but not really seeing, the fledging second families of its resident swans, ducks and coots serenely feeding in the murky water without any apparent care in the world.

Finally he said, "It sounds logical. You go and we stay – but how do you know the villa wouldn't be attacked as a decoy – a pretence of being after me, or even as though they didn't know you were gone – not having been told, as it were."

"As ever, Clemens, you hit the nail right on the thumb. We don't! We never will, with total confidence."

"So?"

"My moving will divide their targets. We should expect our protagonists to come to know that and go for broke by attacking me."

"You mean use all their forces against a half of what we currently have? It doesn't sound rational on our part."

"Whenever did rationality win a battle? On the face of it the outcome's predictable. We will be inferior – nothing less – but our vulnerability will work for us. We shall devise tactics that turn any overconfidence against our enemies."

"We would be too far apart to aid each other!"

"You have the Waerham Police. Devise a signalling stratagem."

"What will you do?"

"Off-the-wall, I'm not finally sure. However, there are a great many time-served men around. Maybe Titus and Julius will arrange work for them – even persuade them it will supplement their gratuities – all good, veteran fighting stock. A centurion and an optio will know how to choose their men. I think it will work. Who goes with whom in the halving is fairly pertinent though."

"Obviously both with you – you need them."

"No. I don't think so – but thank you for your thought. Julius needs to fledge, so you have him. He'll be ever more diligent because of the added responsibility. Make him up, temporarily – he will enjoy the accolade. On my side, Titus will keep the old hands in thrall. After all, he served as optio under Frontus who selected them, too – may the gods continue to bless him – and *his* reputation went before him. He died too soon, but now others have a role model to follow. I think they will.

Once a soldier always a soldier – it's the basic idea of veterans' colonies, after all. As for the recruits the difference is only that they will work for me instead of themselves."

"We know to our cost these renegades can move quietly. Last time Stolus came to the rescue – who the next time? I don't like the idea of dividing our forces," Clemens observed.

Felix drew on some wine and looked keenly at him before saying earnestly, "I want to draw the bastards out! What Firmus tells us about them is good and the false information we feed in return will pay dividends. However, things depend on when they choose to act – if we are to catch them attacking another bullion wagon.

What I am offering them is the chance of getting me. Or you, of course," he added with no relish, thinking of the added risk to his grandson, that swaddled ball with wispy, blonde hair.

"There's a firm chance of the conspirators succeeding, as I see it – especially with you. At least we have the police fort and Stolus down the Swanwic road."

Felix shook his head and glanced up at the sky. "It could rain. Let's start back before the girls send for us.

No. As I've said, I briefly discussed it with Livia and she sees the point. She says she will have to be doubly watchful, but I did have an earful about her leaving Julia and the babe – and that was before she'd seen him!"

"Where was it you said?" Clemens asked the question and, then answered it himself. "On the river Stour near a holly wood? Hol-something?"

Smiling at him Felix agreed. "That's only a locally known place. There's a village – hardly that – nearby, which is called something akin to Throp. I hope to put a small mill on the nearby weir, in good time. We'll see. The river comes out at Twynham harbour, not far from the old trading head at Henburh."

"Ah, yes. That's what I've heard you say at some time or other." Clemens paused and then said, almost with some finality, "If you feel you must, you must!"

★ ★ ★

"So. It's all yours, Quintus." Mercurialis was in expansive mood now. "The quarry, the villa, the string of female gladiators and ownership of the lands around."

"Just some of the lands. There's no point in pushing at the Celtic village – the tribal council in Durnovaria will only appeal to our esteemed governor."

"And he will send that arse, Albinus Felix, nosing in here. It'd almost be worth it to trap him here and end his interference once and-for-all! What do you think?" The tall, lean, close-cropped figure threw himself back in his couch and laughed. "If only dreams became reality so easily!"

"My uncle – whom I think you simply called Paternus – often expressed such a sentiment to me, when he led the group. This man leads a charmed life and I haven't forgotten the shame of my expulsion. The damned slut was only a bloody prostitute – how can you rape a prostitute? And how can an Emperor's servant, no less, find that I did?

That bastard and his friendly governor have it coming – but I cannot put these lands at risk. I would lose all support in the Eternal City – my family and the Marsala family would fall out. No other support would back me if I lose my head and then no revenge would be possible, would it? At least, not easily."

Still smiling broadly Mercurialis spoke from his laid-back position. "You're right, of course. I only teased you with the idea. It was fortuitous that your surviving aunt had only a female child and a deceased father – no male support directly, so the Aurelius Paternus family agreed to relinquish any claim in your favour. Ironic though – I heard that Didius Marsala killed Paternus on Vectis!"

"Had him killed, I heard – but I doubt any of it would stand up beyond hearsay. I ignore it – I am here and accountable to my father, not his brother."

"That's good! That's very good." Mercurialis sat up now and lightly applauded this sanguine approach. "That is absolutely the way to look at it. You may yet be greater than either – especially if our association brings down this governor and we assume control of Britannia sooner rather than later!"

"Where exactly do I fit in? I'm a newcomer. This is my house, my home, my land. I'm not prepared to just be used."

Mercurialis threw his hands wide. "Who said you would just be used? However, I know what you are saying – I was a newcomer, too; but you and I supersede the pedestrian.

I lead, you follow me – but just for the moment. We need Flavius Silus and Publius Lucius – their downgrading now would cause a hiatus. Let it work out as I plan it. Your time is not far off. Trust me. You are vital to our plans."

Quintus beamed at that and inwardly preened. He was vital! What a choice of word. His father would be proud of him.

"You will wait?"

As though awakening from a trance Quintus looked at this aquiline-featured man in his preferred toga, a ready smile on his lips and hands apart in placation.

"Of course," he responded immediately. "These things must be done properly. My father would expect that – however much we shall influence things in the future; I shall wait on you."

"I knew you would," cried Mercurialis as he rubbed his hands. "Time and place, time and place."

"What of One-eye?" Quintus asked.

A deep, guttural monotone asked, "Did someone call me by something other than my name?"

Open-mouthed Quintus half-turned, but in that time Haruld had him by the throat, a strong wrist squeezing gently so that the throttle was slow in coming but just as certain, thrashing hands totally ineffective.

Quintus croaked convulsively and gagged, but his larynx was unable to function and he groped at thin air as his faculties failed him.

Suddenly released to gasp, choke and cough, Quintus fell sideways onto his couch, his hands initially grasping at his throat but immediately recoiling from the pain he caused himself. A hand hit his windpipe and suddenly air flooded into him once again.

His lungs filling fuelled the urge to lift himself and wretch over the side of his couch against the wall, only to fall back exhausted, breathing hard.

"I see you remember Haruld from Thule. He is our hammer. It's best not to be his anvil!"

The spinning world of Quintus suddenly counter-rotated and his eyes focussed on the face of the renowned Norseman, Haruld, known as Haruld the One-eyed to a very few – and to none simply as *The-One-eyed,* or *One-eye,* without retribution.

"I remember," he gasped as he gulped air, "I simply forgot. No slight was intended, I assure you!"

"None was taken – I assure you, too!"

The irony in the response was far greater a warning than any threat would have been. It hit home hard, Quintus acknowledged.

"Haruld, my friend," exclaimed Mercurialis, "You return at so appropriate a time. You must surely be blessed by your gods."

"My men say I am, so I must be."

"So you must be. Tell me, did you see any of the Roman fleet?"

"Nothing. If they were ineffective they would be better than today."

"If I may say so, your Latin is very good."

Haruld beamed. "To speak the language of empire: thank you."

"What method did you use?"

"The most simple. I took captives and tortured some to death in front of the others. Slowly, of course. For some reason I then had many willing tutors. Those I could not easily understand encouraged the rest, as they died, too.

So I learned the new first language of Britannia – though some persisted in calling it Albion. I think I understand enough now. It is a pity for my tutors they could not benefit from what I learnt – beyond my learning it."

"I believe our friend has learnt," offered Mercurialis, smiling as he pointed.

Sitting up now, with a hand to his throat, Quintus croaked, "The language does not make you equal. Only citizenship would do that!"

"I have no wish to demean myself. I *rule* in my land. What do you rule - stones?"

Merculrialis held up a placatory hand and said, "A king and a prince meet. The outcome was predictable. It's sung in your sagas."

Haruld laughed and farted several times. "You have a way with you, my friend. It's why I liaise with you. You like that word? A man suffered a lot for that. I hope he was right."

Laughing himself now to lighten the mood, Mercurialis said, "I cannot think of a better one. Do you have time to visit our Senate in the Eternal City? You could educate them!"

Slapping his thighs Haruld retorted, "I could educate them with my sword! Empire? What do the Romans know of empire? Given the same number of men I would sweep every beehive under my power – the power of Norse."

In the short silence which followed Quintus regained his poise but struggled with a sore throat. "When you enter my lands, lord king, you do so by announcing yourself to my steward."

Smiling Haruld said quietly, "I believe he will tell you I did so. I have already given you his excuse for not announcing me!"

"I will take my sword, I think."

"Sword?"

"The one you took from my uncle. It was my present."

Riled by this Haruld snarled, "Take? You think to take? From me?"

"No!" The snapped word brought both of them up short. "No.! There will be no taking – only giving."

The others looked at him quizzically, wondering what he had meant by the choice of words.

"The sword was given by Quintus to his uncle. It's part of his estate. It clearly belongs to him."

Puzzled, his brow furrowed, Haruld said haltingly, "I understand the words – what do they mean?"

Hurriedly Mercurialis explained. "It's the important difference in meaning between the words themselves and what they mean in Roman law."

"Roman law? I have the sword - with its jewelled hilt. It's mine!"

"In possession only. You came by it. In law it's still in the leavings of the uncle. It quite clearly belongs to our young friend."

"This is Roman law? What law takes from those that have?"

"Roman law. Right exceeds mere possession."

"But how so? I understand that if a Roman takes over someone's land by force, say a better farm, it cannot be recovered in law. At best there is compensation paid."

"That is old law. It would not stand the test now," Quintus spoke up sharply.

"Test? I would test my men against any!"

"And lose! What we stand to gain in the near future," Mercurialis said quietly, striving to dampen the situation, "is unrivalled. A conquered land ready for our administration. Your men would have land, riches and status – as part of the peace-keepers."

"They would desert with riches!"

Staring at Mercurialis Haruld growled, "Much as I would like to slit his throat for saying so, regrettably I have to agree. The little sod's right!"

Quintus made to get up to refute the slur but Mercurialis pushed him back down.

Harold relaxed again and his hand slipped from the knife in his belt, his face a contorted smile as he listened to Mercurialis.

"You both make your points. But your men will be needed in the future army - based north or south – though you would like the north better, I suspect.

As for riches, none of our own rank-and-file recruits will be rewarded finally until they are no longer needed – that is, are replaced. If we have no army it would mean no kingdom. Rome would soon take it back. Any occupying army, one which governs, therefore provides employment for itself.

We must have a well-paid and contented army – but one which realises that loyalty brings its own rewards; land and riches at the right time. Do you see that? It is the present philosophy of the Romans."

Scratching his head and then his scrotum Haruld said quietly, in little more than a mumble, "I have to agree. My men would need occupation – not a fortune!"

"And they will have it," Mercurialis retorted brightly. "*Then* land and riches. You have a small number of good fighting men. Their success will be its own reward. It can be well-afforded: several times over, if all goes well. Tell them that – it has to be earned."

"I shall explain things to them."

"At that time they would be used as auxiliary troops – it will mean less training as they will retain the arms they're used to.

Actually, now would be a good time to enlist. A major battle is likely in the north and men are needed. Entry requirements are more likely to be relaxed, especially for auxiliary troops – but regrettably your Norse are too well known, for now."

"My men are all warriors; fit fighters. They will pass muster whenever."

"Good. I'm sure of it. So, after the battle and heavy Roman losses, let some of your men nominate a leader and they can attend the Deva or Eboracum forts to enlist. Let them understand they are disaffected men to whom promises have been broken.

There's every reason to expect they will be formed into their own squads. Their guard duties will be a valuable tool for us. We can come and go at will through either wall where they are stationed."

"You have matters in hand," Haruld remarked, screwing up his face. "I'm puzzled as to why?"

Smiling easily Mercurialis replied, "These men can go home when their time is up – or desert. Whichever, this group's agenda will be nearer fruition by then."

"I could not go, in any event. I have a contract to fulfil before I winter in Hibernia."

Chapter II

T hey were sat on individual couches round a small, low table covered with what had been described as a working luncheon.

The Governor reached out and took one of several small pastry cases filled with beaten egg and topped with spices. Shaking a generous quantity of pepper onto it he took a large enough bite to leave only half the tart in his hand. He waved airily at the other goods arranged attractively in dishes when he realised the other two were not joining him.

"It's very good of you, Urbicus," observed Admiral Agrippa, unmoved. "However, Felix and I would rather deal with the points we need to discuss with you, first."

"Is that so, Felix?"

"I'm afraid so, Urbicus. Agrippa and I probably have some common points. If so, I wouldn't be surprised."

"Wouldn't you, be dammed? Why haven't you discussed them with me beforehand?"

"I, personally, thought this triumvirate would present the opportunity," interrupted Agrippa, as fleet procurator the second most senior officer in the island. "Presumably Felix thought the same."

As head of the secret service in Britannia Felix had had no such seniority of rank. Therefore, when faced with no alternative, he occasionally relied on the letter of authority issued by the late Hadrian and reinforced by the Governor on his own appointment. However, since his latest promotion, Felix' civil equivalent placed him below very few military ranks.

"I think I must quickly point out, Urbicus, that Agrippa and I haven't had a pre-meeting discussion and neither does he speak for me. It's just that one matter in particular bothers me and I believe it bears debate."

"Raise it," prompted Agrippa.

"I believe you must," agreed the Governor.

"I think it's time that Rome was informed of what's happening here – whilst we still have it under control," said Felix, bluntly and to the point.

"That is *it* – exactly what I was to say," said Agrippa, slapping his couch. "That is it to the jot!"

The words hung in the air and for a few moments seemed as it they might represent a cloud threatening to burst.

"Why?" Urbicus finally asked the obvious question, prompting him to replace the uneaten half of the tart in order to better concentrate on the answer.

Felix sat back in his seat and crossed his hands casually over his abdomen. He did not hurry to answer.

"We can no longer keep this hidden. To use your phrasing more or less, we have tried to for the sake of the new Emperor – but in reality he is no longer *new* and with the change in protagonists involved it will definitely filter back there. Indeed it may deliberately be reported, knowing that we have *not* done so.

Rome must be informed; but not only that, the report must also define why the information was withheld – *for security reasons.* Nothing less will explain the delay."

"Antoninus did not need to be bothered with such minor complications so early in his reign."

"That *is* what you said. However," Felix argued, "as his governor here you have protected his most northerly frontier unblemished for long enough. Now it's time, I strongly suggest, to explain the fallacy of assuming a new wall will, or more correctly will not, prevent this province from being the intrinsic problem we know it to be already.

You have contained the issue magnificently – but despite all our best efforts we must acknowledge that a state of disloyalty exists. Not, of course, with any of your senior officers – nor *all* the tribal leaders by a long shot. But you know of subversive elements at all levels of society here and you can only conclude, therefore, Rome itself has suspects – and these are by no means limited to the upwardly mobile, so to speak.

Our best intelligence suggests that more than just financial aid is coming out of the Eternal City and that this active support will corrupt even some of the currently loyal, if left unchecked."

Urbicus had retreated into his couch as he listened to the advice, noting the almost non-stop nodding of his admiral's head.

He said nothing for a while, apparently unaware of the intense gazes that held him firmly, until and with the utmost sincerity, he sighed, "This Emperor wants only peace. He seeks no border wars.

However, what you have to remember, and which you know very well, no Emperor can realistically lay claim to the actual title unless he has effectively extended the boundary of empire.

For him to push outwards elsewhere would not improve on what Augustus, Trajan or Hadrian did, each of them now elected a god in people's minds. Neither is Antoninus seeking to become another Alexander, though he would welcome trade with far-flung lands as any Emperor would.

So, we push further north to follow previous governor Agricola's trail – as you know the only one to explore Caledonia. You may recall he said he could conquer Hibernia with one legion – but never attempted it. Perhaps his victory at Mons Graupius told him more about conquest than was ever admitted. Still, I conjecture – and don't want to be diverted.

He went in pursuit of the heathen, the uncivilised, the barbarian – call them as you will – and gained a victory. But the land is mountainous and inhospitable as well as beautiful, meaning many of his isolated forts were unsustainable in the long term - to say the least!

It's impossible to deploy our legions in the foothills indefinitely and where cavalry can almost be an encumbrance, with no real room to manoeuvre. Neither are the tribes likely to meet us on level ground again, however cleverly it might have been contrived before.

Hadrian had his wall built, as we know, to be his line in the dust. It takes many men to hold it. Too many.

Antoninus wishes me to build a shorter wall, forty miles in length, taking less men -but closer together. I have explained my thinking before and suffice it to say I want to complete it this year.

The new wall will hold the tribes further back. It will confront them, confuse them and, hopefully, convulse them. Their infighting would help us immensely. It will be a victory for the new Emperor.

As for myself, I can claim at least one more for him between the walls, as we make the area safe to continue building – and possibly a number beyond his wall as we hold back attacks on its construction.

When it's complete there'll be a better road support system behind it than behind Hadrian's. Less men will be able to support each other more easily because of it.

This isn't new to you – I reiterate it, I know – but until it happens Antoninus is *per se*, an Emperor-in-waiting. When it does he will be a true Emperor. It is his due.

Therefore anything adverse I held back, so as not to muddy any celebrations.

As of now, you are right. The wall is being completed and so it *is* time to let the senate know of the problems – not because my eventual successor might uncover the subterfuge – but to let them know it was no easy victory."

"Subterfuge?"

Urbicus spread his hands palms upwards in the traditional gesture, as he replied, "Yes, Agrippa, that's how it might be seen. However, I agree with you both. *Now* is the time. The wall first though. Then, when the senate has granted him his due victory and honours, we shall follow up with reports *ad nauseum* on the treason being perpetrated here and in Rome."

Felix and Agrippa looked at each as though wondering who would speak.

The Governor rode his opportunity and hijacked the pause by waving a scroll. "I also have here a report from the wall's commander, brought down by your protégé, Agrippa. It speaks strongly of unrest and so I have decided to go up there immediately to supervise the New Wall's protection myself. It means, of course, you will need to transport us – so it's as well Gaius Fabullius Macer brought his trireme down. You can split my cohort between you and a transport. Your ninety – no, one-eighty – marines will come in useful, too."

"We welcome the action! Macer will need to revictual, of course. When will you sail?"

"Felix," the governor said seriously, "on this occasion I want you with me. Your son-in-law will have to come to. I want a conference with Firmus – I don't know how long it is since you saw your northern agent, but that's neither here nor there. I want the five of us to coordinate a strike against this Mercurialis and his web before he becomes too bold."

"It's not the right time," protested Felix.

"We have to go immediately or the weather will close in on us. Right, Agrippa?"

Urbicus raised an eyebrow at him.

"That's right enough. Sooner than later."

"Good. Felix you'd best make your preparations and I'll expect you back here, at the Regnum Palace, in three days with Clemens."

Over-ruled, Felix accepted it without further complaint.

★ ★ ★

With Julia once again taking a class of poor children in the small town's market place now that she had recovered from the birth, Livia felt at a loose end and wondered how her husband was faring.

Leaving the villa she wandered idly down to the river and turned along the bank, walking upstream of the fast-flowing body of water to where Felix was having a watermill constructed on what had become a small island, now that the race had been completed beside it. A sluiced channel to take the excess water from the river was on its other side, which then ran around to rejoin the main flow.

Realising that she had wandered some distance from the house she turned about and began to retrace her steps until, suddenly, her intuition told her to look back. It had not failed her and she immediately took in the two hooded figures, in breeches and rough jerkins, climbing from the bank-side reed-bed.

With her heart beating she picked up her skirts and ran along beside the stream, ridiculously thinking it had been a good thing she had not put a short tunic over the traditional longer one, or she would have been too hot.

Wrestling with the flow two other hooded figures competently handled a log using paddles and this, coupled with the current flowing at twice walking speed, soon had them surging past her and into a shallow shingle bank, where they simply stood to allow the log to float off, before stepping up to the path and blocking it.

Livia stopped and let the hem of her dress fall over her sandals, uncertain now what best to do. Should she stand and brazen it out, attempt to dodge through the stand of trees and hope not to be impeded by the fallen trunks, or leap into water and let the river take her where it would – but at least towards the villa. In the instant it took to think those thoughts she realised that to brazen it out was the best of poor options. What a fool she felt, that she had not taken more notice of the fact that no work was being done on the mill.

A deep voice droned in her ear from behind and she twitched in surprise at the silent approach. From his odour she defined him as not a regular bather – probably a tribesman, she thought, but then his Latin confounded her when he spoke.

"My lady. If you wish to survive whole it will be essential you do exactly what you are told – and at once."

She was aware of whispered comment passing between the others but a waved hand silenced it.

"Do you understand? It is important that you *do* understand, because you must remain perfectly still."

She thought she knew what the outcome would be but shivered at the unsuspected touch of a knife that dipped into the halter of her dress and cut down its back, extra pressure slicing into the loose waist sash until it succumbed and allowed the blade its full passage to the hem. A hand flicked each shoulder piece in turn and the now useless covering fell to her feet.

The whispers returned as eyes took in her nakedness, apart from the flimsy drawers she wore.

"Be very still," the deep voice cautioned and she once again felt the cold metal against her body as it followed the line of her right hip, parting the slight fabric as it went, until the now loose drawers slowly slipped down her left leg to join the dress piled on her feet.

Her bare breasts goose-pimpled in nervous expectation as she wondered whether they were disappointed that there had been no uplifting chest-band to cut off as well.

Livia tried to stand tall, holding here elegant neck straight and her head high, ignoring as best she could the excitement in the body language of her captors.

"Step away from those rags and turn to face me. Do it carefully," she was instructed.

Having done so, to add narrow feet and slim ankles to her nakedness, Livia now saw that there were five of them in all.

"You are beautiful, Lady. Stay that way by being careful."

The hooded assailant reached out and brushed his hands over her shoulders, running them down her biceps. As he reached for her breasts Livia involuntarily spat in his face, automatically expressing her contempt for what she expected to take place. Some must have penetrated the eye holes because he barely paused before grasping the back of her neck with one hand in order to pull her blonde-dyed hair towards him for the other hand to use as a wipe.

Letting her go he laughed quietly and then took a breast in each hand, savouring their softness in his palms whilst massaging the nipples with his thumbs. He felt the slightly tanned skin flutter in horror and laughed again, running his hands down her stomach and over her buttocks before sliding a hand between her thighs to prove his complete control of the situation.

"There is no private part of you I have not seen or touched. Remember that, when you lock you door at night. I already know you!"

At his signal two of the four grasped her arms firmly and held them out sideways. Livia expected the worst and was not disappointed, as other hands repeated the previous exploration with gusto, only for it to be repeated yet again by the other two.

Her arms slightly twisted for torsion she was held erect as the four took turns in daubing stinking blue clay across her body in stripes, lingering on breast or thigh as they did so.

Surprised at what was happening she held her head still, as their apparent leader stroked clay across her face from left forehead to right chin by way of her nose and the edge of her mouth, her left eyelid automatically closing to take the colour so that, as it opened again, the light-green eye gazed out from the blue shadow in puzzlement.

At another signal her arms where pulled behind her and the forearms tied together in two places, which also had the effect of drawing up her breasts even more tightly, a fact which did not go unnoticed.

"Your interfering husband should not leave so beautiful a body unattended," the disembodied voice intoned. "Now we wait."

Livia was forced into the shelter of the trees and they formed a small group around her, their evil odour all the ranker for the excitement of her naked closeness.

As time passed one by one they urinated in the trees, the four subordinates each ensuring they waved themselves in her direction. Wanting to go herself, she struggled against the indignity of them watching her and she hoped whatever they waited for would come quickly.

Jerked roughly to her feet Livia was manhandled with relish up to the boundary of the river meadow, now noisy with birdsong in the gathering dusk and she felt the grass damp on her toes.

A thong was passed around her throat and secured to a fence post. Livia, unsure of what would happen, tried to disguise the fear she felt deep inside.

"Now, lady, there is just the matter of the spittle to consider," the leader said, almost conversationally. He held out a hand and the stems of a thick tuft of stinging nestles was placed in his hand.

He traced the leaves round the firm, out-thrust breasts and watched Livia as she twitched and jerked when the barbed leaves bit the tender skin.

"What a shame the clay inhibits, where it streaks you," he said, then quickly thrust the tuft between her thighs, smiling when this time she cried out as she was stung.

A pre-written board of thin wood was suspended from her neck so that it hung from below her breasts to her navel.

"Those who find you will tell what it says."

With those last enigmatic words all five of them sped off in the direction of the mill, leaving nature to finally have its way with her.

* * *

Each fighting back the urge to return south immediately Felix and Clemens studied the report prepared on behalf of Paulinus, who had had it sent by express messenger immediately. They knew the riders must have managed at least fifty miles a day with horse changes at every mansio, to have brought it to the wall so soon.

Paulinus had added a personal note of his regret and anger, also reminding them that his hands were still keeping him from duty after being nailed to the police fort doorway, in the same attack that fired the villa.

"He would not have made a difference," concluded Clemens as he finished reading over his father-in-law's shoulder, "but he'll make a difference to any investigations!"

"I strongly suspect that after all this time he'll be pensioned as unfit. Still, that's another story," Felix remarked before adding, "several things puzzle me about this."

"And me," agreed the young tribune, scratching his frizzy campaign hair. "How did they know, for one?"

"Yes. So presumably they kept a vigil. But does that mean any one of our women could have been a target?"

Clemens clapped him on the shoulder as a compliment, taking liberties with a legate he could not otherwise have taken had they not been friends as well as in-laws.

"I have to admit I'd not taken the *how* that far," he said, "but, yes, I agree with you. It could well be the case. Livia says clearly they were Britons. As they smelled so rank – presumably brigands," he added.

"Let's read it again," suggested Felix, "and see what we *really* know."

Clemens pointed. "Hoods! Britons who didn't want to be recognised afterwards!"

"True," nodded Felix. "But not only afterwards perhaps – what about during as well?"

Clemens hit the heel of his hand against his forehead in frustration. "Damn! I missed that, too! You think someone didn't want to be recognised, then?"

"I think that's more likely, when you think of what happened according to this report – and Paulinus would give a good account even if he couldn't necessarily resolve it."

"I agree with that. What are we looking at now?

"Let's move on to the daubing with clay," Felix said, not wanting to imagine the actual stripping of his wife. "Why use blue *clay*?"

"For Celtic war paint – treating her like a warrior."

Felix breathed out and repeated, "Why blue clay?"

"Well," replied Clemens, "presumably they did not have access to woad."

"Right! So why not? After all, it's a dye as well as battle decoration."

"I see your drift now - and why would they speak Latin to Livia and do the same amongst themselves, so that she would understand?" Clemens frowned then, before adding, "Still, it's possible it was deliberate to frighten her with what they said."

"Possibly – but just think, supposing the stench was to add flavour to the situation. Additionally, they have no woad to paint her with. They speak only Latin all the time. Even the message was in Latin – *next time you will be dead.*"

"For our benefit - but hang on though, you speak Celtic too, your father being a Briton."

"Precisely! The only Britannic-like thing was the log."

"They weren't Britons – but Romans!"

"Most likely – though not necessarily. Most urban dwellers have at least a sense of Latin, so they could be any nationality. Remember Waerham receives foreign traffic on the quay, too.

Whoever they are they killed the mill builders. Would Celts kill their own?"

"So who? Mercurialis and company – or One-eye?"

Felix smiled grimly. "Led – or arranged by. It's only a guess but I shall be surprised if it's wrong. He's doing what I told you I was doing to him by moving house.

He's telling me to come and get him!"

★ ★ ★

"So, the boy's name is, Augustus Iulius Albinus Felix Clemens, then?"

"That's what we shall register his birth as. Of course we, or he himself later, may add others – and I'm not sure of *two* Clemenses in the same family, but you know what women are!" The young man smiled broadly at the Governor, as he confirmed his son's naming.

"I envy you, my lad. It was never my time to be in your position and it's at moments like this I regret it most."

"Will you adopt a successor?"

"I have thought of it. Someone like young Clemens here – or Macer – or Firmus or..... well, I think on it: someone to carry on my estates. Possibly the lad Rufinus. It would be a fillip for him and Romana would love it. He has all the potential of those I've mentioned, to boot. He just needs time."

"You know yourself best," Felix said non-committally.

Urbicus looked at him, paused, then said, "Something is bothering you, my friend. I would have expected great happiness."

"I am happy for others, Urbicus. My problem won't go away because of happiness - but neither am I jealous of anyone being happy. As it happens Clemens knows of the issue. We share problems as well as pleasure."

Sitting back and looking at him afresh the Governor said, "I didn't realise a nerve was so raw. I'm sorry, whatever it is."

"Don't be," Felix retorted quickly. "There's nothing to be done momentarily. There are other matters in hand."

"Your whole attitude tells me it's serious. However, I am forced to take your point. As ever, the Wall occupies me and will do so until completion. Antoninus Pius might be nearly the last in the recent line of humane emperors, that is, apart from his chosen successor, Marcus Aurelius – so putting up this outer wall is my part in keeping the peace he so desperately wants.

History will know Hadrian as The Little Greek, so interested was he in Grecian history. If postcrity knows Antoninus Pius as The Peacemaker I shall die happy for my part in it. I wonder if they will?"

"Only time will tell, my friend. For now, what is our part in it," Felix rejoined.

The Governor looked at them both very carefully. Then, as though on impulse, he said quietly, "As my personal bodyguard."

He allowed the information to sink in before he continued. "Essentially I am baiting a trap, as I did with the traitor you replaced with Firmus a couple of years back."

"Another traitor?" Felix was aghast.

Urbicus laughed. "There are more, my friend. There always will be – but you know that."

"Yes. Yes, of course. What I meant to ask was why you hadn't told me?"

The Governor held up a hand as if to stop the flow. "I didn't because there is nothing definite to tell.

What I intend to do is travel fast along The Wall – well, it's what the military road is for, after all. Your men are Dragooners, aren't they! Each can ride. With you along my presence will be upon the forts before their commanders know it.

I want to confirm our state of readiness personally – though I have a great deal of confidence in Julian Verecundus and his Belgician regiment at Vindolanda. I don't want the troops, or their commanders, resting on their laurels – which might happen after we complete the Emperor's most northern wall of all. Those troops that I leave behind me – I want them all to believe that I can appear out of nowhere and if that myth reaches the Caledonian tribes, so much the better!

However, the penalty for speed is paucity. That is, few men in my escort. So I want you and yours. Does that make sense?"

Felix and his son-in-law exchanged glances before Felix nodded. "Good sense, Urbicus. You believe you could become a target with so small a guard. We shall be most pleased. My men need a new objective, so that's good, too."

"Good, good. I know I'm in safe hands, then. After our race behind this old wall I shall swing hard north and see to Antoninus' Wall. As I said, I want to see it finished so that I can send word to *the common workshop of the world,* as I recently heard the Eternal City is being called."

They all laughed together at that until Urbicus went on, "We shall leave Segedunum, here at the Wall's end, to push on the forty miles to Vindolanda where Verecundus is based, with his Tungrian Belgicans.

I shall be sorry to leave here, in a way. These anglicised Nervian Belgicans of the second cohort are good legionaries – deserving of their grant of citizenship, even though still serving.

I like the site, too. Being in the river's angle there's an excellent view in every direction. Very dominant indeed. Now, I'm for the bathhouse and then the temple. Anybody joining me?"

★ ★ ★

Despite ad hoc visits to forts along the way the fourth day saw them reach their destination as planned. The vicus to the west of the fort was the usual collection of shops, taverns, mansio, bathhouse and whore houses which provided the basic needs of the soldiery and semi-Romanised citizenry around and about. The scouts made a way through the bustle of people and carts in order that the Governor fittingly entered the more important west gate. An altar set up by the council of the local tribe in the name of their local goddess, Sattada, had been erected there and caught their eye as it was intended to do.

Felix wondered on the siting of this civilian settlement, which smelt strongly of damp, thinking there may have been a spring underground and, if so, quite unsuitable for the wooden buildings. But then he was through the gate with the guards snapping neatly to attention on seeing the high-ranking officers in the van.

Grooms rushed out to take the lead horses and then gesticulated wildly that many more men would be needed to cater for the escorting century. Mouths dropped open as they realised the important visitor was no less than the Governor of the province but, now alerted, Julian Verecundus met them on the steps leading up to the commander's house.

Seated comfortably with warmed wine and honey cakes, in the main room of the commandant's house, the three officers tried to put Julian Verecundus at ease, rather than the other way round.

His surprise at the unannounced appearance was obvious and Felix considered it was to his credit that the staff became immediately alert to the hospitality required, without his having to direct the proceedings.

Urbicus, disregarding the social niceties of wearing a toga, lay back on his couch and belched quietly, his stomach reacting to the long, hard and fast ride accompanied by insipid food.

"Verecundus, your hospitality does you credit – but I know from your nickname that *modesty* would prevent you acknowledging it. However, I have noted it."

"I'm honoured sufficiently by your presence, Governor. I knew that the Emperor's wall would bring you north again, but I hadn't bargained on your visiting one of the old Agricolan forts behind Hadrian's Wall – may the gods take care of him."

"Tribune, it is only a fleeting visit – the governor is under immense time pressure," explained Felix. "What he is most interested in is the state and staffing of the wall in your remit. Would you explain it to him, please?"

Julian Verecundus looked away from Felix to the governor as he quickly added and subtracted figures in his mind.

"As you will realise, Sir, nothing in staffing is static. Clearly it varies from week to week – and indeed often hour to hour. You've arrived at a time which actually proves my point strongly. We're adequately staffed, Sir. However, at this particular moment I have half of my garrison present. Pretty much the same thing happened on the eighteenth day of Maius, Sir – that's the last time we collected the garrison's pay.

"Isn't that dangerous? That means the amount is quite high."

"Yes, Sir, it is – which is why I feel able to lend so many men to it. I couldn't justify anything like the number for a smaller amount. If I didn't it could be taken."

"Below the Wall?" Urbicus was incredulous.

"Probably not, Sir, but still a possibility. I have the reports of bullion raids in the south and cannot afford the risk. If the legionaries and the auxiliaries were not paid it would severely challenge loyalties – if you'll forgive my saying so, Sir?"

Expansively Urbicus responded, "Everything you say makes sense. I mean that. You make an excellent point. In fact, I salute you for it."

Exonerated, but embarrassed, Verecundus made to reply, but nothing came.

Gently, Felix said, "Your dispositions, Tribune."

Breathing in hard to gather himself, Verecundus explained, "I have a little short of eight hundred on the register. That includes six centurions.

In view of the raids I sent five centuries, with their centurions, to Eboracum to collect the wagon. With others on wall patrol between the mile forts that is some five hundred men, taking into account the legions' reductions in strength for each company.

In addition I have thirty-one unfit. Six are wounded, twenty-five are on the sick-list, including ten with sore eyes from the cold winds. The recommended eye salve of Axius, the fleet's oculist, will resolve that of course, but it's still a toll as of today, Sir."

"I take your point entirely, Tribune. I've been in similar circumstances in the past."

"Thank you for saying that, Sir. Even when the pay wagon comes in there'll be other calls. Policing duties in the *vicus* – the locals are not all sinless – and we have lost men in pursuit of bandits, sometimes including the Northern Brigantes and sometimes not. There's just no telling whether north and south tribesmen are in league or not, despite the schism that's suppose to exist."

"I wish I could tell you differently. Our local agent has the same problem – you obviously realise we have an agent here?"

"Oh, yes, Governor. I know his name – but will not say it. Some things are best left unsaid."

Urbicus smiled briefly and waved his hand.

"The point is made, I think. All we know is the tribe was split by their Queen Cartimandua, divorcing her consort and marrying her horse trainer decades ago – and is still split. Between the old and new walls the Votadini and Selgovae have every excuse to unite with their previous enemies, the Damnonii."

"Hopefully the Novantae of the north west will see sense and keep their distance."

"I hope you are right, Verecundus - but if we look like losing you can bet your best boots they find a reason for joining in!"

"As ever, Sir."

"As you say, sir, as ever." After the briefest of pauses Urbicus asked, "Can you hold this wall?"

"I am based behind it to do so. It can be relieved in a day, Governor. Any point within my jurisdiction!"

"So long as your pay detail is here," observed Felix quietly. "As we have agreed, they need to go - but they can only be in one place at a time. The oxen will tire, as will the men. They will also be seen to leave."

With a loud sigh Vindolanda's commander capitulated. "The hundred miles we need to go is a nightmare. Convoluted does not describe it! Not difficult – I don't say that – but it takes time. Legate Felix is spot on."

With the exhaustion of continual stress showing through, Verecundus added, scratching his traditionally close-cropped hair, "There's absolutely nothing I can do to disguise the loss of troops – even if I send them in packets. I doubt there's a free spirit in the township outside that does not know when the men are expecting money. Damn it all – they need it by the time they get it!"

"I can endorse that sentiment," confirmed Clemens. "Even now I find it useful!"

His interruption lightened the atmosphere and they all smiled before breaking into laughter.

"Family money is nothing like the sweet joy of what you earn yourself," observed Urbicus.

"A governor who understands that is a soldier's governor," Verecundus rejoined. "A legionary in debt is no man's tool – he's *everybody's* tool. I try not to let that happen by advancing funds, where I can."

In the lull that followed the perennial dilemma, thoughts whirled in Urbicus' mind and he decided to put forward his plans immediately.

"Verecundus. It's in my thoughts to change the stations. That is, with the Emperor's wall being completed very soon I need a commander for it - Vindolanda will no longer be viable as a control centre. I wish you to take command. Naturally it's a temporary promotion for you, bearing in mind Hadrian's Wall's overall commander is still at Petriana. However, you will answer only to me, the Fleet Admiral and the Legate here, as my representative. What do you say?"

"I accept, Sir, without equivocation. What are the stipulations?"

"That you finish the wall, keep it inviolate, keep the peace between the Old and New walls and always without exception keep me regularly informed. In return you will receive monthly supplies by sea and regular pay by the same route."

Just as Verecundus was about to reply Felix intervened. "Naturally as weather permits, Legate. Even Admiral Agrippa cannot fight storms. However, the Governor is committed to this wall. It's going to happen and we shall support you throughout. If necessary I shall bring your pay and rations along the wall myself!"

Urbicus threw up his hands and laughed. "Nobly said, my friend. I shall remember you said that!"

All four were now laughing and the tension went out of the situation, although the newly appointed commander remained wary of being overly frivolous with his Governor.

"As to tactics," Urbicus said finally, "I don't intend to elaborate for the moment. Clearly the Emperor's wall will relieve, indeed already has relieved, pressure on this one. My main task, in order for you to assume the duties of your wall command when I return south, is to bring the *Maeatae* to battle yet again.

Whether I can entice them with the same offering as before I don't know – but I believe I shall offer myself as the gambit – and see!

Assuming so, I shall have half the Second Legion from Isca Silurum, meaning both Deva and Eboracum must look west for a time as well - although I shall take from those, too. These men will be the spine of the force.

Your own Belgicans will also come – joining the Second Cohort of Nervians to the First of Tungrians. Some of the Nervians at the Wall's end will relieve here in order to facilitate it.

Naturally my plan will hinge on cavalry, so I shall take at least the Tungrian First Wing - Belgica is well represented - together with the Iberians Hadrian raised. The First Cohort Hispanorum Equitata, I think it will be. These auxiliaries will support the wing of cavalry. Ala Hispanorum One, raised in Asturia, will be supported by Vardulli Equitata also from Hispana. The Lingonum Equitata from Germania must support, too; the First Cohort initially. There will be a reserve, of course – all fine cavalry - but the reserve's primary role is still to police the Old Wall and northwards.

How does that sound for now?"

It was Verecundus who asked, "What of your camp prefect? He's the logistics expert."

"Petronius Fortunatus? Yes, he is. Regrettably he has a fever and was hospitalised. The four of us will have to make a fist of it without him."

Felix raised his eyebrows with characteristic surprise. "It's so unlike Petronius, I'd taken it for granted he had other duties – another force with the Admiral – and would be joining us. That'll teach me to take things for granted!"

"Take heart, Felix. Even you will make mistakes. When you do we all feel more normal!"

Again the tension eased with the laughter and Julian Verecundus felt able to agree the balance of foot soldiers and cavalry. "I trust I shall be with my Tungrians and hopefully we can earn a battle honour this time round. One wasn't awarded to the Cohort by ex-Governor Agricola, at Mons Graupius sixty years ago. I've often wondered why."

"I cannot answer that either. However, I am sorry but *you* must remain on the Wall at Vercovicium, ready with reserves if needed. Should I fall then you will take the army and win the day. Your Tungrians will accompany me, of course."

Completely frustrated the New Wall's commander was stumped, as he dare not compromise his advancement, which might yet yield a full legion in time.

"Nothing to say, Legate?"

"You know it already, Sir. But as a soldier I shall carry out my orders."

"I never doubted it! Now, are there any other issues?"

Verecundus scratched his head thoughtfully before saying, "Actually, Sir, there is. It's a relatively minor matter in view of your intentions – but it does appear it could involve murder. At Vercovicium - in the Vicus.

"Gods preserve us," observed Urbicus shaking his head. "There are anti-Roman factions behind this wall, there are the same in what will soon be 'twixt walls, plus hordes of woad-painted tribesmen in the high lands beyond – and people are finding time to kill each other!

Well, Felix is my senior investigator – which is why he has the rank of Legatus Iuridicus," the Governor explained to Verecundus. "He must go across with you and see what can be made of it. What is it – a couple of miles?"

The commander nodded. "Two to three, Sir."

"Not necessarily murder?"

"No, Sir."

Turning to Felix Urbicus asked his opinion.

"It'll keep me out of mischief whilst you firm up your battle plan, Governor!" His strong face broke into a smile and his greenish-brown eyes twinkled as he ran a hand through his light-brown hair. "It's about time I used my brain in a civilian capacity again."

Chapter III

In the event Firmus arrived and Urbicus decided to retain Verecundus to be formally introduced and updated, leaving Felix and Clemens to go on.

Trotting their horses as they neared the wall fort they talked briefly again about Livia as they led the century's optio, Julius Julianus, who was accompanied by his temporary duplicarius, Vireius Dexter, in a foursome. Felix had decided the experience would be good for them.

The mixture of semi-permanent and ramshackle buildings stretching from the wall fort's south gate were mainly wooden or wattle-and-daub similar, Felix knew, to those which had originally appeared to service units of the Second Legion when they built that stretch of the wall before returning south. He also knew they did just as good business with the auxiliary troops that replaced them.

Having travelled the dusty road Felix turned and rode back, noting the suspected murder site in particular and how it fronted onto the street. Being rectangular, he thought they would find two rooms in tandem, with a small garden area behind.

Sending Julius on into the fort to see if any foot patrol had noticed anything recently that might have been reportable with hindsight, Felix told Dexter to ask around within the vicus itself – but suggested the brothels were unlikely sources of information.

The man grinned and went off eagerly, hoping he would find answers enough to warrant a permanent promotion.

Clemens took their reins and twisted them around a hitching post, at the same time thinking over what Felix had told them of his discussion with Verecundus.

Apparently one retired legionary had complained to another, who owned a bar, about how convenient the running off of a married shop owner had proved to the abandoned wife. The adjoining shop owner decided to join forces with her, since his wife had left him at about the same time. They had knocked the shops into one and now needed only the one stockroom, which meant more display area for the products they sold.

The ex-soldier held it to be sharp practice, so the report went – presumably since his own wife wouldn't do the same thing to enable him to expand!

An off-duty soldier had heard the jocular complaint and casually mentioned it to his deputy centurion, who in turn had passed it upwards, until it had reached Verecundus, both as a humorous story and as a question mark.

Smiling inwardly at it Clemens walked alongside Felix into the store next to the one in question, their shadows falling over the narrow counter at which a middle-aged woman sat, counting coins.

She looked up at the pair, both in white tunics with a riding cloak thrown over the left shoulder and stopped counting. To her experienced eye they were obviously officers in plain clothes. Calling to the man working on a last at the rear of the shop she resumed her chore.

"Sirs. How can I help? Riding boots, perhaps? Tooled, soft leather, gut-stitched." As he offered his obsequious sales pitch he unconsciously rubbed his hands together.

"Not at the moment. We are here on another matter, sent by the Governor." Felix threw in the last words as an afterthought, to complete their surprise.

It had the desired effect and the motley collection of silver, copper and brass coins, in individual piles, splashed across the counter as the woman visibly started.

The man rubbed his neck as he looked at them but said nothing. He would keep his counsel for the moment, knowing he paid his taxes promptly and was no trouble to the garrison.

When neither spoke Felix said, "We are enquiring after the whereabouts of your wife, sir – and indeed of your husband," he added, glancing briefly in the woman's direction.

"Why so? They upped and went."

"Good riddance to bad times," said the woman, in support of him.

"So you might say," observed Clemens looking around the shop, "for you seem to have prospered."

Licking his lips nervously the shoemaker replied, "You worry us, Sir, coming here with questions. We're the injured parties after all. It's as though you wish to find fault with *us*.

Yes – we have prospered. We each made the best of things, as you must. Life goes on and for us very well. Why is that wrong?"

"Who said it was wrong? It was a simple observation," Clemens retorted. "You pay your taxes, don't you? Why are you worried about our visit?"

Swallowing hard the woman intervened. "You told us his excellency the Governor had sent you. Why would he be interested in us in particular? We are law-abiding people – ask anyone. Everyone knows what happened. Apart from our competitors up the road, one especially, they are happy for us. Ask them!"

"We shall – and what they all thought of your marriages beforehand," Felix responded severely. "The Governor is at Vindolanda and heard of your problem."

"What problem? There's no problem. There was, at first – but we overcame it and you can see, it's had its benefits. What problem?"

Felix shrugged. "Perhaps *problem* is the wrong word. He heard there was jealousy of your success and felt the matter should be resolved. Vercovicium is thriving and must continue to prosper – it's needed on the Wall."

Smiling thinly the cobbler shrugged in return. "When any business does well there's jealousy. It's called life. Fortunately we have nothing to be envious about."

"So I see", Felix responded, with a brief smile of his own. "Still, now that the Governor *is* involved it would set matters to rest if we looked around at your improvements for ourselves. We can confirm that the jealousy is unwarranted and simply due to your acumen coupled with good fortune – something the envious lack, presumably."

"How right you are! Those up the road couldn't succeed if success was given them in their hands. Come in, Sirs, come in by all means and look around. Come woman, close up and be with us. Let them see what we've done. We're proud of it, aren't we?"

Taking a deep breath the woman stopped trying to right the spilled piles and heaved the heavy shutters across, plunging the shop into gloom.

"Let your good lady stay here with the shutters open. There may be more business," said Felix, "I see you also have an interest in copper and pewter tableware."

"Diversification, Sir. One of the reasons we succeed where others don't."

The cobbler led them through a new doorway linking the two shops, effectively turning them into one.

He went on, "There's a forge on the edge of the township and he agreed with me that he would have time to produce more if we displayed and sold them for him – for a commission, of course."

Clemens nodded and echoed, "Of course."

Frowning briefly the man cast his arms around and showed them a living room with a small range in a back corner, which provided heat as well as a cooking facility.

"This is obviously where we live now. Through here is our storeroom. See, when we joined forces we even reinforced the floor with a new layer of clay to make sure there would be no subsidence because of the increased weight of our joint goods on it." He thrust open another door and in the gloom they saw panniers and containers piled up. "Lateral thinking, you see."

Closing the door the boot-maker asked, "Do you want to see our bed chamber and the garden? Everywhere is up together and freshly decorated – just like the new store. I'll be happy to show you."

Putting a restraining hand on the man's shoulder, as he made to turn away, Felix said that they had no need to bother and had seen all they needed to see.

Smiling broadly now the man led them back to the shop area and to the woman who had finally reworked the piles of coin.

"These two officers are satisfied and are leaving now," he said before putting his arm around her as they watched them out to their mounts.

Seeing Dexter coming out of an inn Felix indicated that he should occupy the table under the portico by pointing and holding up four fingers before giving the universal sign for a drink.

Even as they occupied the table nearest to the street Julius came out of the fortress gateway leading his horse, saw them and came over. Tying the reins to a hook he sat with them without seeking permission, wise enough not to publicise their being soldiers.

A serving wench came out to them and very soon each took turns in pouring cold beer from a large jug into their cup, savouring the taste – and waiting.

Several carts rumbled by and they wrinkled their noses at one full of manure whilst envying the owner of what appeared to be wine barrels in another, unlike the bullocks straining up the slope towards the gate.

"I doubt we'll be overheard here," explained Felix. "I have an opinion but I'd prefer to have your reports and views first. Julius?"

"Not a lot, Sir. One patrol did note a load of clay and assumed it was for flooring. They were more concerned with a funeral taking place in the late afternoon."

"Right. Dexter, then."

"Well, it seems most people used to like them but when there were increasing rows it sort of put them off a bit."

"What about?" asked Clemens. "How did people know?"

"Sometimes heard in the street outside, Sir. Not exactly sure what about – but not spending any money cropped up more than once. Could have been about the shop or the wife, I suppose."

"O.K. Any views, Tribune?"

"I did wonder why he wasn't wearing a leather apron when we went in – he was apparently working at a last."

"Good. I wonder if the work was for our benefit? They could well have seen us arrive and knew who we were."

"Yes. The woman was edgy, right enough," Clemens agreed.

"From my point of view I certainly liked the decoration, for a simple house cum shop. All freshly done, of course. It took money for a new floor for their combined store. That seems in contrast to what was overheard. Then again, a unified premises but still only one shop to sell from. Why the need for a *new* storeroom?"

"All true," agreed Clemens, "but supposing the meanness was not about those two?"

"If I may, Sir," interjected Julius, "It doesn't seem likely two skinflints ran away together."

"I wouldn't have thought so, either," observed Dexter, assuming permission to speak wasn't needed.

"However, two have gone and money has been spent."

"I agree, Tribune, it's a puzzle- but I did say I had had a notion." Felix paused for effect before asking, "Now, tell me – what if the two did *not* run off? Supposing the two we saw wanted to be together. How could it be arranged?"

"Buying them off?"

"True, Julius. What of murder, though?"

Julius fiddled with an eyebrow, thinking hard, whilst Dexter looked from one to the other.

Clemens asked, "Why no noise? People rarely die quietly in violence?"

"True – and it made me think. However, the Optio has said there was a late funeral. Its wailing would attract attention to *that*. Anything else could be assumed to belong to it too!"

"Damn me," Dexter ejaculated. "It all fits!"

"Bodies equal evidence." Clemens was to the point.

"That is what triggered me. Then, as I thought it, it was as though I was tapped on the shoulder in confirmation. It's happened before – though if you other two breathe a word you won't live long enough to enjoy it. I felt the clay was the clue. The first money spent, as it were, though it wasn't put that way to us. What if the new, reinforced floor hid the bodies. It's deep enough. Then redecorate, as though it was all in the plan."

The three looked at him, studied him, frowned and smiled. Each thought that it *did* make sense. It could be so.

"Habeas Corpus?"

"You have it, Clemens, my thoughts, too. Will you take the Optio with you into the fort and arrange it. I doubt there'll be any objection. If there is, remember to mention the Governor."

Faced later by a centurion and a squad of soldiers the two shopkeepers continued the bluff, until the floor of the storeroom was pickaxed by the troops using regulation trenching tools. With shovels clearing out the fragmented clay, clothing and limbs were soon exposed.

At that point they tried to convince the centurion that the shopkeeper had defended the woman against her now dead husband, but the shopkeeper's then wife had joined in the fray and the pair were killed.

When the broken point of a sword was found in the male victim's ribs and the woman was seen to have had her throat cut, the two finally confessed that the dead man's wife had at long last inveigled him to repair their living quarters floor and convinced him to ask their neighbours round to boast about it before it was finished.

Having killed their respective partners without difficulty, but not realising the poor quality sword had snapped, the pair had placed the victims in a hole left by the floor-layers, before covering them in clay so they would be buried under the compressed floor the following morning, even as both killers carried on trading.

Hauled away, they were told by the centurion they would be executed for murder in the fort and the settlement invited to watch.

As the four of them remounted for the ride back Clemens remarked how easily it had all been resolved. Then, only half-jokingly, he added a postscript. "You know, I wouldn't be surprised if, when the details become better known, your solving this killing will have provided a pattern for other killings!"

★ ★ ★

"I rather think the young man, here, is right on that score. However, I'm amazed at its rapid resolution. So much so that it need occupy us no further – by us I mean you, of course. Thank you for that," the Governor said, sounding almost relieved.

"So, here we are assembled at last. Everyone knows everyone now? Good, but just an obvious point, Verecundus. No single fact of our deliberations goes to even your deputy."

Vindolanda's commander smiled. "I have no idea what was discussed."

"Good man. Then holding out a hand the governor changed topics saying, "Felix, here tells me I act too soon. If so, so be it – and I trust his judgement.

However, what Firmus has just told me – his report is with your centurion awaiting you – vindicates me, I believe, Felix.

If striking at them now means the pot overflows, then we must clear up the spillage later – to paraphrase a metaphor. What it will do is spoil their appetites for power just long enough for me to take the fight to these Caledonians, in order to protect Antoninus' Wall while we finish it. These native tribesmen seem content not only to remain uncivilised but also resent our civilisation to boot.

It's the priority. Once constructed in its entirety the pressure is off this present wall so we save manpower to be deployed elsewhere." He smiled and added, "No doubt to the great joy of the three legions' legates who are continually seconding men to it."

The clandestine group comprised Governor Urbicus, in his role as overall commander of Roman forces, Admiral Agrippa, as fleet commander, Felix with his deputy

Clemens, to allow continuity, Firmus with his latest intelligence and Julian Verecundus in his new capacity.

"My reasoning," Urbicus began, "in opening this group to our local wall commander is so that he knows, beyond doubt, how our intelligence gathering links with his forays north. Plus with my own efforts – and the anti-government plotting generating from the rich south-lands.

Worryingly, young Firmus has information suggesting there's a great deal of unrest with the Hamians at Magna – as you realise only some ten miles away. Somehow they seem to have heard that they are likely to be pushed forward to the new Wall."

"Will they?"

"Probably so, Verecundus. It seems to me that a cohort of archers would be very useful, to help defend its centre particularly, with cavalry squadrons either side of them. But that is only broad thinking at the moment."

"How did they hear?"

With a shrug Firmus answered, "I haven't been able to pin that down but it seems to have emanated from traders visiting the small settlement there."

"It's so very easy to start rumours and so difficult to stop them," observed Agrippa. "It happens in the fleet, too."

"Who's the commander? Presumably a career soldier as usual," Felix asked.

"Their Prefect is Titus Flavius Secundus. He set up an altar to the health of Hadrian's adopted son who reigned with him briefly, you'll remember, before he died of the white disease anyway."

"Loyal, then?" Clemens rubbed his face thoughtfully.

"Absolutely," Verecundus responded strongly.

"Can you expand, Firmus?" the Governor asked, but then immediately changed tack. "By the way, Verecundus, in these private gatherings we are all equal of view so we each use our cognomen. Please call me Urbicus, too, as the others do."

Surprised, the Wall commander nodded. "I shall do so with pleasure, Sir – I mean Urbicus."

Amid the smiles at the immediate slip Agrippa asked, "As we are forewarned, what is the remedy? Is discipline intended; an example made?"

"Ironic that is was a Hamian deserter who was employed to kill two of the original group of plotters a couple of years ago. It was his skill that betrayed him – that and a lack of background knowledge of the Briton. Now we have them dissenting again," Felix reminded them.

"What are you saying?" asked Verecundus, who had not heard of the episode before.

"The Governor's staff surgeon, Piso Faber, wondered at the wisdom of sending Syrian-recruited troops so far north. They were bound to suffer from ulcera hiberna and even lose fingers and toes to it – possibly worse. Bear in mind that the Emperor's wall is a hundred miles further north still. They may well fear the worst – and be right!"

"What do you suggest then, Felix?" Urbicus regarded him seriously while he waited for an answer.

"Off the top of my head - rotation occurs to me."

"How do you mean rotate them?"

"Apart from the benefits of splitting up the cohort in the circumstances – divide and rule – there could be a system of reward here.

As I said, I've not thought it through but since I'm just back from Vercovicium it's fresh in my mind. They must have one of the largest settlements outside the fort of any on the wall. Consequently off-duty time would provide a great deal of interest – as opposed to the boredom of a wall watch.

Perhaps a century, or a half, could be posted there briefly, in rotation, to give archery instruction to the garrison. If they no longer have such, it's the opportunity."

Urbicus rubbed his hands together with gusto, his deep brown eyes twinkling with pleasure in the broad, open face. He scratched at his new-fashion beard before saying, "I like it. It's simple – and the Hamians must surely like it, too. As you know, I'm from North Africa and I find the northern climes not for me. It'll take their minds off it."

"What if they don't want to return?"

"I'm sure that Verecundus will resolve that when he moves there. Remember, their own will want their turn. Once back, Agrippa, they will soon work out that only good conduct will entail another posting."

"The tribes to the north are holding councils all the time, I'm told," interposed Firmus. "They must know you're coming. Will weakening the garrison there be known, too?"

"It's impossible to mobilise so many troops without word getting around. In any case I shall be taking the Hamians up with me when I go. Let the Caledonians take them on then.

Have we done with Magna now – I want to move on?" Urbicus looked around the group for dissent. "When the Second's detachment arrives from Isca Silura can you embark them, Agrippa?"

"Most of them – all of them, given time."

"Do what you can. However, I want it to look as if you and they are withdrawing down the east coast. At night, turn and come up fast to disembark them as far into the estuary below the Tava as you can – past Cramond to the New Wall fort at Credigone, if possible. Use a minimal number of marines to guard your beachhead and send the others on. Hit them with a dawn attack out of the east – just as they'll be baying for our blood.

Then we'll bring in the auxiliary cavalry with the mounted infantry to support our cavalry strike. I hope to drive a wedge between the tribes and their highland retreat.

Gentlemen. The third issue. To strike while unexpected – at the heart of the conspirators! I've been looking forward to it.

As soon as this battle is done, hopefully once and for all so that the construction can be finished, you and yours will take off south so that you control the strike, Felix. I shall have special orders written to that effect. Macer will come and take you down, in case you need to utilise the navy. Agrippa and I will follow when we feel the time is right."

The young, handsome face of Gaius Fabullius Macer with its infectious grin swam into Felix' mind at his mention. There was every prospect of his marrying Felix' ward Avita. He thought soon. At the moment he was deputising at Portus Ardoni for his admiral. Then, as quickly as it came the image faded.

"Have we definite news of the one-eyed, then? My latest information had him in Hibernia. I doubt he's stayed there. This late summer weather is holding fast. He's mobile, so I can foresee Macer being very much involved."

"That's your prerogative, my friend. However, if things do go awry it will be on *my* shoulders. It's not the end of the world."

"Presumably Firmus will remain here. If it goes askew they may contact him – he needn't be put at risk by being with us. They'll know his work mainly keeps him here," Felix said dogmatically.

"You will have the reins, Felix. You must decide."

★ ★ ★

It was as though the hillsides were alive with ants but the figures quickly grew in size and soon became blue-dyed warriors running pell-mell for the cohorts marching in columns, with weapons at rest.

Urbicus had done everything he could to advertise their presence on the march, to the extent of ordering the camp fires to burn wet wood – even if it had to be peed on. It was essential the tribes were brought to battle, so he held on as long as he dared before giving instructions for battle formation.

The regular legionary troops needed no second bidding and their well-rehearsed manoeuvres immediately fell into place. Shields left shoulders and interlocked as easily as on a practice ground, their covers already packed away with the likelihood of action. Each soldier presented his pilum and that was all the enemy saw as they dashed forward intending to hurl themselves naked at these hated interlopers and potential conquerors.

On command a curtain of the javelins arced upwards to fall onto the oncoming mass of natives. Even as men fell transfixed, blood gushing from them, the soldiers' second javelins performed the same function until bodies writhed or lay still, piled in front of them.

Leaping the corpses, other muscular warriors reached the shield wall now bristling with the short, stabbing swords that were the legion's speciality. Very soon this first wave of uncoordinated attacks faltered and fell back, energy spent, leaving another line of dead or dying warriors as testament to foolhardiness. Very few fell who wore legionary uniform.

As the Caledonians re-gathered orders were given and the shield wall faded away to reveal rank on rank of archers, recurved bows loaded with arrows that, only moments later, seemed like a malevolent rain falling on body and shield alike, where they were carried at all. The charging second wave fizzled out at this unexpected assault from the sky.

What had been howls of bravery now became howls of anger and frustration. What they wanted was single combat – a trial of strength and skill. What they had was a trial of endurance and patience.

Casting around him from his position at the rear of the phalanx from where he could direct the battle best Urbicus said to Felix, "It's going well – but watch for a counter-strike, my friend. Will they really be the anvil for my hammer a second time? I suspect not."

A heady mix of blood, sweat and trampled heather wafted across them as Felix replied, "They look as if they want us to chase them. It's far too early in the fight to do that – it's probably a ploy!"

Taking on another frontal assault the Hamians let fly again and once more blue-streaked bodies fell in droves.

"Do you remember the Greek battle story where their enemies rolled over them, only for the death-feigning Greeks to come alive again and attack from the rear?"

"No," retorted Felix.

"Well, I think we *have* done slaughter here – but I doubt *all* of the fallen are dead, nor some even wounded. That's another reason not to go after them, my friend!"

As though the Caledonians had been listening another wave came on and a number of fallen warriors joined them, triggering the hills to release a further avalanche of tribesmen, leaping rocks and small scrub in their eagerness.

Issuing rapid orders to his aides Urbicus said urgently, "Send the second cohort of Nervians forward of the line to the east and the Germanian first cohort to the west. Let them be bastions in the wall for the shockwave to break on.

Tell the first Tungrians' commander to be ready to support." As his aide doubled away Urbicus turned to Felix. "They are from Belgica like the Nervians, so will want to outdo them!"

In response to this movement of their Roman opponents another hillside disgorged unknown numbers from gullies and clefts to attack the side of the defending box. Immediately local orders were given and files turned outwards to become ranks, in rapid well-disciplined movement.

Titus noted this and warned his men to be alert for any breakthrough to the Governor, whom they were formed behind as his bodyguard.

The sun fell quickly behind the mountains and the Caledonian tribesmen retired with it, their respect for the Night Demons as strong as their hatred of the invaders from the south.

In turn Urbicus drew in his perimeters in order that half the troops could sleep in turn whilst the others formed a defensive wall, since no night camp could be constructed in the circumstances.

"Pass around the order for cold food to be taken. We won't present the enemy with any tempting silhouettes against fires," he instructed, before his aides again raced to do his bidding.

Chapter IV

N othing more than wolf howls disturbed the night and the sleeping men automatically stirred and stretched as the sun thrust itself upwards against the mountain rim, hardly noticing the odour of unwashed bodies, leather and damp earth.

Having deliberately declined to withdraw and build a tented camp in textbook style, Urbicus had counted on the irritation factor of being in his enemies' sight as dawn broke, with their dead still unrecovered.

It provoked a desultory attack which was eagerly received and thrown back with heavy enemy casualties, adding bright, new blood to the brown, dew-frosted patches of the night.

"This time they will come at us hard and in force – I can feel it," observed the Governor." "We've become an itch they can't scratch."

"Let's hope so, my friend. The campaign season is almost over – and we're getting too old for wet grass under a blanket!"

Before Urbicus could reply to Felix, silhouettes appeared along the crests which rapidly took form in uncountable numbers. Shouts carried to the legionaries but very few could understand the words used, although the gist was obvious.

Horns blared on the Governor's signal and the cohorts moved to their allotted places, as given at the meeting their commanders had had with the supreme commander the previous evening.

Watching the flood of warriors cascading down the slopes like a waterfall, Felix checked and rechecked the readiness of his century. The men were unshaven, unkempt and hungry - but he could see fire in their eyes and it warmed him.

"Here it comes," Urbicus said, as the first men reached the valley floor and who could not have stopped had they wanted to, pushed on by the press behind them.

"Advance," commanded Urbicus and the signal trumpet blared its raucous note, urging the legionary phalanx forward.

Crushed between shields with stabbing swords darting from them and their own tribesmen the leading men were barely able to use their weapons properly whilst themselves inhibiting those that followed.

"Throw out the Second Nervians and the Batavians as before, but let the Tungrians fall back to hold these bastards in a funnel," he told his aides.

"Stand by to receive a charge," Felix said to Titus, who deployed the century as a wedge formation in front of the Governor, taking the point himself.

The Caledonians behind were now pushing their unwilling front ranks forward into the wide mouth that had been created, only for them then to be attacked from three sides of a square.

"Are the Sixth Nervians ready?"

"Gaius Julius Barbarus is waiting, Sir," confirmed an aide.

"Well done. Now get over to the prefect and tell him to begin the withdrawal. Stay with him and learn! Let the Nervians fold inwards to join the Batavians and hold the centre, so that we can all fall back in order."

Two more young men dashed away towards the cohorts' commanders. One fell immediately he had delivered his message.

"That was a shame – but aides are not impervious to injury," observed Urbicus shrugging. "His family can be proud of him."

He turned to Felix saying, "Let's see if we remember how to be soldiers. We shall join the Sixth ourselves, so that the others can withdraw to join us all."

Clemens and Firmus returned, looking crestfallen that the fighting had not reached their sector of the line.

"Both of you join the Prefect with his bowmen and withdraw with them. Verecundus may find a use for you."

Watching the readjustments of their enemy below, the tribesmen on the crags spilled over the edge and slid down the shale and scree slopes, eager to be part of a victory that would be celebrated around cooking fires in their glens for years to come.

"Time for the scouts to go up the valley?"

Urbicus grinned at Felix and nodded. "It's about bloody time – the smell of horse crap has been choking me for far too long!"

Felix gave orders directly to the two scouts, Papirius and Aufidius, who immediately unshackled their mounts and got them up. Mounted, they dug in their heels then gripped with their knees as the horses leaped forward loose-reined. The two rode apart so that if one was lost the other would not fall with him.

Urbicus shouted, "There could be ten thousand of them now – odds of what – five to one, four anyway."

"Probably, my friend – how many more hidden?"

"Let's go," the Governor replied, hardly hearing himself about the clash of metal on metal and the hoarse shouts of the combatants.

Withdrawing, Julius took half of the men back covering his centurion as Titus brought the remainder. The governor withdrew at Felix' side, both with weapons drawn, although protected front and rear.

Passing through the Hamian archers, who had strung their bows with the last of their shafts, they rejoined the Sixth cohort of Nervians, which formed the nucleus of the withdrawal, the governor acknowledging Barbarus briefly as they made eye contact.

The naked, blue-streaked, ginger-haired warriors suddenly erupted around the fighting head and surrounded the Second Nervians, the Germanic Batavians and the first cohort of Tungrians.

Battling hard the first cohort of Cugernians, also Germanic, carried their fight to the maelstrom and broke through, scattering the natives by being unexpected. This allowed the Tungrains to withdraw, having taken heavier casualties than expected.

"There will be regimental honours awarded for this fight, be sure of that," growled Urbicus, "and not because I once governed in lower Germania. The Cugernians I only had down as reserves!"

"The Nervian Belgians have done well, too. But then all have held."

"I know that," retorted Urbicus. "What I want most now is the scouts to return."

Spilling out of a valley the auxiliary Hispanic cavalry went hard after Papirius as he rode deep in his saddle, with low reins, towards the hills that still disgorged Caledonian tribesmen.

From another Aufidius headed a wing of crack cavalry based on the Old Wall at Petriana, many hundreds of horsemen wanting to add to their regimental awards dating from the Emperors Domitian and Trajan, but now fighting without their commander who had been required to remain with the residue of his command on the Hadrianic Wall.

"Your men are being overhauled, my friend," Urbicus pointed out phlegmatically.

"Tired horses, Urbicus. They've had one hard ride already. In any case I need them as scouts - not tools: They are no longer cavalry, they're bodyguards."

"Keen though!"

"I've noted it. I expect they'll persuade me it was necessary. They both have silver tongues!"

Temporarily the intensity of the fighting ebbed as the tribesmen saw that they would now be cut off from reinforcements. Some few retreated but most renewed the battle with their Roman counterparts.

However, now it was the turn of the Royal Second Legion from Isca Silurum and they charged down from the hills that divided the fight from the fleet, knowing that their sheer weight of a half-legion would impact on the battle as it hung in the balance.

Driven in from their right, prevented from retreating and still engaged with the three cohorts, the Caledonians fought on stubbornly, somehow expecting their bravery to supplant armour and tactics even though the free flow of replacements had now dried up.

As arranged the first Tungrian cavalry burst out after the others to totally destroying any idea the Caledonians had of reforming on the hillsides and charging again, faced as they now were by some thousand horsemen.

The Royal Second stormed into the melee driving, thrusting and hacking – the overwhelming pressure of over two thousand new soldiers arriving totally confusing the battle plan of the attackers, who had counted on being the overwhelming force themselves as massed tribes.

Swords, spears and axes crashed together, with the occasional Roman legionary colliding with another as lines redressed, but no way could be found into the shield wall and woaded warriors collapsed in heaps of bleeding humanity not long for the world. The cavalry units pursued the fleeing, naked, but still armed warriors up the inclines as far as they could, killing and maiming with total disregard, knowing that every man dead or disabled was another who could not come again at their compatriots.

After what seemed interminable fighting the three cohorts finally flung back the last of the determined warriors and stood free, bloody and gasping for air.

It was an eerie silence that fell over the battlefield, with the trampled heather throwing up its fragrant scent to confront those of stale sweat, blood, warm metal and hot leather harness.

The red, green and blue uniforms of fallen soldiers added colour to the natives' grey bodies and the litter of battle was everywhere. Dropped and discarded weapons dotted the ground while some men simply stared into the distance wondering why they had survived, with others wishing they had done something, somehow, to have saved their friends who died beside them. Too exhausted to think and drained of feeling, any foreign body that moved was thrust through. No chances were taken.

Orders came from battle-weary officers to check the state of fallen legionaries. Surviving medical staff drew on their reserves to confirm death or whether help was needed, be they a field orderly capsarius or a medicus miles. The dead were drawn off somehow in blankets and the living on litters made from uniforms and cloaks with spears through the armholes. Everything seemed to be unreal until the insidious effects of fresh air and relaxation restored normality, even though the far-off sounds of conflict still resounded around the hills.

Sheathing their weapons, Felix and the bodyguard stood awaiting orders. Theirs was a feeling of anti-climax. They had been ready but not needed.

"I believe the field is ours," said Urbicus clapping him on the shoulder. "We are unscathed, but I felt safe with you and yours. You did what was asked of you. You would have done more, I know."

"As you say, we are unscathed. May the gods be praised."

Even as Felix echoed his friend, a rush of natives erupted through a gap in the surrounding troops and came for them. The long, sharp, lethal blades swung and whirled as the bodyguard desperately wrenched their swords from their scabbards to defend this unforeseen situation.

Men long-known to Felix fell dead without reply as the two groups clashed, set aside shields unusable in the speed of the action, their short swords now a different proposition in the circumstances.

"Step inside the swing! Remember your drill instructor," Felix roared. "He told you what to do!"

As he finished his exhortation he went down on one knee, ducking under a slashing sword's trajectory and immediately cut hard backwards, feeling his sword bite into the unguarded body of his assailant. His arena days were well spent, he oddly thought. Coming to his feet he was instantly faced by an incredulous warrior, who paid for his hesitation.

Both Clemens and Firmus had automatically followed Felix to support him and he had to fling out an arm to indicate they should go back to the Governor who, just behind them, was now deliberately blocking scything cuts with his own short sword as he retreated. Felix soon saw that intervention was not a quick option so he threw his own weapon at Urbicus' opponent, only to see it gouge a lump of flesh from a muscular shoulder and spin off to the ground.

Driving his sword into the distracted warrior's abdomen with some satisfaction, Urbicus shouted congratulations to Felix on his throw as he withdrew it and wiped it on his downed opponent's body in contempt, before facing up to another.

The man collapsed in front of him as both Clemens and Firmus independently made killing thrusts that covered their hands in bright-red blood.

"Well, that was invigorating while it lasted," crowed Urbicus, vaguely remembering his days as a junior officer. "I hope you enjoyed yourselves, too!"

"A suicide group! How they thought their own deaths made a difference is anybody's guess," Felix growled.

"You mean if I had died another would follow?"

"No, not at all – although that would be true, of course. I meant they are dead and nothing has been gained." Angrily rubbing his forehead Felix grunted, "I suppose they see it in reverse in reality, but I don't see it that way."

Clapping him on the shoulder Urbicus exclaimed, "I know what you meant. They would not be able to get me – but even had they done so the status quo would exist."

"Exactly so. The Emperor is dead – long live the Emperor."

"Let's pick up your brave men. They didn't flinch. Here, let me," offered Urbicus, as he sidled past a wounded man attempting to roll a body.

Felix knew every name as the dead were carried back to the mortuary area and he regretted every one of the horrendous killing blows that had presented themselves. He felt he should have been more alert.

Vireius Dexter, the temporary duplicarius he had intended to elevate, had died without knowing of his promotion. Iolo, the shipwreck survivor taken into the army for his archery skills. Demetrius, the Greek, the one he knew least about but who was always on hand - a run-of-the-mill good soldier.

"Felix." It was Clemens who interrupted his thoughts. "I can guess what you're about – but didn't you tell me once of your former centurion, Frontus, who mourned the dead but said the living were more important? Will you address the century?"

Clapping him on the biceps Felix grinned. "So he did, may the gods continue to bless him, so he did!"

★ ★ ★

On suitable ground a large temporary camp was ditched and palisaded, each century and cavalry troop allocated a section whilst others mounted guard or patrolled. Very soon rows of tents carried in the baggage wagons were erected in the same pattern as huts within a fort.

Brought by the fleet messages finally reached Urbicus to inform him of the complete recovery of Petronius, his logistics expert, to Felix concerning Livia, as well as to Clemens with news of his baby son. Worryingly the Governor also had news of another bullion robbery.

Finding the governor sitting at his campaign desk Agrippa explained his late arrival at the battle, with the Second Legion and his marines, citing an adverse sea followed by his coming across tribal reinforcements, which had melted away after a delaying skirmish.

Urbicus dismissed his apparent failure and explained how the battle had flowed prior to his timely arrival, which had worked better than the original plan.

As soon as the admiral had left a busy Urbicus allocated postings and duties to the Isca half-legion and to the auxiliaries. He then posted the cavalry units to various points on the new wall where they would undertake guard duties, whilst the craft-skilled legionaries continued to build the wall and forts, as other units were still doing elsewhere. The archery cohort he sent to the wall's centre as he had told Verecundus he would.

Agrippa left with his marines and a cavalry escort to return to his fleet, leaving the governor to mull over the question of awards to individuals and to obtaining the Senate's agreement to unit citations for display on their standards. He decided he would seek permission for three unit awards of citizenship to mark the bravery of all the men against strong numerical opposition, plus one of Civium Latinorum to the Tungrian Equitata, the next thing to citizenship. Having made that decision he then sat in his tent and wrote the report whilst the detail was fresh in his mind.

It was evening before he finished and he went out into the dampening air to stretch his limbs and invite Felix and his son-in-law to join him for a meal. "We will be alone", he explained to them, "since neither wall legate is with me and I have also sent away both of the prefects with their regiments. Neither can I ask Firmus as he is a centurion and it might compromise him."

★ ★ ★

Pleased as Agrippa always was to return to his naval base - particularly so after a successful campaign - this was by contrast a tragic homecoming.

Sabina was dead.

As he paced the low water shoreline under the wall of the fort he had to keep reminding himself of it. She was dead. She was gone and to a soldier or a sailor death was nothing new; *nothing new* he kept hearing himself repeating.

The great white slash on the hills above had provided the chalk for the lime cement that joined the stone blocks he walked beside. Now it seemed to stand guard over him as he turned away from it onto the small jetty that barely took the vessels that brought their stores.

Agrippa acknowledged the sentries' salutes from the seagate as he paced past it, but it was as though he were an automaton – one of the machines that did something if you did something to it first. Unsmilingly he remembered one even delivered a cupful of water if you put a coin in it. Then he dismissed the image. He did not want to think about novelties. What he wanted was a machine that gave the past back as he simply wished it.

Agrippa stood and looked across the water towards the islands that hid the governor's summer palace beyond them, but he really did not see them. What he was visualising was Sabina and himself finding each other – and their eventual physical union. A woman who had had so much taken from her and yet had enough left of herself to give him.

Kidnapped, raped and tortured they had told him. She had been found tied to a fence where she had bled to death and round her neck had been a notice, '*next time it will be her sister*'.

He blinked away a tear, as the incoming tide lapped against the outermost posts of the little quay, before he continued round the corner of the fort to where the shingle had built up in the tidal flow.

As the tide hesitantly explored the stones that his sandals now touched, the breeze stirred his hair as though she was running her fingers through it again.

"Sabina," he whispered and the word floated away. He said her name again more loudly and once more it seemed to float on the breeze, before disappearing with it as it died.

Agrippa swallowed hard and saluted with his fist held across his chest in soldierly fashion. What he had done was towards his favourite medium, the sea, and in doing so had acknowledged her to his gods.

He turned and retraced his steps before walking on to the docking area, with its warehouses and messes, glancing towards the other vessels of the fleet moored off, before stepping up the gangplank of his flagship to spend the night on board, as he usually did. Fleet Procurator Marcus Maenius Agrippa Lucius Tusidius Campester was once more in control.

★ ★ ★

Felix smiled to himself as he lingered over the completion of the final draft. The conversation he had had with his gardener, such as it was, came back to him. They had been discussing whether to let the bean flowers pod for next year's seed.

"We have plenty in the kitchen gardens, Sir, but I know the ladies enjoyed having these for their colour in particular. Shall I keep some of them back?"

"It's a good thought, master gardener. Do so by all means. How long will colour stay in the enclosed garden – to change the subject. I want to make it safer, but not while it can still be enjoyed."

"Be changeable weather, Sir," he answered, putting his trademark finger alongside his nose as though to keep a secret.

"How do you know?"

"See they clouds, Sir. Half-high – but broken up. Has to be wind what did it. We can't feel it, Sir, but wind blows all sorts of things hither-and-thither."

"It's not a mackerel sky, though."

"No, Sir – it's not predictable."

The conversation ended as most of them did – nothing said. The man knew his work inside out – but never seemed to explain how he knew what he knew! Still, Felix thought, it was usually worth a smile.

As though now free to fly, his thoughts went back further. To their homecoming, in fact. Just as she had always done when he returned, Julia came flying out of the gate – only now it was Clemens she ran to. Sometimes he missed it, he thought, but of course the welcome he received instead from Livia had added sexual overtones.

But not this time. Where was she? He turned to ask Julia but she was preoccupied with the now dismounted Clemens and the century, further back, were smiling broadly and each wishing they were he.

Felix slipped a leg over his horse's neck and slid off, walking quickly in but he was anticipated by Comazon Valerius, his steward and one-legged ex-soldier.

Unstrapping Felix' chest armour as he spoke the steward said, "Welcome back, Sir, and in one piece. The lady Livia is in the garden. She rests a lot these days, Sir."

"Does she? Anything obvious?"

"It *is* obvious, Sir, but nothing physical." Valerius had no qualms about speaking out. He knew his old commander well enough to do so. "It's ever since that business, Sir. It was me that found her. Good job it was me – could have been anyone. She's sitting where Miss Julia was sitting when her waters broke."

"Well done, sir," Felix called over his shoulder, as he strode quickly towards the small, enclosed area they all enjoyed when time allowed.

She was sitting looking at the smoke-stained wall as her step-daughter had done and, had both women only known it, thinking along similar lines, although Livia had not actually been there during the attack.

As Felix entered she looked up and smiled a broad welcome, then stood to receive his arms around her in his typically strong embrace.

"Are you ill?" he asked, holding her at arms length when he felt her warm tears on his face. "What can I do?"

She pulled closer to him and spoke into his chest. "You weren't here when I needed you. After they stripped me I thought I would be raped and killed. As you know, I wasn't – only for me to find that that had happened to my sister!"

"Sabina is dead?" Felix held her at arms length again as tears rolled down her white face. "How... when did this happen?"

She clung to him as she answered, "I'm not sure – but she was tortured as well. It's horrible! They put a notice round her neck saying I would be next! Poor Sabina – she'd been through so much. I was hoping she could find a life with Agrippa. All she found was death – and I've a death sentence hanging over me, too!" The final words were racked with sobs and Livia hoped Felix had understood them.

Holding her tightly now he asked gently, "Is there any clue as to who did it?"

"No. *I* don't know, anyway." Shaking, she tried to carry on but could not. All she managed was, "Them?"

Gritting his teeth Felix retorted, "Yes – it does sound like the same bunch. Your late brother-in-law's left a den of vipers. It's as though in removing him, as the snake's head, the body grew two others. One dead – but Mercurialis still lives!"

"And now Minerva is the partner of Quintus. My niece made it clear whose side she's on when she heard the news. Tabitha told me of it – shopping gossip, apparently – she'd gone out with Valerius when the steward shopped."

"I'm not surprised Valerius was there to greet me, with knowledge like that. He realised I couldn't have heard.

So - much as I don't like to admit it, Urbicus might be right about going in with force and finding evidence later. We know they're conspirators, at the very least."

Rex came running into the garden, his tail wagging happily at the sight of Felix, dark eyes wide open and his mouth looking as though he was smiling. As he always did his tongue protruded through his teeth when the backs of his ears were tickled.

Almost immediately Julia followed him to finally greet Felix, putting her arms round his neck and kissing his cheek. "If only you'd been here, Father. Even Rex was with me, in the market place class."

At that, pushing back in his chair, he stopped thinking of his return. How many times had he heard those words in his life? *If only.*

He heard Clemens striding up the hallway, the slap of his house shoes failing to disguise the length of his step.

As his son-in-law came into the room Felix handed him the final listings. The battle had cost the century dear, following other previous losses and retirements.

"I see you thought long and hard on this."

"How come?"

"Aurelius Victor was expecting a step up from standard bearer to Optio. He was counting on the extra money to go towards a higher pension. I heard he was expecting you to form three squads of eight, with a deputy centurion in charge of them."

Felix frowned at that and then laughed lightly. "Well, you know the saying – *expect little and you'll seldom be disappointed.*"

"But Paulinus? It's a big step back up from his demotion. Didn't you tell me your old oppo, Frontus, chose him for his metal-working skills?

Nodding Felix agreed. "That's so – but he was an optio as an armourer. He ran his fort's forge and armoury. Apparently very well until he couldn't hold his tongue. I need experience in charge – not desire!

Victor will still march behind us, as any signifer does. Then, if a replacement optio is required he will get his chance. Make it clear to both it's only a temporary promotion at this time. Will you see Titus and make it clear to him, too?"

"Of course. Titus as centurion with two large squads each under a deputy. Julius Julianus to remain the senior. Right."

★ ★ ★

"Just look at me, Clemens! My breasts are so big – and look at the blue veins in them. Expressing the pap doesn't seem to make any difference. Then I've got stretch marks all over my stomach! How can you still love me, looking such a mess?"

Clemens reached over and kissed a nipple. "You were a lovely wife before and now you're a lovely mother as well. Of course I still love you."

"I wonder how I'd look if I fed him?"

"A wet nurse is traditional – and wouldn't you have to bind yourself up to stop the milk marking your dress?

Julia grimaced. "I suppose so. They tell me it'll go soon – but it's taking its time. Anyway, I thought you liked my boobs as I was?"

"They're hardly pushing me out of bed, are they? You'll be creamy-skinned again and your tabs will go down. Believe what you're told, will you – and go to sleep!"

"How come you think you know all about it? I'll give you *go to sleep,* tribune," she retorted, reaching a hand to his groin.

Chapter V

J ulia eyed the sky thoughtfully as her class of young children gathered round her once again in the market place that doubled as a forum in the small town. She was pleased the townsfolk – and even a few of the outlying farmers – sent their children along to learn to read and write, however perfunctorily, in Latin. Because they did traders provided a brazier for the cold weather and a quiet corner away from the main bustle. It was rain she dreaded most, but it looked as if they would get away with it for the time being.

"How many remember the name of the king with the golden touch?" She asked them, watching their faces light up as they remembered.

"That's right – Midas," Julia agreed with a boy's answer.

" Now, I've a goose story to tell you and, afterwards, I want you to write down the answers to some questions. Do you understand?"

A chorus of positives rang out as she pulled them in closer to her, so that the rattle of a cart would not blot out her voice. Rex looked around, could see no problems, wagged his tail a few times which hit her chair and promptly went to sleep.

"This girl – not much older than your older sisters – found an injured goose down by the village pond." She paused for a chorus of childish disgust, before going on, "She caught it and was stroking it when a soldier rode by, saw her problem and dropped down off his horse."

"Is he going to eat it?"

"Now don't interrupt, young man – or I'll eat you!"

The boy coloured as the others all laughed.

"The soldier tells her it would be kinder to kill the goose because it looked as if a fox had got to it, but the girl said she wanted to help it. Fortunately the soldier is one who helps wounded soldiers – a capsarius – so he fetched some bandages from his saddlebag, while the girl found some strong sticks.

While he splinted and tied an injured leg the goose glowered at him and squawked loudly once, when he straightened it. After that it sits still.

He told the girl he did not know what would happen and, even if it worked, how long the goose might live."

Sad cries interrupted her so she paused and then smiled to cheer them up.

"Then he told her she would have to feed it and what to give.

The soldier takes the goose home for her and her parents despairingly put it in a shed for the night, fearing the worst. However, in the morning when they all peered through a crack they saw it seemed to be asleep.

They went in quietly but the goose opens its eyes and stood up to waddle defiantly sideways away from them – until it recognised the girl and stood still.

They put the goose with some ducks and chickens and hoped for the best.

This went on for a month or two, but sadly the goose died – probably it was quite old."

Julia had to stop again when the children reacted as she had expected them to – as children usually did.

When they were paying attention again Julia finished the tale, smiling broadly at them as she began again, "We started off talking of a golden ego – well, this goose had some golden months, didn't it? To the goose they were better than gold."

As the class chattered about the sad-and-happy story Julia thought back to when she had told the story to Faber, the Governor's staff surgeon, seeking for his opinion.

Tiberius Piso Faber was short, rotund and strong, but had the careworn look of years of trying to save lives. One of his joys was being able to truly relax with Felix and his family where, although he was of lesser rank – albeit a senior centurion – he was on chosen-name terms with family and guests alike. It was a house rule that he totally endorsed.

Julia understood all this and she kissed his cheek after thanking him for listening.

"Well," he said cheerfully, "We have been talking of gold and golden months – I've just had a golden moment!"

★ ★ ★

Rain splattered on the window glass, driven onto it by the gusting wind, which also battered the trees – whipping them to and fro without mercy, causing weaker branches to snap off.

Although howling round the house and outbuildings it was still not the hurricane they had experienced in the recent past but they knew the heavy rain would take a wicked toll of the flower garden and the bushes in bloom.

Livia and Julia sat in the solar, a light room but without the sun it should have enjoyed. They sat together holding hands and thinking about the possible danger to their men out in the storm.

Seeking what shelter could be found against the outbuildings Felix explained to his men what he and Clemens had agreed.

"We are relatively few in number – few enough to escape notice, on a day like this. We can reach them without warning and so surprise them. The estate guards will be enjoying the warmth of their quarters and those on duty will be hiding away somewhere, knowing no one would be stupid enough to be out in this!"

The throwaway remark brought weak smiles from some, but others looked forlorn – it would be a good day to be in the arms of a tavern woman, they were thinking.

"He's right about what he said," observed Victor, in a whisper to the man nearest him. "We *are* idiots!"

As they listened to the detail of the attack their proofed cloaks kept most of the water off them, but some still seeped under as it ran off their helmet peaks where they had thrown back their hoods to hear better.

They rode halfway along the Waerham Road to Corf before turning right and climbing up to the old ridge way, where they returned to their southerly trek.

The ridge lived up to its nickname of 'windy ridge' and each of them had become cold and wet by the time they joined the track running up to the quarry – a track well known to those who had visited the villa before.

As suspected no gate guards were in evidence and Silva, their Balearic slinger, was up and over the gate in moments, unbolting it to let them through on foot. The horses were left in the care of the two scouts, Papirius and Aufidius, not only good horsemen but also skilled in their medical care – as they often proved.

Silva hissed and Clemens signalled a halt, watching the man slip a stone into his sling then, whirling it only once, let fly. The Tribune heard a groan and the thud of something heavy falling to the ground – then silence.

Drawing his knife the unarmoured slinger slipped into a clump of trees, only to return almost at once.

"We were lucky, he whispered, "One was taking a crap and the other was asleep against a tree!"

Felix signalled the group on and made a mental note on the apparent potential of the Ibithencan as a scout.

The rain subsided as they approached the large house, but they were now grateful for the wind as it covered any vestige of noise there might be.

"Who the hell are you?" They were the last words an estate guard uttered after slinking round a corner of the villa, only to receive a slingshot in the middle of his forehead which sent him over backwards.

"What a shot," whispered Echo, an accomplished knife thrower.

"A poor shot – I was aiming between the eyes!"

"Quiet," growled Julius, the deputy centurion.

"Draw swords" Clemens quietly instructed Titus, who made gestures indicating what was required.

Silva found a cellar hatch and Paulinus was signalled to come up and inspect it. One of the skills he had been recruited to provide was his ability to pick locks, a side issue of making keys as an armourer and metalworker.

He drew his dagger and levered it into the latch, his arm strength forcing the bolt back out of the lock with only a small sound. "Poor quality, Sir, no need to bother with anything else," he said easily.

Holding one of the two doors open on an angle they watched, as he peered in and then let himself down on his arms.

After a relatively short time, which seemed forever to the waiting men, a side door opened soundlessly and his head peered out of it.

Felix went over to the doorway and was told that the lock had needed to be persuaded this time.

"Where does it lead?"

"Into the kitchen and then, I suppose, into the main corridors, Sir."

"Anyone?"

"Only one servant sleeping in the kitchen. I had to help him sleep deeper, Sir."

"Good man – go and get your squad and give my order to the optio that you are to follow his."

As the big man moved quietly away Felix knew that Clemens was at his side without looking. He whispered, "I wish there were through-locks – he could pick them all from the outside then. I don't understand why not."

"Must be a problem or there would be. Nobody would miss half the keys not being needed. Here they come," Clemens added.

"I want this door relocked when we're all inside. Don't bother with a guard on it – we need everyone."

Felix was reminding them of their orders when pandemonium broke out, with women screaming and men shouting, as extra torches were lit in the hallways.

Heavy sandals clattered along the passageway to the kitchen and immediately a guard was pulled in by his spear as he made to come through the doorway.

As the man slumped to the floor Felix said loudly, "No need for silence now – go for your targets. You know who I want alive! Must have been another slave in the kitchen who heard our armourer and reported to his steward. Too late now – let's go!"

Leading the race, his hobnailed, military-style boots grating on the kitchen flags, Felix went through the doorway fast. He wished they had their shields with them to hold a corridor easily but it would have been impractical to have brought them.

Any residue of the chill outside left them in the combination of kitchen warmth, residual heat in the corridors and fire in their bellies.

In the atrium Felix met his first guard, parried a thrust and stabbed under the chest armour, doubling him over with a cry. The poorly-armoured man staggered away and fell against an almost burnt-out brazier which had been keeping the entrance hall warm, knocking it over and spilling the still red hot ashes over the tessellated floor, an odd one or two hissing as they died in the fountain's pool.

His two squads went different ways and he was left there with Clemens, as sounds of occasional fighting came to them.

Someone came out of a room off the atrium and Felix believed it to be the steward's. He told the man, in both Latin and Celtic invective, to go back and stay there until told otherwise.

A head peered round a door jamb further down a third passageway and Felix went after him, calling to his second-in-command to follow. He had recognised Quintus, which meant Minerva was in the vicinity, too. He wanted to save his wife's niece if he could, but Quintus was his main objective.

As his feet pounded the tiled patterns and the sound echoed madly off the walls, he was thinking of how the death of the Emperor's wife last year had let Quintus off lightly for his part in Tabitha's gang-rape – many crimes being forgiven in the Empress's memory.

The sprawling villa was a rabbit warren of passages and Quintus had a distinct advantage over them, with their needing to check each room as they passed.

A raucous, almost manic, laugh was followed by the thud of a heavy door slamming and its lock turning. Reaching it they frustratedly pulled at the door but immediately gave it best and retraced their steps to find another exit, since the passageway was clear of people.

They found a secret passage in a bedroom they had raced past to the door, a section of the floor swinging away on pivots to give access to a short tunnel leading from the other room only to go under an outside wall, the external exit disguised as a stoke hole for the hypocaust system.

Quintus did not get far, walking straight into the two scouts. Cursing them he was frogmarched to the house by Aufidius, meeting the two officers outside.

"Where's Minerva?" Felix demanded, his sword pointed at him. "If she's been harmed…"

Swallowing, as Felix let his implied threat tail away, Quintus' thin lips curled, giving his otherwise aquiline, haughty face an evil look and exposing the broken canine tooth which had matched a bite mark on Tabitha's breast, exposing his claimed innocence as lies.

"Find her, if you can! We parted outside in the dark," he growled before groaning, as the scout tightened his grip on Quintus' scrotum from behind.

They knew it was true. The overcast sky had brought dusk already and it was going to be impossible to find anyone hiding in undergrowth.

"Where's Justinian Mercurialis?"

"Gone! You heard him laugh at you!"

"Right", snapped Felix, "put him with the freemen under guard for trial, Centurion. The slaves will go to auction. Put the house to the torch in the morning – delegate half a squad to it. This place will harbour no more traitors!

"Very good, Sir," replied Titus. "And our men, Sir?"

"We shall spend the night here; we will be the best occupants this place has had for a long time."

As Titus turned away Felix turned to Aufidius. "Go and tell Papirius to bring the horses up. Then both of you return to Waerham and tell the ladies Livia and Julia that we shall return in the morning. Then tell Valerius that you can put the bathhouse to use for your trouble. I would appreciate one of you being awake on rotation during the night."

The scout saluted and whirled away, the wind dragging at this cloak.

Dawn broke and the house was at once alive with boots clattering on stone and tile as a half-squad under Paulinus began to lay tinder and kindling near any wood in the villa.

A reluctant Aurelius Victor was pushed into the atrium by an irate Titus, his face black with rage.

"Centurion?" Clemens was intrigued.

"This man calls himself a soldier, an aquilifer, a budding deputy-centurion! He couldn't find his arse in the dark!"

"Translation?"

"The prisoner's escaped. He let him!"

"No!" Victor gave an anxious shout.

"Silence!" roared Titus in his ear, as Felix noticed the standard bearer wore no sword belt.

"Tell it," ordered Clemens.

"This man was in charge of the guard detail on the prisoners. He gave permission for the prisoner, Quintus, to visit the latrine – but, as far as I can tell, did not issue instructions to the guards to check his clothing on return."

"And?"

"He must have secreted keys away because the connecting door to the room he was held in was closed but no longer locked. It appears he somehow let himself out when the guard on the door patrolled the passageway – it's a long one, Sir."

"It wasn't my fault," screeched the aquilifer, only to receive a blow to the kidneys and a further enjoinder to be quiet.

"Any sign of him?"

"No, Sir. I have men out but it could have been a long time ago. He probably used that hole again. There was no reason to close it down with the house being burnt, Sir."

Felix sighed. It was easy to be wise after the event – but Titus was right. Why bother with it? At this time recrimination was of no consequence.

"Very well. Recall the men. On return this man will have a month's detention. Find another man to be standard-bearer – have in mind he has to keep company records. There will be no question of any further promotion for Aurelius Victor – he'll be lucky to hold his rank when I've had your written report."

★ ★ ★

"Isn't it annoying when you can't get shit off your sandals?"

Felix was walking towards the restaurant opposite Londinium's forum and the voice stopped him in his tracks. He spun round and recognised a face from the past.

In front of him stood Geta Marcus his centurion and comrade from Rome – before his fall from grace.

"My old friend – I had no idea," he said, astonished, as he made to embrace him.

However Marcus held his ground impassively, with his toga draped over his left arm as the style was.

Picking up the conversation again Felix asked, "How are you? You seem to have prospered."

"I wasn't rescued by a mentor," Marcus grudgingly replied.

"I heard about the galleys – I'm sorry. I was held in custody after our arrest and could do nothing; Marsala arranged it, so I was told. He was a magistrate with influential friends – more than I could muster."

"No vacancy rowing next to me, then?"

"I became a drunk!"

"I wasn't given the opportunity to be a drunk!"

"I tried to help!"

"I survived, anyway."

"So did I."

"Useful to be the son of a freed slave, though – with his master on hand."

There was a pause and they were buffeted by other pedestrians in much more of a hurry, prompting Felix to suggest they had some midday food together.

"I missed out on talking to that arse-hole Didius Marsala – I'd have liked to hear how sorry he was before he died. I owe you for that, too!"

"Why this?" asked Felix, completely bewildered that an old friend was talking like a new enemy. Pointing, he said "Let's at least get off the street! Have a cup of wine in this tavern."

Buffeted again despite the authority of his toga, Marcus condescendingly agreed by moving in its direction. Felix followed and signalled to the bar. They were immediately given the best table available and, seated in a corner, were soon served with the finest Falernian wine – one of the capital city's benefits.

"I'll drink with you – not to you," Marcus growled, then added taciturnly, "I'll drink your wine – but not your health!"

"Why this?" asked Felix again, trying to keep his tone even, hoping for some form of reconciliation. They had challenged Marsala amateurishly and lost. It was his fault, he knew, but there was nothing he could have done to change anything. Even his late father's master, Augustus Julius Maximus, had not felt able to interfere. Rescuing Felix took all his efforts.

"While you were being discharged I was chained in a galley," Marcus said vehemently, then drained his cup in one and held it out for Felix to pour another from the pewter jug. "I took lashes and built muscles, until I was able to bribe a time-beater with the prospect of half my wage if I was freed to row on my own account. It got me up on deck, too, where I could see what was happening. I replaced a dead man, so I was lucky – at last!"

Frowning Felix asked, "How did you come to be here, in Britain?"

"We were seeking pirates – but they attacked us first. Bloody navy – useless bastards in command! Can you believe it? We were outnumbered – and we were the hunters!

I told those I knew around me that we were all dead men if they didn't follow me. A couple refused and fell overboard: careless of them.

I led them at the war galley's marines. They were all facing the pirate boats so we pitched them overboard, or held them down and strangled them. Obviously the galley lost way and manoeuvrability – so it was easy meat to be boarded.

Their leader was a pirate of reputation – Corbillo. The navy wanted him badly and there he was, facing me. I had no option but to face him down and take the consequences.

He said he had seen my charge and needed men like me. He made me one of his lieutenants and asked who my second was, so I picked a rower at random. Then he had him flogged to death by the time-beater from my boat as an example that no one was immune from punishment, if they disobeyed him.

Then the time-beater was thrown to the sharks that had begun to circle us – blue, grey and white they were – as big as a man, too. Corbillo laughed like a fool as he was torn apart and swallowed in great, bloody chunks!"

"Bastard!"

"I should have thought of it earlier – it would have saved me money."

Then Marcus paused and gulped again before continuing, "So. I was a corsair – with the master pirate. We raided where we liked, land or sea. I made money – he liked me.

Money made friends and I spent high on them, until I reckoned I had a good number who would follow me.

But then the bloody navy caught us and we were lucky to get away. We lost a great many men but worse – we lost boats. I found out later their commander was a Gaius Fabullius, called Macer, who I'd very much like to meet, too. He cost me money and reputation!"

When I eventually took over Corbillo's boat – and made him my lieutenant - I had three of his men whipped to death. It was a lesson to him. He would have been one of them, but he could navigate as though born to it.

Then the bastard escaped and somehow agreed with the Romans not to pirate the inner sea; no idea where he went. There was nothing left for me so I went ashore. I spent money on myself by buying a cargo boat or two of my own. After all, there were no pirates worth talking of, were there?"

Against his will Felix smiled at that but, even as he fought it, he knew Corbillo wasn't the first pirate to be bought off: chasing them was even more expensive of naval time.

"Now here I am in Britain. I came looking for a dead man, apparently, so I'll try to find this naval captain and reward him suitably. Finding you was something I was not expecting." Marcus leaned back and laughed quietly, before pouring his half-filled cup onto the floor. "Funny how life comes around, isn't. Next time it won't be wine that gets spilt!"

Then he stood up, tossed his empty cup onto the table and stalked out.

★ ★ ★

Later in the day, over a pre-dinner drink, Urbicus remarked, "We'll talk some more on this Geta Marcus later

– when Agrippa arrives. For now, I want to talk of something else."

Felix raised his beaker in salute and waited.

"As you know, the Senate empowers me as governor, on their behalf, to arrange and sign contracts with manufacturers, suppliers or their agents as well as local tribes, to provide for our needs. Minerals, of course, mainly go to Rome – apart from what we use ourselves, like iron for weapons and stone for roads and buildings. You know all that – so I won't go over old ground."

Again Felix raised his beaker.

"The two gold mines are, of course, like all silver, lead, tin and copper mines our world over, under Imperial control. I like that personally – it makes them safe and administration easy.

However, the time comes when they begin to play out, with all the inherent problems of falls, flooding, etcetera. It's then the Senate sees it as better business to put them out to contract. A sure return on a problem investment, I suppose. We have an annual rent and they, the contractors, get to keep a percentage of the product.

That, now, is the nub of my problem. So I am told, by this particular mine superintendent and his surveyor, the *easy* gold is petering out. It's about time to put aside our production costs and let a third party explore further. If they want to share the profits then they can accept the dangers.

The Royal Second Legion provides the guard post and we must let them stay – all gold mines must remain secure. So, of course, must the lead mines for the silver content.

The gold mines are some sixty miles apart, with a lead lode in between. The Twentieth Legion can cover the northern gold mine as well as the lead and copper mines around it.

Our southern gold mine in Cambria lies in a triangle of small forts – and the lead mine has a fort nearby, too. However, it wouldn't be impossible to disguise discoveries and smuggle the gold away into the coastal belt. That's why we must retain a barracks there. In addition, though, I need a man who has an eye for intelligence information – gossip, unexplained changes in routine - all that sort of thing."

"What are you suggesting?"

The Governor eyed Felix cautiously and waited for an argument. When the question was not followed up he continued. "You'll be relieved to hear I'm not looking in your direction."

"I am," agreed Felix, once more saluting his friend.

"I'm wanting your man Firmus."

Felix raised an eyebrow "Why?"

Urbicus expanded is arms briefly, almost sending wine flying as he did so. "Why not? He's exactly what I'm looking for. He's your northern agent, so understands our methods – and codification to some extent. Additionally he's, I nearly said only, of centurion rank so it would not seem unusual for him to take command of a guard post. It all fits – he's ideal!"

"Are you saying the north should be denuded?"

"Not at all – if needs be Clemens can go up – on an inspection, or some other pretext. In any case, while we have additional legionaries up there building the wall there's not likely to be any trouble, is there? Now, what do you say?"

After toying with his wine Felix finally said, "I see what you're saying. How long for?

"Well, that depends who gains the contract and how they meet it. However, I think I see your drift. It's remote and hardly a place to win battle honours – every young officer's dream. Neither would I want him to become disaffected and seen as a candidate for revolt. I'll think on it, but six months at a time comes to mind – with promotion when the time's right – say two to three tours. How does that sound initially?"

Felix' greenish-brown eyes clouded briefly and the frown emphasised the childhood scar over his left eyebrow. Then he smiled and his eyes lit up.

"Why not? He'll be in command. Independent. Promotion will be a spur – and we can trust him! I, for one will be pleased to see him withdrawn from his under-cover role as a feed to Mercurialis. Of course," Felix added with a wide smile, "he has an interest in Julia's childhood companion, Dorcas, who is still my responsibility – having freed her. If they were to marry they would have every opportunity to get to know each other well, in a remote spot like that!"

Urbicus laughed loudly at the comment before saying, "My friend, it's no wonder I sought this relationship with you. We've always got on well and you make me laugh – for which I'm always grateful.

In one breath you agree with me, expect me to grant exemption for him to marry in service, at his rank – and lift a burden, of sorts, from your own shoulders! Only you could do that successfully!"

"So. Shall we drink to that?"

★ ★ ★

"They all ride horses, of course. Do you know why?"

"Have you seen their woman – they practice on the horses!"

The four stopped, turned to the tables the comments came from and, after noting the humorists were from the Londinium fort, turned away and continued to the bar to order.

"If you ride, at least you're on top of something decent. You only need to press with a knee and it knows exactly what to do!"

At that the tables erupted with drunken laughter and drink went everywhere, as they rocked about and beat the table top, or simply collapsed against the backs of the benches.

Paulinus made to turn but the fierce hold on his arm by Cassius Magna, perfected by long practice with juggling clubs, reminded him of his loyalties to Felix. No trouble.

Amatus, the seasick ex-marine crowded him, too, whilst Jason stood ready to restrain him with a wrestling hold, if necessary.

Choking back their raucous laughter the tables' occupants kept up the tirade, clearly wanting trouble by provoking it.

"Why do they wear blue uniforms – so that you know who's *woad* into town!"

It was as impossible for the four members of Felix' off-duty bodyguard to order as it was to ignore the shouted comments.

"I heard someone *woad* the legate's wife!"

Immense hilarity erupted at that, causing other customers to leave the tavern by any exit available. The landlord put his hand on the pick handle he kept under the counter, as a means of asserting his authority in just these circumstances.

Pauilinus went over to the bar and suggested to the landlord that it would be wise to have work in his cellar, words that were heeded with vigour.

As the drunken soldiers reeled about in their helpless laugher Paulinus upended one table after another in quick succession, liquid and uneaten food going in all directions.

Startled by the activity and noise the revellers stopped giggling and looked at the four men in front of them, each separated by an arm's length and standing-square on.

"What was that you pointed out to us? Do explain it fully, *please*," Paulinus said levelly, looking the man in front of him straight in the eyes.

"I think you should ask me that," said a well-built soldier on the end of a bench. "I'm used to shovelling shit where it belongs!"

Jason moved across and countered that with, "I suppose you use your hands, do you – make a big pile round yourself, I suppose?"

The man laughed, then growled menacingly, a smile breaking down into a leer. "I shall enjoy breaking your back – and I've just the shit pile to let you rest on."

At that all six leaped forward to grapple with the four, only to find that Cassius Magna and Paulinus had worked together before, when the villa was raided, so the two took one attacker each, to use both as a defence and a weapon against the others.

Jason took one of the arms reaching for him, grabbed it, ducked under it and twisted it up behind the soldier's back, then propelled him head first into a doorframe.

At that, he was immediately clubbed on the neck from behind and went down under fists. He was rescued when Cassius dropped to one knee, tossing his opponent over his shoulder, before coming to his feet with a goblet in his hand and letting fly with it at Jason's attacker.

As payment for his awareness of Jason's plight, Cassius was hit viciously on the temple by a clubbing fist and knocked senseless to the floor.

Paulinus grabbed the man and, lifting him high, threw him into the two remaining soldiers so that the three crashed over backwards in a heap.

Amatus, shoulders muscular from years of the swimming that had made him a legion champion, grabbed two of the dazed men by their hair and cracked their heads together noisily, before letting them drop and brushing his hands together as though to rid himself of any dust.

Paulinus kicked a prostrate form squarely between the legs, enjoying the scream as the feigning soldier rolled over with hands grasping futilely at the agony.

Picking up one comrade apiece the two big men made for the entrance, well pleased that their assailants had no realisation the four had all been selected for skills beyond pure soldiery.

Chapter VI

"It's taken a long time to negotiate but the gold mine is now leased to us. It's *ours*!"

"The mine is played out. What skills do we have to dig deeper or look further? What of our other interest?"

Geta Marcus looked at his inquisitor sympathetically. "You do remember why you invested, do you? We have *employees* to take the risks – we bought them with the mine. Their skills are our skills."

"But what about selling other lots – for us to share the purchase price?"

With studied patience Marcus said nothing, whilst all the time his eyes roamed from face to face. Eventually he said, quietly enough for each to strain to hear the words as he used the ploy to catch their attention, "We are *all* in this to make our fortunes, if we're lucky. If not, on the way to independence for this island, we shall make profits where we may – however, that does not mean we act rashly or injudiciously.

To cover the point made – we *shall* be selling lots in our venture and we *shall* pocket that money but, and mark my words here, *when the time is right*! That will not be until we have our feet firmly anchored there and can be seen to have improved our *own* investment."

"Seen to have? That could be months, years – or never, if no new seams are found!"

"Claudius Venuto! You are a senior chieftain in your tribe – a councillor in your town's ordo even – but you are far removed from Durnovaria and have overlooked the fact that I originated and formed this group. By all means make suggestions –but I will not be dictated to! Keep your dice in your cup. I will tell you when to roll them – and then you scoop the pot."

The other member of the trio coughed gently. He smiled as he looked at Venuto, still amazed at his educated Latin but immensely irritated by his habits of scratching, as well as picking his nose. Even as he made to speak he watched the Romanised Briton scratch his beard, as though it was full of lice.

"As you remember, I'm sure, I come originally from across the water – from Northern Gaul to be precise. I was a small carrier of sea goods there. It's because I was patient and waited for opportunities that I became a bigger shipper, to the point where I say nothing wrong when pointing out that I am one of the most influential in the Londinium port.

Consequently I can say to you, in all conscience, *wait*! Let's see what develops. We shall accumulate money to buy land in this most recent state of the empire – and land represents power. With enough of both we shall be rulers of our own *kingdom*, not only of a town."

"Tiberius Celerianus is right in all he says," Marcus agreed. "If the mine gives up no gold we shall seed it. One way or another we shall acquire what it is you want.

Say nothing, do nothing – and believe me your silence will be *golden*!"

* * *

The governor's parting words to Felix were of his being able to put the theory to the test at last. He was referring to the years Felix had been pressing for a canal system to link the rivers Uxela and Stour, which would transport men and stores to where they were needed quickly, as well as the trade goods of civilian manufacturers.

Urbicus had finally put the work in progress, citing it as an additional security measure, much approved by the navy who would now be called upon far less to weather the conditions around the toe of Albion in order to access the Sabrina river and beyond into Cambria, from the south.

In allowing the false assumption to stand that he would also utilise this connection, Felix and Urbicus had hoped to confound any possible security leakage. In reality Felix took Clemens and the remainder of his century across country on horseback to Glevum. From there they utilised the Sabrina and, although their normal forced-march speed of fifty miles per day was reduced to the speed of the vessel, it could travel all day – which their valiant steeds could not, Felix well knew, anymore than they could – meaning that they saved a day in reaching the mine in the Cothi valley.

* * *

Dust hung in the air as they arrived, since the waterwheel hammers that shattered the mined quartz had barely shut down.

They were challenged by the mine guards, which pleased Felix as his century was in uniform, but immediately admitted on sight of his own authority. He made a note to commend them to Antoninus Sextus, the newly-confirmed legate of the Second Legion in Isca Silurum – where for protocol's sake, he had already sent a messenger from Glevum to notify his destination.

The open-cast workings had long since given up their treasure, as had the hillsides when the sluices from the aqueduct were opened to cascade an avalanche of water down them, stripping them bare of cover to reveal the occasional seams of gold hidden below. Then the earth had been opened up as these seams were followed underground.

As they went through the great open pit that was fast becoming a dumping ground for slag, beyond the mine buildings Felix noted the rough-carved rock pillar denoting the three highest deities, Jupiter, Juno and Minerva, which he saluted briefly by way of homage.

A regular sloshing sound came to them as water was pumped up from a lower level by means of paddle buckets on a scoop wheel, several arranged in a tiered series. He was always intrigued by the thought that went into the technology involved – even to the saving of the water for later use in sluices, when tiny nuggets and even grains of gold were panned.

The mine superintendent and the surveyor came forward to meet them, given no notice of their imminent arrival in order that Felix could judge the mine's outward security.

They each hailed him with a raised hand since they were civilians, before the superintendent said, "Sir. It's both a surprise and a pleasure to have you visit. I trust there is nothing wrong and that you had a good journey," he remarked guardedly, knowing that senior officials did not journey for the views alone.

Felix dismounted while Clemens indicated to Titus that the men should do the same. He said cheerfully, "What could be wrong? We hear only good reports of the mine. Firstly though, will you see to the quartering of my men – I expect the Second have tents to spare?"

The superintendent quickly signalled members of his staff forward and hasty instructions were given to them on various topics.

"Sir. Please do come into my quarters, though I strongly regret you will find them sparse and spare by town standards."

"Thank you for your consideration," Felix responded, "But I have campaigned like every soldier. Comfort is comparative – any comfort desirable!"

The superintendent smiled. "I'm sorry, I had no idea."

"Why should you?" Felix rejoined gently. "I know as much of you."

Felix and Clemens were led into a comfortably, but not generously, furnished office complex and the legate was put into the place of honour, much to his protest.

"I am Gaius Pertinax and this is Lentilus Septimus – a skilled surveyor. How can we help?"

Felix explained why they were there and what his intentions were. "You won't yet be aware that this mine has been leased to a consortium, under contract. It's not open-ended – naturally. The both of you are integral to its operation so it has been assumed you will stay – no doubt at enhanced arrangements."

"I don't know that I want to," interrupted Pertinax. "The administration will be entirely different. It will be a different perspective altogether. I work for the Government, not private enterprise."

Felix raised his eyebrows at Septimus, who took the hint. "It's a question needing time, Legate."

"It was your joint report which indicated that the *easy* gold was coming to an end. The alternative, it was naturally assumed, was to dig deeper and across stopes. You also mentioned arsenic deposits and that there's no facility for recovering the gold from arsenic – in addition to what would be the toxic effects of extracting it."

Revising his opinion of Felix the surveyor replied, with an exhaled breath, "That's all true. The superintendent is fully appraised of all that – the final report was in his name, of course.

However, with the advent of your understanding gold mining in the light of your comments, with the approval of Gaius Pertinax I'll escort you underground – to see for yourself."

"You seem antagonistic," observed Clemens, causing both miners to scrutinise him, wondering what he might understand of mining.

"Not so," countered the superintendent. "Not at all. A little defensive, perhaps, bearing in mind that we had no warning, or notion, of your coming."

"Gentlemen," interrupted Felix, ensuring his features relaxed. "We come in good faith – though a tour is welcome. However, I need to check on my men and hopefully there are minehead baths. Tomorrow would seem a good time to pursue our discussions."

As it transpired the bath complex was down the hill road and neither had felt willing to go down and back after the hard ride, so both settled for a cold sluice in the morning mist, before nibbling hard tack and taking their helmets with them to the mine entrance, which stood out starkly, halfway up a long rise. In both their thoughts was the oddity of walking uphill to a mine.

★ ★ ★

"I was sorry to hear about the lady Sabina, Admiral," Macer said sincerely. "It was a great shock to everyone.

"Yes," agreed the Prefectus Classis, looking momentarily into the distance, "it was. However, I have commended her to the gods and can do no more. Now – what about you, sir? We have a madman at loose, it seems. Another shit-pile is the last thing we need. A vendetta? Against a naval officer? What is the man thinking of?"

The young navarchus shrugged. "I don't remember the man particularly – but I *do* the action. He seems to resent my having removed his livelihood."

"I think the time's come to remove more than his livelihood, don't you?" Having said it Agrippa then laughed out loud at the innuendo. "I rather like that idea!"

Again Macer shrugged. "Clearly we cannot let him make threats openly – but we don't know that he is. Since he's well known to Felix he may have overstepped the mark for effect, given the circumstances of their meeting."

The Little Admiral, as he was sometimes referred to out of earshot, threw his arms wide in disbelief. "Here we have a man offering threats to you and you seek to defend him."

"He was Felix' man, Admiral," Macer retorted, careful to retain the formality his senior preferred on his own territory. "It's likely he has his own ideas."

Snorting disdainfully Agrippa replied, "When did the navy ask the army to do its dirty work for it? We may be paid less – but I still outrank all, bar the governor."

"Naturally I agree, Admiral – but this charge isn't open and shut. The governor will require some evidence to establish at least a prima facie case against him.

Not only that but the legate is the governor's official investigator. Not that you, of course, Admiral, nor the legion commanders, cannot act in your own right, should you deem it necessary."

"What are you saying?"

"No direct threat has been made to *me*. Equally, if anything happened, the legate would know where to look. At the moment it's all hot air."

"Like a fart in the breeze, you're saying?"

"That about sums it up."

"My boy," Agrippa said, his liking for his protégé coming to the fore again, "You must captain your own ship – in both senses. Does your intended know of this?"

"No, Sir – and I'd like her not to. There's no point in worrying her unduly. If anything happens, we'll see."

"She's the legate's ward?"

"One of them, yes. Apart from that I like to think of Felix as a friend. Neither disturbs my loyalty to you, Admiral."

"Very well put, my son – very well argued. As you say, one step at a time."

* * *

With large candles fixed to their helmets Felix and his son-in-law followed Lentilus Septimus down the tunnel lined with slow-burning but spluttering torches to rough steps, hewn out of the bare rock, irregular in height and uneven under their sandals.

Five shafts led off the main, all leading to different levels, each as dark and droplet laden as the others.

"We're about a hundred feet away from the open-cast area now," explained the surveyor, holding out a torch to illuminate a vertical shaft, where two young boys sat watching, waiting for another fall of quartz rocks to be tipped down to them.

"Isn't that lethal?" exclaimed Clemens, wondering about the lack of shelter for them.

"You get used to it. They recognise what's happening and step into this shaft. When the last lump is still, they get to work sorting."

"What about natural falls?" asked Felix.

"No supports are needed because quartz is immensely strong, so is self-supporting. However, for safety's sake we install *screamers* to give warning of any movement."

"Glad to know you have the workers' welfare in mind," Felix observed.

"Bugger welfare! They're all skilled miners – and valuable," retorted the surveyor and waited while his charges coughed as another load of mined quartz fell somewhere behind them, throwing up a cloud of choking dust.

"Sometimes we have to create stopes to follow a seam upwards – when a tunnel isn't necessary."

"Yes, I see. Why isn't that one being pursued?" It puzzled Clemens, peering at what seemed to be gold fleck in amongst quartz.

"Don't touch!" Lentilus Septimus snapped. "That's mixed with arsenic crystals – it could kill you. We can't separate it out, so we leave it."

After what seemed for ever in the damp, dark and dangerous shafts, with both having hit their helmets more than once on projections, they finally stumbled up a different set of irregular steps, holding the fortuitously placed ropes to steady themselves, on their climb towards a rough circle of light.

As Felix and Clemens left the cold confines their relief was palpable and they wondered if all the workers felt the same at the end of the day's work.

"Except for slaves, each day's work is another day's pay. I expect they see it that way," said the smiling surveyor, taking off his helmet and extinguishing his candle before snuffing theirs.

"It takes about ten tons of scree to produce one ton of quartz ore – which yields an ounce of gold, or so – though considerably more is not unknown. It's not an easy job, but the rewards are good, all round"

"What did you mean *screamers*, by the way?"

"Ah! They're squared timbers at intervals across the shafts. Tightly fitted, so that if they are compressed any more the wood sings or creaks – screams, if you like. It works well, reassuringly so when it's silent."

They walked back down the slope to level ground and the surveyor escorted them in to Gaius Pertinax. When they were all seated the superintendent asked about the tour and was pleased with their response. At that he changed tack.

"Now we come to the other part of the process," he said happily, "the lucrative part!"

"Will you also discuss security?" asked Felix.

"Most certainly – I believe I understand what you are seeking, now that I know of the leasing."

"Excellent."

"So. The gold is mined, crushed, extracted and sometimes panned. It can, of course, be sold as it is, but for easy storage and transportation it's normally formed into ingots – bars of gold.

This process is heavily guarded and random searches of workers after shifts is regular, as you would expect.

The gold is heated in a furnace until it liquefies. Then it's skimmed for dross and poured into moulds. Obviously the hot gold pan is moved using wooden tongs – wood does not pick up heat very well, of course.

The moulds are left to cool – but are still very hot when the ingots are tipped into water to finally solidify. The process is timed – and the ingots are stamped with the imperial mark while they cool, in the same way the coins are hand stamped as they cool.

Because of the high heat involved shifts only last about an hour before a rest and water break is allowed."

"Not welfare breaks, I suppose?" Clemens asked rhetorically.

"By all the gods – no! It's to prevent silly accidents occurring because of heat exhaustion. We must keep the process going economically – accidents don't."

When the pair said nothing, but looked thoughtful, the superintendent added wryly, "We do have a hospital for injuries – of all types, of course. We use ex-orderlies who understand first aid. A retired capsarius is a very useful man."

"You'll be getting another useful man soon. Your current centurion is being posted for a stint on the New Wall. I shall see him shortly to inform him."

"Actually he's in transit to Isca – yesterday, as a matter of fact. You probably passed each other. He was escorting a shipment of gold down the river Cothi from here, then up the Sabrina."

★ ★ ★

"Did you use any contraception, when you went with Clemens?"

Julia studied Avita but there was only an expression of concern on her face, so she did her best to put the question in perspective.

"Have you talked to your mother, at all?"

"Romana, as you know her, spends a great deal of time at the palace. Londinium appeals – let alone the governor. I rarely see her to discuss anything – in any case, as your father agreed for me to be his ward when my father died, she probably expects him to arrange what is necessary. I know he keeps mother informed, but she never questions anything.

Not that I'm complaining - your father's concerned about me. I'll lead my own life soon with Macer and mother's entitled to rebuild her life. Don't forget, widows are encouraged – no, required isn't it – to remarry?"

Julia sat in a high-backed chair opposite Avita and crossed her ankles to be more comfortable.

"I wasn't thinking of crossing my legs," the future bride remarked casually, causing them both to burst into laughter, lightening the atmosphere considerably.

"Well, we did try some," Julia said almost conspiratorially, as though someone else might be listening. "Washing, or sluicing out, takes away the fun, to be honest. The pastes are all right but you live in hope with them, of course.

It gets in the way a bit but, with practice," she paused to bite her lip at the implication, "using a skin seems to work best."

"Do you have any evidence of that?" Avita asked impishly, and the two giggled like children at the innuendo.

There was a knock on the door-frame and when Julia called out the steward drew back the curtain before entering.

"Yes, Valerius. What is it?"

"Excuse my disturbing you but a fast messenger brought this tablet for you. Presumably it's important – and it's your father's seal in the wax."

"Thank you," she said, and broke the seal as soon as Comazon Valerius had left the room. Several tablets were laced together to allow enough space for the message, which was from Felix.

Julia exclaimed, after re-reading it, "Well, that gives food for thought – literally! What we were talking of – no, not that," she added only to tail off with another fit of the giggles.

"Marriage, I mean. This is about that. My father says he has heard from Macer that his father has consented to his marrying you. That being the case, when they arrive here – they're coming via the new canal for speed – he says he will marry you!"

Avita had jumped up, her fists in her mouth and eyes wide. Sitting down again, her eyes now wet with tears of happiness she managed, "I don't know what to say. I mean it's wonderful – but so sudden!"

Julia went over and knelt in front of her, taking her entwined fingers in a firm grip.

"Long expected or quickly arranged, marriage is always sudden, my dearest Avita. On the day it seems unreal – perhaps it actually is. But if it's what you really want, the one thing in the world you really want, then you'll walk across glass and nettles to achieve it."

There was a pause, which to Julia seemed interminable, until Avita said with passion, "I do believe I would go mad if Macer and I did not marry!"

"Oh, my dear girl," said Julia, burying her face in Avita's lap.

* * *

By good fortune the plan worked and Firmus was discharged on the Cothi river from the vessel carrying Second Legion soldiers returning from their stint on the Antonine Wall to their depot in Isca Silurum. He was in time to pick up Macer's ship bound for the Uxela and the canal to the Stour.

"Young man," observed Felix, "You've done well – but even better than you know! Macer and Avita will marry on our return. I have promised that. Will you marry Dorcas – a joint wedding?"

"I've not spoken of it. You knew what my schedule was. Why?"

"There are orders awaiting you, I'm afraid. They're good orders – will stand you in good stead. To marry is optional."

"As a centurion I cannot marry until my discharge."

"I never offer what I cannot deliver. If she agrees – will you?"

"I pray the gods will be on my side!"

The homecoming was a riotous affair with the young women dashing out to meet their betrothed before rushing to offer respective congratulations, agonising what to wear and greeting groups of guests as they arrived at the Waerham villa for the marriages.

"Quite normal, really," remarked a smiling Petronius, now fully recovered from his fever. "Of course, I can say things like that because your girl called me *avuncular* years ago – or so it seems."

The two embraced with mutual respect as well as friendship, Felix well aware of this centurion having completed almost fifty years service, encompassing thirteen different legions in his time and now serving the governor as his camp prefect.

He had arrived by sea with Urbicus and Agrippa in a vessel captained by Marcus Julius Draco, who had moored in the great Pwll harbour and they had been brought in by lighters to the small town's quay.

Felix next greeted the governor's staff surgeon, Tiberius Piso Faber, a small, rotund yet strong man in his forties whose grey-green eyes twinkling with pleasure.

"I love this place," he said, not for the first time. "It, with your family, always welcomes me to the point it feels like home."

"You're always welcome, my friend – you know that." Felix replied, then asked, "and who is this handsome young man you've brought to assist you? Surely it's not that young scallywag, Carinorum Rufinus!"

The young man, here in his own right as Avita's brother, stepped forward to embrace his mentor, aware of the debt he owed the man who took him as his ward when his father died. "I'm fine, Sir, and getting on very well as the doctor's surgical assistant. The old wounds don't bother me at all."

Holding him at arm's length Felix looked at him, saying, "You do so look the part, young man. I'm proud of you."

"As I am of you, Sir," he replied. Feeling uneasy with so many senior ranks on hand, he then added, "I had best find my sister, I think."

Felix watched the increasingly confident young man walk away with just a slight limp. Then he was greeting the

Little Admiral who, after grasping forearms in the more formal welcome, introduced Draco.

"He lives up – or should that be down – to his nickname! The *dragon*, here, is becoming adept at sinking or frightening off the wretched poachers from Hibernia. He's sure they're not *all* from Thule originally."

"Macer has often referred to you, Navarchus. The two of you should make a good team – your Sabrina and his Tigris."

"We do, Sir, we do."

"He turned down the opportunity to be the executive on the Trireme to retain command of his Bireme," observed Agrippa. "Can't say I blame him – command is good."

"We'll catch up later, young man," Felix told the young naval officer, whose beard effectively hid his age, giving the appearance of an older man. "I must see to the governor."

At that Felix turned away to Urbicus, who had been conversing quietly with a small group until his host became free.

They embraced enthusiastically and Felix remarked as they broke away, "My friend, I can't believe there are many governors of provinces willing to stand back while their juniors are seen to."

"You and I, Felix, conform to no mould – perhaps one of the reasons we get on well together," he retorted.

"Romana has joined the ladies, so I think a cup of your best in the gardens wouldn't go down amiss."

* * *

"As you all know," Felix said to the throng in front of him, "no formal ceremony of marriage is required – not even a plain statement, taking things to the extreme.

However, this is a special occasion – not only because my ward is marrying Macer but also that my daughter's past companion is also marrying the centurion Firmus. A double wedding."

He waited while the clapping died away before continuing, "And that is why we meet on the garden slopes here – there are quite a lot of us!"

After more clapping he went on, "Each couple has agreed to accept the ceremony as binding on them jointly."

At that he called them forward and each pair stood hand-in-hand on either side of him, the five in an open vee, in order that they could be seen.

"Do you each wish to marry your partner freely?" Having asked, he noted all four nodded as they confirmed it and looked at each other happily.

"Do any of you have a reason that would make this illegal?" Felix listened to all four negative answers before asking, "Do you then wish to exchange tokens as a sign of marriage?"

Each produced a ring to exchange and Felix asked that they be placed on each others' fingers.

"I now call on all here as witnesses to the marriages of Gaius Fabullius Macer to Carinorum Avita and of Marcus Cocceius Firmus to Augusta Dorcas."

There were some inhalations of breath as the applause began, from those who realised that Felix had given his family name to the girl slave he had freed in order to become Julia's childhood companion.

"You may kiss," he added, indicating the already embracing couples.

Chapter VII

Livia lay against Felix' left side, her head resting on the shoulder of the arm around her, while her fingers gently stroked his chest.

He lightly kissed her forehead and she spoke for the first time since he had lifted off her after their climax.

"It was a good wedding celebration, wasn't it? Everyone was just so happy."

Felix knew she had felt him nod several times so he simply replied, "I was very pleased to be expected to officiate. It makes so much more of the occasion. I'm sure the girls, in particular, will look back and remember."

Livia observed quietly, "All you men are so hard, of course. Well – *you* can't be now," she added wickedly and he felt her laughing into his shoulder, as he smiled to himself.

"You did well arranging all those dishes. Urbicus said he would have been happy to see them all at the palace," remarked Felix, pleased to offer the compliment.

"Yes, I heard him say so. He's very generous with compliments."

"He means them, too. Urbicus called that mixed meat compilation a real soldiers' meal. What was it? Beef, pork and mutton?"

She nodded against his shoulder. "All the meat was boned and rolled in pieces, then oven cooked before it was gently grilled. After that it was simmered in a spicy sauce. It was served without the juices - as you saw - sprinkled with pepper. It's a bit fussy."

"Apicius' cook book? You like his recipes."

"Yes, I do. Mind you some of his sauces are a bit pungent – I don't like them all, even though I serve them."

"Cook did well for you, then."

Easing herself against him, as a muscle resented the pressure on it, Livia said, "That's true, too. I tell her the what – Julia & I on this occasion – and she really gets the kitchen hands organised with cutting, peeling, pounding, grinding, grating – the list goes on. Do you think we ought to reward her? I mean, look at all the dishes we asked her to do. There was even a spit by the servants' quarters for the venison."

"I get them in the wrong order," Felix replied, cupping his right hand round Livia's left breast," but that multi-bird collage *always* impresses. What is it? Quail inside pigeon, inside guinea fowl, inside pheasant, inside duck, inside goose, inside swan?"

"The type of bird doesn't matter, my love, as long as each is boned, fits inside the next in size and all slice well together to look good."

"Whose idea was the baked oysters?"

"To go with the hake fillets and sea bream? It was cook's actually. Then Julia thought of roast suckling pig, because the asafoetida essence was going to be needed for the hake and bream sauces, anyway. *I* wanted the venison – men like it."

"By the way," Felix said, "thanks for sending up a side for the century to do themselves."

"I hope they kept some for the men on duty."

"They would have – and some of the ale I sent up. The police post joined them, too."

When there was no reply he added, "I wonder if sly old cook had the occasion in mind? The oysters were bound to go quickly – they always do."

"I know why men like those, too – in fact I'm going to have to revise my opinion about you being a hard man!"

★ ★ ★

Julia groaned with pleasure and held Clemens tightly as the ultimate wave swept over her, coinciding with his breathing out, seemingly in relief. As their chests heaved and then relaxed, she still clung to him so that they turned on their sides together.

After a little while Julia whispered, "I did so need us to do that – it seems so long ago we last made love."

Lifting himself slightly so that she could free the arm she had underneath him, he sank back and said softly, "It did for me too, but it doesn't anymore. That was good."

Pretending to punch him Julia retorted, "Good? What do you mean only good – it was bloody marvellous, as you bold soldiers say!"

"Where did you pick that up?"

"I married a rough soldier. That's why I had a rough soldier's child recently."

Clemens laughed quietly and said, "Is that what caused it? I thought you'd put on a bit of weight."

Julia rolled on top of him and giggled. "If I wasn't still a bit uncomfortable I'd show you what I meant," she said and tried to pummel his chest, but he put his arms round her to hold her still.

Once she was lying quietly on him Clemens asked in a low voice, "Changing the subject somewhat, I never quite got hold of who that woman was with the naval captain - surely too old to be his wife?

Julia whispered back, "She's Draco's sister. She brought up her brother after their parents died, being quite a few years older than him apparently. Well, obviously actually.

There was a tutor about – an uncle, I think. Why?"

"I saw the Little Admiral looking at her. Still, I expect he already knows Draco's history."

"Ssh," Julia cautioned him. "You shouldn't call him that – he's a wedding guest and he might hear. By the way, her name's Aelia Aeliana."

* * *

Marcus Maenius Agrippa had made short work of meeting Draco's sister.

"Admiral," she greeted him, as he moved up to her, "thank you for taking the trouble to meet me – of course, my brother has told me much about you."

Agrippa took one of her hands between his great paws and gently squeezed it.

"I can't understand how we've never met before."

She laughed at his seriousness before explaining, "Earlier this year I decided to see some of our empire that Draco has seen so often and made Londinium a port of call, since my brother speaks so highly of this island's beauty. However, he did advise me not to circumnavigate it but to explore the southern and easterly coasts," she added, almost as though it was a secret.

Letting her hand go Agrippa nodded. "Good advice. Both the western and northern capes can be problems. Not a few ships have come to grief."

"It's the forty-fifth state, I believe; we've been here some ninety years?"

Agrippa shrugged quickly. "Give or take a year or two – about a hundred.

"Why so far north of Rome?"

"Several reasons, dear lady. One of them was that these most northerly tribes were a thorn in the side of governing greater Gaul. Another is that this island's full of various metals and marbles that are of great value to the empire. Now," he continued, "changing the subject, I should be delighted to escort the sister of one of my most promoted young officers along either coast."

She gave him a broad smile which exposed even, white teeth and her brown eyes shone. "Admiral! You sound like a young man proposing a relationship. Do you know, it makes me feel about seventeen, too.

I had to decline any such offers before because our parents had died and I was responsible for Draco," she explained. Then she went on quickly, "However, I'll not decline now and thank you for the thought!"

"Good," the little admiral exclaimed. "Excellent! When I return to my headquarters, will you travel with me?"

Laughing again Aelia Aeliana nodded enthusiastically. "A lovely idea and one to be put into practice straightaway. Thank you once again."

★ ★ ★

"So," Geta Marcus said simply and rubbed his fingers on his chin, as he considered what he had just been told.

This Caecilius Urbanus was seeking to turn his coat – for a few coins every month, naturally. When asked why, he had come up with an entirely plausible story that he was being overlooked and undermined.

It was plausible because it could be checked.

Apparently he had become a *capsarius* and, after assisting surgeon Faber, to remove a soldier's leg, had been taken up as a medicus miles to Faber, which raised him to surgical assistant. Since Faber was staff surgeon to the governor the promotion had come with added kudos. This Caecilius had even looked further and wondered whether a doctor's training might become possible.

Then, completely out of the blue, the century's new capsarius had been badly wounded in an action and instead of being invalided out, as the one-legged soldier had been, he was being offered the very doctor's training that he, Caeilius, had been coveting. Clearly there was room for only one, condemning him to remaining a surgical assistant

– maybe even to the usurper, eventually. It seemed that could not be borne.

And so to this, thought Marcus.

"If – and it's only an if – I return to the century as capsarius, I would be in a useful position to offer you tit-bits of information about goings-on. Men let a lot slip when they trust you!"

"Yes", Marcus replied flatly, drawing the word out. "And what sort of coin is going to interest you?"

Licking his lips the turncoat replied, "An aureus a month!"

Marcus laughed abruptly. "I was looking to reward an informer – not a comedian!"

"Twenty-five denarii is a soldier's pay per month. One Aureus."

"A soldier could be killed."

"Do I run a lesser risk!"

"You still talk too high a price," Marcus observed, an annoyed edge to his voice. Then he added, "However, I shall see what crumbs you pick from the high table. You will remain on the surgeon's staff – at whatever rank. In the palace you will also have access to servants – they can serve a rich sauce, too. Communication will be easier. It will be up to you to find a way to remain if – as you say – there is any risk of your removal."

"And my fee?"

"If I give you gold I expect gold in return. Be aware, I am not interested in glister!"

* * *

"I see why you feel this is the place for your new villa," Clemens remarked.

They had reached the hamlet on the Stour River that Felix thought was called Throp.

"The natural weir is easily bypassed and will form the spillway for your mill. Are you still of that mind?"

Thoughtfully Felix nodded. "Since the mill builders were killed Livia is on edge in Waerham. I shall leave the fish pond for the town, of course. It's a good source of food for the poorer families."

"Should I take it over? After all, you want Julia and I to stay there."

Felix looked at him. "I'm not sure you're a miller inside, young man. Anyone you employ would know that. Still, it's a business opportunity going begging – I leave it to you."

"Julia has a lot of interests. Her cooking and housekeeping book – Livia is sure it'll be a success – the teaching, to name only a minimum. It would be strange if I neglected a means of livelihood for some of the townsfolk."

"You're right, Clemens. It would look as if you didn't care – and you will be one of the bigger landholders in the area."

"Presumably you will stay with us when you meet with Stolus about the pottery and Valerius about the chain of shops Livia wants him to run. Then there's the Carinus quarry over Durnovaria way. It would be nearer and so a good base for you, at least periodically."

"Probably more shops in Durnovaria, too. The oysters in the Great Harbour – again via Stolus – the Corf winery, the pewter works as well. It'll be a butterfly existence for a while, I suspect."

"Did I mention your grandson?"

"You cheeky young sod! Do you think I'd forgotten? Livia will obviously want to come with me when I come over – she'll miss Julia as much as I will. But it'll be good for you to run your own house. It's what a man needs to do."

"I don't know about me running it," Clemens said in mock anguish, " I'm married!"

"Anyway, back to this site," Felix replied, avoiding that issue entirely since Julia certainly knew how to run a house, having done so for him since her mother died suddenly when she was fifteen. His son-in-law was a lucky man.

"This raised area will form a base for the house and see, over there, that's ideal for a small quay – it's well below the ox-bow. Of course, the canal passing the weir will need a pound-lock to raise for the traffic – as all the river's weirs will. We can't keep building rock dams behind us!"

Clemens remembered the Tamarus episode but put it aside saying, "I digress again, because I had an idea last night."

"Should I know your private life?"

Laughing at the innuendo Clemens retorted, "I do have a range of ideas! This one's about recruiting more guards privately. What of Paulinus? He probably won't return to policing Waerham, with his injured hands. Why not let him recruit, train and head up your house guards?"

"Brilliant! A brilliant idea, young sir. Any time you want to remain my son-in-law, I'm on your side! Even so, I should have thought of that myself. He'll keep his eyes open, too. He's a good, steady soldier – a man you can reply on. Will you put it to him – or shall I?"

Clemens blandly replied, "I think you should. He respects you for your detection skills – I believe that should sway him, should he decide to think on it."

Nodding Felix commented, "A good point. He might have his own ideas by now. I'll see to it."

★ ★ ★

"You do realise the man who insures your cargo is just a Briton from up near the first wall. The Parisii tribe?"

"He's a Roman Citizen by dint of his being an Aedile of Petuaria. All top officials are granted that reward."

Tiberius Celerianus looked at his fellow shipper as though he was a child. "Marcus Aurelius Lunaris – Lunaris – listen to me. I know he's a distant relative of yours by marriage, so it's natural to be loyal – but he takes a third of your profit."

"And *all* the loss if a ship founders!"

"How many have? You run a modern fleet."

Lunaris nervously licked his lips before asking, "What are you saying here? You can do better?" The vague possibility of a better deal was always worth listening to, he well knew. He also knew Celerianus was a rich shipper and nobody's fool.

"No, not insuring your ships. I'm talking about you having your own insurance policy. An independent insurance against a rainy day."

Lunaris licked his lips again. "You spoke of shares when you said you insured your own losses, before I reminded you of my deal with Ianuarius."

Nodding rapidly now Celerianus went on, "You have it – shares. Shares, of course, in something special – so special in fact, we can afford to be highly selective, very highly selective of whom we invite to join us."

"Why me?"

"You recently dedicated an altar to the gods, so you will be well looked on by them. It never hurts to have someone the gods look on favourably."

Not entirely convinced, Lunaris still said, "I see that."

"Your ship losses tell me you're no fool. Look at this," Celerianus said quietly, looking carefully about the best restaurant off the docks to make sure he was not observed. All the shippers used it, but he did not want an audience on this occasion.

Lunaris gazed down at the irregular lump of quartz that had been tipped out of a small, drawstring bag. He peered at it in the half-light and then hit it hard with a spoon.

The Gaulish ship-owner quickly covered it with his hands and looked around the room, smiling reassuringly at the few who took any notice.

When he took his hands away Lunaris looked carefully again. "It didn't spark, but the spoon probably wasn't hard enough – but it didn't scratch either. That's *fools gold* –it didn't fool me, though!"

"Are you sure?" Celerianus asked ingenuously.

"I've seen it before – in Italia, Roma to be exact. Why did you show it to me?"

"I hope I haven't misled you – or been misled myself. I was given that – and this," he explained, "to show people I thought would be interested in shares. *I* have some."

Lunaris was now staring intently at another piece of quartz rock. He picked it up, dug a thumbnail into it and then drew his knife and nicked it. "Where did you get this?"

"I told you – I was given it as a sample. It looks good to me."

Lunaris looked at it again. "It *is* good. It's very good, very good indeed. Shares, did you say?"

"I'm not able to tell you where the mine is – it's only for actual shareholders to know. But since I know you, I'll tell you it's in Cymru. How's that?"

"The rumoured Roman mine?"

"Ah, now," replied Celerianus smilingly, "You're not a shareholder yet!"

★ ★ ★

Mercurialis was in Durnovaria with Quintus, both looking over each other's strings of female gladiators.

Neither was concerned over being caught by Roman soldiery since the small fort there was long-since closed and the town's ordo ran its own policing, staffed by their own Durotrigian tribesmen.

"I'm glad you brought yours down from Corinium," said Quintus, "I've been wanting to see how we match up, ever since I inherited mine from my late uncle."

"I see your Lanista trains yours naked, as mine does. I'll tell you what, chain up your best and I'll chain up mine beside her. We'll compare notes and if we see it as a business venture we could match them. What do you say?"

His face brightening Quintus agreed willingly. He needed to glean more about showing them for profit, feeling his trainer was picking his purse. A few good contests in the right quarters would show a tidy turn of coin, he thought.

Mercurialis had already discounted the local arena as too small. He had talked of Corinium or Isca Silurum, the home of the Royal Second Legion, then of both Londinium and Verulanmium, citing how large the latter had become. He would simply follow his suggestion, Quintus thought, until he knew more.

Temporarily housed together and under tight guard, the gladiators looked warily at the older and younger man as they passed through the rough-furnished quarters towards the cell where the two were chained, arms above their heads.

"I see you fight her long-haired. Is that never grabbed as a restraint?" Mercurialis was puzzled by that although his gladiator also had shoulder-length hair, as blonde as the other was dark, but with his it was used to deceive.

"It can be, of course," replied Quintus, "but she'd never let you – unless it was too late to worry about it anyway."

"We think on similar lines, Quintus. Why make life difficult for opponents when you can make it impossible!"

They both laughed and Quintus ran his hand over the shoulder and breast of his gladiator. "Sturdy and strong. See how the wide feet allow her weight to hold firmly to the ground. She resists a heavy charge well – I've watched."

"As you see, mine is leaner – slightly taller, I know – so she's lithe. A fast mover, too."

"A Samnite versus a Thracian, then?"

Mercurialis laughed abruptly. "Well put. Solidly armoured – against speed. Mind you, I like the full tits on yours. They're almost weapons in their own right!"

"It's the long slim legs on yours that catch my eye," Quintus volunteered. "Very narrow feet. Shapely knees, too."

"Yours has shapely knees, for so full a thigh. I also suspect she's the more comfortable ride," the older man admitted grudgingly. "Tell you what, why don't we try them, as they are now?"

* * *

Venuto had invited them both to his town house where they were joined by the tribal chieftain, Hadrianus Caradoc, who was also the town council leader by virtue of his rank. A solidly built man of average height and moustachioed, he might have been called suave.

Scratching his beard Venuto suggested in his cultured Latin that they should eat, showing them through a fresco-decorated main room to the small dining room beyond.

Octagonal mosaics were set in the floor within a complicated border of guilloche with tendrils, though in places the pattern was missed and some tesserae were irregular in shape. Mercurialis thought it might have been a copy of something grander but practiced by less skilled local workmen.

They took the couches allotted to them and servants, the usual mix of free and slave, brought in food on platters for the low tables. Venuto sat at the head of the room, as befitted his status as host.

"You really should try these," he invited them, pointing to a plate of what looked like cooked fingers. "These are grilled bear paws, that is, the knuckles with the claws removed. I managed to get hold of some after an arena show. It's an old recipe from beyond memory, but handed down from mother to daughter. They're basted with honey and mint."

He was not sure whether his Roman guests were impressed or not so he went on, indicating bowls of hop buds, sprouts and roasted bean seeds in vinegar, "Those bean seeds are a distant recipe, too. If the food gives you colic they'll rescue you!"

Whilst they dealt with the cursory midday meal Caradoc remarked during a lull in the conversation, "Venuto tells me he has shares in a gold mine – and some to sell to boot."

Their two guests looked from him to Venuto and back again, then at each other. This was too good an opportunity to miss – if it was genuine.

"Why?"

"Why not, Mercurialis? I have some to sell to wise men. The type of person who invests in development costs to open up new galleries, with an eye to the future. We defray the costs – so it is only fair that an investor shares the proceeds."

"Do you have samples?"

"Naturally," responded Venuto, "Actually some in my purse now. Here they are."

The others watched as the small quartz rocks tumbled and slid on the polished food table in front of him, one of them glowing impressively in the half-light.

Quintus picked that up and turned it in his hand.

"That looks impressive," he said, passing it to Mercurialis.

"Yes, it does – it also fumigates rooms as well, if it's burnt!" The elder Roman tossed it back onto the table as he made the disparaging comment.

"What do you mean?" Venuto looked hurt and on his couch Caradoc smiled.

"This was given me, too. It's not as large as the other sample but it's still there to be mined. Would you?" Venuto pointed at the other sample, which Caradoc reached for and passed it to Quintus.

He eyed it suspiciously then said, "Is this better?"

"It's real gold," interrupted his companion, now interested. "The other's pyrites – it's for fools to faff over!"

"Well, I've no idea myself," Venuto retorted glibly. "I have some shares and it seems a good idea to me. If anyone wants to buy some I don't mind selling at a small profit – hedging my bets, as you sportsmen say. Still, I'm not worried, either way."

"Is there much of this sample?"

Venuto shrugged and then picked his nose. "So I'm told – but I'm interested in the other bit. As you say it'll burn and there's a market for fumigation."

"You don't want shares in this particular sample then?"

"I do, of course, but I'm not so interested in it."

"I'll have some shares, in that case," volunteered Mercurialis, "and so will my young friend here. You're right – it's a good business opportunity."

It was also a good opportunity to fleece that fool of an upstart chieftain, Mercurialis thought. More interested in stink than purity – what an idiot!

Caradoc reached out for an apple, the smile on his face hidden as he leaned forward.

Chapter VIII

T he small flotilla of vessels formed a line to pass Branksea Island and kept to it between the two sandspits that formed the harbour's exit to the sea. As they reached it the boats began to ride the taller waves, pitching and tossing as each helmsman kept a straight course by leaning his weight against the steering oar.

They headed for the water between the mainland and Vectis safe in the knowledge that any bad weather would be broken before it reached them, although none had been suspected.

As they turned to port the pitching and tossing became a sideways roll, which any poor sailor like Aelia welcomed as the lesser of two evils.

Leaning on the rear deck rail Agrippa said, "I was told in later life by my old wet nurse, who seemed to have a better memory than most – please don't jest about mammary, it's been done – that true love comes but once. She said it bites, hurts, intrudes - then either dies or ignites. There are no half measures.

I didn't believe her – she was a slave, when all's said and done – but she did say it a long time after my last supping.

Actually, I pensioned her on the strength of it not long ago. She died soon after. I wish I'd done it sooner, she was a devoted woman."

"We all wish different actions," Aelia said quietly. "Regrettably, until we're older and wiser it isn't possible to look backwards and benefit."

""You had a difficult life, then?"

"I cannot possibly tell you, except that now I'm able to take my own path. It wasn't always possible."

Agrippa frowned into the sea as it frothed passed the stern to leave its mark well into the distance.

After what seemed to him to be an age, he finally said, "The woman I was with lately had a chequered past. It wasn't something I resented. My own past was no more perfect. Whether something might have resulted from our coming together I don't know. It wasn't to be. I was away on a voyage when she was killed."

As she drew in her breath, Aelia asked, "Killed? How so? We have peace – at least in the south. That's what they tell me."

Snorting disdainfully Agrippa agreed. "So we do. So we do. You *are* safe – don't worry."

"Worry? Why not - you've just spoken of killing?"

"Regretably there are robber bands out there, so always travel in a caravan. You are safe then – and otherwise in towns. On board ship you are very safe, believe me."

"How was *she* killed, then?"

Faced with the direct question Agrippa found it hard to answer. His thoughts floundered and there was no way he could rationally deal with the enquiry in its present form.

The pause was a long one until, as she let the boat rock her sideways, Aelia asked, "Was it violent?"

Looking out to sea, emotions ran their full gamut with him. Unlike Aelia, the motion of the boat was of no consequence. It was his thoughts that sickened him.

Eventually, as they held the rail side by side, Agrippa managed, "It was a deep relationship. I make no apology for it. Things might have gone further – but I'm far from sure of that. She always hated what had happened to her and she may never have come to fully trust me."

"She had a traumatic experience?"

"Yes. Oh, yes – but after marriage."

"Rape?"

"No. Not exactly – but yes, in a way."

"It's an enigma – not far short of a riddle, Agrippa".

He quickly turned to her and was grateful for the sea breeze, which kept him cooler than he felt.

"She acquiesced to her husband's requests to service other men – in pursuit of business deals. At a later time she was raped. That wasn't what she'd agreed."

"Ye gods!"

"Much later than that she was raped and murdered. It was a warning to her brother-in-law!"

Aelia leaned well over the rail to be sick into the passing froth, the two mingling inextricably.

Breathing deeply as she recovered herself Aelia accepted a cup of water from the water bucket. It made her belch but, after that, her stomach seemed to settle.

"Thank you," she said, handing back the deep cup on its chain. "I had no idea that so senior an officer would ever had had such problems – much less tell them to someone he hardly knows. Is that your wet nurse's influence too?"

"Probably," Agrippa acknowledged grudgingly, shrugging his shoulders, "If what she said turns out to be true, then clearly I would have absorbed other philosophies of hers."

Aelia laughed obviously, but quietly. It was a truism, she thought – you either accept it or deny it. Then she wondered what he would say next.

Equally quietly he said, with a soft smile on his more often severe countenance, "If something is true it proves itself. Maybe that's why I opened up a recent, personal and sad – almost soul destroying – experience because I feel so extraordinarily at one with you. Lamely – I don't know why!"

"It's a shame your wet nurse isn't here," she retorted enigmatically. "It's yet another example of the intellect that slaves frequently have. We so often neglect to enquire of their earlier status. If we do it's usually only their more recent history."

"You think her intellectual?"

"Not so – though who knows? But she does, did, have an insight into human feeling. It's strange how many owners don't seem to grant that slaves have emotion."

"She talked of instancy. I didn't believe it then – but I do now! There was no way that I couldn't have introduced myself to you at the wedding. The fact that you responded in the way that you did just now only reinforced my view – my wet nurse's view, if you must – that when like minds meet, sparks fly. Until that time we pass the days as best we may."

Aelia leaned against the rail and then let herself slide into Agrippa. She felt him firm against her, but as though he could admit to it being an accident.

"I would deceive you if I said nothing now" she condescended. "You may form your own adverse view and I shall never argue against it. How you see it is up to you – but what I tell you now is the full, unwholesome truth. I'm far from a virgin!

When our parents died so suddenly it was my view, being so much older than Draco, that we could cope with our lives together.

However, Roman law being as it is, it was decided because of our ages and our having living relatives that my uncle should, or rather was required, to be my tutor. I prefer the word mentor, but so what?

He did guide me as to house management, how to treat and deal with servants and, of course, the always pecunious trades people. In return he increasingly forced himself on me and his visits soon had as much to do about sex with me as instructing me in bringing up Draco. More, even. I'm talking rape, of course.

Finally, as I grew of an age, I rebelled and he had no option but to leave me to my own devices.

It's not a past I like to relate. In fact, you are one of the very few – and the first man."

Blowing very gently between his lips Agrippa digested what she had said and what had been implied. It was even more horrendous than Sabina's story, he conceded, since it was involuntary. It was when he felt he could have killed the uncle nastily that he realised his nurse was right again.

Agrippa was vaguely aware of the ship's captain issuing an order to his executive officer and his passing it on to the helmsman, but his thoughts were elsewhere.

He realised he had feelings for this woman in a way he had never expected. It was as though he had experienced a savage sea battle, only to return to a safe harbour and all that that offered.

★ ★ ★

"I cannot believe what is happening. You confirm that workers are refusing to work?"

"Just that, Urbicus. All the free workers."

Slapping his hands down on the arms of his chair in frustration, the governor shook his head frequently. Then he turned back to Felix and said, "You soon solved the unrest on The Wall – what will you do here?"

"This is a different kettle of fish entirely. Most work on a daily basis in the docks – they unload or load, transfer cargoes to warehouses or barges, then pack, store, etcetera. Any skilled men ply their trades on a different basis, insofar as they are sail-makers, carpenters, storekeepers and the like, since the work covers a period of time. All may choose not to work on any given day."

"No work – no pay?"

Felix shrugged expressively. "That's their prerogative as free men – craftsmen as well as labourers. Not unexpectedly though, there are agitators at work."

The governor raised his eyebrows and then scowled. "I must remain within the rule of law – unfortunately – as you have not described a riot situation. What of these agitators?"

Felix grimaced. "Encouraging someone not to work is hardly an issue of state. If, of course, property's damaged to prevent work being undertaken by those who don't wish to withdraw their labour, that would be an entirely different matter, as you realise."

"I shall send in troops to carry out the work. Cargoes cannot stand idle. We may not be the Common Workshop Of The World – as Rome itself is known – but Londinium is a busy port nevertheless. Imports and exports are equally important and imports need to be distributed quickly, to boot."

"Will you send the Londinium garrison? If so, my men can stand guard in the palace."

Urbicus smiled at the offer saying, "The troops are losing their edge here in the south. They're becoming police, not soldiers. The work will do them good. I accept."

"The century can also carry out any patrols that're necessary."

"Right", agreed Urbicus readily. "That's what we'll do."

★ ★ ★

Clemens went into the room that Felix used as his office at the palace. His smile brought a return one from his father-in-law.

"You look like the typical proud father. Is my grandson reciting Plato suddenly?"

Laughingly Clemens replied, "Your grandson is in fine voice, so I'm to believe – and Paulinus is in fine form recruiting old soldiers for our new guard on the house. Obviously what you said impressed him.

No. It's none of those things. In the circumstances – better."

Felix's eyebrows went up as he asked, "Then it's good news?"

"Absolutely – that is, for the governor, actually. I've been down to the dockside in plain clothes to cast about and there's resentment of our troops presence."

"Only resentment?"

"There are two huddles going on and it won't be to discuss the chariot racing at the arena. Mischief is being plotted – or I'm Peregrini!"

"It doesn't show when you're sitting down." Felix commented light-heartedly. "That *is* good news. I'm going down there myself shortly. Go round and tell the governor the good news, will you – and I'll see him later."

Felix wore an exomis, the rough, sleeveless, toga-like slave garment often favoured by Urbicus in private but, as though anticipating the coming chill of the changing season, he also wore a short tunic under it so that the waist wrap of the exomis was then thrown over a covered shoulder. The effect was of a slave who had risen above mere labouring. What seemed like a pair of old army boots, well made but worn, complemented the picture.

Eyeing the the scar that ran across the forehead and down over one, half-closed eye one loiterer called out, "You look like you've used your head for something – use it again and join us for more money!"

Felix stopped and half-turned. "What do you mean by *more* money?"

The man pushed himself off the wall using the leg that he had drawn up under him. "What line are you in?"

"I asked you what you meant," Felix retorted bluntly, now turning to face his inquisitor.

"I can see you're used to asking the questions," came the reply. "What I meant was, are you looking to recruit a gang for a job? All here are looking for better pay"

"What's your role in this?"

"If *you* look for better money then you can pay your gang more. I recruit people."

"If I don't want to join?"

"Then you're wasting your time here."

"I'll be the judge of that," Felix retorted sharply. "I've my duties to carry out."

The man signalled to a group of idlers huddled furtively against a wall out of the breeze and they mooched over to him, half surrounding Felix who, like any slave past or present, took a pace backwards. In reality he was balancing himself against a sudden assault.

"Well now," the man began again, "I and my friends are against cheap labour. If your master wants any goods shifted we're certainly the boys for it – but it'll cost more than yesterday."

"How much more?" enquired Felix, now careful to adopt a less-than-certain pose.

"The bastard soldiers who're stealing our jobs earn a gold coin a month. We unload the food that feeds them, so why not the same rate?"

Now Felix laughed out loud. "I like your sense of humour. An aureus for labouring? Nearly a denarius a day?"

"Four sesterces for a fair day's work. Take it or leave it!"

"Then I'll leave it. I'll try another dock."

"You do and you may not see another dock!"

"Are you threatening me?" Felix stood on his dander as would befit a promoted slave. "My master will soon settle this – you wait and see!"

The gang moved towards him so Felix turned and fled, his exomis trailing out behind him, looking every inch a man frightened to lose his position.

At the next wharf he adopted a different tactic. He approached the watching guardian and asked, "I've heard the rate being asked is a denarius a day. I like the sound of that – gold in my purse by the end a month. Could you use a pursauader at all? I'm between jobs – especially now this strike's biting."

The man looked him over and smiled. "Well, we might. There's still some who don't want to agree."

"The troops are taking their work. They'll go back."

"You seem to understand the issue well enough. They will – if they're not persuaded otherwise, but why are you dressed like a supervisor?"

"I thought I might look the part more. Actually I'm a tally-man in disguise – but you'd not think me able, if I'd come dressed like that."

His companion stepped forward and slapped him on the shoulder. "You look sturdy enough to me. All I want's for you to look hard at any waverers – warn them off. Anything else and I'll tell you."

"And wages?"

The man laughed and slapped his shoulder again. "Like I said, you see the issues. Of course we're paid – a denarius a day, paid daily. No point in us going hungry is there!"

"I'll settle for a piece of silver – I like its feel."

"Good. I'll leave you to it, then. I've got to report in."

"Where do I report?"

The man looked at him quizzically, then said, "You ask a lot of questions – but that's a sensible one. You don't! You meet me here in the morning – I'll give you your coin and you carry on. I'm looking you out a mate. Until then be careful."

Felix watched him stride away and smiled to himself. Tomorrow he'd follow him and find the next link in the chain.

He'd barely decided on that when two obvious dockers approached him and stood glaring, their eyes narrowed.

"What's your game?"

Easing his leg down from where he had adopted his pseudo-employer's pose Felix stood against the building's wall, prepared for an attack on himself.

"Who wants to know?"

One of them poked his face forward and almost spat as he growled, "This is *our* dock and *we'll* keep the men out! We've heard the rumours some newly-arrived Roman moneybags is trying to muscle-in – so bloody push off!"

Immediately picking up the inference Felix' mind worked quickly and he replied, poking his own face forward into the other's and speaking in as poor Latin as he could, "I don't take orders from no stone cutter's lackey. Now *you* can bloody piss off!

As expected the man brought his fist up in a sucker-punch which Felix easily sidestepped, only to grab the arm and heave his opponent into the wall where his face hit it with a sickening crunch.

The second man cursed vitriolically behind Felix' back but, sensing the expected, he crouched down on one knee and let the man tumble over him to crash full length on to the stone quay.

As the startled man tried to rise on grazed knees and elbows Felix knee-dropped onto his kidneys. Even as his man groaned loudly he looped an arm around his neck and tightened the crook on it.

"Where'll I find the man you report to," Felix grunted gutturally into his ear as he tightened the crook of his arm even more.

Dazedly the man coughed the answer, half-choking as he mouthed, "He works for the quarryman. We meet him…. where the dock road goes into town…in the morning."

"You two had a fight with some other workers. Tell him it was me and I'll come back to bloody finished the job!"

Almost throwing the man's head away Felix stood up and brazenly peed on him as a further warning. It was what he would have understood, he thought – dockworkers were a tough breed and respected greater strength.

★ ★ ★

"So" remarked Urbicus thoughtfully, "you put yourself in the lion's den when there're others to do that for you? What would've been the outcome if you'd been murdered?

"You'd have replaced me and carried on."

"You know too much that others would like to know. To be killed might have been a pleasant outcome."

Felix spread his arms. "If we thought too much about likely outcomes we'd not get out of bed – and die of something else! What we do know is that Mercurialis is involved with this strike and outsiders are being used to enforce it, along with willing hands."

"Intimidation's a good enough reason to police the docks so that the labourers can go back," observed the governor, belching inwardly and reaching for a beaker of watered wine. "Is that what you propose?"

Shaking his head Felix retorted, "No! Definitely not – until I've tracked this contact. He'll be there in the morning and I've arranged a team of followers."

"You'll be recognised."

"I'll go in a toga and I won't have a scar. They'll be looking for someone else. When I see him go to report, I'll trigger my optio to follow him. Already along the road

Julius will take over and after that the centurion will hand over to Clemens. Just in case of trouble a few of the century will be loitering along the way, too. They can also pick up where a man of substance would not follow, should he slip off into a grubby alley or back street."

"How do you know he won't take transport?"

"This strike's being coordinated, so if a change of tack's required then so is a quick, local decision. Our quarryman is lurking somewhere in the metropolis – I think I understand Mercurialis *that* well."

"Who were you supposed to be working for?"

"I suspected the involvement of Marcus, Geta Marcus that is. I thought the pair to be his men. If they were, I did have that dubious pleasure – fortunately at a distance!"

Urbicus huffed and scratched his beard. "I'm going to have this off, come the winter's end," he remarked divergently, his brown eyes seeming to smile out from the rugged, yet gentle face. Then he laughed as he wondered if that sounded as though he was going soft.

Felix cocked his head as Urbicus let his laugh evaporate.

"Anyway, well done. In one swoop you've identified the probable ringleaders and confirmed that your old oppo has activated himself. Pity the two can't kill each other off, though," the governor added as an afterthought and they both laughed at the casualness of the remark.

★ ★ ★

The short, rotund figure of Tiberius Piso Faber bustled in and the look of consternation on his face immediately interrupted the discussion between Urbicus and his camp prefect, Petronius Fortunatus, once again in full flow having recovered from his fever.

"Doctor! Whatever is it? Your brow's wrinkled enough to be a bolt looking for a nut. Do sit down."

The earnest, grey-green eyes peered solemnly at his governor, wandered onto Petronius and back again. "I've spent my life soldiering as an army surgeon – and, I dare say, worried too much about what I cannot do. Now, I'm afraid we have this."

"Old friend," began Petronius, "Remember – I've served in thirteen different legions and done my own share of worrying, including where my *next* fifty years of service will come from! Just tell Urbicus what it is that's causing you such discomfort."

"That was a long speech and good advice from our friend. What is it?"

Faber took a deep breath, let it out and said simply, "It's marsh fever."

"The ague?"

Nodding Faber agreed. "The bad airs. They're with us. I think you, we, should be prepared for the worst."

"How can you be sure? Surely it's just an odd case." Petronius suggested.

"I wish I could be that uncertain, my friend, but all the conditions are there. The brackish river estuaries – at least the banks of the tributaries – produce a saline impregnated mud. You can't mistake the odour, once you know it. It's a sulphurous smell. Malodorous."

"So you're definite. It's the same thing as the epidemic of Roma, about twenty years ago, then?"

Looking at his governor Faber answered the question solemnly, nodding in emphasis. "Yes, I fear so. The Sickness of Galen it was called. He led the fight against it but, renowned physician that he's become, treating the result is still hit and miss."

"We're draining as much salt marsh on the east coast as we can – though, of course, we expect to use the reclaimed land, too."

Faber shrugged, his tiredness showing all too well. "It's all that can be done. Whether it's the airs, or the tiny flies in it, that are responsible we don't know yet. There are some remedies – some better than others." The exhausted surgeon paused but no questions came.

"I thought you ought to know" he added resignedly. "There are already a number of cases displaying all the symptoms. It's the late, mild and damp spell that's caused the problem. Pray for frost!"

"My friend – I shall! It's not good news but I needed to know it. I shall start a drainage programme of the southern rim immediately!"

"We're already fully committed in Britannia, old friend," observed Petronius, donning his logistics hat. "At the very best we have to wait until the New Wall is finished."

"The New Wall," exclaimed Urbicus thinking laterally. "Is that secure?"

Tiredly Faber said, "It should be, if you drink good water."

Urbicus crossed to the now almost comatose surgeon and, lifting him up, said, "You shall have a couch in a dining room – no one will trouble you. When you feel able I shall be here. When I awarded you the *Corona Muralis* on the Empire's behalf, during the White Disease, it wasn't half enough. You will rest – it's my order."

"I need copious amounts of feverfew, parsley, jasmine, strawberries and juniper. The fall-back of poppy seed," Faber said faintly, "and plenty of space. Pray for the men to be strong."

Urbicus carried the sleepy Faber to a nearby dining room, stretched the short, portly figure on a couch and left him to regain his strength with sleep.

Having summoned an aide the governor demanded, "I want the admiral and the legate – *now*."

Chapter IX

Wiping beads of perspiration from his forehead Rufinus felt the chest of one of his patients. Feeling no movement he pressed his ear to the sweaty torso and confirmed his suspicions. The man was dead.

Knowing that the small hospital in the fort had long since overflowed its one cell to a century allocation, Rufinus rang a brass bell. Immediately a soldier came, hefted the inert body and took it outside. The bed was immediately filled.

"How do you feel?" It was a question Rufinus dreaded asking after so many virtually unbroken days of routine labour, when only a few were taken away to convalescence as their attacks diminished.

The man lying in front of him exhibited the usual combination of weakness, lack of intellectual response and high fever, the general malaise he had come to expect.

"Sage, vinegar and fennel drink," Rufinus instructed an aide, citing a popular remedy. "If he regains his senses then give him feverfew, parsley, strawberry and juniper mash: I hope you know a sympathic god."

The pungent odours of sweat and vomit permeated everything and he briefly wondered whether he would ever get the stench out of nose.

At the very same moment, escorted by a guard, a totally exhausted messenger from the Celtic chieftain, Stolus, staggered into the palace ante-chamber, holding out a rolled bark in front of him. Immediately it was taken from him he groaned and dropped dead in front of them.

As soon as they read it Urbicus said, "He must have run more than twenty-five miles a day for four consecutive days. What a feat of endurance!"

He was amazed at what had been achieved and immediately ordered the body to be preserved for a formal burial.

Petronius looked sternly at his governor, old friends that they had become, before saying, "We need all our resources here. He cannot, under any circumstances have Faber – their White Disease saviour or no!"

Urbicus scratched at his annoying beard, then replied, "You are, of course, absolutely right. There's no way he could be released."

After a long silence he looked searchingly at his camp prefect whom he seemed to have known for so many years. "If you or I let one another down – how would we feel?"

Petronius simply shrugged at the rhetoric and waited for the next observation.

"Stolus is close to Felix. It was Felix' man who died working with Faber on the chest disease. It was also another man of his who held the peace between our medic and their medicine men. I can't believe you are against me in sending help this time."

Petronius retorted, "I recall this prince saved Felix' household – so why do you think I couldn't be moved by this request?"

"Then we have only one recourse."

It was a classically long stare that Petronius laid on his governor, without a word passing between them.

"Rufinus?"

"Rufinus," endorsed Petronius. "He *is* the automatic choice. It has to be him. He has the skills – or nearly so, at any rate."

"He is young, to be exposed – but then no more so than he is already. Will you arrange it?"

"I shall – as soon as I speak to Felix. He's his ward and so will probably go with him. It's likely he'll take his century as well, though."

"If he does go – he must. It's a long journey. We'll just have to mount any watch that's available in the circumstances. Hopefully, our enemies are just as taken by this outbreak."

"Unfortunately we can't logically make that assumption. They may even be immune, as some of us appear to be. As your camp prefect I have to assume the worst scenario – particularly as Felix won't be here."

"Organise it as you wish. My regret is that we failed to catch that devious bastard, Mercurialis. Now he could be anywhere and we need to start again."

Petronius nodded thoughtfully. "It *is* strange that, having carefully arranged the trailing of the suspect, Felix found the bird had flown. It's as though he knew Felix was coming."

Exasperatedly Urbicus rasped, "You have it. I can't believe any of his men would leak information – but that does seem the most likely scenario.

However, you had better go and sort out Rufinus. You can see to a guard roster at the same time. Presumably, what's his name, Urbanus, can resume his old duties?"

"I shall make it so."

As he marched to the boat behind his centurion and what remained of the century, holding their standard aloft Aurelius Victor smiled to himself as he recalled a recent conversation. He had not delivered gold to Mercurialis – he'd delivered life.

★ ★ ★

As soon as the boat docked on the pottery wharf Stolus embraced Felix and then looked disappointedly around for the little surgeon.

"This is Carinorum Rufinus. He's studying under Faber and brings his skills instead."

Embracing him too, Stolus said tactfully, "Then I welcome you as well. Thank you for coming. Did you journey well?"

"Actually I slept most of the way – so I'm fine," responded Rufinus.

On the way to his new house the young chieftain explained that it was largely the pottery workers on the small island and along the fringes of the harbour that were affected, but it had also spread into his village and to some of Waerham's population who worked the harbour banks.

"I am particularly concerned about my wife, Galina," he went on, "but also whether it might spread to your lands around the town, if it's not checked."

"So our families are well at the moment?"

Vigorously nodding at Felix Stolus replied, "In rude health – the boy, too. You must go to them," he added turning back to Rufinus.

"I must see your wife and villagers first," retorted the young man "That's what I'm charged to do."

As Felix hurried away the young chieftain smiled broadly and then laughed. "And you came to this island to enslave us!"

"Not me personally – I was born here."

Stolus slapped him on the shoulder and grinned. "It's still what some of our people say and it'll become part of our folklore. Come, here's my house – see for yourself."

The building was a single-storey structure under thatch but, in deference to the increasing influence of Roman society, the walls were built of local Purbic stone and faced in painted plaster.

As they ducked through the doorway Stolus explained that such was a Celtic tradition. He described it as paying due respect to the owner. "Actually, the senior chieftains,

Caradoc and Venuto, applauded my decision. It's done me no harm," he added.

It was obvious there was no central heating hypocaust system but, as they passed through the plastered main room, Rufinus noted a fireplace with a raised heath and an iron-dog to the side. A pitcher of wine stood beside it to increase its nose and flavour. In a small recess, halfway up one of the side-walls, a skilfully painted picture seemed like a statuette and represented their personal house god.

Shown through to a bedroom off the corridor Rufinus saw Galina lying in the bed, the sheet pushed down from her chest to expose her breasts. Turning away he was caught by Stolus and pushed forward. "You're a doctor and seen it all before, I'll warrant. Forget she's my wife and examine her."

Feeling slightly embarrassed nonetheless, Rufinus suggested it would be easier if he were left alone but that Stolus should remain within call.

Understanding the issue Stolus replied, "Then I will leave you. I'll talk with Amatus who is guarding the door. I awarded him the freedom of Purbic for his work during the White Disease. It's been a long time."

Rufinus approached the perspiring figure carefully. She appeared to be sleeping but she could equally have been comatose.

He stared down at her, noting her breathing, her pulse – something Faber had counselled him in, from his association with the renowned physician Galen – and her body language. He rolled down the cover and explored her naked body, touching salient parts and gauging her temperature.

After some time and much rechecking, he came to the only conclusion he could. She had a fever – but she was also pregnant.

Called back in Stolus was astounded. He could hardly take in both sets of good news at once. She did not have the ague – and she carried his child.

Rufinus explained the differences as best he could, not knowing whether the information actually registered. "The extended abdomen is vaguely similar – but is definitely not an enlarged stomach gland."

Casting about his mind for meagre knowledge he fixed on, "Feel here, to the upper left of the soft abdomen, it's *not* swollen. Do you see? It would be hard, otherwise. Now down here, do you feel a bump? It's your child. I'm as sure as I can be!"

Stolus stared into Rufinus' face and no words came. He gulped and still no words came. Then he opened his mouth but still no words came.

"It's a double shock to you, my lord chief, but I do think I'm correct," Rufinus said quietly. "I have a gift with pregnancy – I don't know why."

Almost stammering, as he grappled with his tongue, Stolus finally asked, "But she is still. No life – no life force. How will she survive?"

Rufinus gritted his teeth before saying, "My lord chief, I didn't say she would survive. What I said was that she has your child in her."

"Can she?"

"Has she had headaches, pains in joints, swelling of feet and hands and sickness? Does she pee a lot?"

"Yes – all of those, plus she sleeps a lot and she's difficult to wake."

"I don't recognise that symptom – but all the others I have been shown. It's a particularly difficult problem in pregnancy."

"What can be done?"

"The normal way is to deliver the child. It will save your wife and sometimes the baby, too."

Stolus held his head in his hands. "How can I choose between my wife and our baby. How can I?"

Putting his arm around Stolus' shoulders as though he was the elder Rufinus said, "Galina's not very far pregnant. It's very unlikely a child would survive. Helping your wife would mean you have another – many other – opportunities to try again. But it's your choice."

"Save Galina. You must save Galina!"

"I'm supposed to be saving the ague suffers," Rufinus reminded him. "But this *is* an emergency and I am the one to take the decision on priorities. Faber has always been clear on that."

"Please do it," Stolus pleaded. "Now."

"It won't be pain free."

"Do it, please!"

Faced with the urgency of the request his inexperience evaporated. Rufinus found inner strength, felt taller, more commanding and confident.

"Send for a midwife. I need her phlegm."

Because the bloom on her abdomen was so immature Rufinus could not bring himself to perform a caesarean delivery. He considered it to be an unnecessary risk. He had to interfere with the delivery mechanism, he decided – then sweated at the thought, as though he had the mal-air disease himself.

★ ★ ★

"She has lost a lot of blood – it was inevitable. She's asleep again, so you'll not be able to speak to her. Let her rest, it is her best defence. When she wakes I've given instructions to the midwife to feed her chicken gruel – please be there to ensure nothing else is given.

As she improves then minced chicken. Also watered wine – half and half. She can have strawberries if she wishes – they're good for the blood. If I am still here, then send word and I'll come and see the way forward as best I can."

Stolus had tears running down his cheeks as he tried to respond. "Freedom of Purbic is not enough. I don't know what *is* right. I am for ever in your debt."

"Not so," retorted the young doctor. "I'm in yours for entrusting me with your wife."

"As a Briton I am for ever in your debt," he repeated. "Simply ask."

Rufinus took the liberty of embracing the young prince and then stood back. "I have duties."

"If there is criticism or obstruction refer it to me. If you need anything at all, day or night, send for me. I will ensure it."

"I thank you, Prince Stolus. I must go."

"Only return if you call me Stolus," rang in his ears as Rufinus almost ran for the gate.

★ ★ ★

Arranging burials took most of the day some days running so, with his two optios, Julius and the temporary Paulinus, Titus took on the task of liasing with the village elders and the small town's ordo.

Rufinus used up his meagre supply of medicines and fell back on some of the old Celtic remedies, hoping that the mixes and strengths were of the right order, since they were supplied to him. Artemisia and allium figured highly, as their properties were considered to be anti-malair and anti-parasitic. Even if they did not fully work, he thought, at least the patients had a good turnout!

As the attacks of fever lessened in frequency and duration Rufinus hoped that the worst was over. Far fewer new cases were occurring and he was, at last, able to regularly sleep, though not always for long. What did cheer him, though, were the occasional glimpses of Galina sitting outside her house, enjoying what was probably the last of the unseasonable sunshine, her hair dressed with wild flowers.

★ ★ ★

Ianuarius sailed into the small port one morning and Felix was delighted to welcome him.

The small, sheltered garden was picking up and reflecting whatever strength was left in the sun so they took watered wine out into it.

Dutifully the shipper admired Julia and Clemens' baby and discussed the joint weddings of Firmus and Macer, before Livia took the baby away to leave the two men in private.

"The pottery wagons being attacked some time ago I put down to bad luck," Ianuarius began, "but possibly there is some connection with this strike. What do you think?"

Felix frowned. "Have you been especially targeted?

"Not that I am aware of, but I heard recently that Celerianus has sold some goldmine shares to Lunaris. Nothing of that nature has ever disrupted our shipping interests before. That is enough of a gamble in itself, without chasing moonbeams!"

"Are you telling me you doubt the efficacy of the shares?"

"How can I? I haven't been offered any, but I understand they are being sold on the production of gold. That may sound poetic – but the sales may be poetic licence, if you'll pardon the pun. I mean, who has gold interests? Normally the state runs all mines."

Felix rubbed his jawline as he pondered not the question but the answer. Should he tell what he knew, which was a private matter between contractors, or keep quiet.

Breathing out heavily he decided to hedge his bets and replied, "This must go no further – but I know you'll understand the reasons for that. One of the gold mines has been put out to contract."

"That smacks of it coming to the end of its working life," Ianuarius observed. "In the same way as a vessel is sold on."

"You have it in one," agreed Felix.

The one feature that stopped Ianuarius being handsome, his large nose, flared briefly and his boyish face fell. "I would have wagered on the shares being false. As it is, they could just be a means of raising working capital."

Felix looked at him sympathetically and said softly, "You may not be so off-track as you now think."

Startled the astute young shipper stared back. "How so?"

"By definition, the mine is not thought to have any reserves to speak of. If samples are being hawked around it would be surprising if a rich vein has already been found – in the unlikely event of one even existing."

Brightening at the thought Ianuarius picked up on the inference. "My instincts were all against. They still are. You're saying – no, suggesting – that the samples aren't genuine?"

"Not as strongly as suggesting, even. These samples may be genuine – you can tell – but not necessarily from the proposed source. However, that opens up another vista altogether."

"Fraud!"

"Just so"

"Where did the samples and shares originate? I mean, you'd need some evidence of ownership – or should do – before parting with any metal of your own."

"That's as far as I can go for now – I have a name – but I suggest you look around your shipping association again and keep me informed of your findings. When I can I'll give you more."

* * *

Later that day, after Ianuarius had taken the next tide back, Felix was talking with Clemens about the visit and related what had been said.

"One thing we do know now is that since Tiberius Celerianus was the unloader of shares he must be in league with, or at the very least associated with, Geta Marcus."

Clemens slapped his knee and remarked, "It's one of his group, of course – but he'd know what was going on! Can we get him on fraud? Obviously the samples are false – not from the mine on the Cothi River – for the reasons you gave."

Felix shrugged, but smiling said, "If we arrest Celerianus the shipper first! We'd need his testament."

"Would he convict himself?"

"I dare say we could barter a deal. It would do no real harm – after all, the shippers would freeze him out. He'd probably go back to Gaul."

"Pity Mercurialis' man didn't come up with his whereabouts when he was questioned. All that following for nothing – even he was surprised the bird had flown."

"Well, *he'll* get his comeuppance – Urbicus is all for him working out his time in the docks after the workers go back. It'll not be easy for him."

"More effective than a flogging. A better lesson to others, I suppose – if anything does deter those bent on self-destruction."

"I'll leave philosophy to Faber I think, young man. We must talk to Urbicus about the shipper as soon as possible."

* * *

"But they *were* soldiers! They had uniforms, badges of rank – awards or whatever! They chased us off - said we had stolen the goods."

Having taken over the police post temporarily due to Lucius Paulinus' injuries, Salinus was only too aware of the difference in rank. Suddenly he was stepped up from duplicarius to acting–signifer, making him virtually the centurion-in-charge, since he was the senior non-commissioned officer.

He looked balefully at the complainants and wondered what to do with this unlikely story. Had they themselves lost, or even sold, the carts and pots? He was rudely awakened from his dazed state by a furthering of the complaints.

"You don't believe us, do you? You weren't bloody there, were you? They laid about us with the flat of their swords and we ran for it."

Salinus scratched his helmetless head in frustration. If it wasn't true why were they making so much fuss and drawing attention to themselves?

"What colour uniforms were they? Regulars or auxiliaries?"

"We don't bloody know and care bloody less. They wore blue – that's all we can tell you. Now, are you going to get the carts back?"

He rode out to where they said the attack took place and was able to confirm cart tracks and footprints. When he followed them he immediately came across dead mules, overturned carts and broken pottery. A quick check confirmed that every pot was broken. No attempt had been made to disguise the destruction.

★ ★ ★

"So I did the best thing I could think of and came to see you, Sir," said Salinus, standing stiffly to attention.

"You're not the first to do that, optio. All right stand easy," Felix told him. "This is definitely a pottery sherd from one of the carts?"

"Yes, Sir. Definitely. I took it myself – I was the only one there."

"Good – but it wasn't *under* a cart?"

Salinus shook his head forcibly . "I took it from a cart."

Felix turned to his son-in-law and handed him the salvage. "It's from the pottery. It has the stamp on the base."

"Yes – so I see."

"Optio – leave this with me. Do your report but leave any conclusion alone. Right?"

Snapping to attention he agreed readily, only too pleased to have passed on his responsibility. Then, turning smartly about, he left the two behind him.

"So", mused Felix, "someone is definitely after destroying our pottery. It can be replaced, but it's money out of Stolus' profits. Is it them or us that's the target?"

"Well," Clemens said and was immediately annoyed with himself. The word was unnecessary. "Obviously killing the mules means they were under orders. We don't know if any pots were taken – but it's unlikely. Burning the carts would have called attention to them. That may mean they're local and needed time to disperse safely. Maybe there's a joint target."

"Well reasoned, young sir. I follow your drift. But the uniforms – he was told, *blue*."

"Our colour," agreed Clemens. "I don't believe that – at least, not our men."

"If not our men then, by definition, who's?"

"Where did they obtain the uniforms and where are they now? We have an awful lot of questions and so very few answers."

Chapter X

"I'm of a mind to force feed you your balls," ranted Geta Marcus to Venuto. "You sold shares you should have sat on until the market was right. Instead of that you sat on your brains!"

Venuto grunted. He was not used to being spoken to in that manner – no tribal chieftain would be, he concluded. Only pride prompted him to break the silence that had followed the outburst in order to continue his argument.

"Mercurialis is a wealthy importer who inherited land, has interests in a quarry and has a string of female gladiators which he has fought in Durnovaria – a man with links to a man who rejuvenated our amphitheatre. I took him down on behalf of the Durotriges – it's our way."

"Bugger your way", fumed Marcus. "Double bugger it! Roman law applies now – not some tribal one-upmanship! No stealing of a few cattle will put things in balance! If you'd waited it would still have happened – but no! You know best. You speak educated Latin – but you don't know the law!"

Venuto unhurriedly scratched his rectum then picked his nose, habits that disconcerted many more than just Marcus.

"Now I have to try to put thing right. I'm a shipper with contacts – though not in his consortium, because I don't ship stone. But, somehow, I must let him sell *me* the shares, though I have no idea how. He may even know of our buying the mine by now. These things get out. If so, he has recourse to law."

"Bugger the law – and your opinion of me! My money was good enough for you – now I want a return on it. The offence, as you would term it, occurred here in tribal land. We are the council and we provide the magistrate."

"Mercurialis can make claim to citizenship. He can argue to be heard in a Roman court!"

"Don't let him!"

"Don't be ridiculous! To interfere with the law increases the offence!"

Claudius Venuto shrugged. He had had enough of the argument and it showed in his voice. "Go back to Londinium. You've finished your business here – I am not important enough to have come before it! I shall wait with interest for a return on my investment!" He laughed at the unintentional pun as Marcus spun angrily on his heels and made for the door.

* * *

"Am I going mad or simply insane? I have two people selling shares in gold that doesn't exist and you can't see any problem in doing so! I said to wait. Let people see how we spend our gold, then let *them* persuade *us* to sell – not the other way round! You, of all people, Celerianus – the leading shipper of Londinium, so they tell me."

Tiberius Celerianus spread his hands, then reached for his wine cup and took down a draught while he contemplated his reply.

"Marcus Aurelius Lunaris is a distant relative of another influential shipper – Marcus Ulpius Ianuarius. There's a deal of money there. The first dedicated an altar and the latter a new stage for the theatre in Petuaria. They all work out of the Abus at some time in the year and have their own web. I wanted Lunaris to be indebted to me by being the first.

It could well bring us all the funding for land that we need. Remember, when we succeed all the shipping taxes will be for our pockets – like they are for this damned governor!"

"A long speech, Celerianus. If you had waited I might have agreed with you – but how could we have worked enough gold at this point? When Lunaris' greed abates he will realise it."

"As a shipper – though, of course, I mean experienced – you learn to have patience. Markets open up. You speculate to accumulate. Buying *more* shares is his most likely decision."

"Good – I'm pleased to hear it. So go and buy the stone shipper's shares and sell them on to Lunaris. That should get Venuto off the hook!"

★ ★ ★

"Yes, I see what you're saying, Mercurialis, it was my being led astray by the fools gold that prompted you to latch onto the gold nugget the Briton then produced. But I don't see why that invalidates the shares."

Gently shaking his head as though talking to an obtuse child, the older man tried a more direct tack. "I cannot exactly blame you for my buying the shares, but I was influenced by your naivety, nonetheless. I was putting my money where my mouth was. It wasn't until later that I began to use my common sense."

Quintus looked perplexed so Mercurialis continued, "They've not long had the mine. If development costs are needed then the product is not self-sufficient. It would be a happy coincidence if they'd found nuggets – plural because there must be other sellers – enough to sell, without a seam to go with them. If there had been a seam, they would not be wanting to share it so easily."

"You're saying the nugget was false, then?"

"Nearly. What I'm saying is that the sample is genuine…"

"But not from the mine in question," interrupted Quintus, brightly he thought.

Breathing out noisily Mercurialis sighed, "You have it, at last."

"So will you go to law to recover your money? It's fraud – obviously so."

Putting his hand to his forehead the quarry owner elect said nothing for a few moments before replying, "Quintus, in the name of all the gods, learn to think before you speak! I'm temporarily in hiding – you cannot have forgotten, surely? Am I likely to reveal myself for a few shares? Clearly not.

What it does mean though – if you *do* think for a moment – is that this new arrival, Geta Marcus, is a devious man."

Nodding the young man agreed. "If what you say is so, then why? Is he raising relatively small sums to fund another cause? As, in fact, my uncle did before his death and before you assumed control."

"My dear young associate – that's masterful! And what do you think *for*?"

Happy to have saved face Quintus gnawed at his lower lip until, suddenly, he said, "Land! Again as my uncle did. Raise sums to purchase land without it being obvious."

Clapping his hands together Mercurialis smiled as he retorted, "You have it! That is almost certainly the answer. So what I plan to do is to return the favour he did me. If he wants conflict he shall have it!"

* * *

Walking the Londinium Palace's formal garden the governor shared his thoughts with Felix. "Now that the bad air epidemic is under control – what a pity we cannot eradicate it completely – the dockers are drifting back in larger numbers. I had wondered – expected even – that we could have opened the docks again anyway because of property being damaged to prevent work being done, by using the Riot Act or something akin to it. Still, it's an ill wind that does nobody good. The workers need the money and there is work to be done."

Felix nodded and said, "As you say, it's turned ill to good. Will you be talking to Agrippa about a final fling for this season – searching for Haruld the Horrible and the two strike promoters? Things have rather got in the way."

Now Urbicus was nodding. "It's in hand, my friend. We think alike. It may even work to our advantage, in that such a move might be unexpected so seasonally late.

I shall invite Agrippa to dinner tonight –assuming he berths later, as expected. The three of us will discuss it then."

They walked on, with Urbicus stopping every so often and reaching out to pull a rose to his nose, smiling as the scent pleased him. It prompted him to acknowledge that the unseasonably warm weather, which had encouraged the ague, had done the same to his favourite flower.

As Felix ran his hand through a stand of lavender and its aroma temporarily filled the air, Urbicus remarked, "The senior law officer tells me that Verulamium is now the second largest city in Britannia. He wants to officially acknowledge it."

"That's a pity, in a way – I don't mean the recognition – because it lies only just north of Londinium. Having Corinium as the second city worked well,as it gave the middle lands some status."

"It'll still rate as third – but I see what you're saying. However, the senate in Rome will wish to have it exact – like distances between cities."

That evening the three officers, who formed the triumvirate seen necessary by the governor, sat or lay on the couches after they had served themselves – all servants having been dismissed for security reasons.

"Before we look at the darker side," said Urbicus "I'd like you to know that I intend to promote Faber for his efforts during the outbreak. It'll be of more use to him than another corona. I thought prefectus medicus, to put him amongst the hierarchy. He ought to be acknowledged as that – however senior in centurion rank he is now."

Agrippa nodded. "Yes, that's a fair rank for him to hold. Good."

"I don't believe rank's ever worried him," commented Felix. "No one's going to disagree with him on medical matters – he's a leading expert. I think he'll take it, though – the pension will be far greater when he finally does retire. He's a long way from destitute – but I can see him wanting to set up a medical school and that doesn't come cheaply!"

"Good, I'm glad we're agreed on that. Then there's your young ward, Rufinus. As I can't very well promote him until he's fully qualified I intend to award him the same as I gave Faber during the White Disease – a corona muralis."

"That's very good of you, Urbicus. He did sterling work – I saw him."

"He seems to be making his mark," observed Agrippa. "Do we have another Faber in the making?"

"Very probably", agreed the governor. "Now, I'm going to make light work of these oysters – do join me."

The three fell to and proved their credentials as trenchermen, soon finishing off the picea, the dark brown rounds of flat oven-baked dough topped with pastes, spices and slices of truffle, before going on to the pasta ribbons in meat juices and then complimenting Urbicus on the quality of the lagana they were eating.

The mulsum ran out with the seafood so Urbicus himself poured them Falernian and Caecuban wines from

Naples. He took the opportunity to tell them his steward had found a supplier of truffles from an area not far from the great stone henge.

"So they haven't travelled far," he said proudly. "No question of what can happen to our homeland ones, going off after a few days from Italia. I, personally, like the nutty flavour of these grey and white local ones. What do you say?"

Both nodded in agreement and Felix suggested that Livia would probably like to take some back with her.

"Better still, my friend, I'll send my steward round with some and the suppliers details – then your man can obtain them."

They settled back in the couches with a dark, sweet, Greek wine and began to discuss their game plan.

"Where are they?" Agrippa asked the question looking directly at Felix.

The answer was as directly given. "You, presumably, have been keeping spies out for the One-eyed. As for the other two, my information is scant on Geta Marcus – but Mercurialis is in Purbic again – with the boy, Quintus."

Intervening Urbicus observed, "I suppose we shall have to call *him* the quarry owner, since it's his estate now. This Mercurialis may influence him but he has no claim."

Clearing his throat, Agrippa went on, "As and when we find pirates *we* go after them. Our discussion will follow that rule. Felix, here, needs the authority to do the same – on land at least."

In the short silence that followed Urbicus frowned for a while, before brightening to say, "Yes. It's unusual – but necessary. At sea, of course Agrippa, you are fleet commander – which makes a difference. However, it *is* ridiculous for Felix to always seek my authority before acting. Mostly, anyway," he added with a laugh.

"Good," said Agrippa and swallowed his wine, enjoying the taste on his tongue even as the thick, red liquid hit his stomach.

"What of One-eye?"

Returning his governor's friendly gaze Agrippa nevertheless realised a point was being made. "My last report placed him on Silura, in the Sabrina channel. I've said nothing as the report is, as yet, unconfirmed. However, I suggest we storm it on principle."

"I recall the last storming, I believe – one way up or down and we didn't penetrate the island." Felix ended his comment with a strug.

Agrippa nodded. "What you say is only too true. It would be too costly to storm, in that sense. No, what I have in mind was suggested by Macer. We should firestorm it."

"Yes, I remember him telling me that himself," agreed Felix, "after we'd both concluded that a permanent presence there would be wasteful in men and ships. Obviously it was only conversation, because both of you would need to endorse such a plan."

"Weather?"

"It would be touch-and-go," Agrippa conceded to Urbicus, "but the tinder on the plateau should be dry after the warm spell and, if we have no rain beforehand, we should carry it out."

"You would go round the toe?"

"As the last thrust of the season, yes."

Now Felix coughed quietly, drawing their attention. "You will probably already have discounted the idea, but I understand there are often warships at Isca Silurum – and further up the Sabrina, sometimes."

"Go on," said Agrippa, non-commitally.

"If those were used to avoid the journey round the toe of Britannia both sailors and marines could be taken up the new Uxela-Stour cut. Neither would your sailing be noted – a potential warning to our enemy."

"It was unlikely we'd have a meeting without Felix' favourite canal being mentioned," laughed Urbicus, "even though it's finally been cut!"

" I'm not sure it's my favourite canal," Felix said dryly.

Agrippa said nothing, his fingers drumming gently on the side of his couch. Neither interrupted him.

Eventually he said, "Naval tactics are my realm and normally I stand no interference. However, in all honesty, I'd forgotten that damned canal *was* available. I like the idea of surprise, since our sailing would not otherwise go unnoticed.

I'll take a vessel eastwards with more pomp than secrecy. The marines can go first up the canal and the crews can follow – that'll confuse the spies!"

"I like your plan, Agrippa. Boldness was always my own friend. And you'll toast them?"

The little admiral sat back with his empty cup and said, "If I had wine I'd already have toasted our victory."

"Forgive my hospitality," Urbicus responded rapidly and, getting up, retrieved two jugs of their current drink. "May the gods bless victory."

"I'll even sit up to drink to that," said Agrippa eagerly and he noticed Felix joined him.

"I believe my men can help you."

Looking sideways at Felix Agrippa asked, "With one ex-marine?"

"That sea-sick ex-marine saved one of Macer's men on your last attack – as you recall, our being rescued coincided with it."

"So he did. I acknowledge him for that."

"As I was saying, I think we can help. Please remember that, apart from my century impressing the public with wordless drills, they were all recruited to my commando with individual skills."

"So," challenged Agrippa, feeling that his battle plan was under threat. "What are you suggesting?"

"It's only a thought but, whereas an assault is obvious, perhaps a few of my men could scale the cliffs unscathed, as one did before, to give siting reports."

"Siting reports?"

"Yes – on the ranging of your fireballs."

"How?" The prospect seemed incredulous to Agrippa.

"Torches. If you attack at dusk you'll easily gauge the overall effect yourselves. My men would only signal your *accuracy* by semaphore – Macer is familiar with it, obviously. Naturally he would need to teach mine some basic figures to signal."

"Before the debate goes further, my friends, I like the idea. The island needs to be rendered inhospitable over the winter and into the new season. That'll screw the bastards!"

Agrippa thought for a while, then said, "How do we get your men there unannounced?"

"Take us close, then we use coracles while you provide a diversion elsewhere. Once a torch is thrown in a high arc – twice if we can – come in to take *us* off at the dropping point. The men will be in the water – so don't miss them!"

"The fine detail I leave to you." Urbicus waved an airy hand as he continued, "I'm also concerned about the use – misuse – of army uniform, Felix. What else do we know about it?"

With a laugh Felix responded, "Would you believe it? We have a captive who's dead!"

"Dead?" Both men echoed each other.

"That's right. He's dead! That's how he was caught."

"You're having a laugh at our expense," protested the admiral, sitting bolt upright.

"Now come on, my friend," cajoled the governor, also sitting up to confront his chief of intelligence who already favoured sitting. "Dead men tell no tales. You obviously have something to say. Say it."

Smiling broadly Felix explained, "It was a stroke of luck on our part – but well spotted and reported by one of my men, the ex-armourer, Paulinus. He apparently had served with a cohort which went north shortly after he was demoted and allowed his being recruited to my commando–cum–century by the late Frontus – may the gods bless him still."

"What was spotted?"

"That's the observational bit, Agrippa. My acting-optio came across a soldier in an inn, not in blue, purporting to be a certain person. It transpired that the optio knew this man – the named man – who was a different build altogether. A few questions soon revealed this impostor knew nothing of his so-called background other than cohort, name and age.

So Paulinus took him in hand – you may remember his size – and round the back of the hostelry the man was keen to tell the optio what he wanted to know."

Urbicus asked, "Which was?" Then he reached for his wine cup, found there was nothing in it and pushed off his couch in search of the jugs.

"He confirmed he was a dead man."

Agrippa hit the couch with his hand, causing the governor to look round to see why. "You've said that! How can he be?"

As Felix waited to continue the governor tittered while he poured more wine for the other two. He had seen the issue now and said so. "Apparently dead men *do* tell tales. Carry on – it's fascinating."

"Apart from stealing uniforms this bunch have been stealing identities to go with them. They take names from gravestones which give age, unit, name, sometimes rank and even family names, on occasion."

"What a scheme," remarked Urbicus. "I can almost admire them. Your man did well."

"How did he fathom this man was *undoubtedly* an impostor – I see how he proved it afterwards?" Agrippa was still puzzled by the discovery.

"That's where the luck comes in," replied Felix, pausing to drink. "While we were on Hadrian's wall – behind it at that time – he came across the friend of a friend, who told him of this identity's death."

"So he was the walking dead – I see it now, I don't know why I was so slow," conceded Agrippa. Then he asked, "Why was this prisoner in different uniform? The impersonators wore blue before – as yours."

"At the moment I can't answer that. However, we were about so clearly any of my men would have known an impostor in blue. What it does tell us is that other uniforms are in their possession. We must tighten security and change the passwords religiously."

"Who does he work for and where is he now?"

"That's another interesting facet. He's under the general auspices of Geta Marcus – another stone on his grave."

"Your disaffected friend," observed Agrippa, making it sound like a question.

"Afraid so – that's why I think he chose blue before. He's attempting to discredit us – me in particular. As to where he is now, the suspect is being questioned in the fort. They'll be even heavier-handed than my optio. Still, any sympathy would be misplaced and if he didn't realise the penalty he might incur he shouldn't have become involved.

Since he's in the fort, though, I suspect any information he's given out will find its way to our friend Petronius, before it comes my way."

"I suspect you're right on that score," agreed the governor. "However, it won't be withheld – you obviously know that, of course."

"So now we have grounds beyond doubt to take this in-comer," remarked Agrippa, who drained his cup as though in celebration.

"When we find him – or learn of his whereabouts."

"You and your team have done well so far, Felix," said the admiral, "but this Geta Marcus is a shipper, so my *frumentarii* will be more used to dealings in the docks."

"Your secret agents are your own concern, Agrippa. But remember what we agreed long ago," Urbicus reminded him. "It was that all information would be pooled. We cannot return to the situation where we each duplicated the other. However, I agree your reasoning, so prioritise them here for the moment. Felix, you can move against this Mercurialis in the meanwhile."

"I accept your reminder," Agrippa said. "It was unnecessary – but timely, since it works all round. We must nail these conspirators before they gain a real foothold."

"A *real* foothold?" Urbicus looked at Agrippa. "Do you know they have one?"

"No," Agrippa responded positively. "But we cannot assume they don't!"

"I agree," Felix said immediately. "Mercurialis probably has more than one. I shall naturally raid the villa again – but the boy Quintus has every right to be there."

"Harbouring criminals is an offence and these men are traitors. He can't be innocent," Agrippa growled.

"They've yet to be tried, Agrippa," responded Urbicus.

"Find them, try them and execute them. Let's be rid!"

"I tend to agree with you – but economy of scale has nothing to do with the legal requirements," observed Felix. "Of course, it could well apply to One-eye. I wish you well in that."

Chapter XI

They played a fast game of handball before dropping into the main pool to swim the comparatively few strokes it allowed a number of times. After going through the sequence of baths they ended up in the hot pool, supporting themselves with their elbows on the edge as they enjoyed its therapeutic effect.

"They cover their tracks well, these traitors – unproven as yet they are, of course," Urbicus observed casually. "We have two operatives, one from each group, but neither knows anything worth a pinch of salt."

"The impostor told us where to find the other uniforms – but they'll get more," agreed Agrippa.

"I'm wondering whether any of these stolen identities have been used to infiltrate guilds or associations. They could stir up a nest of vipers. Even the Council of Roman Citizens could be at risk."

"Do you, Felix? I'd have thought them to be self-sufficient," replied the governor. "They'd look after their own interests – being Roman citizens and tradesmen."

"No doubt they think they represent their members' interests fairly – but what mischief could be stirred up with even one agitator griping about others getting better deals, or paying less taxes?"

"Taxes are universal," Agrippa said pointedly. "How would they benefit from saying differently?"

"The concept is all I'm proposing for now. What about warning the principals of these organisations that false identities are about – though how they would check them is a conundrum?"

"You've answered your own question, Felix. However we must be aware of falling into the same trap. Have we *confirmed* our captives' details?"

"The only sure way would be to trace a letter of recommendation – or if they've served. The latter in their case, " Felix replied. "Clemens is seeing to the record check as we speak."

"Your son-in-law's a thorough worker. We must hope his team finds something," commented the governor.

"Why don't we storm the mine? I've no doubt this Geta Marcus, may the gods rot his cuts, is protecting his interests there."

"Agrippa, don't forget that Firmus is the guard commander there. He will report to us."

"Has he received your message yet, I wonder?"

"He'll reply immediately he does," Felix stated firmly.

"Well, I'm for the changing room," Urbicus said, breaking up the discussion, "and I think I'll miss out the baths in reverse order. See you and yours at dinner."

They returned the smile on the broad, open face and watched the once-muscular buttocks disappear through the doorway.

★ ★ ★

Aelia Aeliana was waiting for him as Agrippa came through the door of his room. The neck-length halo of hair framed her smile, which showed her white teeth to advantage.

She stood in front of him and, as he paused uncertainly for a moment, swiftly reached her hands behind her neck to undo the clasp of her dress, which then fell to her feet. There was nothing else to remove and she enjoyed his looking at her, from the rather shapeless ankles she wriggled free of the dress, up past her full thighs to her small but shapely breasts and then to her brown eyes, which she hoped were encouraging him.

Breathing heavily the admiral asked, "Are you sure?"

"Oh, yes. Quitc sure," Aelia replied, slowly and positively.

Agrippa undid his bathrobe, quickly shrugged it off and took the few paces necessary to embrace her, but not before she had seen his arousal and the look of desire in his eyes.

★ ★ ★

Felix felt Livia's already erect nipple come up harder under his caressing thumb and he kissed her on the nose.

"You know," she said as she stroked his thigh, "we've been married long enough now for eyebrows to be raised if we go to bed before evening – and I don't care!"

Taking Livia in his arms Felix ensured they came gently together, enjoying each sensation as it became available until the peak was over and they lay side-by-side again.

"We mustn't be late, my lovely man. We'd keep a lot of people waiting," she said snuggling into him.

"Do you think we should go as we are," Felix asked, "or do you have some other plan in mind?"

Playfully pinching him she sat up and Felix watched her firm, high breasts sway briefly and then settle, the light-coloured nipples on the milky skin matching the slightly tanned shoulders.

"Shall we risk the baths? Everybody should be finished by now and dressing. We would need to hurry though."

Laughing quietly Felix nodded towards her and said, "You just want to show those off!"

Rolling out of bed Livia rummaged in a trunk and threw him one of the two bath- robes. "Just in case," she chuckled.

However, they noticed that there were two other robes in a wall niche, purple-edged, promising the governor – which meant Romana would be there, too.

Stepping down into the bath they were not fazed in any way – neither with Urbicus and Romana hauling out together nor in the admiring glances the couples gave each other. They had all been naked before in Felix' bath suite or in the suite at the Regnum Palace. The rules were simple. Each trusted the other and admired the beauty of the moment.

When they were alone in the water Livia pressed back into Felix and his hands almost automatically cupped her breasts. When he did, she stretched out her long legs and floated, relaxing completely.

Dreamily she said, "When we're home again we must talk of opening shops. Julia has her babe and her fledgling cookery book, you have your soldiering and your business interests. I must have some work besides running the household. We agreed Valerius would supervise them – it would be an adjunct to his stewarding, after all. I would deal with the stocking, ordering and financial side – overseeing all."

"Come here, woman," he said in a feigned growl, pulling her back to him. "I've been overseeing all for long enough, without a cuddle!"

★ ★ ★

It was an enormous feast by any standards, one table alone supporting two baked hares boxing, and two roast boar going head-to-head, whilst pheasants, with carefully replaced tail feathers, apparently watched.

Urbicus had requested several particular dishes so Romana had surreptitiously infiltrated the kitchens to ensure his fads were provided for. The end product was worth her efforts, she thought, as she looked around at their guests' expressions.

The constant half-smile was there as she once more looked at him as he liked her to. It was as though their one thought was to be close together, whether or not sex was involved.

Livia nudged Felix and he took in what she had seen so obviously – only to look away immediately, not wishing to even potentially embarrass his governor. He wished Urbicus well but such a situation might cause problems for him he could have done without, as the mentor of Romana's children.

Felix' thoughts centred on last year when he had lost Carina to suicide prior to her traitor lover's execution, though the positive aspect of Rufinus being well on his way to becoming a qualified physician – and probably a surgeon – somehow helped with that. His other ward, Avita, he had personally married to Macer at their request – a union he had high hopes for.

However, the prospect of his wards' mother, married or otherwise, following his governor back to his North African birthplace, or even to his senate seat in Rome, far from thrilled him. A young bride could well need her mother's support, especially since her late father obviously could not help. The latter was a stupid thought, he chastised himself!

Relaxing in order to breathe more easily, he then realised he had Livia to advise him – and thanked his personal deity for that blessing.

His thoughts ran on Macer and Draco, who were leading the late season attack on the puffin populated island of Silura.

He remembered Macer taking his battered century off the north Dumnonian beach after their fierce clash with Haruld One-eye's men and levies – a far more numerous force – only then to request their help in storming the island that stood out to sea. Felix remembered thinking him a cheeky young sod but he had had a debt to repay and so had agreed. In the abortive assault his men, Amatus and Silva, had dived into the rock-strewn sea to save marines, from which had grown a mutual respect between the two senior officers.

"Isn't that right, Felix?"

The disembodied voice somehow invaded his subconscious and he peered around in the direction he thought it came from.

As his eyes focused it was on the smiling face of Ianuarius. Then he realised everyone was smiling and joined them.

"Sorry to interrupt your reverie," the shipper said, "but we'd be interested on how you view giving contracts to Britons."

Felix paused, blew out his cheeks and pulled at his chin before replying, "I don't know that my view is actually worth that much – it's essentially a legal matter, as I see it.

However, I do have a vested interest, insofar as you know I'm involved with Stolus of the Durotriges in pottery, oysters and vineyards – the pottery for the army."

"Why?" The question came back before Felix could finish.

He looked at Agrippa and took his time before answering. "Why what? Are you asking why my contracts are with Britons?

If so, my answer to that is simple – it's basically because their product is good. Purbic ware may be less sophisticated than Samian ware but it wears well – no pun intended."

"Better than Terra Nigra? The highly-polished grey ware is superb."

"So it is, Agrippa. Price?"

"Terra Rubra?"

"Price?"

"Our own Arretine from Arretium? The northern Italian product is good."

"In terms of local products Purbic black-burnished pottery is even better, in my view, than that from Durnovaria for the price."

"Like the black slip by Liberticus of Lezoux?"

"Only in the mind. Ours is cheaper and more durable. I wouldn't sell it to anyone – let alone the army – if I thought differently!"

"That's why I ship it for Felix," interposed Ianuarius. Then he added, his eyes raised to the ceiling, "It's a good product – *too* long-lasting, if you ask me."

In the laughter Urbicus said, "So you don't think me ignorant of pottery I know you're using red sand, from the red cliff near Waerham, in your terracotta ware."

Raising a hand to the governor in acknowledgement Felix agreed. "This State is the better that you are so well informed, Urbicus. However we shall charge the army no more for it!"

"I believe we should import ware – as we do wine, olives, dates. Samian ware – or Arretine, at least!"

Urbicus looked at Agrippa and took some time before answering. "I've no doubt of your loyalty to Italia, admiral. Nor have I doubt of your commitment to defend this forty-fifth state of the empire. Sometimes, though, I wish I had your determination to adhere to Roman superiority – and before you rise, Agrippa, it was a sincere comment. It would make my job so much easier. However, Pax Romana does entail embracing whatever is reasonable of Britannic civilian society – perhaps not society as we know it - but as much as is possible.

"Including cheap goods?"

"Yes – highly desirable. Locally produced, too, so no long distance transport."

"Are you now wondering about the navy's ability to protect merchant vessels in these waters?"

"Agrippa. You perform wonders with much limited resources. You cannot very often convoy, but merchants accept those risks. Am I right, Ianuarius?"

"Unfortunately, yes, Governor. I mean Urbicus, of course. We lose ships – and their crews to slavery - as close as along the Iberian peninsular. Total losses."

"We need more ships," Agrippa said pointedly.

"Pirates evade fleets," Ianuarius remarked casually. "Hit and run is their stock in trade, which I know to my cost."

Romana sensed an impasse and, raising her eyebrows at Livia, asked, "Surely at least the east coast is safe? Roman ships are up and down it all the time, supplying the New Wall."

Livia had not wished to involve herself in the men's' debate, believing it to be something for their own resolution – and she knew it was surprising what could be divined from listening.

However, she dutifully supported Romana by adding to the previous comment, "And what of the south? Just across the way is the main harbour of Bononia."

"My dear ladies," Agrippa said quickly, "I have no wish to frighten you – and you are right, Ianuarius, about hit and run – but the proximity of a few naval vessels is no deterrent to a large fleet of pirates unless, of course, the navy is under strict orders to destroy them at all costs."

"As happened some years ago – and more recently against a fanatical pirate called Corbella, I believe," rejoined Ianuarius. "I heard about it with relish. The middle sea was awash with them – particularly North African. No offence intended, Urbicus."

The governor looked at him, saw no guile in his face and said simply, "None taken. It was fact."

"He was called Corbillo, just for the record." Agrippa looked directly at Ianuarius as he added, " His pirate fleet was tracked and attacked. Annihilated actually, which is why piracy is once more hit and run."

"Your protégé, Macer, was involved, I believe."

Agrippa turned to the shipper, but then decided not to go into detail. "Yes, he was. That recent victory did him no harm."

"So we can sleep easily in our beds, then?" observed Aelia, finally slipping in a contribution to the debate.

"I wish I could wholly agree with you, my dear," Agrippa said softly. "Though do, by all means, sleep easily. However, history does have a way of repeating itself – if not sooner, then later."

"In what way?" Romana was puzzled. "Surely we are deep enough up the Temesis to be safe from raiders?"

"I would say so, my dear. The fort in Londinium is well manned and not far across from the docks in reality." Urbicus felt the need to reassure the ladies and hoped he had done so.

"I naturally agree with the governor," replied the admiral, lapsing automatically into his preferred terms of reference. Then he added, "Urbicus is probably right – as you both are, Aelia and Romana. We almost certainly *can* sleep softly, so far inland."

"Then what of history?"

"Well, Livia," Agrippa began, "with Urbicus' permission I will tell you about Rome's home port of Ostia, some two centuries ago."

The governor wondered about refusing but nodded instead. It was an interesting story, he conceded to himself.

"It was in the 685th year from our founding, as I recall it…."

Urbicus interrupted before he realised what he had done. "That's 68 years before the new-fangled Christian calendar begins – if anyone's interested."

"….when our main fleet was at anchor some fifteen miles south-west of the Eternal City. Ostia at peace, you could say.

It coincided with two very senior members of the senate, Bellinus and Sextillius, visiting the port to assess value for money, to put it bluntly. Naturally they had a score of assistants, scribes and lictors with them. The lictors were heralds, of course, but also were meant to protect them.

Just imagine the calm water, a still night – nothing happening," he added for dramatic effect.

"Had anyone been awake, which seems unlikely in retrospect, there would have been open-decked myopiarones appearing out of the early morning water-mist. As it was these sailing barques met no resistance at all and the low shapes escaped detection, especially as they must have moved quietly, as well as quickly, across the harbour.

The first warning was the torching of our major warships, just before the docks themselves burst into flames. They even had their priorities right.

In the ensuing chaos both senators, Bellinus as well as Sexillius, were captured with their ineffectual retinues.

Whatever the City thought of the flames in the western sky is not known. Possibly, in their complacency fifteen miles away, they might even have admired an extended sunset.

The aftermath was as important as the act. If the City's harbour wasn't safe, was Roma? Even if the City, what of the Baiae – the beachside of Napoli Bay? What of a life's interest in developing property there?"

"Surely not," Aelia gasped, "they wouldn't attack?"

Agrippa shrugged and a smile briefly played on his lips at her naivety before he continued, "A pirate fleet raided Croton, on the heel of our mainland, and carried off the temple treasures. Worse than that the island of Delos was raided and the whole population was taken prisoner, to be sold as slaves."

The admiral paused as the ladies looked shocked, placing their hands on their faces or, in Livia's case, a hand to her mouth. He took a draught of wine and looked at the governor.

"You'd best go on," said Urbicus. "The story needs an ending."

Agrippa took a deep breath and carried on, not now looking at the women but into his beaker. "As a final insult they raided the naval base at Misenum and captured, from her villa near the port, Admiral Antonius' daughter – his was the latest of our fleets at that time to be sent against them."

He felt it best to pause again, while his female companions regained their breath, so he signalled a servant to bring him more honey–roasted ham and a pepper pot.

"Their treatment of some of the Roman prisoners was vile, especially the mind games – for the pirates' particular amusement – before the unfortunates were then unexpectedly tossed overboard miles from land. The Greek, Plutarch, wrote a short history of it.

Personally I find it a strange thing to do, since they were effectively tossing money away – but who fathoms the minds of such dross. The dregs of society is a title too good for them.

At any rate, these excesses spurred our senate to take action and Pompey the Administrator – of Julius Caesar fame – was put in charge of anti-piracy measures. His very effective plan was to build several fleets of boats and attack all of the pirate bases at the same time. It worked and piracy was all but eliminated. Hence my plea for more ships," he added as an end piece, looking directly at Urbicus.

"So you see, ladies, there was a happy end to the tale, after all." Urbicus gazed around at them with a large smile that showed his teeth.

Having listened quietly to the story and noting the relief on the women's faces, Felix reminded them that Macer and Draco were at that very time throwing balls of fire, from the onagers mounted on their vessels, up onto Silura's plateau to burn any dwellings, storehouses and dry grasses, in order to make the place uninhabitable to pirates. He did not add that it would only be temporarily, since they were barely reassured as it was. Felix wondered how Livia felt, having been in Haruld's sight several times already.

★ ★ ★

The next day he heard of the successful attack on Silura except that one boat, pulling hard, escaped. It was thought to be heading for Hibernia or possibly even Monavia. Macer had not authorised pursuit in case the idea was to divide his force, which would have prevented the satisfactory firing of the island.

Later that day, off duty, some of Felix'century were attacked again.

Chapter XII

The unseasonable weather continued into the winter proper until the eventual frosts, followed by ice and snow, finally nipped the confused flowers in the bud and the leaves turned colour before being whipped off their dormant branches by the fiercely persistent winds.

So it was not until springtime that a directive reached the governor, who immediately had copies made and passed to his admiral and his head of security.

As he often did Felix found a sheltered corner of the walled garden, put his cup of mulled wine on a small table, then settled down to read what was obviously an important development.

'You may wish to grit your teeth,' Urbicus' personal note began, 'before you read on. There appears little, at least pro tem, that I can do about this directive from the emperor's office and it must therefore be put into practice. By reading between the lines it seems apparent that the family concerned has been flexing its considerable muscle.'

Felix put aside the rolled note and picked up the accompanying scroll before realising that he was, indeed, gritting his teeth. Trying to relax he leaned back and began to read.

'Following protracted representations made to my legal officers and a petition to myself, the family of the late Aurelius Priscus Paternus has presented a convincing argument that the nephew, Aurelius Quintus, has a just claim to the Britannic estates of the said Paternus. Having never been convicted of any crime, nor personally involved in any such crime as may be construed as being against the state, he has the right to reoccupy the said estates in the

Purbic area on the south coast forthwith, without let or hindrance.'Felix let go the breath he had been holding as he realised the implications of the directive. There was no need to read on further since it was only dedications and similar over the signature – or where that would have been on the original document.

It had always been a possibility, as he remembered remarking to the governor more than once, that the Paternus family – and possibly that of Marsala – would seek to become involved to save their own. Now they had.

What galled him most was that, in the final analysis, Quintus had *not* been convicted – nor indeed Mercurialis or the Norseman, Haruld, since the two could not be caught for trial.

So be it, he thought, resigning himself to the fact. Now the little bastard would have to be careful! That he may not even realise it was Felix's parting hope, as he re-rolled the parchment and replaced it in its tube.

Julia came out into the garden and asked after the scroll, seeing that he had put down the official looking package. "Was it important, Father? The messenger clattered up the road with loose stones and earth flying."

"It was, is, an instruction from Urbicus. Is your husband to hand – I'd like to see him? We've something to put into practice."

* * *

The four of them had a quiet evening meal, plainer than was often the case and certainly less animated. Finally pushing away his platter Felix looked at them. There was no question of anyone saying anything except himself. "Let's remove to the solar, it's the lightest room and the most comfortable."

When they were seated, with wine and nuts, Felix explained himself. "I've had to talk to Clemens already, on empirical business. What I shall go on to say is what I've only alluded to on other occasions. The two things are not unconnected – but let me say Clemens and I have *not* already discussed a final outcome.

It's been decreed, and Urbicus cannot avoid it, that the little turd, Quintus, has to be – must be – allowed back onto the quarryman's estate. It is deemed his now, by law.

That, of itself, is not the issue. We all know, as the governor does, it's what the incumbent will allow to happen on his land that matters. That, after all, is why we burned it. Now it'll become a rat-hole again."

Livia and Julia both paled. Each had been captured and stripped, on separate occasions, by bands everyone believed had been based on, or succoured by, the estate in question. Its burning was to have been a turning point.

Now it was all to happen again.

"My belief is that they – whoever – are coming for *me*, in one way or another," Felix said bluntly. "If so, then you and I, my love, have to move on. I can always protect myself, but I cannot always protect you."

Livia twitched as the point was made and turned to him. "But what of Clemens and Julia, if we go?"

"The problem will follow *us*. You are bound to me – our offspring are not. Clemens will also take half the century. They will be safe."

"No!" Clemens was forceful. "No. Dividing our forces won't work – it never does! You have devised a plan to help us – but have you ever wondered what your reaction would be if Julia was ever taken as a blackmail pawn? What would a father do? Is there more than one answer?"

Initially taken aback by the unexpected outburst, since he and his son-in-law had previously touched on the issue, Felix quickly regained his composure.

He said pointedly, "Yes, there is! Of course I love my daughter dearly – as I love your baby, my grandson, Felix

Clemens – but they are *your* responsibility, my son. Mine is Livia! Livia first, then you and your family. That's how it works. *I* don't matter.

Caught out in turn by his father-in-law's animated response Clemens could only retort, "and *I* will die for *them* – as, apparently you will for Livia! No! I didn't mean that as it sounded – obviously you feel as I do – we would both die for all of them," he hastily added, dismayed by his own ire.

"Those bloody bastards have already succeeded," observed Livia, her barrack room litany jerking them back to reality. "We are fighting amongst ourselves!"

"The gods bless you, my love, for your acumen. They have done exactly that! May their guts rot in Hades! What a fool I am! Let me better explain what I meant," Felix conceded.

"Livia and I can remove to a little place with the name, I think, of Throp – something to do with having been an outlying farmstead of a small settlement near there. Whatever, it's ideal for a mill and another fishpond – so we wouldn't starve!

I tend towards a house built as a fortified villa and, as you know, have a permanent guard of veteran soldiers, commanded by ex-centurion Paulinus, who have just recently been recruited."

"Can he hold a sword now?"

"My darling daughter – no, he can't. But he can manage a centurion's spear, held against his body – and a dagger. He's no pushover – plus he knows how to command and deploy men. They respect his awards, too. In actual fact, if he went down and his medallions were lost the loss would be their shame, too. It's how the army works. Veterans are veterans – pride never dies."

"He's right, dearest," agreed Clemens. "We stay here to run the estate and the mill, as before."

"No!" Julia was as adamant as she was vociferous. "If it was you and I then, obviously, I would agree. But what of young Clemens? The risk is too great. We must all go!"

"Two points to the bastards now," Clemens observed. "They have instilled fear."

"Your son's life, husband! How can you play with it?"

Livia moved over to Julia and put a motherly arm round her. Julia pressed into her for comfort – she was in unfamiliar territory.

Then Livia said, "Your father believes you will be safe here. He wouldn't say so otherwise. However, you and Clemens, with Clemens the younger, can obviously move with us if you wish. We just thought you'd want your own home."

Clemens thought exactly that so commented, "We would have half our men as guards, too. It would be just us – like you and your father used to be."

Bridling, Julia retorted, "Then, yes. Not now! Things are volatile again – with these roving bands nothing is safe. We cannot risk our son."

Clemens moved over to console her and she left Livia to hug her husband. "I'm sorry. You *are* brave and strong. I don't doubt you, honestly I don't. It's our baby I worry on. I've been stripped *and* thoroughly frightened, though no one other than you knows that – but *he* cannot defend himself."

"My love," Clemens said, holding her to him, "what is it you want?"

"We must stay together – just as you said earlier. We must!"

"Then we shall," Livia said adamantly, looking determinedly at her husband. "We shall remain one family – not become two!"

"Livia!" Felix was amazed at her single-mindedness. "The point was that only I would then be a target."

"Do you really think so? Isn't that what we've been saying – we each are *still* targets. Whole families are targets. Think on that!"

Dumbfounded, Felix said nothing. He looked at them all, one by one, and each simply looked back at him. What was the point of saying anything, he wondered? How could he draw his enemies to him if it would imperil his whole family? Bad enough his beloved Livia. What to do now, he asked himself?

Livia decided it for him. "We remove as you wish, Felix, but we all go. That is an end to it!"

★ ★ ★

Caecillius Urbanus still raged within himself. Overlooked for an honour once before he was again overlooked during the malairs outbreak – but not that upstart sod, Rufinus. He had not only taken his place and with it any chance of promotion, but had even been awarded a corona!

They were all bastards – double-dyed bastards, all. Still ranting to himself he bustled down the street and pushed down the narrow alley, careful not to turn an ankle on the cobbles.

Inside the low, dark, dingy room he waited until the vague outline of a face appeared through a dimly-lit inner doorway.

"Yes?"

"I am Caecillius."

"Yes?"

"I have news."

"Ah! Come forward."

The medic inched forward and reached the doorway finally, where he was escorted inside.

Publius Lucius faced him. "You have something useful to sell?"

"I have priceless information."

"Why so? We haven't dealt before."

"I come from Geta Marcus with a gift."

"Are you Greek? I was warned off taking gifts from Greeks!"

"I know of the Trojan horse! Geta Marcus will have your balls while you still live, if you jest further!"

Chastised, for all his senatorial wit, Publius Lucius asked, "What of your coming today?"

"Tell your leader that Marcus has the greater vision – cooperation."

Lucius' eyebrows shot up at that, but he managed to contain himself and said quietly, "Go on."

"You have a traitor in the midst of traitors!" Caecillius laughed at the concept, but let it fall away as Lucius' eyes bored into him. "Your esteemed friend, Firmus, is an agent. He manipulates you all!"

With his teeth grinding together, his jaw muscles working hard, Lucius still managed, "An agent from whom?"

"That is the gold with the gift. He's the legate's man. Albinus Felix is his keeper!"

Sucking in his breath Lucius took a while to embrace the idea – though there was no way he would admit that to his low-life informer. The would-be Britannic senator simply grunted, "We know that. How much coin did you expect?"

"None. It's the gift of Geta Marcus – I told you that." With his confirming statement the disgruntled soldier turned away and carefully edged back to the healthily illuminated street.

★ ★ ★

Stolus and his retinue were seen approaching the house and were greeted at the gateway by Valerius, the steward, who escorted him through to Felix' office.

The greetings over Felix instructed Valerius to arrange ale for the men and then to bring Italian wine out to the secure garden. Then he changed his mind and said "No. Better still have the men taken round to the century's barracks with the ale – I've no doubt a competitive spirit will surface."

The young chieftain laughed at that and nodded. "I've no doubt either!"

When they were both seated Felix asked about Galina and was pleased to hear of a good recovery from the effects of the induced birth.

"As a matter of fact Faber is with her now. He's paying a quick visit to the malair patients, too. It's a routine follow up of the work Rufinus did on his own, so he tells me!"

"He did say something about that – but I had no idea when it would be. Another surprise," said Felix, smiling at the thought of seeing the surgeon again. "So. To what do I owe to this visit?"

Stolus smiled broadly – and again when he was prevented from starting by the arrival of wine and picea, round, scorched flat-breads topped with herbs and spices.

"You will have me as fat as a pig in litter," he said, taking one of the slices and biting it in half. Swallowing he went on, "Living as you do in the heartland of the Durotriges you will not be surprised that I acquire a great deal of information from a variety of sources."

Felix nodded his agreement and pursed his lips.

"This is fine wine, my friend. I'm grateful for it."

"It's Caecuban – from the Versuvius region."

"Ah, yes. A major catastrophe I'm told. In it's own way, of course, we have a catastrophe of our own to deal with."

Felix looked at his young visitor enquiringly but still said nothing.

"The quarry estate is to be reoccupied and the house repaired, I hear. A shame it exists at all."

"Where did you hear of that – and it *was* a pity the rains came to put a damper on the destruction."

Stolus tapped his nose in the classic way saying, "I know it to be true. However, the main reason I've come is to discuss a different issue. I think my new grasp of Latin will take us through. As, of course, it does my senior, Venuto."

"It *is* good, Stolus. You've obviously worked hard at it. My compliments," Felix said sincerely, then added, "this issue?"

"Yes, of course, the issue. So I'm told, you will move elsewhere and this rather lovely villa will be leased."

Felix leaned back comfortably against the seat's cushions and joined his hands over his abdomen – which he hoped would hide the paunch that made him more of a pig in litter than ever this junior chieftain would become, he thought.

"You do, certainly, know much. Can you tell me when I'm leaving, too?"

Chuckling and sipping his wine Stolus replied, "I don't believe you have a day in mind yet. However, that is the point. I am in time.

As you know from when you solved the murder in Welle – and saved his life – one of your retired soldiers had married into the little village there. Flavius now has several children and I would like to show our gratitude at his never having resented the fate that would have befallen him, but for you. I wish him to manage this house and run the estate for me whilst you are away – permanently should you decide not to return. Lease, or purchase, I have enough coin."

In the course of digesting the long speech Felix retreated behind his wine cup and thought hard. Irrespective of how he knew, Stolus was presenting the best possible resolution of the dilemma which he himself had never debated but which had concerned him greatly. What to do with the villa?

"Much of your life has been spent here," Stolus continued gently. "Because I couldn't do it, neither can I conceive how you could totally relinquish this place. On that basis I'm looking at leasing it. You, of course, would always dictate the terms. It is your home."

Gradually Felix began to realise the intensity with which Stolus was pushing for the lease. Whatever the reasons he clearly wanted it.

"My friend. It never occurred to me that you were ever likely to be interested," Felix said finally. "Estates like this are alien. Are you sure?"

"I couldn't run it," Stolus admitted. "The disciplines are too great. We operate on utilising the land as it's available. You attempt to govern it."

"Do we?"

"Absolutely – though I have to admit, privately, you tend to succeed."

"What does Flavius know of an estate?"

"He's a good hand – better even. His many acres work for him well. Sometimes he has a surplus for the village. That is, the less fortunate."

"Are you determined, my friend?"

"Yes."

"Then the deal is done – when and if I move. There are conditions, though."

Stolus said resignedly, "As ever."

"Your lease of the land is covered by the profits on our other ventures. So just harvest – no payment, no argument."

"I cannot!"

"You were there when we needed you. Your men saved my daughter. This is my repayment."

Stolus replaced his cup and stood. "We complete a bond on our word. It is final – unto death."

Felix hauled himself to his feet, not understanding his weariness, to face his young Celtic friend. "The lease is yours, but you must talk to my estate manager. Estates have vagaries."

"Are you ill?" Stolus was concerned.

"No," replied Felix, then the world spun around him and he collapsed in a heap.

"But we ate and drank the same," an agitated Stolus told Faber a little while later. *I* am well.."

The rotund surgeon accepted the statement and, frowning, he balanced the time lapses between the last meal and Stolus arriving, then rechecked the symptoms. A food poison would have worked earlier. The only exception would be a long-term poison. This was not that – for obvious reasons.

Tipping more of the tincture made from southernwood mixed with wine between Felix' lips, Faber excluded Stolus from the sickroom and sat down to await events. Unknown to him whilst he slept Livia kept watch on her husband.

Felix stirred and moaned, and Faber took that as a good sign. Then he thanked the gods that his good friend had put several fingers down his throat even as he collapsed, provoking violent sickness. Time would tell.

★ ★ ★

Weak and pale, but very much alive, Felix was propped up in bed, pleased to be discussing the case with his friend the surgeon. Relieved to have something tangible to contribute he said, "As to what we've discussed – I'm sure I was poisoned."

Faber nodded. "Your eyes, pallor and pulse all point to that. Why are *you* certain?"

Taking a breath Felix replied as positively as he felt able, "It's not the first time."

Completely taken aback Faber asked the obvious question "Why?"

A wan smile crossed his face as Felix recalled the event. "I've been doing this work for many years, my friend. It's not hard to make enemies. I was close to that late bastard, Marsala, on several occasions and on this one I was working incognito – or so I thought – in a bordello. No jests please! A companion and I ate and drank but when I left I keeled over, though not before I forced myself to puke. It saved my life on that occasion, too, back in Roma."

"Was that around the time you associated with the girl you suffocated?" Faber frowned before adding gently, "The one in your bad dreams?"

Felix nodded sadly. "You know all about it."

"She was madly in torment from the rabies, my friend. Don't bring it all back – you did what you thought best. It's done and gone. But I didn't know of the poisoning. It's no wonder your unconscious erupted from time to time."

"And this?" Felix let the question hang.

The rotund little surgeon shrugged and sat at the foot of the pallet.

"It beats me," he confessed. "It couldn't have been in the wine or Stolus would have been affected as well. I think we're in your territory here, my friend. Detection."

"According to Clemens, Varerius hadn't poured the wine when he took the men to the barracks. Obviously he didn't take long, because he served us soon afterwards. We'd barely started our discussion."

"So where does that leave it?" asked Faber. "Not in the earlier food, nor the wine, nor the picea. I can't accept it was a curse on you," he added lightly.

Felix kneaded his forehead with his fingers and gnawed at his bottom lip, annoyed that his brain did not seem to want to work at all. Then it came to him in a flash. Once again it was as though he had been jogged into life.

"That's it! That must be it," he said, as though to himself, then smiled broadly at Faber. "No curse, old friend – a blessing."

Puzzled, Faber said nothing but while Felix explained he raised his eyebrows several times, smiled to himself and shook his head.

"It was a gamble - but a no-lose situation! Opportunistic, of course, but the means must have been available for some time. That, of itself, means it had to have been planned –albeit loosely. Possibly not even planned – just an idea waiting for its opportunity."

"What was?" Faber asked patiently, not understanding.

"The wine was unattended – don't you see?"

"Frankly no. We'd ruled out the wine."

Felix spread his hands. "Yes – not the wine. It was the cups."

Shaking his head Faber said he still did not understand, since only Felix had been affected.

"Not cups – a single cup," said Felix. "One cup had been treated. Poison had been rubbed around its inside – maybe only the rim was necessary, I don't know."

"But which would you take? Possibly even not have drunk from it."

"As host, I was always going to drink, too, even if it was only a small amount."

Faber grimaced. "I suppose so," he said.

"But it didn't really matter, did it?"

Silent, the surgeon shrugged uncertainly.

"If I drank, as I did, then I was the victim and their plan was wholly complete. If not, then the cup went to Stolus. If he died I might be accused of murder. If I wasn't then the

Durotriges would be alienated - and candidates for civil disobedience – on the Mercurialis and Quintus alliance's doorstep. They must be kicking their own balls, having come so close."

"I think we could say you are well, my friend. A few days rest and back to the treadmill."

Valerius was totally distraut about what had happened and attributed it to carelessness in his stewardship. He told Felix he would leave immediately but Livia, sitting near him, was able to reassure the agitated ex-soldier that no such thoughts were in their minds. Later she took Tabitha aside to insist she and Valerius were irreplaceable and that the legate trusted her husband implicitly. Livia saw tears in her eyes as she left the kitchen.

★ ★ ★

Bryn and Dyfed were found dead the next morning, apparently having taken poison in a room at the tavern. An immediate assumption was made of their guilt and again when a bullion moneybag was discovered in their possession.

"Two crimes in one, then," Faber advanced, but both Felix and Clemens shook their heads.

"The local optio has the facts, but not the picture. Why commit suicide – why not run? The rest of the conspirators have gone to ground, so why not them? In any case neither of them is particularly physically active – why choose either of them, let alone both, to attempt a crime of this type? In and out quickly and silently required."

"Had they been seen hereabouts they would have been taken," explained Clemens. "Both are well known."

"How were they not known at the tavern?" Faber's brow wrinkled at the obvious.

"We shall never know. Was the barman distracted – in one of many ways? Were they taken in bodily, as though drunk? You know, heads down and half-carried. Maybe yet another way. Neither would it be difficult to get a drunk to take something poisoned."

"True. He probably would neither taste it nor smell it," Faber agreed.

"We think it's a job lot, Faber. It was meant to be several for the price of one. Mercurialis wants to start afresh," said Clemens. "Someone unknown knew Stolus was coming."

"Will you leave Firmus in the melting pot? Could he be next?"

"We shall pull him out – he's posted away, in any case," Felix replied.

"A marked man?"

"We all are, my friend. You take care, like the rest of us."

"I shall give Urbicus the good news," Faber said, tongue-in-cheek, "that all we have to do is take care!"

Chapter XIII

"What hat you need, my friend, is a good hunt. It will make your blood flow and stimulate your appetite," Stolus cried cheerfully, slapping Felix on the back as he continued, "and I have just the one for you! Locally – at harbour's end – so you'll be serving your own land, too."

They were walking through the market place of the small town, which was bare of anything bar a few stalls, under a grey and threatening sky which did nothing to raise Felix' mood.

"It's what I came to talk to you about. You'll remember a lynx sniffing the wind when we rescued your ward, Rufinus? It might even be the same one – they have large territories."

"I've heard they're growing scarce – I think that was why the governor had a pelt wall-mounted after he'd killed one."

"Maybe so," Stolus agreed cautiously, "but one is too many when they find the taste for your calves and sheep."

"I'm not saying don't hunt it, my young friend – as you intended I was roused by your enthusiasm – like you said, it'll probably do me good."

"Fine then," beamed Stolus, reassured. "This one's a big one – probably four feet long. It's taking a couple of calves a week. It'll move fast – be a hard catch!"

"Right," laughed Felix "I'll bring my son-in-law with me. How do you want to organise it?"

Stolus grinned at the jest he was going to make as he replied, "We'll take a boat from the quay and row across to the Lytchett Bay – not far from where your Roman centuries landed a century ago!" Felix raised his eyes skywards as Stolus went on, "We'll land close to the farm concerned and can begin the hunt on the way to it."

Under a duck-egg blue sky, with the rowers pulling hard, the barge made its way out of the Frome and across the northern inlets of the Great Harbour, all the time the sea shimmering like so many small jewels glinting in the sunlight as they danced on the surface. Finally turning north they were soon into the small bay, its musty smell revealing that the tide-water did not scour it often enough, before cutting through the reed beds to push hard into the shoreline mud.

The two beaters Stolus had brought with him leapt ashore to hold the codicaria's bow which allowed their chieftain and the two officers to step out onto shingle, each carrying their own weapons and with swords buckled around their waists.

"We must push on, my friends. The vessel will return in the mid-afternoon, to enable us to be on the quay again before nightfall."

As they nodded their agreement Stolus sent on the two men to scout for spoor, with instructions to way-mark rather than keep reporting back.

"We shall pick up dogs at the farmstead – though I can't vouch for their skills. However, they could well drive the cat towards us – if we can find its hiding place."

"Won't the dogs pick up the scent and seek it out?"

"It's a good question, Clemens. The problem is that a lynx can see wonderfully well and it's said to hear a twig snap at about sixty paces."

"Is that why the dogs can't protect the calves, then?

Stolus grimaced. "Yes – and no! They have the weight to do the job although, as you know, the cat's about the size of a roe deer and also has wicked claws, but dogs will be dogs – as they say. The damn things sometimes go off on their own."

They trudged on and soon were walking carefully in hunter silence, looking around them for a sign to follow. However, nothing transpired and they approached the farmhouse, a long, low building in wattle-and-daub, with thatch greening on the side of the prevailing wind. A red totem stood a short distance away and Stolus acknowledged the house's guardian spirit.

When, at last, two dogs began to bark Stolus remarked, "Do you see what I mean about doing their own thing – sleeping or shagging most like."

Both the Romans smiled at the brevity of the comment, which pithily put things in a nutshell, before concentrating on two mastiffs attached to rope leads bodily pulling a young farmer in their direction.

Stolus threw an arm upwards in their general direction and positively instructed them to stop. This gave the young man the opportunity to lean back and haul on the leads.

"I have come to hunt your lynx," Stolus told him. "It is my duty as your chieftain and I have brought two others with me. I shall take your dogs along – it will do them good."

"So it will, my lord Stolus. You are very welcome to them. I thank you for your help."

With no more ado Stolus grabbed the ropes and passed one to Clemens who took it with more than a little trepidation, since he knew of their fearsome reputation as war dogs after his father-in-law had told him of their use against an army wood detail outside Corinium a year or two ago.

"The secret," explained Stolus, "is to be firm with them. Certainly they are as powerful as they look – but they do look to protect their own. They see me as being their pack leader."

"I hope they've been fed," Clemens observed quietly.

"Not likely at this time of day. The dogs needs to be keen!"

Both animals regarded the men quizzically, their black face-markings emphasising the crinkled eyebrows as they studied them, their straight, heavy, front legs placed solidly shoulder-width apart.

"Now we shall see," commented Felix. "Which of you is going first?"

At that moment the two beaters came quickly into the fenced clearing around the house and looked at their leader for permission to speak, whilst also eyeing the dogs.

Given a wave of approval one pointed with his hunting spear towards the bay further on, which Stolus also knew to be deeper and wider.

"The big cat sits on a tree stump, lord, as though he owns the land!".

"In a way, he does," Stolus remarked to his two friends, "but not the cattle he eats!"

He added, pointing with his own hunting spear, at one beater, "You. Take the two dogs and chase around the other side of this house, down towards the water. There is a tree line between the shore and the field sloping down to it. When you reach the edge of the field release the dogs. No, you both go – take a dog each, I think."

As the two men disappeared into the woodland, their charges pounding along behind them like small mules, Stolus dismissed the farmer and turned to the somewhat relieved pair beside him.

"You both hunt so you know stealth and speed are sometimes linked together – this is one of the times. If you head directly down the nearside of this field you'll come to the tree line, too. Hopefully this lynx will drive towards you – and you may well be in shadow.

"You?"

"Felix, my friend. I shall wait a very short while, until I hear the dogs, then go straight to the field's edge this side. Our quarry should reach one of us!"

Not arguing, Felix and Clemens ran through the wood with their spears at the trail, ready to throw them as they made for the lower trees as suggested.

"The damn thing's still sitting there," muttered Clemens, as they slipped from one close of trees to another. "Odd!"

"Yes, it is. I was surprised to find us anywhere near it, after those dogs went off like charging bulls."

They stopped and hefted their weapons loosely as they studied the still animal, which was apparently oblivious to everything except soaking up the sunshine.

What sounded like a battle developed as the beaters and dogs suddenly broke cover – but still the lynx did not react. It was alive, they knew, because it kept its head moving.

Suddenly the dogs began baying as a beater went down screaming, a large boar taking his legs away before ripping a thigh to the bone with a tusk.

One leapt at the boar and held on to its neck for some time before being thrown off. Coming to its feet it faced the boar again. The second then threw itself into the fray, but its fawn coat was soon blood-speckled enough that it withdrew with its tongue hanging from a gaping mouth.

The boar charged but its target leapt sideways, leaving the back of the animal available to both mastiffs. Their jaws grabbed and tore at the muscle layers protecting the wild pig's vital organs, causing it to squeal in vexation as much as pain, before they broke away again.

Twice the size of the dogs it had no fear and charged once more, the blood trail now some of its own.

The uninjured beater picked his moment to throw and suddenly his spear protruded from the animal's side. He grinned and made for his inert companion's weapon.

Squealing a challenge the boar made directly for its tormentor who, seeing an overhanging branch, wisely jumped to grab it. Wheeling around and around it lost interest in its invisible target and resumed the fight with the dogs.

"That cat hasn't moved," exclaimed Clemens and Felix looked to see that it hadn't. It was as though it was deaf.

They crept low along the foliage and each launched their spear at the lynx.

Both went home and the tawny-coloured animal was torn off the stump.

Both mastiffs had the boar by the back of the neck and were crunching their jaws into it whilst it wrestled and twisted to escape. Eventually dislodged, but with blood now pouring from the pig's wounded neck, they faced it once more.

No less convinced of its victory it slowly paced towards them, but stopped when they did not move. Its poor eyesight let it down and it failed to find a moving object to fight.

As it turned away both dogs leaped forward, one grabbing at the testicles whilst the other bit into the exposed spine.

Transfixed by the pain of moving the boar stood still until the rearward mastiff mistakenly crunched its prize, galvanising it to leap and roll, throwing both dogs off yet again. Pouring blood from several deep wounds the boar charged once more, but the spear, which had moved easily until now, caught in its rear legs and tore a massive hole in the animal's side.

Now in blood frenzy both dogs attacked and knocked it over, grabbing for its throat and jowls, one to immobilise and one to kill.

On the other side of the field Felix and Clemens looked down on the carcase of the lynx and wondered.

Both had thought, at first, that the cat was simply keeping high for safely but now, seeing the savage head wound, wondered what had kept it alive.

Stolus came up and complimented them. "A wonderful charge. My compliments!"

They indicated the head wound but Stolus simply shrugged. "Would you have said it was an unequal contest if it had taken a child? The point is it's dead. No more lost calves and sheep for my countrymen."

"It may have had damaged hearing or even worse, just as soldiers can do from blows. Had it been caught by the boar?"

"If it had been then my compliments to the boar. No more than it deserved. Do the strong never defeat the weak? No, wrong words. The more able, the less able?"

Felix leaned on the spear he had withdrawn from the lynx before saying, "This seemed wrong at the time, my friend. I felt demeaned because of its injuries. But, of course, you're right. The calves would have preferred to be the victors, too. It was dog eat dog, if you'll forgive my poor choice of example. Your dogs did well. Will they heal just as well?"

Stolus smiled. "They will. Herb poultices and red meat. They'll come again – like the rain. So will the beater."

"Say a prayer at the totem for us," Felix said – and was assured one was already being framed.

The homecoming was strange. There had been small talk on the way, discussion on the beater's roughly-bound wound, the dogs and life in general, but all muted.

On the quay Stolus said to Felix, "It was not what I thought it would be. There was no glory in it after all: no superiority of man over beast.

However, I stand by my original suggestion. It was to be good for you – and it has been. Your blood ran in your body and you achieved our objective. I personally did nothing – if there has to be a failure it was mine. But who failed? Do we always know why we succeed or fail? I don't. My tenant is happy – we should be too. We were willing to face danger and did so. What more is there?"

★ ★ ★

A few days later Felix received a strange missive from Firmus, still on duty with the gold mine guard although he was aware of Geta Marcus' fall from grace. He also pointed out that Dorcas was still pregnant.

'Ragwort' the message began. 'I don't know it personally – I'm not a farmer – but the name was given to me. Whatever, herds on Marcus' estate are being affected. Horses are just dropping dead, along with cattle. Not sheep, though. Sometimes the animals are ill for months. Will you wish to investigate?'

"Whatever ragwort is," Clemens commented, when shown the note, "it's a pity we can't use it on Geta Marcus and Mercurialis!"

"I've some sympathy with that view, young man – but a quick death would solve the problem better – perhaps on the end of one of our swords!"

"So. What will you do?"

"I'd leave it to the experts normally – but as this is Marcus there's probably something behind it. I'll tell you what – go and see our estate manager and pick his brains, like how and why the animals might have come to grief. I'll do the same with our two hippiatros, so send for Aufidius and Papirius as you go, will you?"

The two scouts cum veterinarians came almost at once, having already been in the stables dealing with an injured foreleg. Felix explained the animals' fate and asked for their opinions.

"Well, Sir," Papirius began diffidently, "there really are so many weed and plants not good for them that it always helps to see the victim – signs and that."

"That's very right, Sir, always helps," Aufidius confirmed.

"In general then," suggested Felix patiently.

"Well, Sir," Papirius began again, "ragwort's a strong possibility – though for some reason it doesn't affect sheep. Other animals don't usually eat it but it can get into hay – then they do."

Aufidius chipped in then. "Yew leaves are a problem, too. So's its bark and seeds – except to birds! Strange – but the jelly-fruit round the seeds isn't poisonous. I was told that – but never tried it. They don't chew the seed," he added somewhat sheepishly.

"Of course, Sir, what we're saying, at the moment, is based on an accident. It wouldn't be possible to talk about deliberate poisoning." Papirius shook his head and looked gravely at Felix. "I know little about cattle but you need to realise, excuse me Sir, that horses are trusting. They will take from you, if they know you – and even if they don't, more often than not!"

"How do you mean?" asked Felix.

"If a poison is disguised in something tasty, say an apple, they wouldn't know it – trust, Sir."

"I see. So an individual's poisoning of them would be hard to detect?"

"I'd say almost impossible, Sir."

"The effect would be obvious, of course," observed Aufidius, "nothing clever there. Signs and symptoms might possibly tell us the what – but never the how. Also the time lapse would cover events."

"Small doses? Is that what you're saying?"

Papirius shrugged. "Different things and different quantities would make the list a long one. Some are quick acting, others slow – deliberate or otherwise."

"You're telling me I shan't find out?"

The two looked at each other and paused. It was Aufidius that said, "You may not, Sir, however diligent, if that's the word, you are. If we're with you, we might recognise something – but may be not. We often go on intuition but we can't ask *you* to do that – not only on our word, we know that. We'll do what you say, Sir."

"My life has often depended on you two," Felix answered quickly. "Your opinion will certainly be useful. Keep yourselves local until you hear otherwise."

He dismissed them and sat thinking.

When Clemens returned, having learned little more than Felix, except that they might have eaten ivy or corncockle in their food, they both realised that, because so much was poisonous or ill-making, they were out of their depth in trying to prove the cause.

"We're going to call in our friend, cui bono, I think," Felix stated humorously.

"Who gains? Well, we've done that a few times – its one of the first things you pointed out to the men they should consider, if they investigate a complaint. So are you going to start the discussion?"

Scratching his head Felix answered, "We know, at least second-hand, that Celerianus, one of the Londinium shippers, sold pseudo shares in the gold mine to Lunaris – another one of the Londinium shippers. It puts Celerianus with Geta Marcus. That is, to have them available to sell.

Could it be that he, or another, is taking revenge on Marcus – Lunaris, I mean by *he*?"

Clemens baulked but then, in turn, looked thoughtful. "It's a wild thought of yours Felix – a real grab out of thin air. But you said *another*. Are you by any chance suggesting Mercurialis – that he's been sold shares, too?"

"If you think that, then was mine such a wild thought? You've arrived at my journey's end with the smallest of prompts."

"He's certainly capable of revenge: we both know that. How in hades would we ever prove it, though? He'd need to admit it."

"In his pomp he might just do that – he's full of bravado."

"He's full of shit!"

"I think we've summed him up between us," agreed Felix. "But there's always a vague possibility that someone might just give him away – accidentally or purposefully. We must make sure there are as many ears flapping on our behalf as possible."

"Firmus?"

"Yes, we should get him investigating – no point in us flogging ourselves down to Cymru. Of course, he's probably already looking into it, since he's the senior man in situ."

Clemens changed the subject by asking, "It's strange there's no word of Marcus. He may be persona non grata but the rest of his board are still running the mine. How is it there's no apparent contact – he is the motivating force, after all?"

Looking puzzled Felix agreed. "I've wondered at that several times myself. The mine's still working and there'll always be a small profit as long as it is. You'd expect *some* contact."

"And his shipping line is still going strong, I understand".

Tapping his fist on his pate Felix said agitatedly, "What a bloody fool I am! I'm going senile! All this time I'm wondering where he is and he's on his damned ships! Thank you for your return prompt, young man."

Looking pleased Clemens responded, "Unconscious, I can assure you – but if it's done the trick, that's good. I didn't think of it either, of course. What'll you do?"

Thinking as he spoke Felix said slowly, "We can stop his ships. We're entitled to follow up leads when we search for agitators. Mind you, it'd be better not to make too many wrong guesses. What we need is information."

"Ianuarius?"

"In one!"

"How?"

"He's no investigator, of course, so neither do we want to put him in jeopardy – but he must have seamen he can trust. Men who talk to other seamen."

"Good idea," agreed Clemens, before adding "haven't we got port guards who should be keeping their eyes and ears open? Soldiers talk to each as well."

"A very good point, Clemens – I knew I could find a use for you eventually! Now, I must send messages to both Agrippa and Urbicus – the former to act and the latter to know of the idea. Mind you, I don't suppose our admiral will be thrilled at the extra work."

"Mercurialis ships stone – could the same be true of him?"

"Good thinking, my boy. Maybe, just maybe. Of course his barges aren't suitable really – and I'd expect Stolus to know if either's working from Purbic. But it's worth bearing that in mind."

"The One-eyed might convey him. It's what we've often thought – but now we've brought up this other idea it's highly likely he'd prefer to be independent."

"So do I, young man. Having decided that I think, now, you ought to see mother and child."

★ ★ ★

From behind, Clemens had slipped his hands under Julia's unfastened woollen jacket and into each side of her dress's plunging neckline, a crossed palm cupping each full breast as he kissed her neck.

She smiled and putting a hand up to his head pulled it down so that, by turning hers, they could kiss over her shoulder.

Light from the cross-hatched window fell across the slate she was writing on, as she stood at the kitchen table.

"I wonder which receipt I should put what you're doing under," she asked teasingly.

"Feeling melons for ripeness," he quickly retorted and immediately felt her foot playfully stamp backwards onto his – so he gently squeezed a little harder.

"Livia will be back soon, my love. She's only gone to see Valerius about her shops project."

"I was wondering if you wanted to borrow my stylus," Clemens enquired provocatively, kissed her neck again.

"I thought you might offer – I can feel where you keep it. No thanks, I'll make do with my chalks for the moment!"

He withdrew his hands and ran them down her thighs, feeling their slim strength through her long tunic.

Julia put down her chalk and turned to embrace him just as Livia came back into the room, her house slippers soundless in the passageway. They broke away, flustered but not embarrassed, smiling at her warmly because they knew it was just the sort of thing that she and Felix did.

"No need to stop – I'm always willing to learn," she remarked, smiling back at them.

Chapter XIV

"Right," said Paulinus to the assembled men. "You've all been recruited to serve and protect Augustus Albinus Felix, his family, chattels and property. Being bright and clever you already know that, so I'm telling you nothing new. So what could be new to old soldiers and citizens? I'll tell you."

Their cocky, self-assured faces took on a puzzled look as almost to a man they leaned forward to hear better.

"I see you're all listening – that's a good start. Keep up the good work."

Paulinus was beginning to sound like the centurion he had been until his injuries. In their turn, all being old soldiers, they instinctively listened for an order.

It came. "Get fell into line! You're a miserable, ragtag bunch of misfits. You couldn't even handle doing nothing properly. Admit it – I'm right, aren't I?"

Staring along the newly-formed ranks he went on in his best parade ground rhetoric, "I 'm very sorry, citizens, I must be going deaf because I didn't hear you answer. I'm right, aren't I?

Their shouts equalled his raised voice so now he smiled grimly to himself. Old soldiers are always old soldiers, he thought. Putting on his uniform, with his awards displayed on it, had done no harm.

"You must all have realised you weren't going to get money for nothing. Am I right?"

A chorus of acknowledgement rose and fell.

"Now I *am* going to tell you things you didn't know," Paulinus went on. "The legate is a reasonable man – far too reasonable, if you ask me, so I shall be also. The only thing is, my reasonable may not equate - that means agree, by the way - with your own opinions of reasonable. That does not matter, since it's only my opinion that counts. Are any of you listening?"

Another chorus of consent came.

"Right. So far you're all doing well," the ex-centurion said. "Now, hear this and mark me well. I'm paid, too – and there's no way I'm not going to earn *my* pay.

Like me, you all have pensions. You'll keep them – unless you're hopeless with dice! Like me, you'll all earn a wage. You'll keep it – since all is found, you lucky people! No deductions from pay – you don't know you're born!

Like me, every Saturnalia you'll receive a lovely, golden aureus for every month of satisfactory service, as a festive gift from Augustus Albinus Felix. That means, unless you've just joined or been replaced by a proper soldier, twelve gold coins if you've managed to last the year.

Did I say replaced? Dear me – that'd mean someone has failed! Not failed themselves, of course, but failed me. That'll not happen! If that *is* a likelihood then leave now. No, sooner than that!"

Paulinus paused before asking, "Is anyone still here?" The chorus was as bold as before and it confirmed in his mind that they *had* missed the barrack-room litany. That was a good sign – a very good sign, he thought.

"Aside from *not* being part of the Roman army, you'll be part of the Roman army as far as I'm concerned. That means discipline, standards and rules. I'll not have stealing – and neither will the legate. Do please take *all found* as meaning just that – not all stolen! I hope no one's deaf."

He cupped a hand to his ear and they laughed as they shouted their response.

"You may do, reasonably, what you like off-duty – if you ever are, of course. You will work shifts with appointed duties. I told you it was like the army, didn't I – and if there ever is a need to fight you will do so. I hope that is clear – because there will be weapon drills, too. Is anyone *still* here?"

With their affirmation Paulinus went on, "You'll construct a temporary camp with tents for now. When the house is ready a barrack will be built – you'll build it, so that there'll be no complaints. Stone based and half-wooden walls – just like your mother would want for you."

He allowed the chuckling to subside and then said, "You'll also have a bathhouse - but only a small one, so you don't get ideas above your station!

I don't know why you're so pampered - but beware, because it means if anyone lets down the legate they let me down and nobody lets *me* down. Am I clear?"

A loud chorus of agreement was followed by his saying, "By the way, I forgot to mention that you'll also have field training – so it'll be *just* like the army!"

He allowed the groans and then went on, "You'll all sign contracts, so if you fancy deserting now's the time to do it. After that, I'll personally come looking for you!"

In the ensuing silence nothing moved until Paulinus stated, "Any takers, one pace forward – march!"

★ ★ ★

"The Mummers are out again and hopefully will be as successful as other times. It's surprising how people take to – and talk to – entertainers. Frankly, I was loath to send Tabitha until I realised that Valerius was a candidate too – a chance to show his skills on a wider stage, as he used to a long time ago. She'll be safe."

"So you no longer have a steward," Urbicus observed to Felix. "Yet the house still functions smoothly – and what a cook you have. Three versions of pork, with mouth-watering herb crackling to die for. What price the sauce with the venison and then with the stewed partridge? Followed by swan!

Was the salmon all caught locally – I've never tasted fresher? And you tell me the wine is mainly from your own Corf vineyards? It's probably that that's oiling my tongue, come to think of it. Why didn't you stop me?"

Felix smiled warmly at his friend, the governor. "You were in full flow and telling me how much you enjoy our hospitality – what's to stop?"

The room echoed to the laughter of the men enjoying the post-dinner separation from the ladies, who had retired to the solar for their own company.

Knowing those present as he did Felix was able to recognise each by their brand of laugh. Some were deep and throaty, others full and exuberant, but even within each range the laughs were longer or shorter, some choked off whilst others petered out. He knew them all.

Newly promoted surgeon Faber was there with his sparring partner Petronius, the governor's strategist and camp prefect. Ianuarius had come down with them, in one of his own vessels. Stolus, unusually, had come with his now fully recovered wife, Galina. Then lastly, Clemens.

"Do you remember a year, or so ago, I spoke of forming a governor's council – on the lines of the emperor's intimate council. Not, perhaps, as intimate as that is - but advisory, all the same." Urbicus looked at Felix enquiringly.

"I do," agreed Felix.

"Well, I've the backbone of business and profession. I would ask Ianuarius, here, to join me to represent the sea-faring trade – what do you say?" Having asked the question the governor turned to him with raised eyebrows.

After thinking for a few moments the shipper replied, "It would be an honour – but I'd need to put it before the

Shippers' Federation. I wouldn't want to be seen as taking an unfair advantage."

Nodding slowly Urbicus agreed reluctantly. "I do see that. But the offer is made to *you* – not the federation. I'm seeking an impartial cross-section, not salesmen with vested interests. Understandably, it's difficult to be wholly impartial – but some are better than others. I'll await events."

"Whatever the outcome I'm most grateful for having been considered."

"Good. Now, I'd also like a tribal chieftain from the hinterland. One who's well versed in Romano–British custom – not one who's ceased to get his hands dirty because of title. Would you be sanctioned by the tribal council in Durnovaria, Stolus?"

Startled by the way the statement was made he shrugged. "It's unlikely – I'm a lesser chieftain, after all. I also couldn't spare the time away from the lands I'm responsible for, in any case."

"Will you ask Caradoc and Venuto? Presumably you'd agree if they said so? No," Urbicus instantly corrected himself; "I'll write from here – the council will receive my personal request immediately."

Stolus made as if to protest but sank back, realising the governor was free to write to whom he wished.

"I believe, Felix, I'd already mentioned the idea of asking you for Comazon Valerius. I need the view of the common man, so to speak."

Felix grimaced. "I seem to recall something about it, Urbicus, but I really need his services at the moment."

"So do I, my friend. We're not looking to pass law or statute – but I'd value the opportunity to discuss the effect of those we have already and also what might be needed. Valerius is a disabled ex-soldier and a talented actor/musician as well as a steward, so has a broad view.

Clearly, however, unlike the needs of empire-broad thinking my council might meet only twice a year, or so, say after your Beltain, Stolus, and before your Samhain?"

"*If* it comes to pass," answered Stolus, "then the beginning of summer would suit well. As for preceding Samhain it would have to be between harvest home and then. I cannot interrupt our reaping, though I have no thirst for winter travel naturally.

Neither would I wish to miss any of our festivals that mark the first days of our seasons – which would also include Imbolc, in your month of Februarius, and Lughnasad, that marks harvest, at the start of your Augustus."

"How do you put it, as regards Imbolc – 'the sun awakening from its winter sleep'? By all means celebrate that, Stolus. I'm sure we'd all wish to join you," replied the governor earnestly. "I shall avoid those days assiduously, just as I would wish to avoid Rosalia in our Maius, as Saturnalia with its custom of giving in December, or the kalends of Ianuarius, when our new year begins! Of course, as yours does in our November."

"Then we shall see," retorted Stolus, unfazed by the governor's understanding of each other's different festivals.

"Talking of sea – if you'll excuse the pun – my hope is that you and Valerius would take ship from here together. It would break the ice, so to speak."

"We already know each other."

Urbicus smiled. "Of course – from weddings, plus the battle for the villa – I had almost forgotten. I must be more senile than I thought!"

As the laughter died away Petronius broke the silence. "Now that that's been put to bed, my old friend, perhaps you could press our good host to refresh that excellent Falernian jug – lessons bring on a thirst!"

Chuckling at that Urbicus said to no one in particular, as Felix indicated to a servant that more of the Italian wine was needed, "If our admiral had been here he'd probably have complained that if he was not receiving Greek lessons it was now Celtic!"

"Talking of Greece," said Felix, "who's for a measure of their sweet wine – if the ladies haven't finished it all?"

★ ★ ★

"I just can't believe this man," Felix exploded. "Our quarry's in hiding, but I'm told by our good spy in Corinium that Mercurialis has just dedicated a temple further north!"

"He's tweaking our noses, Felix," replied Clemens. "He also knows we cannot storm up there and tear it down. Not now it's dedicated to one god or another – there'd be a public outcry – probably already in use, too."

"Damn the man!"

It was quiet after his outburst until Felix exclaimed, "Hold hard! Has he been too clever here? How did he get there? By boat – so he must have other than just stone barges," he added, without waiting for a comment.

"You're wondering where he keeps it, I suppose?"

"You've hit the nail on the thumb there, young man. I really must wake up! I didn't think of ships with Marcus and now I hadn't thought of moorings for either type"

Clemens said quickly, "The navy's looking for pirate boats – Haruld in particular – so the same vessels can look for any odd moorings-up, or even the possibility of passing them in a normal anchorage. It won't mean any more work than they do already. Shall I draw up a document for you?"

"Yes," Felix said, "I'll get it off to Urbicus by special messenger straight away."

A book of wax tablets came back to them quickly and they were pleased to note that, although they seemed to have been scribbled hastily and possibly on the move, Urbicus was pleased with the information and endorsed their suggestions. He had also sent to Agrippa to put it in hand.

* * *

The following day a scroll arrived for Felix personally and the seal was Urbicus' personal seal, he noted. Not official then, he thought, as he broke the wax and untied the fastening.

'My very dear friend,' he read, 'there comes a time in life when stock has to be taken for the future. I would not bother you now otherwise – indeed, putting my thoughts on record to you may even be foolhardy. However, I know your discretion and would ask you to burn this when read.

The situation is that I need your advice on whether I should marry Romana – that is, what effect formalising our relationship would have on your wards. Additionally, of course, should we marry I would wish to adopt them formally, as my successors. How would that affect you, my friend? You have done well for them, particularly Rufinus.

I feel sure you will understand my dilemma, not least because Livia married you with your adult daughter, Julia, still living at home. That has worked so very well I would wish for similar in my case.

Should you not pander to me I shall take that as you having no objection, but I really would prefer your views, including reservations.

May the gods continue to bless your house.'

* * *

"I think I must be supporting the mail service on my own," Felix complained to Clemens, but the tone of voice decried his words as far as the younger man was concerned.

"How so?"

"This has come from Firmus today. It says that his men are being rotated by their headquarters in Isca Silurum to the point where he hardly knows them. Here, read it for yourself."

Clemens took the wax tablets and read them through. Then he did so again. "There's no telestich here that I can find," he told his father-in-law.

"No, I thought not – so there're no hidden secrets to fathom. He means what he says. It's strange!"

"What is?"

"The rotation from Isca – and no message. Why not?

"Sorry?"

"No explanation of the rapid rotation. We both know Sextus, the commander there. He would normally give reasons. So why not? Does he know of it? If not – and we might ask why not– perhaps no one has told him. If so, it's similar to what happened to his predecessor. His lack of knowledge allowed a revolt to happen. I told you – I was there at the time. Sextus and I drove spears side by side, naked."

"You've told me. What are you saying?"

"I cautioned Sextus about his support staff. Have they done the same to him, nevertheless?"

"In the name of all the gods, how can we tell?" Clemens was frustrated by his lack of understanding. "Say what you mean – plainly!"

Felix threw his arms wide as he exclaimed, "How do I know what I don't know? That's rhetoric that has been asked for a millennium – probably for all time."

"So?"

"You ask me what? Then let's look at all the possibilities. Is Sextus innocent – or complicit? Is Firmus free to write? If rotation is necessary – why so much?"

Interrupting the flow Clemens asked, "Was that the only thing Firmus was free to write?"

"As you said, who knows? In my mind the only way to know is to go!"

"To do what? What's our objective? How can we justify interference?" The questions came thick and fast from Clemens since, interesting as it was, he did not want his mentor to go in like a bull in a frenzy.

"You're right, as usual, my son. Softly, softly. So I'll go on. *Is* Sextus innocent? *Is* Firmus being used? Are either or both under restraint? If the latter, why no telestich from Firmus? Is its very absence meant to trigger us? Is it a trap? The overall question though, is why rapid rotation in the first place?"

Clemens rubbed his forehead as though to clear his mind. "If Firmus *is* under restraint why was he allowed to communicate? They would recognise the dangers in that – and of our coming."

"As I said, is it a trap? If telestich would give us information would lack of it make us suspicious? Either way my reaction was supposed to be to go there. You were right to question it. As to such rapid rotation of guards, I said I find it strange. They wouldn't know the workforce intimately – perhaps not even each other. Firmus, himself, said as much. Divide and rule?"

"Firmus is still there," Clemens observed.

"Yes. That puzzles me too – although he's the senior officer, of course."

"Training?"

"Possibly, or could he be the sacrificial lamb for whatever's in the offing? Could some of those being rotated be in the pay of our slippery friend?"

"Smuggling gold?" Clemens was surprised at his father-in-law's inference but then realised it was a possibility. It gave some sense to rotating the men to that degree. "Are we coming round to restraint? That'd be treason, if both of them. Complicity in some crime, if only

Firmus. Would Sextus be compliant? I don't believe so, any more than you do. Nor can I see another revolt. The Royal Second Legion *is* the Royal Second, after all. I was surprised to hear of their gullibility the first time around but, even then, it was only some."

Felix smiled at Clemens before saying, "That was a long speech. I think a reasonable analysis. What we both seem to be concluding is that Sextus is not aware of what's happening? Equally, Firmus is possibly under guard – though my gut reaction is not. On this occasion he informed us of the oddity before he found out why."

"That reflects on both of them. Sextus, for not carrying out spot checks and our friend for being hasty. If so, it's just a coincidence of errors then?"

"It would be, except that now we know of this quick rotation – which *is* suspicious.

If it's as we suspect then Sextus needs to know. It's his legion. His domain."

"What if he does know?"

"Then that'll be my error. I think I must write to Firmus, telling him to take Dorcas on a trip to Isca. That'll get her to safety. Then he can see Sextus personally, taking a scroll from me to him in telestich. I must back our judgement on this – that it was expected we would want to find out what was happening. It was a trap for us that Sextus must sort.

The question now is, a trap set by whom?"

★ ★ ★

The weather held fine and the sea had been a millpond the whole way to the Regnum Palace, so much so that baby Augustus Clemens slept the journey, except to be woken for a feed halfway, off Clausentum.

Since this had involved the wet nurse taking out an ample, blue-veined breast in view of the nearest crew, it had intrigued them so much that the sailing master had had to have them reminded of their duties. This vigorous use of a switch had brought a broad smile to the wet nurse's face, in turn.

Helping Livia and Julia down the gangplank Felix and Clemens were greeted in person by the governor and Romana.

A good deal of forearm gripping and shoulder slapping went on between the men, whilst the three women looked on happily as their men became boys for a moment.

"So you went ahead and did it, my old friend. I'm so very, very pleased for you," exclaimed Felix.

"My congratulations to you are just as warmly given, Urbicus," Clemens said, leaning towards a slight formality in respect of their differences in rank, notwithstanding the acknowledge informality between them on unofficial occasions.

"Had to do it, my boy, just had to – after what your father-in-law wrote to me," chortled Urbicus. "I wonder how many governors have such friends as you and yours. Now for goodness sake let me at your women!"

An embrace and a kissed cheek later both Livia and Julia were hurried down the private quay by Romana to a side entrance of the palace.

Urbicus called for wine and the three men walked out through one of the formal gardens, box-hedged trimmed and planted in roses, then past fountains with the dancing water playing from one bowl to another and finally on to a smaller area Felix knew well.

Breathing deeply the governor said, "I thought a pre-prandial libation in the herb garden would suit us as well as anywhere - private, too. I've always considered you to enjoy it as much as me, my friend. We've had a few dinners out here, haven't we," he added, briefly indicating the dining recess lying to one side of the entranceway.

They sat on the wooden, slatted seats and almost immediately were presented with trays of wines, fruit bowls and dishes of olives, by slaves who appeared as though from nowhere.

"I was pleased," the governor began after dismissing the slaves, "to learn that Legate Sextus had two men executed for smuggling gold nuggets into the mine. You'd hardly look for gold going *into* a mine, would you?"

"I wonder who it was they were going to allow to discover them, as it were, before asking such lucky men to invest in further exploration?"

"You're ahead of me, Felix. I hadn't quite gone that far in my own mind. Still, as long as I have people who can think for me, I'm happy." He swallowed a draught of his thin, Gaulish wine and chewed an olive before adding, "I'm also pleased you left it to the legate to manage his own affairs. We may yet learn more from others of the guard who have been arrested – as they're auxiliaries so not yet citizens, no doubt the questioning will be as robust as fits the occasion."

"It was this young man that counselled me on not going in, actually."

"I have hopes for you, Clemens. You have acted well and wisely on several occasions I'm aware of. There are several of you who may do very well in the Emperor's service. Macer and Draco come to mind to join you."

"Then I'm both in good company and grateful," responded Clemens. "Will the admiral and those two be joining us tonight?"

"I don't know why it happens so often," replied Urbicus, "but Agrippa frequently doesn't arrive until evening. Yes, they're due in."

"Something to do with tides, possibly," offered the young tribune.

"I expect you're right. Still, I always leave them to make their own excuses", retorted the governor, but his voice was full of inflection and they all laughed at the idea of Agrippa feeling an excuse was necessary.

"Changing the subject to something we *can* understand, as well as making a private matter public, I really was grateful for your sympathetic view, Felix. I mean, agreeing to Romana's request that you become their legal guardian, when her late husband died, you would normally be expected to decide - dictate even - where the two surviving children live, whether married or not.

In itself it's not a big issue since, although Avita is married, you will always be her father-figure, as is Macer's father to him, in law. Rufinus is an adult in the army medical corps and doing well. You, of course, are still his quasi-father and no doubt he will always see you as such.

Even with that in mind, you bothered to set out the advantages my adopting them would bring. As part of it they would have continual contact with their natural mother. I was particularly impressed by your pointing out that the ownership of the Portland stone quarry would then need to pass to me, too.

The latter, attractive as the prospect is, is not to be. Both Romana and I believe you should retain it – after all you already own half. If you like, for services rendered. Should you refuse it we could not take back the gift, so then it will fall into disuse – therefore please *do* accept our offer. It's already been registered as all yours.

However, I have spoken for far too long and more so without interruption, Felix," the governor said, lifting a hand in his general direction.

Even while Urbicus spoke, thoughts had whirled around in Felix' head – both for and against. He felt his heart beat faster as though he was in battle. What he had written was what he thought best. He would miss the responsibility oddly enough yet, because of their relative youth, he felt they should be allowed to go further on – to climb the hill to see if the grass was greener beyond it. With all Urbicus could offer them the hill was lower and the possibilities greater.

As to their mother – he was not so sure. Sometime soon she would be a governor's wife. Excellent for the job, he knew, but somehow she seemed to have risen above the role of being an ordinary mother.

As though dragging himself back to reality he forced his mind to concentrate and managed to gabble, "I said it all in my letter to you, my friend. My answer is the same."

Looking closely at Felix the governor said, "I shouldn't have resurrected the issue. My apologies are sincerely given. It is extremely emotive. I only thought to thank you – the quarry is a joint gift, insofar as we cannot accept your offer of its return."

Groping for a lifeline Felix managed, "Will you publicly announce your betrothal?"

"Ah! Now *I* have the dilemma! Remind me not to cross you in court," Urbicus said – and even the forced smiles lightened the moment.

The three were first to the baths and were swimming lengths when their ladies joined them very soon after. As now the governor's betrothed, Romana was the first to drop her towel and, not unnaturally to anyone, the men observed her shapely figure, small-busted but with provocatively erect nipples.

Livia followed, very slightly ahead of Julia who was wondering how her lately pregnant body would look to older men. She need not have worried since all eyes were upon Livia's milky-cream breasts, followed by the long legs and tapering calves, leading to slim, sculptured ankles. She knew she was protecting Julia and allowed their gazes to linger before she jumped in to join Romana and the men.

Even with the rapidly fading, but still obvious, stretch-marks on Julia's abdomen, it was difficult for them all not too see how tall and slender she was, with everything in proportion. As ever, they enjoyed the ready smile on the open, honest face.

Chapter XV

Unusually sailing in Draco's 'Sabrina' Agrippa came into the harbour reaches near to the Regnum Palace and had the bireme drop anchor. Macer followed in his larger trireme, 'Tigris', in which the admiral more often went to sea, mooring up further out because of its size.

Hauling in their trailing dinghys allowed the lone occupant of each to clamber out with his unused baling bucket. Then crews took the boats to the little jetty alongside the palace, where the three officers were met by the guard commander and escorted through the formal entrance as courtesy required.

Then, knowing the way well, they hurried off to make themselves presentable.

Having quickly visited the baths, the three just managed to take their places in time, not wanting to miss the banquet laid on as part of the governor's celebration of the betrothal. Unknown to them the governor had deliberately delayed his arrival to avoid any embarrassment.

Couches followed the lines of the walls on three sides, leaving once side open for the servants and slaves to service the low tables placed within reach of the guests.

Whole hams and suckling pigs, goose, peacock, chicken, dormice and pigeon were clustered on silver trays, amongst bowls of fruit and various salads. Some included raw purple carrots, or cooked marrow liberally spiced with pepper and ginger. Pennyroyal or mint was abundant in order to keep mouths fresh.

Just when it seemed that the guests were winning the fight to reduce the amount of food, a horn heralded the entrance of a man-sized sturgeon, carefully borne into the dining area whilst surrounded by dancing flute players with garlanded hairstyles and dressed in brightly-coloured tunics.

Squeals of laughter and simulated groans filled the air as the steaming platter was placed centrally on rapidly cleared tables. Silver slicers soon had the fish portioned, each with a spoonful of its salted, black eggs contrasting with the pink flesh.

As the dancing flautists left Urbicus gestured to those within easy earshot remarking "This was brought live to Britannia, especially for this occasion. Let's do it justice accordingly!"

Romana reached over and kissed his cheek as many tapped the tables in approval. Unnoticed, Aelia squeezed Agrippa's hand and they smiled self-consciously at each other, the short, stocky admiral colouring slightly at his unaccustomed vulnerability.

Because he was also a senior official in Petuaria for the Parisii tribal council, Ianuarius was not over-awed at being promoted to the High Table. Preparing to comment he glanced across at Felix but saw that Livia was holding him in her gaze and so held his wist. Instead he wiped up some of the prized caviar with a small, hot roll and sat back to listen to Petronius and Faber discussing the surgeon's own elevation.

The third couch at the top table comprised Clemens, Macer and Draco, all about the same age, well promoted and from similar backgrounds who, without realising it, had finished eating and drifted into a discussion on the respective merits of cremation and inhumation.

Macer added to what had already been said by observing, "Death is a very arbitrary thing. We each face it periodically, if not every day – and at some time we know we shall have no option. But what does it really mean?"

"I'm no philosopher," replied Clemens and Draco nodded his own agreement.

"Draco, here, will endorse what I'm saying because he's in the same position. Sometimes, when the ship's humming along and it's quiet, you get to thinking all sorts of things. These thoughts run the gamut from pure melancholy to the sublime. I suppose, if I *was* a philosopher, at this point I would question which end of that scale death fits – but I'm not one, either."

"That's so, Clemens. The sea does that to you," Draco confirmed, but then added, "so what are you saying it means, Macer?"

"I'm not sure I'm saying anything – more questioning something. Nobody, including me, really knows. However, I certainly can't equate with whoever cynically said something akin to 'I was not – I was – I am not – I do not care'."

"Written almost as a riddle," observed Draco. "You're saying there *is* definitely something?"

Nodding Macer replied, "Definitely. I started thinking during one evening voyage, about a chair, for example. I mean, it's dead timber obviously – but what if the *spirit* of the tree is still in it? If so, what does it appreciate? Thought? I wonder."

"It will wear out," Draco stated obviously.

"So it will. What then? Would the spirit of the tree still exist? After all, don't children – didn't we – give our toys a life form? Whose to say that it isn't for children to accept what they feel – they make inanimate into animate. They imbue a toy with life – just as if the spirit of the original element remains in it.

I've gone too far now – that's enough of me."

Taking his cue Clemens said, "Cremation is said to release the soul of the departed – yet burial gives somewhere to grieve, somewhere to go to remember. It's a human need."

"Our Rosalia," offered Draco.

"Come on, you three," called Aelia. "This is a celebration – not a wake!"

Quickly jolted out of their intensity both Clemens and Macer looked around at their partners further down the room to receive a stern look and a shake of the head, just as Draco did from his sister.

Just before the ensuing laughter died, Urbicus stood to address them. After thanking the gathering for their kind words and even kinder gifts on behalf of them both, he then told them of other plans.

"Tomorrow I intend to start work on a vivarium."

A buzz of excitement ran around the room before he went on, "A games will take place in Verulamium to celebrate their being formally declared the Second City of this forty-fifth state of the empire.

The town council will, of course, organize and run them. I understand there will be athletic contests in addition to the gladiatorial fighting – but also displays of animal prowess."

Another buzz started up at the thought of seeing potentially exotic animals so far north. In order to continue it was necessary for the governor to raise his hand. "The thoughts you have are those I, too, have.

There will be, of necessity, a pause between any animals arriving in this country and their use in the games. Some training of those animals may possibly be required – but it would be a crying shame to simply have the beasts locked away and miss the opportunity of drooling over them as I shall and, as I hope, you will also be able to."

Applause broke out spontaneously and he was forced to raise a hand again before he could go on. "Exactly where it will be I have yet to decide but my gut instinct, if the ladies will excuse the expression, is here in Londinium – or possibly just to the north. The animals will come into this port and, since Londinium has the largest population, more people will be able to gaze on them before they are transported to our new Second City."

Urbicus regained his seat to more applause and Livia quietly remarked, "You kept that very quiet. It's certainly made an impact on everyone here."

Smiling at her he replied, "No doubt it will get back to Rome. If it does, it will do my standing there no harm at all."

Hearing how he had phrased it Romana quickly said, "The idea was always to please the people, though."

Much later that evening, in the company of his top table guests and others of his hierarchy, Urbicus raised his cup and asked them to toast his future bride.

"Tomorrow," said Urbicus, "we shall have a beach party. We'll lie in the sun, swim, eat and talk – as usual, everyone equal."

Various words of agreement followed and they each drained their cups when Urbicus drained his, thoughts of bed now occupying most of their minds in the circumstances.

Ianurarius took Felix aside by the elbow and asked what a beach party comprised before adding, "Why was I included?"

"You need to be one of his confidants to have been invited. Look around you to see how many of us there are."

Grimacing at the small number, Ianuarius shrugged. "I do understand the honour – and welcome it – but it could be a two-edged sword. I may just as readily lose the confidences of my own associates."

"I see your point," responded Felix, "but it's far more likely you'll be sought out by them – and those beyond your own inner circle. If you involve them in the benefits you accrue I think your standing can only increase."

Pursing his lips for a moment the shipper replied, "Thank you for that – I shall take your advice. However, what's a beach party, as it was termed?"

Felix laughed. "Do you swim?"

"Not well, but yes."

"Then you'll have no problem. Go with the flow," observed Felix. "The important thing is to have no inhibitions. As the man said, on these occasions everyone is equal – say and do as you wish. No record is taken nor retained. It's a time to let your hair down and relax in good company, good wine and good food."

"Just that?"

"Absolutely! No more and no less."

"I have no partner," Ianuarius pointed out, "I shall lopside the party."

"Neither has Faber nor Petronius," countered Felix.

"No, I see that – but they form their own pairing."

"They will circulate. Once you've found your feet it'll all seem easier. The first time is always the worst – we've each experienced that."

"You're sure?"

"As I can be. Believe me, if you've been invited you're gold-plated. As I've said, go with the flow and you'll make hay while the sun shines. There's no need for embarrassment. Just be natural?"

"What do you mean by natural?"

"As nature intended, my friend. Just admire the beauty and feel as privileged as I do."

"Are you saying what I think?"

"Probably," retorted Felix laughing. "Just as long as you remember only to *admire* the beauty!"

★ ★ ★

A boat took the laughing, chattering group down into the eastern entrance of the harbour before turning due east along the shoreline to reach the end of the sandy beach running along the southern edge of the mainland, some distance below the palace on the estuary to the north.

"Interestingly these are called the Witterings," Agrippa said, to the laughter of the few who were able to hear over the hubbub, as the vessel was gently but positively nudged onto the beach.

While the servants carefully unloaded food from a second boat, a third made landfall further down and a contingent of legionaires disembarked, to reassemble in the tall dunes behind their charges. Camp fires were lit and a brew made for those not immediately on watch. They were a mixed guard, some of Felix' century mingled with those from the fort.

The warm sun shone from a perfect sky and was reflected in the placid waters lapping gently at the golden sands, turning their farthest reach briefly wet, only to dry as they immediately withdrew.

Without inhibition the first ashore threw off their coverings and made for the sea, anticipating the refreshing touch of the cool water. Laughing loudly the second wave disrobed and dashed after them, as eagerly anticipating the mild shock as their friends.

Almost dragged along in the welter of enthusiasm that surrounded him Ianuarius heard an unknown voice call, "Forget your fount – just get in!"

As soon as he had Felix appeared beside him and swam a few strokes explaining, "We've all known each other some time. There can be little not seen before."

Smiling at the thought, the still awkward shipper replied, "In this early-season water little is all that *will* be seen!"

Pleased that Ianuarius felt able to pun Felix suggested he join his group initially and then move on when he was ready.

"You're welcome to come ashore now, if you like. The girls are quite happy in the raw amongst their friends. Remember, my own wife and daughter will be there – you'll be welcomed."

"Regrettably, my wife died a few weeks after our baby – it was some time ago," Ianuarius said as he walked self-consciously out of the water, droplets falling feely to remind him of his nakedness. "For one reason or another I've not been like this outside the baths."

Livia and Julia watched the two well-built men walk up the beach chatting and could not help remarking on how handsome their guest was, apart from a rather large nose.

As they came together the two women stood, in order that no one was at a disadvantage in the circumstances, whilst in return Ianuarius struggled to keep his eye on their faces.

Felix told them of the shipper's loss and they sat on the dry, warm sand together, as condolences were offered.

"I was in my middle twenties," he explained, "but I found the double loss hard to bear. Fortunately I was able to throw myself into our – my - expanding business and, over time, I coped better and better. Really, I suppose, I ought to make the effort to try again – there's a good inheritance to be passed on!"

"I think," observed Livia, thinking it best to change the subject, "in that last sentence you have answered all our questions at once."

★ ★ ★

Lying naked on the warm beach Urbicus was expansive and he talked of his plans for when his governorship ended. A servant poured wine into his goblet and, as she retreated, he idly wondered what she would look like unclothed. It was a momentary, mad thought which he banished immediately, realising his old life was behind him – he had the lovely Romana.

"As I was saying, when my term is up it will be my last posting – at least, that's my own intention. Who knows the will of emperors?

At the moment I believe I shall go to Rome and take up my senatorial seat. It's my due. Presumably, may the gods bless him, Antoninus will still occupy the throne and he will confirm my status. I have the wealth – what I need is an end to my travels.

The alternative is to retire to one of my estates. I have them in Italia, Sicilia and my homeland of North Africa. Even then, should I tire of inaction, I may still enter the senate."

They all laughed at the idea of the senate being comprised of tired-of-retirement ancients until Clemens, recently returned from checking the guard dispositions, said, "You always favoured Sicilia – and its wines."

"If not Roma – then Sicilia. You're right. Naxos is in my heart."

"Not Libya then at all? You intend to forego it?" queried Julia, who had adjusted her position to kneeling with her legs apart, heels supporting her buttocks.

Ianuarius inwardly groaned and rolled over onto his stomach as he felt his passion rise. With so many beautiful breasts and bums so close, he could almost breathe the scents of their almondy skins.

Urbicus smiled wanly and waved away a sand fly. "Home? Home is where I find my helmet, these days. In any case I'm an entirely different person to the one who left the old Phoenician shores. I see so differently now – as you must all do. I was with Hadrian in the Jewish rebellion of a decade ago and it opened my eyes, so I tried to bring that experience to my governorship of Germania Inferior, which I was given after that.

I think Rome. Then I think Sicilia – who can tell? Perhaps, even, I could continue to live in this Albion of yours, Felix. I've come to love it. But what, then, of my successor? I would be an embarrassment of riches, to put it kindly.

Of course, Romana may yet hold the key," he added turning to the slim, naked form beside him.

Julia decided to sit cross-legged at that point and the shipper knew he could no longer concentrate on the governor's monologue.

"I have needs," he said, ensuring there was urgency in his voice, though realising he was far from acting the part. "I need the sea."

They watched him roll over with his back towards them and run for the solace of the cold water.

"Was it something I said?" asked Urbicus and they all laughed heartily. "Joking aside, you ladies. I empathise with him. I think I must join him."

* * *

Clothed servants ran to and fro replenishing small tables with wine cups as Livia sat cross-legged with both hands on one shin, obscuring her lower parts from most angles. Julia sat forward, legs irregularly drawn up, her head supported on a hand that required an elbow on a thigh for support.

Clemens looked at his wife and asked, "Are you oiled against this sun?"

She smiled at him and said, "I've herb extracts and olive oil rubbed in, my love – but thank you for the thought. Actually, Romana gave me a paste said to have been a favourite of Cleopatra's. It's beeswax, bee jelly and olive oil. I can't remember what else. She bought it in Londinium –

probably at a cost!" Looking away she changed the subject. "This is such a lovely day in such a lovely place I almost wish we'd brought young Clemens."

Blowing out his cheeks Clemens senior answered, "I know. But the danger is too great. Sand flies, too. We don't want him getting a fever, do we?"

Julia leaned over to him and he glimpsed her breasts hanging down, almost touching her legs as her hand caressed his knee.

Aelia sat up suddenly and, supporting herself on one arm, pulled at the sleepy Agrippa to join her. "Look! Up there – on the dunes to the high left. Someone's watching us!"

"We have guards on the dunes," Agrippa protested. "It's one of them."

"No? It was too far to the left."

Livia stretched her long frame backwards on her arms, one leg drawn-up for comfort, although her breasts were pulled full and wide nevertheless.

"Surely we're safe here, of all places," she said. "We have guards on the ships, guards in the dunes behind us and a good number of virile men-folk all around us. Who did you think you saw?"

Aelia screwed up her eyes and squinted again, "Whatever, it's gone now. I still think it was a man though."

Squirming through the sand on his stomach and taking care to keep below the marram tussocks, Haruld's scout was pleased with himself. Not only had he carried out his mission successfully he had also identified the women he was going to rape and then take back with him – given half a chance.

* * *

Aurelius Victor looked down from the dune top he occupied and sneered to Urbanus, who had been drafted as a medical orderly in case of accident, "There's not one of those middens down there that doesn't screw like a common whore. Yet what do we get by comparison when we're time-served? Any kids we've already got are no longer included in our citizenship award – only those dropped after discharge! Those bitches down there get the lot, simply by marriage."

Not knowing they were both already in opposing camps, the solidly-built, bald-pated Caecilius decided to persuade his old comrade to join him in the Geta Marcus group, but he would be careful to name no names.

His sour face screwed up as he agreed, "We ought to be down there swimming. Army regs state we should swim as often as possible in the summer. Look at them – none of them could care less," the orderly added as he squinted hard to look at Livia in the distance, sitting talking, with one leg sideways across herself. His bull-neck pulsed with passion as he imagined her arms around his naked back.

"If we *was* down there with them middens things would certainly go swimmingly, but I doubt we'd do much swimming – except on dry land!"

"I know someone who'd look after us both if we did him a favour or two," Caecilius observed, disregarding the comment but nodding at the same time. "Shall I drop a word?"

"I'll make me own way, old mate – but thanks for the thought…"

"You're not paid to think, you prat," growled acting-optio Paulinus suddenly appearing, "you're paid to watch – only not the ladies, just the dunes."

Neither had heard him steal up on them and they started, their weapons automatically half-raised.

"You'd both be dreaming dead dreams by now, if I'd been an enemy! Right – you each get your bloody arses over to that dune on the left," he said pointing. "I'll talk to you later!"

★ ★ ★

Her green eyes catching the sun the shapely Romana looked away, briefly dazzled and, leaning forward slightly, her small but otherwise perfect breasts took on a brief fullness.

Urbicus missed nothing and was roused by her drawing up one leg to put both arms around the shin, which increased the fullness of the thigh.

She laughed as she noticed him looking. "I think we ought to swim," she said and made for the sea, pleased that her breasts did not flop about as she ran, but gently bounced instead.

Her betrothed caught her as she splashed into a wavelet and she laughed again, as she realised what he would have looked like as he chased after her.

Avita's long, blonde hair hung down around her ears as she sat with Macer, her hazel eyes adding depth to the thoughtful, almost wistful, expression on her face.Coming to a decision, her nipples stood out as she rose to look down at her husband, one hand on a hip as the other arm hung loosely at her side.

"What I have you see," she began enigmatically. "Do you think the bloom on my tummy shows much?"

Almost dreamily Macer studied her from his prone position. "You're so beautiful I see no blemish of any sort."

Avita briefly touched her navel as she asked, "You still find me attractive, then. That's good," she added, almost pouting.

Realisation came to him and he stopped ogling his partner, reaching out instead to stroke one of her calf muscles, his mind racing as to what to say that would not sound juvenile in his delight.

His face looked serious as he regarded her navel once more. "I never really considered I'd ever have children, after what I told you about just before we were married. Because of that, I never once thought that you would look so wonderful pregnant." As he finished his boyish wide-toothed grin took over and he scrambled to his feet so that he could take her in his arms, locking their naked bodies together.

Julia had swum and then lain back in the shallows facing out to sea, her wet hair hanging down behind her as though a saturated rope. Propped on her elbows, with one leg slightly bent to help balance her against the gentle slope of the beach, she idly watched a seagull spiralling down to something in the water, but actually thinking how strange it was that there were pockets of warm water amongst the generally cold.

Looking up, on hearing the splash of water as someone entered it, she saw Avita standing there with the well-built figure of her sea-captain husband beside her.

Quite unselfconsciously she greeted them and then realised they wanted to speak to her. As she did the languid indolence that had unnaturally prompted her to do nothing left her as quickly as it had come.

Rolling over she drew her knees under her and came to her feet, immediately seeing that Macer, unused to being naked with her, had coloured slightly as she faced them.

"What a lovely looking couple," she remarked lightly, her happy-go-lucky style immediately coming to the fore as her bright-blue eyes twinkled with merriment. "Will you say it, Avita, or this handsome beast?"

Although thoroughly pink now Macer could not resist her smile and he grinned, as he inclined his head to his wife.

"We're pregnant Julia, I mean I am," Avita announced, both bashful and happy at the same time.

"Have you told your mother?"

"I thought I'd tell you first. You're like my elder sister since Carina's death – at least that's what I like to think."

Julia let the smile linger. "Shall we all tell her together? Then there's my father. Guardians need to know as well," she reminded her.

"Yes. Absolutely. At once. We shall," Macer managed in staccato fashion, wondering how he was going to stand naked in front of Avita's equally naked mother and talk of the product of sex so blatantly.

Julia stepped lightly between them and took an arm each. "Come on, let's do it now. The beach party can be your celebration, too!"

Chapter XVI

S tanding knee-deep in the wild-flower meadow Felix put a hand up to shield his eyes from the sun, as he peered down into the tree line at the bottom of the long slope.

In a sudden flurry of activity a dog went one way and his freed slave ran uphill towards him, stooping every so often to clamp a hand to her leg.

Then his dream moved on to her lying naked, sweating and convulsing, struggling against the strips of cloth that held her down. Groaning, her breath came in raucous gasps that he could do nothing about until suddenly, with a tremendous shudder, he realised that he could.

He fought against it but, somehow, the pillow was pushed into his hands and he was unable to stop it pulling itself down over the wet face.

From somewhere he heard Geta Marcus laughing as he called out that it was his rabid dog that had bitten her and now he, Felix, had had to suffocate her.

"Two bites of the cherry, so to speak – even better!"

Felix woke suddenly with those words on his lips and Livia held him tightly until he was fully awake and breathing quietly once more.

"Was it the dream again?"

He nodded and wiped the tears from his eyes with his forearm, remembering that he had freed his slave to marry her, only to end up putting her out of her misery. Then, having waited months to join her, had not contracted the infection after all.

"Faber might be able to help, my love," Livia offered but, as she looked at him earnestly, his response was to shake his head.

"I thought the dream had gone," he said. "I expect it will go away again when it's ready."

Holding him to her firmly, she kneaded the tight, bunched muscles in his back and then massaged his neck with her fingertips until she felt the tension go out of him. As it did he began to caress her body in response.

★ ★ ★

"The acting-optio came and told me, Sir," Titus answered, in response to the question. "But I've had my eye on Victor for some time – he's never enthusiastic about anything, Sir, nothing at all. I feel I need to check whatever he's supposed to do."

"A good optio does that for you, Titus, as you used to do. Was there more?"

"Well, Sir," Titus said, rubbing the back of his neck unconsciously as he screwed up his brow in thought, "Caecillius Urbanus looked in on his old mates, but he seems resentful, too! We spoke briefly and one or two things he said could have meant something else."

"Like what?"

"It was almost as though he was trying to tell me not to be so keen – it had got him nowhere – so he was going to look after himself."

"See himself all right?"

"That's about it, Sir, though he never actually put it into words, as such."

"You did the right thing coming to me. Now, don't do anything obvious, just keep watching Victor. I may want to use this to advantage – if it's what I suspect."

"What do you think?" Clemens asked, when the centurion had gone.

"I think it's the cause of several things happening – from attacks on the century to the pottery wagon attacks."

"He's providing inside information?"

"I would say so. Will you put something in the post to Petronius about Caecillius – use my personal seal on the wax. Same ideology – watch and wait."

"Keep us informed?"

"Yes, certainly – but also Urbicus."

★ ★ ★

"There's an old traveller at the gate, Sir. He's asking for you by name." Valerius was matter-of-fact about his announcement. "I would have had him driven off but there's something about him that might make him genuine – if down on his luck. He said he was a druid, so I suppose that's just what he would be!"

Felix chewed at the end of his pen as he regarded his steward until he realised what he was doing and threw it down, but nothing else was said about the strange caller.

"I'll see him, Valerius."

"Might I suggest you see him in the garden somewhere, Sir. He's been on the road some time."

Felix smiled. "I see. Very well, I shall attend the river garden."

The steward acknowledged the instruction and went out to find his quarry. In a few moments he returned saying in a puzzled voice, "He's nowhere to be seen, Sir. He seems to have disappeared!"

Felix smiled again. "I think I know where to find him."

"Sir?"

"I met one of his kind in Corinium some years ago – or so it seems now. Will you fetch out two cups of watered wine to the river garden?"

When Felix reached it he was not surprised to see the dishevelled old man sitting on a stone bench and looking down the sloping grass to the stream-like river below.

"I hear you come, Legate, although you tread quietly," the stranger said without looking round.

"How did you know it would be me?"

"How did you know I would be here?" came the reply.

"Where else would a mind reader go?"

"Who else would have come?"

Sitting on the bench next to him Felix said easily, "I bandied words with a druid once before."

"Thank you for the thought of watered wine – I have become used to only nature's water on my journey," he answered. Then, for the first time, the straggly-haired grey-bearded traveller looked at his host and there was the faintest of smiles as he registered the surprise on Felix' face. "Forgive me, but as I believe you have now guessed, that man was my father – Emrys Ap Harri."

Breathing out hard Felix leaned forward and put his forearms across his thighs as he looked sideways at him. "I remember him – I could not help him as he would have liked."

"Did you know his name was not as he was named – it was the one he used for Romans."

"Why? He knew I had a Briton for a father."

The mop of hair bobbed as he nodded. "He would have. We both have the gift, as his father did before him."

"You divine thought?"

"Stranger than that, even."

Now Felix nodded. "Yes, that's so – I experienced it. Why have you come? No! That's how I started with your father and he reminded me of my manners then."

"Alan Ap Emrys is my name – I am happy to use his chosen one."

Smiling at the anticipation shown Felix said, "Yes, You have the gift, too. May I now know your reason?"

Before he could answer Varerius came with a jug of cool wine and a beaker of water. His petite wife, Tabitha, swarthy and dark-haired, held a small tray of honey cakes. Her deep-green eyes regarded him over an enigmatic smile.

"You see, " observed the druid, "how your steward anticipated what you wished you had asked for? The gift is by no means only for a few."

Felix thanked them for the courtesy and dismissed them, offering the tray to Alan Ap Emrys who took two. "It will save time and effort later!"

After the druid had drunk deeply Felix again asked the reason for his visit.

"I have a dream to discuss with you – but before I do, let me thank you for your kindness to me. As for your own dream, it is because of the return of an acquaintance that you again feel guilt – do not any longer. There was nothing you could have done once you had chosen your road. Just as he chose his – then and now. It will go, with your help."

"My help?" Felix was at a double loss, as he had often been with Alan's father.

"Will you allow me to place my hand on your head?"

When Felix nodded the old man put down his burdens on the nearby table before turning to place both hands onto the waiting head. Felix was conscious of feeling relaxation running through him and then it was gone.

"You have no more fear of me than you had of my father – but then, as he told you, we are benign druids. We do not seek power from taken heads. Your dream should not return unless you wish it so."

"Thank you." It was all he could think of saying as he struggled to separate father from son.

"I suspect you are your father's son, as I am like mine – as ours would be of us if either had one. Now, to the reason for my journey."

Felix was no longer surprised at the anticipation, given his experience with the older druid.

"I have lived one hundred and twenty-five years. As you know, my father was older – as was his before him. It may be our druidic powers are waning. The storming of Mona took our heart though, I believe, not our spirit.

However, this is my last journey, as I have lived my life now. It is a fitting end."

"How do you know?"

"As my father did, we *know*. I hope to return to my starting point, but my time will come soon, somewhere.

I had a dream and it is a dream you must act on. Can you believe that?"

Felix nodded and the druid said, "Yes, of course. Your father is in you – *he* would have believed.

The dream was of a centurion – one of your own. He was being held somewhere with gushing water whilst his pregnant wife's legs were being tied together. It seemed they intended to beat her womb – it was to be a punishment for his informing on them. Then I woke and knew I must come to you. You would know where."

Felix had clenched his fists while Alan Ap Emrys was speaking. Clearly it was Firmus and Dorcas that were involved, so he asked, "When should I best react?"

The old man shrugged. "I only know what I am told in the dream. However, I would not have dreamt that dream if it was too late. Whatever you do, go quickly – I felt extreme urgency so I came as fast as I was able on foot."

"Druid. You've done well. You should live long – you're needed."

"Some would say I have lived too long already – Rome does not countenance Druidism. No, I have run my span. I can go beyond this life now, in hope of gentler years."

"Is there some way I can help you?"

Alan shook his mane. "There is nothing – but I thank you for the thought. If I may stay to finish the wine and the honey cakes I shall see it as more than my due."

"Alone?" Felix was puzzled.

Nodding his shaggy hair now, the old man explained, "My father had little time left and was pleased to be with you. However, I will sit and contemplate Samhain, when our old year finishes and another begins, if I have that long."

Standing, Felix placed a hand on the old man's shoulder before leaving him to his own devices.

★ ★ ★

Riding hard for the gold mine Felix and Clemens enjoyed the flowing movement of their well-trained mounts, regularly schooled by the two scouts, Aufidius and Papirius, each skilled as a hippiatros. They imagined the horses equally enjoyed the freedom after having been couped up aboard various vessels, as they crossed to the beginning of the Sabrina's western isthmus.

Both scouts had been sent ahead with Silva, the Balearic slinger, and his Ibizan hounds. They were to infiltrate the fort and the dogs were to distract the defenders before quickly retreating, not being fighting dogs. If the men found what was hoped not, they were to use ultimate force to stop it.

Since the legate of the Royal Second Legion had executed two men for treason Felix hardly expected the fort's remnants to be actively involved – but he knew it was far from certain.

Oddly, it was Firmus who met them outside the gates, but his agitation was obvious. "How did you know? Your scouts freed me. They still have Dorcas – she's close to time and they've tied her up. They're in the mine entrance!"

Slipping from his still moving horse, Felix briefly grasped him in his arms. "Now we're here things can go forward. Where are they, exactly. Keep calm, I need you!" Felix was conscious of the lie but it gave his ward's husband something to cling to.

Going past the gatehouse, which was now in their hands, Firmus pointed beyond the rock carving of Zeus with Minerva and Juno in his arms at the mineshaft which Felix still felt was strangely reached by a path leading uphill.

A few ill-assorted guards were half-hidden in the shadow of the entrance, but nothing else could be seen.

"She's due soon," Firmus said, "I'm told she doesn't need shock or trauma."

"So I believe," Felix said. "I've been there with Julia. But, to be clear in my own mind should it arise, your wife's the one to save if you have no choice? Is that so?"

"Yes," Firmus said determinedly! "Save our child – but Dorcas first!"

"Good," replied Felix. "Now we have our objective."

"I estimate about a hundred and fifty feet to the shaft," Clemens advised Felix. "We can make that easily in about fifty paces at the charge, even uphill."

"Is there an alternative?"

"I don't see one," agreed Firmus. "No! Hang on - Silva's dogs. They can harass the guards, who are no good even after more training. I'm afraid they'd be killed, though."

Thinking quickly of Silva, Felix said, "They're his dogs. He must agree before we can put them in. You know that!"

"I do, I do," granted Firmus, "but it's Dorcas. She's already tied. They may be beating her even as we talk! I was to be killed after I'd been forced to watch."

On the slinger's word the two dogs raced up the hill towards the dark entrance, their sharp eyes already picking up shadows. Each knew its role – they were not fighting dogs, but chasers and harriers.

Two spears came at them but missed their narrow, head-on targets. Undeterred, the dogs bounded on, keen to carry out their instructions to harry and worry.

More spears faced them as they approached the entrance so the dogs stood at bay, as they would against horn or antler. Trained, they postured and taunted, natural instinct taking over what training did not cover.

The first sling stone took out a guard's eye and he dropped his spear, screaming for help as he tried to push it back in.

The second shot was between the eyes of his companion and he pitched over backwards, barely knowing of its contact before he died.

Both dogs growled ominously and edged forward, but no one moved – as far as the guards were concerned the disregarded statue of Rome's major gods was working its magic to avenge.

Released by a whistle both fawn-coloured hounds galloped unharmed down the slope to their master, who received their charge rapturously, patting, rubbing and tickling them in their enthusiasm, more pleased than they were in their survival, as he loudly welcomed them.

"Come out now! You're guilty of heinous crimes. If we have to capture you it will go ill – if you surrender note will be taken of your reticence to go further. Some of you may even yet convince me of your relative innocence," shouted Felix. "But you must do it now – with no harm to the woman! Without it you'll be stoned, whipped or crucified to death. There will be nothing easy – but the choice is yours."

Five soldiers charged down the rise but the javelins that took them came from behind, so that they spilled down the slope to end in side bushes.

In the momentary quiet Felix thought rapidly. Then he signalled to Clemens and Firmus, striding up the steep rise with them.

There was only a brief impasse before an array of weapons clattered out into the mottled shadows at the entrance to the gold mine.

"There's only the one way in, for security reasons," Firmus told them. "I've checked that."

Several screams set them back, but none was a woman's and they allowed the remaining men to file sheepishly down to the flat area of the site entrance.

In the rear four men appeared, hesitantly carrying a naked Dorcas on two upturned shields – her limp arms hanging uselessly over the edges. To their relief the three officers saw that her distended abdomen was still intact.

"Get her a proper bed, then find a local midwife and take her with you to Isca. I ask the gods you arrive safely," Felix said to Firmus, dismissing him.

"Put those four over there, when they get down," ordered Felix pointing at one of the sheds.

The two scouts were the first into the mine and, apart from bodies, thought it was clear. Felix accepted their view. They would both have listened for breathing, as well as obvious movement, long before taking a breath themselves and checking for recent signs going into the depths. There was no surety but he doubted any could move in the slippery, echoing darkness to deceive his men.

Clemens ordered the surrendered captives into line and then stepped back beside Felix to allow his father-in-law to address them.

"All you men know your fate. You have rebelled against your officers and those of you who are immunes are particularly culpable. Rebellion against your officers is rebellion against the state. This state is part of the empire and therefore you rebel against the emperor. If any disagree take a pace forward and face your comrades."

No one stood forward. All trusted to luck and their personal gods, hoping their conduct had not offended them.

"I've no liking for my judgement, except that it's our law - a law which you all accepted on enlistment. I cannot accept that your immunes didn't take the lead. They are all guilty, just as you are aware decimation is the law for the rest of you!"

Hearing this the non-commissioned officers made to run but the century took them easily. Everyone else licked their lips and breathed heavily, casting furtive glances at their neighbours.

"In view of your leaders' admission of guilt by attempting to escape, only two others will be selected. You've brought this upon yourselves. The chosen number is fifteen!" Felix made the choice of number based on how many more he had said would be selected.

"No!"

The man who shouted was apprehended as he moved in desperation, having already calculated his place. A second along the line swayed as the count picked him out, but he walked away with his guards resignedly.

Wooden clubs were brought from the fort's store, but Felix regretted the delay in finding them. The death was deserved but the wait was torture and he deplored it.

Surrounded by armed guards the remaining prisoners took their places in a circle.

"Any man who fails to carry out his legal duty will take his own place there. Let the punishment be carried out!"

Forced to watch the required act both officers were sick to their stomachs, as they watched the clubs being wielded by the victims' compatriots. Some were taken high and brought down hard, others in a horizontal mode, only for the blows to change the receipient's posture, causing others to miss their intended target and thud in elsewhere. As screams of pain and howls of fear hung on the air Felix was forced to swallow – he hated the idea that regulations demanded soldiers be killed in this way, for various crimes besides this one.

Blood spattered and puddled until finally there was no movement in any body under blows. At that point Clemens signalled a halt to the execution, breathing a sigh of relief. On his signal the bloodied clubs were thrown onto the corpses for rough burial with them and the men once again formed a line.

"Be aware, you have not redeemed yourselves. I ruled on the law, as I was both empowered and required to do. I now pass you over to your legionary commander for his action. You will obviously be redeployed – I hope to the far north, where you may actually discharge your vows to the emperor.

Under the guard of my century you will form rank and file – then march south to the estuary with full equipment where you will be embarked for your legionary fortress. Should you not arrive your life will be forfeit, as will your family's pension. Single men I shall personally hunt down! Tribune, arrange for this dross to leave my sight!"

"It was necessary," Clemens said later, trying to be supportive.

"I know, but it gave me no more pleasure than it gave you."

On the journey to see Sextus their spirits rose, allowing Felix and Clemens to laugh at the situation that had arisen when Firmus, just before he left, had again asked how they knew.

"A druid told me," Felix had replied.

Firmus had shrugged and as he turned away had muttered," Ask a silly question…"

★ ★ ★

"There are just so many nooks and crannies – inlets, small natural harbours, estuaries and rivers for these ships or boats, or whatever craft they are, to hide in. That's not to mention mists that blind the watch – nor the black of night.

The favoured boats are fast, slim and agile. Double banks of oars give them speed and mobility. My biremes are the only suitable ships to pursue them – if they find them. I don't have enough. By the way, Macer made this exact speech to me!"

Agrippa grabbed his beaker and swallowed, as Urbicus rubbed his forehead. "You've presumably sent to Bononia?"

"Of course. It's my right and privilege. You cannot run the fleet, too. It's why I'm here!"

"I don't challenge your right, Agrippa! The fleet's yours – you were made fleet procurator, quite sensibly. I wouldn't have questioned your action, in any event. The problem, as I see it – not being a seaman - is that we cannot build boats fast enough, in any case. We need ready-mades."

Agrippa put down his empty beaker. "You see it well. That's the very need – and Bononia says they've none to spare. Their own Gaulish seaboard takes all their resource. I was quietly informed we're lucky not to be told to provide relief!"

Urbicus spread his arms. "We have desert recruits manning our freezing northern defences. Warring tribesmen – the damned Brigantes in particular – fighting us, too, if we give them half a chance. The Cambrian tribes – Silures to the front – pay lip service and, as you point out, there are so many miles of concealed coast that any raider can slip into. The Hibernians trade - but I wonder what else they do, with a coastline like ours?"

"You echo my own thoughts, Urbicus." Agrippa would have preferred to call him governor but paid due deference to his wish for private informality. "Can you do anything to rectify things?"

Thinking hard and sipping his wine to gain time Urbicus finally observed, "The short answer is no, I can't. But, of course, that helps less and the one thing that can be of use quickly is, as you implied, to build more ships since there are no others.

To me the east and south-east coasts are well patrolled by us and the main base at Bononia is just across the water, so could not ignore anything they did see. Ergo. That leaves the southern and southwest coasts - as ever, I expect you to say. But that's where we need a shipyard. What do you say?"

"I agree the need."

"You're concerned about money or workforce?"

"Both! Naturally we can raise import and export duty – but where's the labour? Most of our spare forces are on duty in the north."

A further silence followed until Urbicus said, "We'll trawl the legions. There have been inter-legion transferees who may have some experience. I'll have the veteran's lists checked, too. Don't you have sailors who've been involved?"

"So few, I regret. In any case I need them as deckhands," replied the little admiral, he thought obviously.

"Well surely some, if not all, of your marines must have observed how to be shipshape – after all, they don't fight in harbour," Urbicus retorted.

Agrippa pulled at his ear. "I'll see, of course – and possibly borrow a legionary or two, if I need replacements," he finished, smiling at the thought.

Smiling in return the governor said, "A good point – though I'll find you auxiliaries to fit the bill."

Chapter XVII

S itting quietly in his office Felix finished his missive to the governor. He had made several recommendations on the ship shortage, reminding Urbicus that the Celtic tribes in the south still traded with Gaul, going over in small vessels they built themselves. They also built substantial wooden houses.

Therefore a man skilled with an adze, a chisel or a saw could, at least potentially, use those skills in a different theatre, under the guidance of Roman shipbuilders. He pointed out that his own local chieftain, Stolus, built small boats whilst yet others were built in the river opposite Vectis, as he recalled.

Having added various other unrelated suggestions he had then recommended bravery awards for the two scouts and the slinger, pointing out that this was one of several instances which should now be recognised.

After checking his work he rolled the papyrus and placed it in a cylinder, dropping melted wax onto the ties and impressing his ring seal into it. Tossing the sealed scroll into a wicker basket to await collection he leaned back and put his hands behind his head to think.

What had he made of Sextus? The legate had considered the fort safe after the original executions and sent Firmus back there to retake control. He had retained his usual advisers for some reason best known to himself, which meant there were no guarantees that other situations would not arise.

He wondered again whether he should have conveyed his thoughts to the governor, but came to the same answer – that that would have made it official. Although there was a loose friendship with Sextus which they had formed during the impromptu skirmish there, which now seemed distant, the man had since been confirmed as the legion's commander. As this was some time ago now, he should be capable of sorting out any problems that arise himself, Felix concluded.

Had he been right about feeling a certain abstraction on Sextus' part, albeit his denial that anything was wrong?

There again, what of the woman in the legate's life – *had* she vamped him? He saw it as nothing less, laid back as she was on a cushioned bench in the headquarters garden, languidly he would have said since one leg draped indolently over the side, whilst her blonde hair framed the head cushion like some golden halo.

Even had the hanging leg contributed to her dressing gown pulling apart at that moment to slip off the leg and expose its whole tanned length – presumably one of a long pair, he smiled to himself – hadn't she taken just too long to recover the errant garment?

Then he was dragged back to the present by a knuckle rapping on the door jamb. Glancing around he saw Valerius and Tabitha standing in the doorway.

"I'm sorry to interrupt, Sir, but I'm certain my wife has something important to tell you."

Sitting up and turning the chair Felix smiled encouragingly at Tabitha. As always he was pleased it had been long enough since the violent gang-rape for her to have made a full recovery, becoming the capable woman of the present rather than the insolent waif she had been then.

"What've you to tell me Tabitha? Your information's been very useful in the past."

Gently clearing her throat she began, "I'm just a little reticent, Sir, because it involves your niece – that is, the lady Livia's."

"Go on. You've nothing to be worried about – not after all these years."

With a wan smile at his words she thought again of being set up by him as a bordello madam to glean information from her girls concerning particular clients. Then she said, "Minerva came by me in the market place yesterday, Sir. She took me aside and insisted I rehearse a message for you. It was this.

'I know that you have no liking for me but I also know that you pursue Haruld, the-one-eyed. He will be on the Swanwic shore in two days time. He will land to meet Quintus to further the contract he has with him to kill you. If you wonder why I tell you – consider who it was who killed my mother, Sabina. Look for him in the evening as he goes to the quarry for the meeting."

After a brief pause Tabitha shrugged slightly and said, "That was word for word, Sir, I'm certain of that."

"So am I, my girl. You have a performer's memory, after all. Is that everything you have to say?"

"It is, Sir," confirmed Valrius.

"Well done. You obviously realise you must not discuss this with anyone else – you'd be familiar with that, Valerius?"

"Quite so, Sir. We shall go?"

"Yes," he agreed and then added as they turned away, "Thank you, Tabitha. You've proved very useful once again."

* * *

Felix urged his mount to a fast trot down the now poorly repaired road to Corf, with Clemens and Titus following hard on his heels whenever he raised a canter or better.

They immediately turned off and arrived at Stolus' village, where he met them.

"I was informed of your haste," he explained in his much-improved Latin, "so I assumed it was an urgent matter and needed my personal presence."

Lifting his leg over the horse's mane cleared his pommel and Felix slid off, grasping the forearm offered in salute.

"What can I get you whilst we talk?" Stolus asked, as they made for his newly-finished house.

"Anything wet and strong will do me – and I imagine for these two reprobates as well."

Clemens and Titus grinned as they were guided into the main room. They commented on the boldness of the colours and the panelling effect as they waited for the refreshments to come.

Then Stolus said, "I suspect there's no time to waste – we should move on."

"Thank you, my friend," replied Felix kindly. "The fact is, as you might have guessed, I'm looking for your help."

"You always have what I'm able to give – though I owe you more."

At that moment his wife came in bringing wine and sweetmeats personally. Felix took the opportunity to say how good it was to see her well and that she looked so happy.

"Galina is carrying a child again. We're more than pleased about that, as you might expect," explained Stolus.

After spontaneous congratulations from all three the young chieftain, still smiling broadly, asked her to leave them to their deliberations and they watched her leave gracefully.

Handing round the wine and telling them it was a the last he had of Felix' first pressing, he went back to the interruption, saying, "As to help it could only be so. Tell me how?"

Enjoying his own wine in another's house amused Felix, but he answered seriously, "One-eye is due in Swanwic in two days. He'll go on to the quarry. I've enough men to front him but not enough to confine him, if he declines battle. Should he do so, have you enough fighting men to contain his withdrawal until we come up?"

Throwing his arms wide Stolus growled, "This peregrine insults the Durotriges by thinking he can land in Purbic at will. When he attacked your house in a previous incursion I thought we taught him a lesson – but he doesn't seem a willing pupil. You contain him – *we* will front him!"

With a grim smile Felix replied, "I know you would, but he's wanted under Roman law, for crimes against it. Regrettably I am only looking for your help, not your solution. We must try to take him. Will you still help?"

"Of course," Stolus responded immediately, "But I cannot *guarantee* he will survive."

★ ★ ★

The two days passed and Felix had his men hidden in depressions behind the steep hillside leading upwards from the beach, on the side of the bay opposite the white cliffs, which was the quickest ascent to the quarry area.

Eventually a long, low vessel with an ornately carved prow crept around the corner of the small bay and sidled along under the cliffs, before suddenly pulling hard towards the beach, presumably satisfied of its safety.

As it ground on the shingle at the end of the otherwise sandy shore running almost north away from them, men jumped off the bows into the shallows to heave on the lines and drag the fast-lightening vessel further in before making it fast.

With the square-rigged sail long-since furled the remaining warriors grabbed their round shields and released their war axes before slipping over the longboat's clinker-built sides. Most wore helmets that sat on the head rather than surrounded it, some plain and others with varying styles of mounted horns.

"Slip over to your detail and make sure they don't move except on my signal," Felix whispered to Clemens and watched him slide further below the skyline before crossing the depression.

His plan was to allow the group to climb the steep slope and then attack them just before they breasted the scarp. Once the attack began Stolus was to bring his men out of the nearby woodland and sweep down to the beach along the bay's shallow central valley to take the boat, cutting off One-eye's retreat.

Felix signalled and his men rose, javelins projecting beyond their curved shields. Even his half-century looked formidable as its two details attacked from different angles.

A thrown javelin took a man in the middle of his poorly-armoured body and he screamed as he was stopped in his tracks, then again as its impetus toppled him backwards down the slope to collide with other warriors climbing behind him, bringing some down.

Now shouting the infantry cry 'mars ultor' his men charged over the rim, scattering the surprised and ill-prepared enemy. Wearing only chainmail for convenience, instead of their normal segmented armour, they were able to move faster and more freely. Shields clashed together and sounds of battle echoed as axes, swords and spears met in anger, some drawing blood as sweat ran freely to join it.

Felix was conscious of one of his men falling and aware that another in the other detail was about to receive a double-handed axe blow to his back – but he could do nothing for either as he rammed his shield boss into a glowering face and stabbed under it, feeling the familiar jarring up his arm as the blade went home. Then, twisting and withdrawing it, he smelt the odour of warm blood.

At that moment he saw Haruld-one-eye out of the corner of his eye and smiled at the inadvertent pun. Apart from the jagged facial scar Felix would not have recognised him, fighting as though he was a simple warrior and not their leader.

Knocking another man down the rise Felix took the opportunity to slip backwards out of the line without disrupting it only to find that, before he could close on his adversary, Haruld was calling his men away.

The reason, Felix realised immediately, was that instead of charging the boat and so losing their opportunity for revenge, Stolus' force had divided and one unit was crossing the hill laterally to join in the fight.

With the intruders now retreating Felix doubted Stolus had enough men to hold the boat and cursed. A perfectly good plan had been ruined by impulse.

Knowing the difficulty of maintaining a regular line downhill on a steep incline at speed, Felix shouted for his men to throw their javelins and drop their shields, in order to fight with their swords and daggers as they ran down an opponent. It was a risk he thought he could take.

The now even more lightly- armoured Britons leaped boulders and took greater risks, as they sped after their quarries. Individual fights took place, often with opponents rolling on the turf or sliding down the escarpment together.

Felix' men were outdistanced and forced to settle for an occasion strike on wounded men who refused to surrender, or at any suddenly coming to life after feigning death, since neither could be left to fight again.

Reaching the beach the remaining invaders split into two groups, one standing to await Stolus' charge whilst the smaller slashed the holding lines and heaved at their vessel, straining to push, shove and drag it into the shoaling waters. With a final squelch it gave up its berth and floated free, allowing some to climb aboard as crew and others to form a second line of defence, calling the first line back to them.

"It's a shambles, Clemens! We had them cold – now we'll be lucky to wave goodbye," Felix shouted to his son-on-law as they reached the level ground beside the beach.

Waiting only to throw their battle-axes at Stolus as his men charged, the original group of Norse fled backwards in order to be tossed replacement weapons from the boat.

Grudgingly Felix granted that these men could fight, particularly with their backs to the wall, though it was a fleeting thought. It was replaced by a forlorn wish that he had had archers with him – but he had none and Britons only used arrows to hunt.

The boat was drifting off at an angle in the slight breeze with a few oars pulling on the landward side to turn it away. Encouraging his men to charge Felix nevertheless realised there was too much ground to cover and no real chance of clambering up the vessel's sides as it went into deeper water, in any event.

Leeching away, some of their enemy jumped the wavelets before plunging into the water to swim after their boat, where they were offered oars to cling to until they could be pulled in.

Those bravely remaining were cut down and Stolus held back the few of his men who could swim because he also considered further pursuit was pointless.

Felix knew that his own swimmers had no chance of succeeding wearing mail – not even Amatus who could swim in full armour, as all Batavians were trained to do.

Stolus came up to him and in silence they watched the escaping swimmers being pulled aboard. When the sail went up there was a corporate groan from the legionaries.

"I am sorry, my friend," Stolus began apologetically. "Those who broke away were men who had had their farms burnt, or families killed, by these vermin. We'd been looking for them in the woodlands, as you know, when we found your house under siege last year. I'm responsible for this fiasco – but I can't blame them."

Breathing out and holding his temper Felix almost grunted his reply. "Whatever the reasons it's too late now. We had him in our grasp and lost him. However, I doubt we could've taken him anyway without your support so I'm grateful for that, at least!"

"I estimate they lost half a crew. That's a victory, surely," the young chieftain proposed defensively. "That'll be a severe handicap to them."

Furrowing his brow as his mind raced Felix suddenly exclaimed, "It might well – indeed it might. Look, get a boat into the Wych as soon as possible. I want you to take both my scouts across the harbour to save them going round it. They're with our horses, about a mile inland."

"A messenger to your naval outpost at Portus Ardoni?"

"You have it! One will get there, at least. We've had our ill-luck – now, perhaps, it's our turn to throw the dice and find a Venus!"

Stolus thought that a Venus must be the highest throw in dice but said nothing. It was not the time. He knew his men had let him down, causing him in turn to let his friend down, because they were no longer battle disciplined in the peaceful south. All his tribal lands were at peace with their neighbours, just as Roman rule required. It was best left alone now.

They threw their enemies' corpses into a hastily dug pit in a depression and tossed additional earth from higher up down onto it, then stomped it flat.

Their own dead and injured they took back with them – first to Corf for refreshment and repair where possible, as well as to embark the scouts, then on to Waerham for local burial of bodies.

It was Clemens who had suggested direct interment, as it was coming into favour in Rome. Believing the innovation would sit well with the men who regretted any particular deaths Felix had agreed, thinking that remembering the dead at Rosalia would be a busy time this year.

It was full dark when they reached the small town, having travelled the last few miles under flaming torches, whose light sometimes reflected from unknown animal eyes amongst the trees that flanked the road, before they finally crossed the bridge of boats that took them over the lower river.

★ ★ ★

Draco sailed into Pwll harbour and anchored, taking his cutter into the shallows and up to the town quay, where Felix met him having been told of the 'Sabrina's' arrival.

"My friend Draco – good to see you," Felix said warmly, as they grasped forearms.

"As you must have seen from my message I may have some work for your ship. Let's take the chariot back to the house and talk it over – though the decision must be yours, of course."

In no time they were sipping some of Livia's honeyed apple juice in the shady garden.

"Let me see what I know and therefore what I need to know," suggested the young, bearded captain. "You almost caught this Norseman but he managed to escape with half a crew. Last seen he was heading westward. I assume you have an urgent need for action, as your two scouts rode most of last night."

"That's about it," Felix agreed. "We strongly suspect that he uses Silura and Monavia as raiding bases – but probably spends more time on Hibernia."

"Monavia's far to his north at the moment," observed Draco, "and he would need to round the tip of Albion to reach *any* of the places you've outlined. Silura is his nearest base – but I doubt he would have left additional crew there."

"I wondered whether he might have pulled in to reorganise his boat, knowing we weren't able to follow."

Draco inclined his head in partial agreement. "It's certainly possible – he'd probably need his remaining best rowers at the back and his strongest in the middle. Losses may well upset the previous rhythm. What you're saying is that he's likely to have spent precious time on that – in terms of otherwise gaining sanctuary somewhere?"

"Exactly so," Felix agreed and then asked, "but would I be right in thinking that loss of rowers would make the boat lighter certainly – but still slower?"

Draco rubbed his face. "Sea conditions would play a part – but, yes I agree with you in principle. I think the rowers would tire quicker, too."

"Good – excellent, in fact." Felix said. "So, on to my request. I think that if they make it round the tip – and they're seamen enough to do so, apparently – they won't bother with Silura. It would amount to an unnecessary detour, as well as being on the route of our ships in the Sabrina river channel. Yes?"

"Yes," agreed Draco, nodding and smiling. "We may convert you to the navy yet!"

"I'm army through and through," retorted Felix. "Now. My view is that there's a possibility they'll rest-over somewhere well below Herculis promontorium before pushing on from Dumnonia direct to Hibernia."

"They'll need several stops," Draco interjected, "but there are good hideaways all along that coast, if they keep away from the tin mines and our patrols. So, again, you make sense in general – for a landsman!"

"Cheeky young sod!" Felix' smile took most of the sting out of his words, but nevertheless emphasised that familiarity could come later. "For your impertinence, tell me if you can embark what remains of my bodyguard. Without mounts, in case you ask."

Taken slightly aback Draco told Felix he could, but extra rations would be needed. "They seem to be sailors," he observed.

"Most are, now. One will be hanging over the side – always has."

"Not a marine, then?"

"As a matter of fact he was, but transferred for that reason. You may remember he swims well, though. However, I want your opinion on how fast we can reach Hibernia – cutting them off, if possible."

"Across the canals?"

"I discounted that. Although our signal stations could arrange for a ship to be waiting I don't think we'd actually be any closer to Hibernia than now. The land crossing works – but not for that particular destination. In any case it wouldn't be you in command then."

"No, afraid not," Draco agreed. "Still, if they're forced to rest up frequently we could catch up – but it's doubtful, I fear. I don't know exactly how many crew they have – capturing a few inexperienced peasants on the way wouldn't help – so their speed and capacity is all guesswork. How efficient is their sail? What of sea conditions? If they did, as you suggest, hug the coast in the general direction of Herculis Prom it could take them two, three or four days, give or take, but they'd still have a pull of some forty miles, to make even southern Cambria from there. However I'd hate my life to depend on such vagueness."

"I see your point, young sir. However, my view is still that, properly provisioned, we could round land's end and push north, directly to Hibernia. Would we be faster?"

Draco scratched his head. "Again, tides, wind, type of sea – even with our specially raised sides a really heavy sea's an issue. So I can only say – I would expect so."

"That's all I want to hear Draco. Let's do it! How do we get my men on board?"

★ ★ ★

Felix wondered why the gods were so well disposed as they sped northwards under oar and sail, closing quickly with the extreme south-eastern reaches of Hibernia. Turning north-east they made landfall, erecting a shore camp on a headland. From it they would see any vessel close to or, if the light was right, on the distant horizon.

Making fires behind shields, to disguise the bright flames, they lay back, ate, chatted and, for the first time, drank wine. The warm food, pleasantly washed down, released their tensions and enabled most to sleep well. It was the three officers, Felix, Clemens and Draco who were fitful, waking to check on each change of watch and to look at the horizon themselves.

Dawn drove them on, sail and oar combining easily in a following breeze, every man willing the ship forward. It was as though, Felix thought, each man had a personal interest in anticipating this upstart northern raider so that, defeated, the sea routes of Rome's most northerly outpost would be the safer. He hoped so, as the ship crested waves in the Hibernian sea and he readied himself for the next swell.

The trading promontory they sought, with its supportive inner sandbank, was the logical destination of the One-eyed, situated as it was about a third of the way up Hibernia's eastern seaboard. Whatever its true name Draco knew it as Drumanagh, which Felix unconvincingly translated as being akin to 'The Lookout'. Fluent in Celtic he was still unable to place the name accurately in Erse, the Celtic variation of Hibernia.

As they neared it without having sighted their quarry, they were surprised to see a narrow boat, its sail in tatters, make for the isthmus behind the headland and ground there.

A cross section of expletives came from more than just the 'Sabrina's' officers, as the drumbeat eased off the pace. Now, they all knew, it was up to diplomacy.

Felix and Clemens put on their parade armour, personally polished and packed by Valerius as a precaution, as the 'Sabrina' watchfully reached for a mooring and dropped anchor. That the power of Rome had now to reach this far, was in Felix' mind.

Put ashore in their cutter they stepped down onto the sand before finally putting on their helmets, the transverse plumage marking them out as officers.

A small group of tribesmen waited for them, whilst Haruld and his men stood off to one side, just beyond their own boat's prow. Though tired and blooded they were still interested in the outcome.

As the two officers walked up the shingle-mix one of the tribal group detached himself and came forward to confront them.

"I am Osian Mac Ior, Osian the son of Ior, the Lord of the North," he told them, in halting Latin. Then he asked them directly, "Why do you come in armour to my lands?"

Clemens stepped forward to introduce Felix in order to emphasise his importance. "This is Augustus Albinus, Legate to Quintus Lollius Urbicus, governor of Britannia and friend of Antoninus Pius, Emperor of all the Roman Empire."

"I am the Taoiseach, accepted leader you would say, so I ask again, why have you come armed when we trade with Britons and Roman-Britons?"

Osian Mac Ior stopped speaking and watched as the century dropped over the ship's side one by one and waded ashore. He also saw that the ship's complement of twenty marines remained at readiness on board.

Clemens said, "We come in peace to talk, since we wish you to return these men to us who have broken our laws."

The Taoiseach smiled at that and pointed in the direction of Haruld. "These men are of the north – as was my father. I have no sway over them to give them to you."

The pursued group grinned as those who understood this muttered amongst themselves.

Felix spoke, slowly and evenly. "We come in peace, but if you harbour our enemies you put our intention at risk. Have the men drill," he instructed his son-in-law, without losing eye contact, then heard the order passed to Titus.

The group of tribesmen looked at the assembled men with suspicion and their hands moved to their weapons, resting there without drawing them.

Given the command the men performed their wordless drill on the firm surface of the beach, impressing the watchers as they impressed an audience anywhere, although on this occasion, as they completed the last manoeuvre, there was no clap of appreciation.

"Very pretty," Osian commented, "A welcome dance I assume?"

"My men fight better than they drill," Felix said quietly. "I don't expect them to have to fight!"

Only Osian heard that and wondered what to make of it. Was it a threat – or did it remove the threat, he pondered? He knew a horn call would bring hordes of warriors to him, but that would be provocative, he decided – and there was no point in antagonising what he knew to be a greater power than his own.

Felix went on, "It's not my intention to offer you the chance of a place in your Great Tomb. I come in peace."

"You know of it?" Osian Mac Ior questioned, almost in disbelief.

"I'm told it's from the ancient past, say three thousand years – but what is time? It is, perhaps, even older than the great stone henge in Albion."

"I've heard our magicians speak of that place," he replied. "I know nothing of it, except our storytellers say that two beaten-gold earbands were taken across the water to appease the gods when it was finished. Why do you talk of Albion's stone henge?"

"Doesn't your Great Tomb also tell you the longest and shortest days? Does not a beam of light come in and retreat, to link the living to the dead?"

"It's more than that. There are discs the magicians use, aligned to the horizon.

Their magic number is eighty-two – I don't know why. Only they access it. I do not, since I am neither magician nor priest."

"Neither am I, Taoiseach. I just change the living to the dead, if that is what they crave. These men have killed – women would say worse – so they must be judged."

At the mention of the original point Osian realised he had been sidetracked. Thinking quickly he said, "These men trade with us regularly. We know them. In fact, we welcome them."

Cutting across the homily Felix said, "I'm sure you do and it's not difficult to guess the trade. I assume you have all manner of visitors who seek other than metals, dogs and plunder!

So, surrender these men or blow a horn to summon your tribe – and see how Romans die! Then you can wonder how short a time it will be before a legion lands to take you *and* your kingdom. What reaction would there be by the other tribes? The Cauci, the Darini and the Robogdii, I believe – to name only a few. Is that what you'd prefer?"

Osian Mac Ior wished he had time to think, but realised he did not. He was now on the defensive and he knew it.

Seeking compromise without losing authority he countered, "You speak of Roman justice. What would you call it – Iustus Romana? So I give you a just verdict. These men are under my protection. You may go without offence – they stay! When you're no longer on the horizon they will launch, too. After that, you do as you please – as they shall."

Felix warmed to the scnse of that decision and agreed. "It's done. The horizon will determine the outcome!"

Chapter XVIII

Quartering the sea behind them, in the dimming light, Draco remarked, "We can hope their sail's up, but it won't be. When it is though, it'll be bright and shiny like any new one!"

Felix said, "If they don't have another boat, I shall be surprised. We were told they're well known here!"

"Damn," offered the young captain. "How can I have overlooked that so easily?"

"How often have you negotiated a fight? They weren't about to be given up that easily."

"I see your point – it's one I'll remember. Macer said you were a man to follow. Right – back to the moment. We must keep down moon."

"Now that's a good sailor's point," Felix observed encouragingly. "We have to spot them or we'll give them too much sea-room to be caught."

"Where will they go?"

"No idea. None! Possibly try for Mona or Monavia? If so, we have to be in a position to prevent it. If they make landfall there or another island it will give free access to Britannia. We *must* prevent that, at all costs."

"Where do you think, then? Stay north-east for now?"

"Yes. We must drive them southwest, if possible, away from Albion. I'd love the southern pirates of Iberia to have them – poetic justice – but I suspect not. They probably forage slaves for them.

Our best opportunity would be to push them on and isolate them in the Sarnian islands off the point of Gaul. What do you think?"

Draco looked puzzled. "You're not a sailor, yet you repeatedly discuss sailing destinations. How is that?"

As the ship drew further away from Hibernia Felix explained, "I was once told in the legion – know your enemy. After I absorbed that gem I thought about it, because it worked well. Then I produced what I thought was my own gem - *know your friend.* That is, be well prepared. I looked at charts Macer had sometime prepared for his mentor, Agrippa. He'd kindly copied them to me. It's horrendous what we don't know – you sailors have my heartfelt appreciation – but equally, to a landsman, marvellous what we do.

If we can drive him by our presence – or even suspicion of it – to those islands they are small enough for us to find them. At least one island, marine Amatus told me, is so reef-bound as to be dangerous – even to the regular traders and naval vessels. It's Lisia, he said – the nearest usable. Apparently it's a normal call on the Inner Sea to Northern Gaul route, via Iberia. No doubt you know it since we obviously have marked charts. I doubt One-eye has".

"Good – I'd love to nail that bastard."

"What do we have on board as weaponry?"

Draco grimaced. "Nothing. Well, that is, we still have the scorpion Macer had had mounted in the bow. I couldn't get on with it, so it's stored below in the bilges."

"Get it up! If it's dirty get it working! Yes. That's just what I want!"

"You know it?"

"Oh, yes. I've seen it used. Each century has a single shot version. Macer favoured the repeater. The gods bless young Macer!"

Felix beckoned Clemens over from where he had been inspecting the men and told him to supervise the weapon's restoration.

★ ★ ★

In the event they saw nothing warlike come out from land and hung about anxiously until Felix said, "We're being taken as fools here! It was obvious we would be looking for a warship, so we're being shown geese instead of swans! We haven't see anything remotely aggressive have we?"

"Right."

"Then we'll sail south – after that trader we saw. I think we'll find our quarry on that. Whilst we're looking for another longship he's off on a civil one. I'll remember Osian Mac Ior – he's too clever by half!"

Draco issued rapid orders and the rested rowers pulled hard with the beat of the drum, so that their ship gathered way smoothly on the swell, calm by Hibernian Sea standards they all realised.

Fed and watered while they had waited every rower now put their backs into it, so that mile after mile was covered with comparative ease, with some smiling at the number of times the ex-marine was allowed to the lee side to vomit with the wind, away from the vessel.

Running only under sail men slept as well as they could, in the knowledge that the following day would bring the same – unless they sighted the trader.

They did not, until the sun lowered again and the watch officer squinted into the orange glow. He spoke as he pointed and they all squinted with him, some under shielding hands.

"I think it is," ventured Draco. "I think so."

From between slitted eyes Felix concentrated, then agreed. "In silhouette it seems to have the same shape"

"If my watch officer says so, I'll take it as so," Draco said. "I'm pleased you think so, too."

"Then take us west as fast as you're able – sail and oar. We must put pressure on the west now, to make that vessel turn southeast towards the islands. If we close, keep between them and land. I want them to go for Lisia. Ideally I want them wrecked, because it's a cargo boat – but, if not, we'll turn them into a wreck ourselves!"

Caught up in the excitement Draco urged his officers on who, in turn, worked on the crew and the rowers. It seemed they flew across the water and they did close the gap, only to take the western seaboard to the surprise of the sturdy trader, which immediately escaped to the east.

With more hard work they were finally able to slip inside the vessel's new course and the exhausted rowers, sitting out-rigged, were cheered by the sight of the trader shearing off and groping for a wind to take it in to Lisia.

Felix applauded the crew and all the officers took the opportunity to join with him, whilst he laughed out loud.

"They must be as tired as us, that sail needs constant adjustment and there aren't many to do it. That means bastard Haruld hasn't taken his men with him – they could at least have manned the sheets," Felix cried happily. "Do your men have a reserve? Can we catch them as they enter the harbour that's there? Is the scorpion readied?"

"Clemens tells me it's as well as it will be, my friend. What do you want to do with it?" Draco's face was eager as he asked for directions.

"Let them turn in towards the harbour. Slow off, so the men can catch their breath. If I'm right – and in all the gods' names tell me if you think I'm not – they will then be caught between a rock and a harbour. We will have them!"

"My memory tells me you are right, Felix. This great rock rears up – if it was properly used in defence it would prove formidable."

Almost sidelined for a long time Clemens walked across and asked, "Why was it so important that he escaped alone? What is it he fears us taking from him – apart from his life? Surely he would normally have gone with his men – lives for the taking?"

Felix drew up short then wandered the deck, pondering on why their quarry would have abandoned his men.

Why was the question he kept asking himself until finally he smiled and said, "He could not take the chance of losing something!"

Clemens cried, "Then he has something valuable! It can't be *for* Hibernia – or they would already have it. That means he's *collected* it and so he could not leave it behind. In any case, he thought he'd have made the mainland before we realised he'd gone!"

"My son, you have the mind of an investigator! We're definitely chasing something valuable, not just him – you are absolutely right, I wish I'd thought of it without being prompted!"

"What, though?"

"We'll know that when we catch him."

"He's a slippery customer, so I'd better go back to the men and prepare them," said Clemens and turned away.

Felix looked at Draco. "Drive in beside him – they won't want to be boarded, so they'll turn away."

"Sir," acknowledged Draco and gave the command.

"Close them hard!"

"Sir." Draco issued the further order and immediately their target turned away from them towards the great rock.

They saw the neat central hatches and the small deck cabin at the rear of the boat clearly, as it heeled over in its tight turn, one end of the broad sail almost touching the frothing water, with two men leaning on the steering oar as they ran before the incoming tide.

Now rising behind the boat the almost conical island, beyond the distant harbour's entrance, threatened destruction and the sheets were hauled to turn the sail away.

"Fire at the sail, Sir. It'll mean they will lose motive power and most of their steerage way, if it rips."

"We'll do that, Draco. Well considered. I'll tell Clemens."

The repeating ballista, disliked by operators on land for putting too many bolts in the same place, was a weapon favoured by Macer because of the natural motion of a ship. It was this very same one that opened fire on the solidly built merchant vessel.

One bolt hit the sail full on and the pointed missile went straight through the taut canvas. The second glanced off the centrally placed mast and lodged in the fabric. All subsequent bolts hit home in the wide target until suddenly a long rent appeared, followed by another and another, until the wind that had previously filled the sail gave up and passed through.

"Cease firing," came the order and whilst the ballista's crew reloaded it, all other eyes were on the target as it yawed out of control, the steering oar having no compensating side pressure from the sail.

"Will it clear that guarding rock, Draco?"

"Nip and tuck, Sir, but I think it will. However, with the tide flowing like this, it means the water could be three hours away from full – that is, not far off low tide – and with little steerage there *is* a chance of it leaving the main channel and ripping out its guts!"

They watched for a while as the vessel battled the cross currents until Draco's premonition became reality. With a rending crash the boat struck one of the barely-covered upthrust rocks, stopped its flight for a moment, then tore itself free and ran again, listing heavily as water poured into the hold.

They watched all the deckhands pick themselves up, but one of the steersmen stayed where he had fallen, after hitting the small cabin.

Suddenly smoke billowed sideways, only to dissipate rapidly in the wind. Then flame reached up from the burning wooden cabin, set alight by the ship's altar fire in the collision.

The wind that cleared the smoke fanned the flames and the crew ran to the bows to escape them. They watched as the fallen steersman was engulfed, whilst the other jumped overboard with his tunic alight.

The burning boat neared the harbour entrance, but the odd combination of fire and water finally told. It listed more heavily until the weakened timbers at last gave way and with a creaking groan capsized, throwing the reduced crew into the water. Those who could not swim were pulled under and those who could fought the cross current in the vain hope of avoiding being torn by the razor-sharp, granite rocks lurking just below the surface.

Peering beneath hands that shielded their eyes from the low sun, Felix and Draco finally picked out the struggling form of Haruld-The-One-Eyed. Not previously seen, they wondered if he had been below for safety and then not been able to bypass the fire to regain the deck. They acknowledged it was all conjecture, except the fact that he was now flailing with only one arm to stay above the water.

No longer needed to direct the ballista, Clemens rejoined them and all three officers gripped the side rail that held spare weapons, knowing there was nothing to be done. There was no question of risking their own vessel, even if One-Eye did have something of importance.

As they stared at their adversary it seemed that he had no leg movements to help his one arm and his head frequently went under water. Eventually the arm appeared to be less mobile and less energetic, so that he rolled and twisted in the tidal surge until he no longer resurfaced. Just once more they thought they caught a glimpse of an arm in the water and then saw no other sign of him.

"He didn't seem to have a bag or pannier with him," observed Clemens disappointedly.

"It's probably with the ship," Felix replied. "It did look as if our man was ejected rather than making a planned exit, to put a fine point on it."

"Unless he's swept into the harbour the currents could put him anywhere – even shredded on the rocks for the fishes – so his body may never be found," Draco explained. "I hope that's one problem behind us."

★ ★ ★

"So we cleared the outcome with the harbourmaster, rested overnight and then hugged the Gaulish coast, before crossing to Vectis and Portus Ardoni soon after."

"You did well in the chase, Draco. I commend your handling of your ship and economic use of the rowers," Agrippa remarked. "A small action - but one to be proud of."

Felix said positively, "I've no hesitation in putting forward a request for a ship's citation - all the crew performed well."

The governor thought briefly before replying, "I see no reason not to award one. The effort the crew made over a protracted period is different to the seamanship required by their captain. It will not affect an award to Draco for ridding us of a bloodsucking parasite. What do you say, Agrippa?"

The little admiral nodded enthusiastically. Having made the request for an honour for Draco he realised he could do little else, because he actually supported the crew's award – it would mean a plaque on the mast and hopefully encourage other ships' companies to emulate the feat.

Draco smiled self-consciously and it was as though his beard widened with it, causing several smiles in return. "It was a joint effort, gentlemen. Felix had good ideas, which I managed to put into practice."

Urbicus turned to Felix and raised his eyebrows. "Have you hidden your light under a bushel, my friend?"

"I hadn't – but it was put out by the wind! Breezy platforms – ships," he replied jovially. "Any ideas would have been useless if they hadn't been property carried out. An award is rightfully his."

"Then that's unanimous. So be it," said the governor and ended the debate.

Felix observed, "Changing the subject, I'd like to have known what he was carrying that was worth dying for."

"Yes," agreed Macer. "If I'd been there I'd have wanted to know, too."

"You haven't spoken, Clemens. Any ideas?"

Shaking his head and making a fine spray of the water in his hair Clemens responded simply, "None, Urbicus. I simply realised he had to have collected, not delivered, something."

Sitting around the largest bath's marbled edge they fell quiet and one by one regarded their governor, waiting for what it now seemed he would tell them. They were not disappointed.

"The treasury told me, whilst you were off on a sea trip," he began mischievously, only to be rewarded by their splashing water at him, "that there are increasing numbers of counterfeit coins in circulation. Obviously there will always be some, but I'm told it's become more blatant of late.Had the emperor not authorised the casting of a *special* issue, to celebrate the northern wall's success as a triumph over the barbarian north, they say it might have been worse."

"You think it's down to the dead man?" asked Agrippa. "I saw him as more of an adventurer, eyeing the main chance – not averse to rape and pillage whilst about it!"

"I wonder," said Felix, thoughtfully looking down at the marbling and running his fingers along its wet surface, "whether he might be responsible – indirectly, that is."

"Say again", requested Agrippa, pursing his lips as he puzzled on the remark, brow furrowed.

Felix went on slowly, his fingers still tracing a pattern in the splashes, "It *is* just an idea. No proof, of course. However, when I was speaking with the Taoiseach he mentioned their having made beaten gold ear-bands – presumable hanging from the ears rather than through them – at the time of the Stone Henge's completion. So, if that's the case, they may now actually make far more of the crafted metal objects they trade than we've perhaps stopped to consider. On a par with those in Britannia and Gaul Magna, in fact, in terms of skills if not of scale."

"Why are we thinking of ornaments? Urbicus mentioned coinage," Agrippa pointed out.

Looking up Felix spoke directly to the governor. "If able, as they must be, to work to that quality it isn't likely they'd have much of a problem producing counterfeit moulds."

"So he *was* collecting something," ejaculated Clemens. "And that's what is was."

Felix square chin was tense as he nodded amid the doubting voices. Then he went on, "Why not? Debased metal is poured in, titivated as necessary – and one side forms in the mould. While it's still warm it's turned out and hand stamped on the reverse. I've seen it done with gold in the mine, up to a point."

"You must have a devious mind, my friend," chuckled Urbicus. "The gods were good to you! It fits well enough as a theory. I like it."

"So who had the coins made from the moulds?"

Again Felix was serious as he said, "Once more all supposition. But remember, this bandit is, was, Mercurialis' man. No wonder he could dedicate a temple! *He's* behind it. Flooding false coinage onto the market would undermine the economy. Trade would shun coinage – well most. The army – nor the navy – would not be best pleased, either.

"What a throw of the dice – if it's true!"

"It would lead to revolt," agreed Agrippa. "But I've not see any to speak of, as fleet procurator."

Urbicus turned to his fleet commander. "Would you, though? After all, you either pay out coin or take in goods as taxes. The trade's the other way."

"Damn me if that's not so," exclaimed Agrippa. "Too obvious to be noticed!"

"I had a somewhat classical education," Macer said, rejoining the conversation. "Even now, but especially in the old days, smiths were seen as miracle-workers, converting rough alloys into fine metals – tools, weapons, intricate jewellery. What Felix suggests makes a great deal of sense, in that light. The skills are handed down in families. Why not be able to make moulds?"

"And they went down with the boat?"

"As best we can tell. One-Eye didn't seem to have them," confirmed Draco nodding.

"You tell me he drowned," Urbicus said, looking for confirmation of that, too.

"I can't see how anyone could stay under without breath for that long in those crosscurrents – the strain would be too great."

"I'll tell you what," Urbicus said. "Let the swimmers go under, here, and Draco can judge the length of time by comparison."

"The open water would be cooler there, too," agreed Draco. "It's more difficult to hold your breath."

Felix, Macer, Clemens and Agrippa took deep breaths and submerged, while Urbicus kept time with the bireme captain.

A rush of bubbles passed Felix' ears as he let out a small quantity of air through his nose and he even felt some kiss his skin. As always, shadows flickered in the disturbed water.

Looking around him as he sat on the tiled floor of the pool he studied the intricate patterns to pass the time, then saw the other three were doing the same.

Agrippa went up first and Clemens blew a bubble from his mouth as though counting. It caused Felix to laugh and having lost his retained air, he pushed upwards to break the ruffled surface in a spray of froth. Annoyed with himself, he hauled out on his arms and once again sat on the side.

The four looked at each other and wondered whether the two still under would make a competition of it. However, when the surge of water came both broke the surface together.

"A shorter time, all," Draco commented. "I'm sure our quarry was under longer – in colder water."

"We weren't using our limbs, either," Felix said. "Exertion would take more air."

"A valid point," agreed Agrippa.

Even as they accepted the verdict the sound of voices came from the ladies changing room, as the women emerged to join their men.

Appreciative glances were cast in their direction as breast and thigh were fully exposed without embarrassment, including Macer's pregnant Avita. Draco soon found his eye drawn to his sister, unable to avoid noticing that she had no pubic hair to disguise any detail whatsoever. Immediately averting his gaze he realised that that was for Agrippa's benefit. Then it came to him that he alone was alone – but he was not excluded. That thought gave him a great sense of belonging.

Chapter XIX

When news came to Felix in his mail that Firmus and Dorcas' baby had died, he read to Livia from the brief note. "The delivery started but faltered, then only restarted some time later with the help of the fortresses' surgeon. After not feeding for three days, the child died peacefully in its sleep."

Tears coursed down Livia's cheeks and she clung to Felix trying not to sob her heart out for his ward, Dorcas.

"It sounded so flat and matter-of-fact, my love," she managed to whisper. "It sounds as if Firmus has taken it hard."

"Yes, I think you're right – so much so he does not mention my ward, nor how she is. Unlike him not to be objective," Felix observed tight-lipped, as he tried not to show his emotions.

"Do you think when she's able to travel she could come here? You're the nearest she has to family – you and Julia. Army life's going to be no help to her, is it?"

Felix put his arm round his wife's trembling shoulders and she snuggled into him on the settle. Then, looking up at him, Livia said softly, "I know you fell out with her when she did not warn you of what poor Carina had asked her – but you did marry them, after all."

He looked down at her and gently kissed her readied lips. It was almost an automatic reaction between them. He said, "I've forgotten about it. There was no guarantee I could've stopped Carina's suicide. Even her sister had no idea."

"That's so true, my dear. She obviously loved Gaius Lucius and wanted to be with him more than she loved her mother Romana, or Avita – and you as her guardian, for that matter. Dorcas was an unwitting ally."

"Yes – to both ideas."

"She can come? That'll be wonderful – I hope she sees the sense in it."

"Will Firmus? He's been able to branch out where he is. Taking command of the fort at the mine, I mean. He'll be even more of a target back here – so will Dorcas."

"Oh, no! I'd overlooked that – how silly. That's why she was attacked there as well – and here's me thinking she'll be safe with us."

"She'll be safest in Isca Silurum and the vicus that's sprung up around it provides a deal of shops for her."

She squeezed his arm. "I know you're right, my love, but there's a downside to her being reminded all the time, by her environment, of the reason for her grief. I was thinking of a change of scenery for her."

Felix put his hand over hers and replied, "Even with a bodyguard I couldn't guarantee her safety. In any case, the century's so reduced now I can't even spare enough men to do other jobs."

"Can't you get more?"

Shrugging Felix said, "The short answer's no. They're all needed on the New Wall or as replacements in the three legions. I don't think the Twentieth or the Sixth, or Sextus' Second, would thank me overmuch if I looked to Urbicus for favours. That's why I recruited our own, under Paulinus, for the new house."

"I see," Livia responded flatly.

"I'll leave it to you, as to whether Dorcas comes back. You understand people better than me – women anyway!"

Livia sat up and looked at him. "I'll take that as an admission of men's natural failings," she said and flounced exaggeratedly out of the sitting room, turning to smile at him and blow a kiss from the doorway.

★ ★ ★

In the event Firmus took leave of absence and they both returned to Waerham, though Felix was unsure just what part Livia and Julia had played in persuading them. However, he accepted the situation.

It was after the midsummer festival had passed, to which Stolus had invited them all, that he felt the need to take Firmus aside.

"I'd almost forgotten how beautiful these river meadows are," the young centurion said, as just the two of them walked the riverbank below Felix' house. A lot of mountainous scenery in Cymru. Impressive - but not always friendly."

"You have an option not to go back."

Firmus stopped and regarded him seriously. "What option? In any case I'm beginning to enjoy my job at the mine. What are you suggesting?"

Felix gave a shrug before saying, "I'm not making a suggestion, but there is something I can discuss with you. Still, if you want to return I can understand that."

"The only thing that would tempt me away from the Second, bearing in mind at the mine I'm far enough away to have autonomy, is to stuff something nasty up Mercurialis personally – and permanently," he added venomously, his face dark at the name.

"Not only for me but for poor Dorcas. The fort surgeon tried hard enough but he said the baby had become wedged due to the treatment she'd received, he thought. The baby had to be removed he told me, or she'd die. He did all he could, massaging and manoeuvring it – I don't really understand the technicalities. Dorcas did suffer, though.

All that bastard's fault – I'd like to meet him face-to-face!"

"It's funny you should say that, because it might be an outcome." Felix smiled gently to ease the atmosphere.

"You are serious? Deadly serious?

"Deadly would be associated with the work."

Astounded, Firmus did a double take and swallowed, his face lightening perceptibly as he thought on it. "Well, he wouldn't welcome me back into his group, that's for sure!"

"I'm pleased about that. I'd rather you gave *him* a warm welcome instead."

They walked on then in the direction of the still unrepaired mill and site of Livia's attack before Felix continued, "You'd feature in his worst nightmares, if things went well. The other bastard's too, I hope!"

"How? I mean, how would it work?"

"Are you sure, now? What of Dorcas?"

Stopping again Firmus said with feeling, "Look. You represented me in that treason trial, when it looked gloomy for me. I'll never forget that. So I'd not say this to anyone else – but Dorcas and I haven't had it since our loss. We put on a front – but that's all it is. We don't do it any more – she finds it difficult to adjust to getting pregnant again.

I wonder whether the score being settled would put matters right – don't know, of course, but it might. It certainly wouldn't hurt! Even my being away might be a good thing. I take it I'd be away a lot?"

"Sometimes. Initially with the Mummers – as you were in Corinium."

"When we arrested Mercurialis! How long ago and so wasted an opportunity that seems now. But you said deadly?"

Walking on again Felix replied, "So I did, but I want the deadly to be outgoing not incoming. I heard somewhere that giving is better than receiving – make it so!

We'll talk of it again, with Cassius the juggler, knife-throwing Echo and wrestler Jason. Pluto will lead them as before. He's a natural trickster. Clemens will need to talk to you on codification – telestich in particular.

Now, for the moment, I want to look at this mill's state."

★ ★ ★

After dinner that evening, at which it was noticeable that Dorcas had had little interest in what was said although she smiled frequently, the men sat quietly waiting to hear from Felix what Urbicus had sent down from the Londinium Palace.

Momentarily Firmus thought of the three women who had retired to the solar in order to talk about the two gold necklaces he had bought Dorcas, only to be lost at the mine, as well as Julia's cookery book, which was nearing completion. He hoped that the other two would draw something out of his wife, now that she was back where she had spent the greater part of her life and so might feel more secure – but he was not sure enough to wager on it.

Then Felix began his summary. "He says that the Paternus and Marsala families have joined forces to push for the boy, Quintus, to enjoy a higher profile in this forty-fifth state of the empire. It seems there's no love lost for the renegade, Mercurialis, whose bosom friend, the late and wholly unlamented One-eye, stole the jewelled dagger which was a gift from Quintus to his uncle."

He went on to quote, "It remains to be seen what pressure will be applied in Rome and through whom. It is not beyond the realms of possibility I may, even here, receive a deputation with proposals!

It does not appear that the families are backing Geta Marcus, at least for now.

Naturally, I welcome any information you may unearth.

Then he ends with the usual dedications."

"Can we afford to ignore Mercurialis? He is still a traitor," Clemens both observed and asked, "even if what's said turns out to be true."

"I was hoping he'd be my first target," said Firmus, almost as a grumble. "Ignore is the wrong word for what I'd like to do!"

"I take both points," replied Felix. "He's still a target, as far as I'm concerned.

Don't forget, too, Geta Marcus is only a threat whilst he's at large. Neither Urbicus nor I are worried whether he's taken or killed. If the former, we'd find out if he's involved with the families. *He'll* be worried though, so if he's caught make sure he doesn't take his own life!"

"This Quintus. What *greater* threat is he by being supported?"

"None, Firmus," replied Clemens. "He'll still be a little turd – just in a larger cesspit!"

"If only they could all be summed up so aptly," mused Felix out loud.

"If I'm to be reunited with the Mummers," Firmus remarked, "what's this about telestich?"

Clemens raised his eyes to the ceiling before saying, "I suppose I'm the nominee to explain it."

Smiling as he said it Felix quickly retorted, "Obviously a mind-reader is a prime candidate!"

Looking down at his hands Clemens began, "It's a form of code, of course – though of itself it's rarely the full item. We use it to indicate whether the main missive has a code or not. Even then we use a nominated copy of one of surgeon Faber's medical books to provide the wording of the actual message. It's more time-consuming than cumbersome – and it works well."

"I understand the principle," Firmus agreed nodding.

"Right. So, telestich is an agreed number of lines – we favour six – of text or verse where the end letter of each last word is used to form a word. It's normal to use consecutive letters, but we jumble them to be sorted into a previously agreed word. To make it interesting – and less obvious – we usually agree a four-letter keyword so the two other letters are misleading to anyone else. It's possible of course, to use the *first* letter of each line, but every steganographer would look for that immediately. Occasionally it might be agreed that every last word makes a message of itself in code – etcetera.

So, if a keyword is present there *is* a hidden message."

"Didn't I hear something about Caesar inventing a cipher?"

"That's so," agreed Felix, "but it's ancient history now. Science has moved on vastly, since then."

"This one either triggers action or indicates a message in the overt letter," Clemens observed. "What do you think?"

"Is it too late to apply for a transfer?"

★ ★ ★

Flames reached up to play along the roof of the farmhouse, as though enjoying being the cause of the pillar of grey smoke rising from the burning building.

Men's bodies lay in awkward shapes where they had crumbled in life – and death had left them unaltered.

Two women lay in the building. One had died under rape, whilst the other had been killed when she had outlasted their amusement. A third woman knelt with her head on the ground, her arms clasped in pain around her stomach, the well-toned, naked body dirty and bloodied from when she fought to save herself.

"Let her live as an example that virgins, especially, are not safe on farmland," the hooded leader said. Then he watched dispassionately as the young woman barely twitched when the trademark of their outlaw band was etched into her upper arm. He smiled in the knowledge that not only would others see it but she would have a constant reminder of her unsuccessful battle.

"Time to go," he said as the roof collapsed in a welter of sparks causing black smoke to billow upwards into the darkening sky. "We've got all the food we need, so we'll find a night camp and move on to tomorrow's target.

The Moonshadows have made their mark."

★ ★ ★

The meeting had been called in the Regnum Palace and Urbicus was pleased with his decision to come south, away from the heat and odours of Londinium.

He was looking forward to telling them of his marriage arrangements, which were to coincide with the celebratory games at Verulamium in honour of its new status, plus his plans to adopt Rufinus and Avita on marriage. Then he would congratulate them on Haruld's demise with its associated reduction in forged coins. After that there was the updated progress on the New Wall and the need to plan the capture of the two main traitors – not to forget, of course, his vivarium.

A full programme, he thought, as he washed his latrine sponge in the fresh water channel that ran the length of the chamber. Even as he did so he thought he heard a trumpet announcing the first arrivals.

Livia and Julia were in front of the group greeted by Petronius and Faber on this occasion, which pleased them just as much. The two old friends led them all into the audience chamber to be warmly welcomed by the governor, who sat on his throne-like seat as though welcoming royalty to the palace.

Standing, he called out, "Hail the conquering heroes – or at lest some of them, for ridding us of that damned Norse pirate at long last! You will be pleased to hear that young Draco's award was approved – and one each for you two, my friends, for such persistence over time," he added, indicating Felix and Clemens.

Firmus led the ladies in their applause, joined by the portly surgeon and camp prefect without reservation.

As it died away the governor added, "Corona for you both. Two to you Clemens, with three to Felix plus three Vexilla, as is relevant to your ranks. Draco received the same as Clemens and his bireme a gold disc, to be fixed to the mast as it would be to a standard."

After waiting for the second round of applause to abate Felix thanked the govnernor on their behalf and whispered to Livia, "Three more little silver standards for you to clean!"

She whispered back, as Urbicus approached, "At this rate, you'll need the three crowns made into one to fit!"

* * *

The centrally placed tables overflowed with all manner of local and imported produce including joints of meat expertly carved to represent other animals, succulent seafood which almost appeared to be escaping from the bowls and a whole array of rich sauces.

Palace servants hurried amongst the couches, filling or refilling plates and exchanging the cups that had contained mulsum with fresh ones, for the following wines.

It seemed clear to most that the governor had arranged a feast with a purpose so that, although it flowed, the conversation was reserved as though not to overshadow what would follow.

Avita was there with Macer and her brother, the young surgeon-to-be, had also been invited to join the feast, although Rufinus sat with Draco, Faber, Petronius and Firmus, on this occasion there without Dorcas, forming a bachelor group.

"I think I know what's coming," Livia whispered to Felix, as Urbicus spoke to Agrippa, "Don't you?"

"You always do have an unusual insight," Felix replied, "but yes, I think I can guess with both my wards here."

On the other side of the top table Aelia, like Romana, wore a sleeveless dress with narrow straps that almost left her shoulders bare. When Urbicus turned away she held Agrippa's hand, after he surprisingly brushed his lips against her as he leaned forward on the pretext of stealing a seasoned prawn from her plate.

Livia excited the men with one completely bare shoulder, her dress daringly cut low over the bodice on that side, as though emulating the one-time fashion of baring a breast. She pressed against Felix and the feel of her strong thigh roused him to the point of wishing Urbicus would make his announcement as soon as possible.

As though reading his mind the governor raised a hand and the room quickly fell silent, except for the muted swishing of the large fans plied by slaves to keep the warm air moving.

"My friends – my very dear friends – I have several announcements to make, so I shall be brief as to each one," he began, as he stood in order to be readily seen by everyone. "As this is the usual informal gathering I shall put personal matters first.

The personal matters are just that – personal. I say in front of you all as witnesses to the fact that, from this moment, the Lady Romana and I should be treated as married."

As he sat every gaze fell on Romana but, smiling happily, she simply nodded her head several times, which was a signal for much applause and happy laughter.

Rank making no difference it was Petronius who felt it his responsibility to reply and, as he stood in turn, the room again fell expectantly silent.

"Notwithstanding this crafty old reprobate not even telling his best friends," he began, briefly looking at his good-natured audience before turning back, "I'm sure I speak for all here when I say that Romana is far too good a catch for him! However – you lucky old dog – she's willing to put up with you, so we raise our cups to you both and wish you a long and happy union! To the happy couple."

Cups were drained and immediately refilled by servants seemingly appearing from nowhere, while the chatter began again as Petronius regained his seat.

Felix and Livia looked keenly at each other and a slight movement of their wrists was all that was visible, as they privately toasted themselves.

"What do you think of that?" Julia asked, as she turned back to Clemens. "Did you know anything?"

"Nothing, my love, I assure you – I would have said something," he answered reassuringly.

Urbicus stood again, his broad-featured face opening up into a wide-toothed grin as he began, "My second – and indeed third – announcement is, I mean are, connected with my first."

Another undercurrent of whispers started, a mixture of question and prediction, causing the governor to hold up a silencing hand.

"My friends, since my wife has children and I have none, I feel it would be right for me to formally adopt them. Of course, for several years, Felix has been their legal guardian at Romana's request, so I made my request to him which Felix, being Felix, agreed would be best for them."

In the pause everyone regarded Felix cautiously, since they each knew he had taken his duties seriously and was respected by both wards, with a deal of affection shown by each side to the other. He looked steadily back and gave a slight shrug.

Sensing the mood Urbicus explained, "Felix had no knowledge of this public announcement and I suspect he is as surprised as the rest of you.

What it will mean, though, is that Rufinus and Avita, despite her marriage to a lusty seaman, will inherit my property and estates, here as well as in my adopted homeland of Italia."

Hesitant applause broke out until Felix stood, when it immediately died. There was absolute quiet as he spoke.

"What has been said is true. However, what it will also mean is that Urbicus and Romana will be a family – not simply two people. As you all know, I already have a daughter and am also responsible for the freed slave who became her companion. Unfortunately Dorcas is unwell and was unable to join her husband here."

Rufinus was staring at him and a startled Avita was looking down at her lap as Felix continued.

"I am as fond of my wards as though they were my own. I shall continued to be. Therefore I wish I could have forewarned them. However, that shouldn't detract from the honour of his formal adoption and they will gain much from it."

Both men were still on their feet when Rufinus stood, the young man's jaw muscles working hard. In the hush both his seniors conceded the floor and a dramatic silence fell over the room, which many felt could be cut with a knife.

"I, too," Rufinus began slowly, trying to pick words which would not be misunderstood, "would have preferred to have had some warning – and I'm sure I speak for my sister in this. However, such is the nature of surprises.

We both, myself in particular, are in our guardian's debt and we've always looked upon him as a surrogate father, with fondness and respect. Because of that I know he must believe it's for the best. On that basis I accept the kind offer made to us. What do you say, Avita?"

Realising he would be looking at her as he waited for an answer she raised her head and met his gaze, holding it for several moments before nodding her agreement.

Both looked at Felix and he nodded his approval, at which Rufinus took his seat again as Macer put a comforting arm around his wife.

"That was a mature speech from your ward – protégé, I suppose I mean now," Livia said. "He has the makings of a fine young man."

"I hope he finds a wife like you, my love. That will complete the making of him."

Taking the moment Urbicus rose once more. "As this eloquent trainee surgeon has said, such is the nature of surprises. I have to concede it was too great a one on this occasion and I am personally culpable for warning no one at all that I intended to announce it – not even their dear mother. No blame attaches to anyone but myself for any dissention but, as has been said, I hope that in no way diminishes the goodwill in my intention, nor the pleasure it has given me – I believe, us – in its acceptance."

For a few moments there was an uncomfortable vacuum until Felix regained his feet to applaud, respecting the way in which his friend had steered any liability clearly towards himself. It was a noble gesture, he thought. Following Felix' lead the others also gave a standing ovation and servants were signalled to recharge any empty cups.

"You are all invited to the games at Verulamium, which I am offering as a thanks to the gods for my marriage. It will coincide with the celebrating of that place as the new Second City of Britannia," Urbicus announced to his re-seated audience. During more applause a wine cup was knocked over to much laughter, with Firmus the one to colour.

"If you choose to go via Londinium it would be an ideal opportunity to view Continental and African animals in the vivarium parklands, north west of the city. These already include several varieties of bear, panther and leopard and, with luck, soon a giraffe, a camel and an elephant.

However, that's enough of personal things. When the feast is over, if the ladies will retire – I'm sure Avita must be tiring, carrying as she is – the men will discuss progress on the Antonine Wall and some additional matters of security."

Chapter XX

A part from Rufinus, who had returned to the fort to take charge of the hospital in Faber's absence, the men had gathered in the principal room of the North Wing and formed a rough semi-circle, facing the governor and his admiral.

The chill of the evening went unnoticed because the large room basked in the warmth of the newly installed hypocaust system. Satisfied that overheating could be avoided by opening the doors accessing its courtyard and peristyle, Urbicus was in a contented mood. However, he decided to cut to the chase.

"As I said earlier this year, I want those two miscreants captured or killed. I want the banditry stopped and this area returned to peace and tranquillity. The northern realm will provide all the fighting we require for the foreseeable future.

Of course, I realise there will always be ad hoc outlaw bands from time to time. It's inherent that those outside the law will often join together – but what we have presently is organised, sometimes synchronised, mayhem. Only yesterday the signal stations telegraphed further attacks on farmsteads. A messenger brought me details."

Urbicus paused to let them look from one to the other while they digested this fresh information. He noticed the resolute look on Felix's face and pressed on with his monologue.

"It seems their trademark is to leave a young woman or child alive after each attack, previously a virgin, to inform us of the band's identity by carving it on the victim's upper arm. The symbol appears to be a crescent moon, with underlying shadow in the form of a line below it. This violence has to be stopped before fear causes wholesale selling."

Felix took the initiative as the governor finished, responding, "Up until now we've been hampered by assiduously keeping within the law. Evidence that would stand scrutiny has proved difficult to come by – except when both Firmus and I, individually, infiltrated the organisations in one way or another. Firmus, of course, over a longer period.

This is old news, I know, but the thought of the problems it caused our protagonists prompted me to think of going further, which led to my brief discussion with you as to putting it into practice."

The governor nodded and observed to the others, "This is so and the concept is interesting. Will you enlarge on it now?"

Realising the question was a directive Felix adjusted his position and did as he had been instructed. The room was silent and it appeared that each individual was holding his breath as they looked at him, though he knew it was not so.

"We have been – and still are – at a legal disadvantage. I believe this must cease and we should take the fight to them, so to speak.

They appear to be large bands and a fair number of troops will be required to dissuade them, in the normal course of events. As you realise, a large body of troops is easily detected. Consequently they are their own worst enemy.

What I propose is a commando - a small unit capable of penetrating deep cover quickly – and silently. The idea is that they go in hard and fast without warning, to snatch the ringleaders of whatever level, then hold them against possible counter-attack until a relieving force arrives. Noise will not matter by then, obviously."

Agrippa muttered, "It sounds reasonable. Who will lead it?"

Felix indicated his ex-ward's husband. "Firmus. He has agreed and accepts the dangers willingly. He has much to seek redress for."

"Yes, he does," replied Urbicus, then looking concernedly at the young man added, "I'm deeply sorry about your loss. It's not surprising you wish to lead this what, snatch squad?"

"An apt description, Urbicus," Felix agreed, interrupting. "However, I've already stressed that the desire for revenge needs to be controlled. Taking them for information – not to speak of their hostage value in terms of negotiating – is important."

Agrippa led the nodded agreement around the room as Felix continued, "However, if this cannot be achieved then over a mule will be the result. I think it imperative that everyone agrees that."

As they all nodded emphatically and looked at each other for mutual confirmation Agrippa asked, "Who will lead the follow-up – if enough troops can be found?"

Felix spread his hands as he answered, "I intend to."

Before he could say more Urbicus sprang into the breathing gap with a questioning, "Is that wise? What would be the result if you were taken by them? Intelligence mayhem." The governor was clearly concerned as to security issues and his facial expression confirmed it.

"I agree."

Felix was quick to rebuff the admiral saying, "Would it be different if you were captured – or you, Urbicus? In fact Agrippa is at risk twice, at least in theory, on land as well as at sea. Actually, any one of us here has useful knowledge.

No. The main advantage of my being involved is to use the remains of my century. All can ride. We shall be dragooners, able to act as cavalry when necessary. A fast follow up is required – horsemen can achieve that!"

Rubbing his nose with a finger Urbicus looked at Agrippa and then around the room. It seemed the right moment to him, so he asked, "What do you all have to say individually. Speak your minds," he added as a rider.

Petronius observed, "Initially, I agreed with you, old friend – and your reasons are still right. However, Felix has a good point and good points make good plans. I think he should lead."

Faber nodded before deciding the moment was now his. "You're all used to each other. That leads to mutual understanding which should mean less injuries – and on that score I should like to volunteer young Rufinus to look after any injured soldiery. I would volunteer like lightning, but would only be a liability on a fast horse at my age, I regret. Also, he is from the century himself," he added as makeweight.

Agrippa spoke next. "Let's not forget one thing. You can only be in one place at one time. Who'll coordinate the overall strategy if you're bare-arsed riding somewhere else?"

"That *is* a very good point, gentlemen," observed the governor. "What's your answer to it Felix?

Gently teasing his forehead, as he appeared to be thinking, Felix replied, "That bothers me, too – but the obvious answer's for it to be Agrippa. He has the naval intelligence resource – as well as the coastal telegraph system.

Now *that* leads me very smoothly into a suggestion I want to make. Will Agrippa lend me Draco and his bireme? I won't ask for Macer as his trireme is too important for transportation of troops north, as well as managing the Gaulish sea, if the east coast weather turns."

"Well, Admiral, your deputy – or his deputy? It's a fair summary," Urbicus remarked.

Agrippa had immediately pursed his lips at the original request. Now he frowned as he retorted, "I can't spare either! On that score, I refer back to a previous discussion on coastal security and my point of not having enough ships as it is."

Urbicus raised a hand for silence as several tried to speak at once. "Let's go back, for a moment, to our round robin. Macer, on the original topic?"

"My first thoughts on not being required in support were frustration and disagreement. However, to answer the original, if Felix is to fly then he must be there. Yes, to Rufinus, too.

As to the second, any ship must be able to close land more easily than my 'Tigris', so Felix is right there as well. With regard to too few ships, I can only agree. However, we're looking at a short, sharp campaign, as I see it, in which case a very brief leave of absence for 'Sabrina' might just be possible," Macer added diplomatically, offering his mentor a route back.

"Well put, sir," complimented Urbicus. "Of course, it's your final say, Admiral."

Seeing the governor turn to him Agrippa shrugged. "One place at a time applies to the navy also. But I take Macer's point. A short absence is possible – subject to instant recall, naturally."

"Naturally," agreed Urbicus. "So that's settled, Felix."

"Equally naturally you would expect me to support my father-in-law," Clemens interjected. "I do, but not because of that. In actual fact, my own argument is that we have two excellent scouts, recently decorated, who will prove invaluable to both Firmus, a cavalryman himself in the past, as well as to us. We shall have fast communication through them – plus any surviving signal stations in our area of operations. We also understand codification, should it be deemed necessary."

"And well put to you too, sir," said Urbicus smiling. "We seem to have the most intelligent young whelps in our midst! Draco. Your views?"

In the informal atmosphere the bearded young sailor smiled at the description and retorted, "You flatter us, Sir, but I agree with everything said so far, coming down on the side, though, of Felix leading the troop and calling on naval support where possible. I believe my marines might yet prove valuable, too."

"Another good point, young man. Thank you," Urbicus said. Then he turned to Firmus "Almost last but not least, my boy. You will be at the cutting edge – do you have a view?"

Clearing his throat Firmus answered, "Clearly speed is of the essence – both in my actions and with the support group. Felix can provide that speed in support. In addition to that, when we have prisoners it will be vital to get them to a secure environment as soon as possible. What's more secure than a naval vessel – with a plus factor that, should we ourselves be involved in a holding action, the sudden appearance of Draco's marines would make a pursuer pause for thought. Even if we're inland the 'Sabrina' could still be our objective. After all, it's the quickest means of conveying captives, as well as being safe."

"Yet more sense," commented Urbicus, happy that his young officers were clearly thinking men with a future. "What additions do you have, my old friend, from your logistics viewpoint?"

Petronius regarded the governor for a brief moment before replying. "As you say, all good sense. I have just the one concern – coordination. As we heard from Agrippa, a ship can only be in one place at a time. It has to be proximous for any plan to work. I suggest an attack plan is given to Draco and his sailing plan then given to Firmus and/or Felix. Securely, of course."

"Words of wisdom from the expert. What do you say, Felix?"

Quickly responding he said, "A great deal of common sense has been applied this evening. May the gods give us the opportunity."

"Good use of your ship, Admiral?"

Agrippa nodded as he replied to Urbicus, "I believe so. However, I again stress the short period of availability."

"That's understood," agreed Urbicus. "Good. Let's attack my best Falernian on that note!"

★ ★ ★

"Before Firmus left with the Mummers he told me something quite interesting – in fact, it answered a question that's been lingering in my head for some time," Felix observed to Clemens, as they strode round the large ornamental garden leading down to the small quay's gateway.

"Are you telling me that something smells more than this box hedging?" Clemens wrinkled his nose to emphasise his dislike. "To me it smells like cat's pee!"

"You've a good memory, then. The only cats round here are up in the granaries keeping the mice at bay – hardly round here at all – so I doubt you've seen *them*."

"True – it was some time ago. I don't miss the smell, though!"

"So, anyway, he said that Sextus has a bit of a problem. He's got this woman there and his wife's sent a message to say she's coming to stay at the fortress with him – changed her mind, apparently."

"When did he get the message?"

"Several weeks ago – she's coming from their villa in Iberia. That's why he was off-key when I saw him last, according to Firmus. I've only seen, never met, this woman of his – but I think he'd be well rid of her."

"How so, then?"

"When she saw I'd noticed her I was presented with a leg show. Not that they were special either – just long. Man-hungry – that's my guess. Maybe for power and money, too. Anyway that's enough of her."

They had walked the length of the sea wall side of the garden and turned up towards the palace, before Felix spoke again.

"We must use Caecilius and Victor to pass on false information – or question one to learn their master's last known whereabouts. Either or both know how to contact their respective paymasters – they must do!"

"Questioning them takes them out of the circle, so they'll lose their usefulness," Clemens replied, "though there's no guarantee any false-fed information would be acted upon anyway, of course. Do you think they represent more than one band, then, from what you said?"

Nodding at him Felix explained, "I have to. Outlaws do cover vast tracts, of course, but south of Corinium is quiet country. With comparatively few troops in the hinterland there's no need to move away far. If that's so, then I believe there are at least two. Possibly a sub-division – but anyone can carve a logo."

"Quite disparate bands?" Clemens was surprised at this view and his voice showed it.

"Possibly – making it look like the work of one."

"Both our wealthy traitors on the same treadmill? Accident or design?"

"That's for us to find out – or more correctly, for the moment, Firmus and his Mummers."

"What's their planned route, again?"

They stopped short of the palace to maintain secrecy as Felix expanded on what he had said only briefly before.

"Their first performance will be in Venta Belgarum, then on to Calleva, if necessary. After that to swing north to Corinium, then south west to Aqae Sulis and Lindinis before turning east again to Durnovaria and ending back in Waerham. I expect the circle to be broken at some point by ferreted information – or by my old optio, Septimus, if they go as far as Corinium. His inn's a good source of intelligence."

"Yes," agreed Clemens, pursing his lips and whistling. "Hopefully still, otherwise it's a very large but rather empty net."

"Only too true. What I'd hoped, though, was to pick up something before we use our two disaffected legionaries to spread the word to tempt whichever band it is down to Clausentum water. Draco can get his bireme up the river and well above the town, to be the mouth of the trap. He can remain there after disembarking us."

"Will it work? There're a lot of ifs and buts."

Shrugging his shoulders hugely Felix retorted, "Why not? This is good, fertile land – just the place for them to find helpless targets, all the time they think they're one jump ahead."

"I'll make sure what's left of the century's on standby. It had best look like an exercise, so I'll put something together.

★ ★ ★

Finally able to get into the nearby town of Noviomagus Aurelius Victor immediately made for the mansio, in order to send a message upcountry by one of the official couriers, disguising it as an underclothing request for himself via a friend.

Cursing his ill-luck he saw that his optio, Julius, was already there, writing what appeared to him to be a world history, judging by the size of the parchment.

Damn them all, he thought viciously, when he saw that the acting-optio, Paulinus, was also on his way there. Giving up at that point Victor turned towards the nearest inn hoping that, whilst he drank some ale with a whole picea topped with onion, garlic and pepper, he would come across his local contact there.

Woken from a doze by a tap on his shoulder the rebellious signifer started, to a sonorous voice intoning, "My friend, they're working you too hard. Will another beer refresh you?"

Licking his lips Victor nodded and his contact's hand went up towards the bar, with a rigid forefinger pointing downwards at the empty tankard on the table.

"So," the man said, seating himself to face the door, "What's there to tell me?"

"It could be what you've been waiting for," Aurelius Victor began, only to be stopped by his companion.

Looking around, he warned, "Speak softly, walls have ears – as you well know!"

The ale came and Victor thirstily drank from it, the onion, garlic and pepper wreaking their revenge on him. After slaking his thirst he leant forward to whisper, a decision his benefactor was not altogether grateful for in the light of the stale odours.

"The Mummers, that is the entertainers in my century, have been sent off to Venta before going on to Calleva. If you can get the information away you could grab them."

"They won't know any more than you, will they?"

Noting the caution in his contact's eyes Victor quickly replied, "No, they won't – but they'd make useful hostages to draw the legate into a trap!"

Raising his eyebrows briefly as he evaluated the suggestion, Victor's companion nodded slowly. "You have a devious mind, my friend, a very devious mind. Good. Very good – if you're sure of your facts."

"I was put on guard to keep anyone from the doorway. I heard it all, whispered though it was. The fools!"

"You've done well. Here, the full bag's yours," said the man, putting a brown pouch onto the table near his informer's tankard hand.

At about the same time Caecilius made his way to the temple, on the pretext of offering prayers for a patient they had recently lost. Going up the few steps to the platform he made his way to the gods' niche and stood there, apparently in prayer.

Soon afterwards a toga-clad figure entered and, walking over, stood slightly behind him as though waiting his turn.

"What do you have that I'll find interesting?"

Unsurprised, having heard the sandaled feet, the medical orderly stared straight ahead as he replied, "I think I have what has been wanted for some time. I risk much to bring it."

With a grin on his face the second man said, "That's what you're paid for. I'll see what this seems to be worth – when I get to hear it, of course," he added with edged sarcasm.

"Do you want the legate enough – does your principal, I mean – to pay well?"

The hissed breath escaped before it could be stopped, causing the toga foldover to tremble slightly from the anger and tension in the supporting arm. Geta Marcus knew the breath had told his informer too much to bargain.

"Tell me," he grated, "and I shall see."

"The legate has sent his Mummers out looking for you – and your rival, Mercurialis."

"That has no value!"

"They are under the control of Marcus Cocceius Firmus. I believe you'll agree he has value."

A few steps in the doorway interrupted them but the penitent saw he would have to take his place in the queue and withdrew to try later.

"He has some limited value."

"Married to the legate's ward? Good value, I think."

The bearded chin quivered at the impertinence but Geta Marcus held his temper, asking only, "How do you come by this?"

"I was sent from the room but I heard the whispered voices well enough. Hospital rooms echo."

"Good. Where will I find him?"

"My reward?"

"It's valuable information – you're right. This time what I give you will be life changing, I think. You've done well."

"They're probably already in Venta by now – I couldn't get away quicker. After that, they go next to Calleva, then Corinium. Taking the centurion would bring the legate to you. I've earned what you intend to give me."

As Caecilius half turned for confirmation, the army dagger went deeply under the soft ribs and up into the ribcage. The shock was such that the orderly could only gasp before the world turned grey around him.

★ ★ ★

"Can you believe how easily they fell for it?"

"Thanks to your acting ability, Clemens. Your whispering had just the right element of drama about it. Well done, young man."

"Comedy more like, in retrospect," exclaimed Clemens. "They were so keen for secrets it was a shame not to oblige!"

Felix laughed at that, his face mischievous. "I have to say, how could Victor imagine we'd ever put him on guard – with *his* record?"

"And Caecilius," added Clemens, "did he really believe we'd not check he was beyond hearing? So. Have we done it?"

"I think so. It was a pity we had to come on to Londinium to catch our medical orderly – but it did mean Victor could not release his titbits earlier either, so it was useful as well."

"The scouts are on standby. Shall I send them on?"

Felix nodded as he said, "Spare mounts must be taken at the halfway stage on the Calleva Atrebatum Road. They must do it in a day. Then they can rest up in the mansio overnight and slip out unseen by the south gate for the relatively short ride down to Venta Belgarum to warn Firmus."

"They'll be tired on the way to Clausentum," Clemens observed.

"They will. However, make sure they understand that they're our eyes and ears on that road, if Firmus is not to be ambushed by our quarry."

Chapter XXI

S ince both officers deemed an attack cum sailing plan irrelevant on this occasion Felix embarked the remnants of his bodyguard, boosted by Rufinus as his surgeon, plus Victor, who had been arrested by his optio, Julius.

Hard rowing and a sympathetic wind for the sail brought them into Clausentum water a day later, Draco knowing that the whole crew would then be able to recover their strength while they waited.

Put ashore some two miles up a tributary running north to south, Felix calculated that, using the road to their left, it was less than a half-day ride to Venta Belgarum. Therefore they had to find a high point to oversee it, since any attack on Firmus would not be within sight of the town and probably would happen about halfway along the road.

He sent half his remaining men to find a defensive point some miles on, with a directive to have a man ready to ride on contact, and was pleased that Clemens did not query why he had not been put in charge of the detail. Like his men Felix wore chain mail, doubled over the shoulders, because of its flexibility combined with its relative noiselessness. Each had a cavalry shield slung across their backs, although these were not favoured by his men since the protection was negligible if they were dismounted.

Reconsidering the original plan, having now viewed the ground, Felix opted instead to follow a line under the low rise of hills. Never doubting for a moment that one or other of the protagonists would attack Firmus, he started them alongside the road slowly to give the detachment time to get ahead, but remained aware of the need to close the distance in order to provide support when it was required. When the attack came Firmus would ride like Hades towards them. Felix hoped there would be no premature casualties.

Rain began soon after the start and the breeze quickly grew to a wind which drove it in on them to the point where their horses twitched their ears against the irritation.

It was much later than he had expected when the sounds of pursuit came to him as a confusion of clattering hooves on the road, a thudding of hooves on grass and the hoarse shouts of men closing their prey in expectation of a kill.

Felix had retained the comparatively inexperienced Paulinus as his optio knowing that Silus was an experienced enough centurion to lead the others whatever happened. Hand to hand he considered Paulinus to be worth two men in a fight and now he would prove his worth.

Shouting the single order to charge Felix heeled his horse savagely, regretting the suddenness but satisfied of the need and aware that Clemens had done exactly the same.

Leaving the hills they reached the road as Firmus came into view, long reining and low in the saddle, seeking speed not style. Letting them pass Felix ordered his men into two lines, giving his son-in-law command of the second. Then, hardly allowing them chance to free-off their shields, he rode them fast into the pursuers who, taken aback by their sudden appearance, reined-in and fumbled with their own shields.

The clash quickly became a confusion of shouts, screams and the grating of metal on metal. Fear and exhilaration produced mingled odours of horse and human sweat, which competed with the cloyingly sweet smell of newly-released blood.

Faced with a ferocious, untrained horse his own reared and brought its hooves down in the deadly, self-defensive strike that any predator feared, smashing bone and flesh as its metal shoes enhanced the power in each leg.

Horror-struck his opponent pitched over his mount's neck and Felix slashed at him for good measure. Not knowing whether his own blow was decisive he left Paulinus to deal with him.

Somehow sensing an attack from the rear he skewed sideways which allowed him to fend off a lance blow. Instinctively he knew the man was an old soldier because of the choice of weapon and he realised he was lucky to have taken the counter-thrust on his cavalry shield.

All around him Felix was aware death was happening, as groaning men pitched from their horses and others' mounts collapsed from wounds, in the organised chaos that a mounted action often became.

A snatched glance took in Clemens dealing with a threat to Paulinus but his own opponent was determined and having wheeled hard, came at him from a wide angle. Digging in his left heel and pulling right on his reins, Felix met him head on. Deflecting the lance with his sword in the classic defence enabled him to cut down below the offered shield deep into a thigh muscle, relishing the scream of pain that meant his antagonist was more than just hurt.

As he pulled on his reins again and turned, he was aware of mud splashing across a leg and Firmus surging past to cut viciously at the man's exposed neck. His head almost severed the rider toppled from his horse, lifeless but oozing blood.

"About time, too," shouted Felix, who, receiving a similar reply but in the vernacular, then asked, "how do you want us to form?"

The cavalry-experienced Firmus quickly issued directions and his bloodied Mummers joined Clemens in the line, Felix happily relinquishing temporary command to the ex-decurion, as he rode beside him.

In one body they drove at their attackers, shattering the pretence of a defensive line with ease, their inept opponents unused to fighting on horseback. The few one-time cavalrymen amongst the brigands fought on for a while, unwilling to surrender their pride but, with no support, were soon cut down.

With a fiendish scream a demented Geta Marcus came at them both, his frightened horse lathering as it was goaded into a mad charge.

Titus and Julius smashed into the retreating band almost unseen and the withdrawal quickly became a rout, even as Felix was trading blow for blow with a madman who had once been a friend.

Firmus used the flat of his blade across the rump of Marcus' horse, the stinging blow causing it to skitter sideways unexpectedly and pitch its rider to the churned-up ground.

Coming to his feet winded, but not unduly handicapped by it, Geta Marcus faced his mounted enemy. His mouth twitched into a snarl as Felix slipped off his horse to confront him on the wet and slippery grass.

Firmus was hesitant. They could easily take this man, yet he did not want to interfere in an obviously long-standing feud – at least from the crazed ex-centurion's standpoint.

The rain drove in again and trickled down their necks inside the mail, entirely unnoticed in the tension of the standoff.

"Take him," ordered Felix, but before anyone could move Geta Marcus was dying from a slashed throat, having cut in deeply and determinedly.

Rufinus reached him as he sank wild-eyed to the ground with blood running from both corners of his mouth. The young man looked down, then at Felix, shaking his head because there was nothing to be done.

"See to the others, boy, they might be worth saving. This shit pile isn't!"

Firmus looked keenly at Felix, whose jaw muscles were flexing, but he did not know what to say. By rights his role was to have taken the fugitive and held him but, in being called back from Venta to be the bait in the trap, he had been unable to identify his target soon enough.

Sighing, Firmus realised that there had been no guarantee of capture. Suicide might still have been the result. As it was they had an end product – and one that would satisfy Urbicus. Any governor welcomed the demise of a terrorist, so he would see it that way, too.

It had been a short, sharp, bloody action but when the sound of fighting suddenly died away Felix clapped the now dismounted Firmus on the shoulder. "Next time, eh, young man? You did well."

"Mercurialis tops of my list now. I wonder where he is?"

★ ★ ★

They returned to the ship with four dead, but no serious injuries otherwise, to find that Draco's marines had intercepted some escapees trying to make for Clausentum.

"If they were looking for a boat out, they've found one," he said laughing at his dark humour. "Sorry about your men, though. It hurts – even when you've won the day."

Inclining his head Draco indicated the body draped across a horse and added, "One down and one to go, then."

"The governor may very well want to display him in Londinium to prove that treason does not pay. Presumably crowds will come – but out of ghoulish interest. Frankly, I don't care what happens to him – but I wish I'd killed him myself, bearing in mind the outcome."

"You did the job as directed, Felix – alive or dead."

"He lost his head to revenge and his life to over-confidence. A sad combination."

"Former friends make the worst enemies," Firmus remarked philosophically. "It was for the best."

"He was born a citizen, so he's saved himself the public trial that would have been necessary", observed Clemens.

Felix shrugged. "I'll try to view it that he saved *me* his public trial."

Everyone aboard swayed as the 'Sabrina' rocked and rolled in the current while it was turned, using both sets of oars and its rudder, causing Felix to catch hold of a crossbeam. He looked down the whole length of the lower deck to the manacled prisoners, wondering if they were contemplating the same fate for themselves as had once befallen their dead leader.

"Rather than sailing on Londinium, I thought it'd be a better idea for us to call at Portus Ardoni – the men would enjoy a night in their base. What do you think?"

The four officers were leaning on the poop, looking at the headland slipping past, as they left the Clausentum river heading east between the mainland and Vectis.

"It's a remedy for much," agreed Felix glancing at Draco. "Why don't we do just that? We could all use a bath, a good meal and a landlubber's bed."

The other two nodded a vigorous agreement and Draco issued the necessary order to veer towards the narrow harbour entrance that lay between the headland they were now almost past and the large island that looked its mirror image.

Once through it they made due north towards the small fort and the dock, some two miles distant though they found it hard to believe it in the clean, clear light.

Having gone forward to investigate, after listening to his second-in-command and the watch officer an agitated Draco rapidly returned to the three.

"The bow lookout thinks there's a fight going on around the fort. I've ordered the sail down just in case – we'll be less conspicuous, too."

"Incredible – his eyesight, I mean," remarked Clemens. "What sort of fight – in general terms?"

It was the question Felix was going to ask so he kept quiet.

"He's never wrong! Better educated and he'd be made up as a reward. Ironic though, isn't it? Promoted – I'd lose a good lookout! He'll tell us what, soon enough."

As Draco had promised, with the distance rapidly closing the lookout reported an attack by ground troops, which appeared to be a mixed bag he had said.

"Steer for the warehouses – that's what they'll go for. He's right about a land attack – there're no boats moored off or docked," the young, bearded captain confirmed.

"They're presumably taking advantage of the fleet being away with the governor," Felix suggested.

"That's about right." Draco threw the words into the headwind, as he peered anxiously at the quay in front of the storehouses and messes. "Stand-by to ship. Ship!"

The oars rapidly withdrew, to allow the 'Sabrina' to berth against the quay's fenders with the faintest of bumps.

Firmus was surprised they hadn't been seen and remarked, "Are they stupid or playing with us?"

When the gangplank was put out marines began to file quickly off, forming a defensive arc alongside their vessel.

Following their example Felix instructed Clemens to disembark their own men and form a small phalanx.

"Form it up in squads, as far as you can. Take one and Firmus another – Titus, Julius and Paulinus taking the others. I'll lead any leftovers and combine with the marines."

Draco joined him. "I've arranged for the sailors to secure the ship. How do you intend to deal with this?"

The sounds of fighting came and went, louder when the attackers formed up on the nearside of the fort.

"Good thing they were preoccupied," commented Felix, "They weren't expecting us, obviously."

"The gods are certainly on your side today, my friend. Who are the *they*, do you think?"

"Either another part of Marcus' men or Mercurialis' – I fancy the latter. Let's advance and see."

The phalanx moved off ahead of Felix, Draco and the marines, with Felix wishing a bireme carried more than twenty regular fighting men.

A sudden cry went up, followed by howls of rage, as the attackers thought they had been tricked. Urged to attack the phalanx they were wary, knowing that every man in it covered another making it difficult to penetrate. In addition some of their own were falling, with no apparent cause.

Silva reloaded his sling and, guided by Felix, aimed yet another metal bullet at an apparent leader, smiling as he saw his target reel away injured but still wishing he had dropped to the ground.

Noticing a group forming Clemens immediately led an attack and had the satisfaction of seeing it break and run although, with weapons rebounding from their shields, he knew there was resistance somewhere else.

Felix and Draco took the marines and the residue of legionaries away from the shelter of the phalanx's rear to charge those attackers still hacking at the small fort's wooden door.

The usual shouts and screams of pain-generated invective swirled around them as sweaty bodies met fire with fire and metal glowed in the evening sun.

Draco intercepted a blow aimed at Felix and thrust his man through, surprised at the poor armour he wore.

Felix protected him from a similar attempt, first holding the slash, then ducking under its counter to stab into the man's belly before chopping down as his opponent hunched away.

Marine spears arched in the air and a line of targets fell grotesquely, their attitudes depending on how badly they were hit. A hiss of metal indicated the marines had then drawn their swords.

From the cleared doorway the defenders burst into the fray, finally able to fight as Romans preferred – in the open.

This proved the final straw and the attackers, harassed on three sides, turned and ran for the line of hills backing the small port, though not without leaving a man or two more as testament to Silva's skills.

★ ★ ★

The four officers relaxed in the quarters rarely used by the admiral, pleased to have soaked in the small bathing complex beforehand.

Frankly amazed at having taken so few casualties, with no deaths and only minor injuries, they had seen the men settled, fed but only rough-wined, as regulations required. However, Felix and Draco had conspired to send across flagons of beer to the messes as makeweight.

"I wish it could have been to the ship, too," Felix said, "but obviously you're right. It would be too dangerous."

"We'll see the rowers and crew are suitably rewarded for their day's work, don't worry. However, they'll not get time off until the job's done. But where *is* the sod?"

Pursing his lips briefly, Felix ventured, "I wouldn't wager my life on nearby – but it's short odds! Apart from it being a balls-up – he's no soldier – why attack the fort at all? Go for the warehouses straight away. He had enough men with him for the fort's small complement to know they had to stay inside.

But I'll tell you what – they would have succeeded, if the fates hadn't been against them. Now he'll be taking advice. The question is, whose?

"Will we go after him?"

"You will, young Firmus – with the Mummers. My first guess is that he'll either go for Purbic to hopefully disappear, or Corinium to pick up money from his estates. Who's running his string of female gladiators? You go there and find out. Press after him – but don't follow too closely in the sward. Let him realise he can't spare the time for ambuscade. Keep him moving until we can snare him."

"Good. What's the end product?"

"Who does he see along the way? We'll pick his contacts up later. If, *only if,* you can safely take him – do so! If so, stay in town. Hole up – get a message out to Septimus at his inn. He'll probably send to Sextus at Isca Silurum – or get you there."

"What if there's no trail?"

"Come on back to Waerham. We'll see if our families remember us before we go hunting for him on Quintus' estate."

Firmus smiled and said, "It's not the one about finding our quarry in a quarry again, is it?"

"If it is, I hope he'll see the humour of it, so we can make him laugh on the other side of his face!"

★ ★ ★

As Felix absently stroked the milky skin of Livia's firm shoulders with his fingers, her light-green eyes regarded him mischievously and a ready smile played at the corners of her mouth. Lost in thought he found himself wondering what he would do without her and the stability she brought to his disjointed existence. It was no wonder he looked to the spirit of the house to protect her in his absence. He was ever more sure that, like him, she touched the niche containing their nominated god figurine in gratitude as they left the house. Without question Eros had been their obvious choice.

Almost automatically one of his hands wandered down to her breasts and his thumb teased a lightly-coloured nipple. Then his hand closed around the firm yet soft flesh, gently kneading it and feeling the erect nipple pressing into his palm as he did so.

"I much prefer to have one of these in my hand than my sword," he suddenly found himself muttering and realising that he had spoken out loud, looked at her.

Livia burst out laughing and then held him close, for him to see that she was laughing with him, not at him. "You were so far away in thought, I wondered how long it would take you to notice that I'm naked!"

"You always are," he replied, puzzled.

"Well, my dear man, what are you going to do about it?"

In a room further down the house Julia was lying against Clemens, perfectly satisfied and smiling inwardly at herself for ever wondering, before their marriage, whether she would be frigid following her inexperienced and fumbled cuddle one evening.

Closing an arm tighter Clemens whispered, "He's a good, strong lad, my love. I'm proud of you for giving us

Clemens Junior. He's someone else I look forward to seeing when I'm away."

She snuggled closer in and whispered back, "I'm pleased, too. I hope he'll be like you when he's grown. But I'm surprised you still like me so much – I mean, my breasts seem much fuller than before. They're not a young woman's any more."

"My darling girl! I'm not going to risk saying anything about your advancing years," Clemens began, only to expectantly break off as she dug his ribs, "but I loved you pregnant and I love you now. Unlike you though, I do need my beauty sleep. I suspect tomorrow will be another day."

In their own guest room Dorcas pranced about in a tassled bikini, hands on hip and with her head tossed confrontationally, the hazel eyes flaming.

"You obviously didn't like the off-the-shoulder dress I bought in Durnovaria – something to do while you were away – so now I'm dressed like an athlete. Or would you prefer me naked, like a gladiator?" As she said it she pulled the two pieces off and threw them at him.

Letting them hit him and fall to the floor, Firmus could not help himself but admire her shapely body. He took in her long, blonde hair – worn native style, falling past her shoulders – to her small, round breasts, the shapely waist and, what roused him the most, her full and rounded thighs.

The challenge was there, mockingly full frontal, until Dorcas crossed her legs, though still inclining her body erotically. The lips pouted slightly, then parted to show slightly pronounced front teeth. The imperfection complimented, rather than emphasised, the small bump on her nose from a childhood injury.

"If you touch me I'll scream," she said, noticing the way he looked at her. Having followed his eyes she somehow knew that he was remembering when they had first met. She had worn a bare-shoulder dress then, too, citing the Greek women who had run races like that in years gone by. Anyway, she thought she had said it. After that she had talked of athletic costume and teased him about gladiatorial nakedness – which he had replied did appeal to him in her case.

"I *shall* scream," she repeated.

That comment spurred him on and in a bold stride he had her to him, pinioning her arms even as he put a precautionary hand across her mouth.

Pushing her backwards across the bed he took her fully, but gently, as she offered no resistance. Afterwards he kissed her lips and then stood to go.

"Please don't" she pleaded. "Please don't go. I don't know if things will be all right now, but at least we've – I've – tried again. I dared you out of devilment but, when you looked at me the way you did, how could I not try? Please! Come back."

Firmus looked at her, relaxed on the ruffled bed, arms outstretched towards him, hazel eyes wet with emotion.

Jerking awake clammy with perspiration Dorcas lay there, momentarily startled, until realising she had been dreaming. How strange, she thought, that it was possible to be both of them so realistically, when, of course, Firmus had not even been there – he was away in Corinium, on duty.

★ ★ ★

"So it seems that Tiberius Celerianus isn't taking his involvement in the gold mine any too seriously," Ianuarius observed, having sailed into the small port to tell Felix of his discovery that the shipper had been allowing Mercurialis to use one of his vessels.

"Presumably not disinterested enough to refund his shares money to your friend, Lunaris?"

The boyish chin bobbed as Ianuarius'otherwise handsome face broke into a broad smile. "As you say, he hasn't. Strangely enough Lunaris is keeping quiet about having been sold a pig-in-a-poke, too."

They were talking in Felix' small office and broke off when the steward's wife, Tabitha, brought in honey cakes and watered wine, with the pepper the shipper had asked for to sprinkle over them. She smiled as she placed them on a small table within easy reach, before quickly withdrawing.

His eyes following her shapely but elfin figure as she left, Ianuarius commented, "What a lovely smile that girl has – and green eyes, where you would expect dark to go with her black hair. Lucky man, your steward."

Smiling at the memory of seeing her naked when she had performed in the market place for her then owner, a fire-eater, Felix answered, "He thinks so, too – and I must say I've never regretted buying her freedom so that she could fit into a role I had in mind for her."

"I suspect many had a role in mind for her, my friend! Yours was clearly the best for her, that's obvious."

"She has been very useful, that's for sure. Now, what of Celerianus? Where is he now?"

Smiling again the shipper replied, "As it happens he preceded me out of port. I held his course for a while but when I eventually turned back for the Great Harbour he sailed on. Unless he's for Swanwic bay he'd have been too tight to the shore to swing wide and avoid the shoal water at its point – that's where I think he is."

"With the bandit?"

"I didn't see him but I believe in the balance of probability. It's the basis for my insuring cargoes – providing the ships are seaworthy."

Felix asked, "He'd have anchored about the same time you arrived here."

"Give or take."

"He'd have no transport from the bay – unless he *was* met. That's about a five mile romp up the valley – two hours walking, at least, for someone like him. No, he's been met so," Felix paused briefly, "he's probably about to arrive at the villa – if that's the objective. What price the baths for him?"

"I suspect you're right," Ianuarius agreed, unsure of its importance.

"Unfortunately the villa overlooks the Corf road so a sally will be seen. Do you think if you take the honey cakes with you, you could take some men round to the bay? I want to cut off his retreat. It would mean starting now, though, I'm afraid."

Momentarily laughing about the bribe his face became deadly serious. "Will the vessel be at risk? I like our governor – but ships don't come cheap! I mean, of course, I'll take you, but there's a livelihood at stake."

Equally seriously Felix responded, "I wouldn't have thought so. The other vessel's not a warship either. I take your point – but if it sails, crowding its exit would do well enough."

"The bay's too open for that – it could be taken out easily enough around me," the experienced sailor retorted.

"Damn," Felix said vehemently. "Still, if you can beach some men it'll help considerably."

"I'll leave at once to ready the ship and sail as soon as your men board. I'll have an extra tug take us down the river to save time."

"Good, thanks," Felix said hurriedly explaining as he rose, "I have to get the men rousted out and mounted."

He hurried off shouting for his son-in-law, leaving Ianuarius open-mouthed, not realising the real urgency until that point. Grabbing a handful of cakes and, shaking a good helping of pepper over them, he rushed out himself.

With only forty men available and now no medic, Felix simply divided his force between the boat and the Corf road, sending Clemens to lead the charge up it with Titus.

Instructing him to send a scout over the hills to Stolus, in the hope of supplementing the meagre force, Felix took his men, under Julius and Paulinus, down to the small quay where they quickly embarked. No sooner had they done so than the two tugs, six rowers in each, began to ease the vessel into the main stream before pulling heartily for the river's Pwll Harbour mouth.

The breeze tugged at any clothing not covered by armour and their host told them it was a good sign. "Talking of signs and omens, it's a good job it wasn't a Friday or the men wouldn't have sailed in the first place. What we need now are some gulls in the rigging – that's an excellent omen!"

Some time later Rex, the Canaan dog, stood with his mistress and Livia at the gate, watching Clemen's group as it disappeared down the road. His tail was curled alertly over his back as he did not pick up any signs that it was a time to wag it.

Running fast with a full sail the boat was sheering away from the deep indentations in the fragile cliffs, in order to escape the chalk pinnacles lying off the foreland. Clearing them it rounded the next point to turn for the run into Swanwic bay.

"A good trip so far," observed Ianuarius, as he scanned the sky for weather signs. "If our luck holds Celerianus' vessel will see us from the far side and up-anchor. Then I'll put you on the beach and try to keep it from coming back in. How's that."

Felix laughed and said, "If you do and you can, I'll settle for that. Finding out too late should adequately depress Mercurialis – he won't have seen it go as he runs away from Clemens down the valley. He may even think you're him."

On the sand Felix observed to his carrier, "You ought to become a seer – it went exactly as you forecast!"

They watched the scurrying vessel dart for the bay's far reach and disappear south, presumably to later run along the southern coastline of the Purbic hills.

"I hope he keeps off the reef in his haste – I don't wish Celerianus any harm, even though I doubt he's personally on board."

Felix formed his men across the already decrepit road and stood with Julius, idly looking towards Corf and trusting that things had gone according to plan.

Quite some time later the thudding of hooves jolted them all to awareness, as several riders came into sight riding out their reins and heeling their horses on.

When the group finally saw their welcoming party each of them hauled back and brought their heaving, sweaty mounts to a sliding halt.

"You, you bastard!" Mercurialis stormed, as he fought to regain his breath. "Move aside – or we'll charge!"

His words were immediately rendered meaningless as Clemens and Titus led the pursuing group down at a gallop to swell the growing throng, before drawing rein.

"I think we might take your weapons now, don't you?" As he said it Felix approached the stone shipper and indicated where they should be thrown.

His brow tensed, as though in acute pain, Mercurialis palmed his sword hilt but thought better of it and undid his weapon belt, tossing it to the ground. His men quickly followed suit since, being largely villa guards on loan, a scrap with serving legionaries did not sit well.

While Titus told off troops to collect the discarded arms Clemens came over to Felix and said, "Stolus provided some men to secure the hill road back into Waerham. He said he had no intention of letting anyone harm Amatus, the soldier he granted the freedom of his lands to – nor to let our adversary escape. He wanted no more of his quarry workers killed for another's greed."

"You won't keep me – even if your nickname does mean *lucky!*" Stepping down from his trembling horse Mercurialis threw the reins at Felix who, instead of grabbing at them, let them fall to the ground.

"It also means successful," he said.

When his nemesis made no further comment, the stone shipper continued his rant. "I was released last time you took me – remember Corinium! I shall be again. What actually have I done personally, eh? My family has the emperor's ear – so does the boy Quintus'. You won't last long!"

Ignoring the comments Felix asked, "Are these horses from the estate? I assume you stole them."

"You poor demented fool," snapped Mercurialis. "You're living on borrowed time, don't you realise that? They were lent – like these men!"

"For the boy's sake I'll believe you stole them," retorted Felix and signalled that Mercurialis should be restrained, but the captives were to return with the mounts the way they had come without delay.

With their fuming prisoner secured, Felix led his men back to the dinghy that would ferry them to their transport, saying quietly to Clemens, "The trouble is, I have a premonition that he'll be proved right."

THE END

Appendix 1

<u>Glossary of Towns, Tribes and Countries</u>

Whenever possible Roman names for towns are used, otherwise the oldest known name.

Alauna	Ardoch (Scotland)
Anderida	Pevensey
Aquae Sulis	Bath
Arbeia	South Shields
Barrow Tor	Countisbury (Devon)
Bononia	Boulogne (France)
Bravonium	Leintwardine
Calleva Atrebatum	Silchester
Camulodunum	Colchester
Cilurnum	Chesters (Hadrian's Wall)
Clausentum	Southampton
Corf	Corfe Castle (Dorset)
Corinium	Cirencester
Deva	Chester
Dubris	Dover
Durnovaria	Dorchester (Dorset)
Eboracum	York
Glevum	Gloucester
Henburh	Hengistbury (Dorset)
Herculis Promontorium	Hartland Point (Devon)
Horrea Classis	Carpow (Scotland)

Isca Dumnoniorum	Exeter
Isca Silurum	Caerleon (Wales)
Lindinis	Ilchester (Somerset)
Lindum	Lincoln
Londinium	London
Magnis	Kenchester
Malaius	Isle of Mull
Mona	Anglesey
Monavia	Isle of Man
Nemostatio	North Tawton (Devon)
Noviomagus	Chichester
Orcades Insulae	Orkney Islands
Petriana	Stanwix (Hadrian's Wall)
Petuaria	Brough-on-Humber
Pinnata Castra	Inchtuthil (Scotland)
Portus Ardoni	Porchester
Purbic	Purbeck Hills (Dorset)
Pwll	Poole
Ratae	Leicester
Regnum	Fishbourne
Roma	Rome (Italy)
Scitis	Isle of Skye
Silura	Lundy Island
Stollant	Studland (Dorset)
Swanwic	Swanage (Dorset)
Twynham	Christchurch
Vallum Hadriani	Hadrian's Wall
Vectis	Isle of Wight

Venta Belgarum	Winchester
Venta Silurum	Caerwent (Wales)
Verulamium	St Albans
Waerham	Wareham (Dorset)

Appendix 2

Glossary of Rivers

Abus	Humber
Birgos	Barrow (Ireland)
Buvinda	Boyne
Sabrina	Severn
Tava	Tay
Tamarus	Tamar
Temesis (Isis)	Thames
Tynea	Tyne
Uxella	Parrett (Somerset)
Wych	Wych (Dorset)

Appendix 3

Glossary of Countries

Belgica	France/Belgium
Caledonia	Scotland
Canaria	Canary Islands
Cymru/Cambria	Welsh/Wales
Gaul	N. European Collective
Hibernia	Ireland
Melita	Malta
Taprobane	Sri Lanka
Thule	Iceland

Appendix 4

<u>Glossary of English and Welsh Tribes</u>

Precise tribal boundaries are not known so those used are suggested in other works.

Atrebates	Wilts/Berks/Oxon
Belgae	Hants/Wilts
Brigantes (Southern)	Yorks/Firth of Forth
Catuvellauni	Northants/Beds/Herts
Dobunni	Glos/Wilts/Oxon
Durotriges	Dorset/Somerset
Dumnonii	Devon/Cornwall
Iceni	Suffolk/Norfolk
Ordovices	North Wales and Border
Regni	Hants/Sussex
Silures	South Wales and Border

Appendix 5

Glossary of Scottish Tribes

Picts/Scots (both invaders)	Western Lowlands
Venicones	Western Lowlands
Brigantes (Northern)	Eastern Lowlands
Caledonii	Low Highlands
Maeatae	(Combined Tribes)

Appendix 6

Glossary of Irish Tribes

Brigantes	River Barrow
Cauci	River Boyne
Darini	Lough Neagh (South)
Robogdii	Lough Neagh (North)

Apprendix 7

GLOSSARY OF ROMAN ARMY RANKS AND APPROXIMATE MODERN EQUIVALENTS

The Roman army had a complex system of seniority throughout lower rankings as well as within officer grades. These have been simplified in order to compare them with approximate modern equivalents.

Rank(Rough)	Service Equivalents	Duties
Governor	General Commanding	In the field
Legatus Legionis	Brigadier General	Legion Commander
* Tribune Laticlavius	Colonel 2 i/c	Snr Tribune/Dep. Commander
Prefectus Castrorum	Lt. Colonel 3 i/c	Camp Prefect/Logistics
* Tribune Augusticlavius	Lt. Colonel	Snr Cadet/Adjutant
* Tribunes	Acting Lt. Colonel	Cadets– Gen.Aides/admin
Prefectus Fabrorum	Lt. Colonel	I/c Ordnance & Workshops
Primus Pilus	Major	Snr Centurion-Admin/training
Centurion	Captain/lieutenant	In Charge of Century
Cornicularius	Reg. Sgt. Major	HQ Deputy Centurion
Aquilifer	Co. Sgt. Major	Eagle Standard Bearer/ Legion Accounts
Optiones	Co. Sgt. Major	Deputy Centurion
Signifer	Colour Sgt.	Century Standard Bearer/ Company Accounts
Tesserarius	Sergeant.	OrderlySgt./Sgt Guard
Duplicarius	Corporal	Double Paid as Relief NCO

Immunes	Lance Corporal	Craftsman/Specialist Excused Duties
Miles/Pedes	Private	Infantryman/foot soldier
Prefectus Equitatus	Lt. Colonel	(Unusual) Commander Of Cavalry Wing
Decurion	2nd Lieutenant	Cavalry Troop Commander
Eques	Trooper	Cavalryman
Prefectus Classis	Brig. General	Admiral
Navarchus	Colonel	Large Warship Captain
★ Kybernetes (Tribune)	Lt. Colonel/Major	Exec/Quartermaster
Proreus (Centurion)	Captain/Lt	Watch Officer
Miles Classicus	Marine	Soldier/Seaman
Nauta	Seaman	Deckhand/Sailor
Medicus Ordinarius	Major/Captain	Qualified Surgeon
Medicus Miles	Orderly Sgt (Hospital)	Surgeon's Assistant
Capsarius	Orderly Cpl (Field)	Trained First Aider/ Bandager

★ (Career diplomats on short service commissions)

Appendix 8

Glossary of Unit Sizes

Unit	Rough Equivalent	Nonimal Strength	Usual Strength
Legion	Regiment	5000	4,800
Cohort	Battalion	500	480
Century	Company	100	80
Maniple	Half-Company	50	40
Turma	Cavalry Troop	30	30
Ala (Alae)	Cavalry Wing	500/800	400/700

Schola Optiones	Non-Commissioned Officers Mess
Schola Miles	'NAAFI'

Appendix 9

Glossary of Ships

Roman Ship Type	Modern Function	Usual Strength
Dekares (600 oarsmen)	Battleship	40 Crew + 400 Marines
Trireme (170 oarsmen)	Cruiser	30 Crew + 90 Marines
Bireme (50 oarsmen)	Fast Frigate	10 Crew + 20 Marines

Appendix 10

Main Character Profiles
Selective List

Augustus Albinus **Felix**	Main Character
Quintus Lollius **Urbicus**	Governor of Britain
Marcus Maenius **Agrippa**	British Fleet Commander (later Procurator)
Gauis Iulius **Clemens**	Deputy to Felix and Son-in-law
Tiberius Piso **Faber**	Staff Surgeon (previously second legion)
Claudia Juno **Livia**	Wife of Felix (step mother to Julia)
Augusta Frontera **Julia**	Daughter of Felix married to Clemens
Dorcas	Julia's maid/companion
Comazon **Valerius**	Steward to Felix (disabled legionary)
Tabitha	Ex-madam wife of Valerius
Titus Aurelius **Antoninus** Pius	Roman Emperor
Marcus Cocceius **Firmus**	Ex-legion agent to Felix
Gaius Fabullius **Macer**	Captain of Trireme 'Tigris'
Carinorum **Rufinus**	Ward to Felix

Lentila **Romana**	Wife of Governor Urbicus
Aurelius Priscus **Paternus**	Main conspirator (quarry owner)
Aurelia Flavia **Sabina**	Wife of Paternus and sister of Livia
Stolus	Minor chieftain of Durotriges Tribe
Galina	Wife of Stolus
Quintus	Nephew of Paternus
Geta **Marcus**	Conspirator (shipper)
Marcus Ulpius **Ianuarius**	Shipper of Petuaria (ex administrator) and friend of Felix
Justinian **Mercurialis**	Conspirator from Corinium (Cirencester)

Appendix 11

Locations

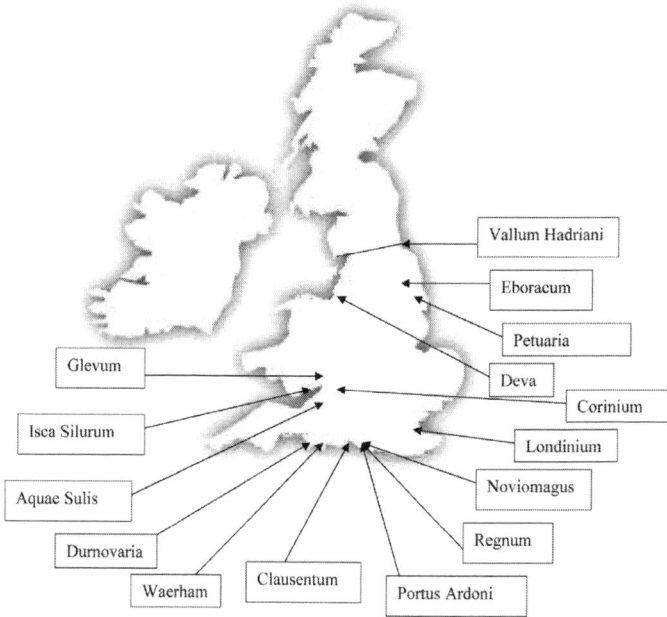

Vallum Hadriani

Eboracum

Petuaria

Glevum

Deva

Corinium

Isca Silurum

Londinium

Aquae Sulis

Noviomagus

Durnovaria

Regnum

Waerham

Clausentum

Portus Ardoni